BONEMAN'S
DAUGHTERS

TED
DEKKER

BONEMAN'S
DAUGHTERS

CENTER STREET®

NEW YORK   BOSTON   NASHVILLE

Copyright © 2009 by Ted Dekker
Article "Are You the BoneMan's Daughter?" copyright © 2009 by Ted Dekker
Excerpt from *The Bride Collector* copyright © 2010 by Ted Dekker
All rights reserved. Except as permitted under the U.S. Copyright Act of 1976, no part of this publication may be reproduced, distributed, or transmitted in any form or by any means, or stored in a database or retrieval system, without the prior written permission of the publisher.

Center Street
Hachette Book Group
237 Park Avenue
New York, NY 10017
Visit our website at www.centerstreet.com

Center Street ® is a division of Hachette Book Group, Inc.
The Center Street name and logo are trademarks of Hachette Book Group, Inc.

Printed in the United States of America

Originally published in hardcover by Hachette Book Group
First mass market edition, March 2010

10 9 8 7 6 5 4 3 2 1

For Rachelle

BONEMAN'S
DAUGHTERS

1

THE DAY THAT Ryan Evans's world changed forever began as any other day he'd spent in the hot desert might have begun.

On the move, on the double.

Redeploying, as they liked to call it in the army. Changing stations, changing units, changing rank, and all at a moment's notice because when command said *jump,* you jumped. When command said *lock and load,* you got up, geared up, and went where command ordered you. It didn't matter if you were an E2 washing dishes or a lieutenant on the fast track to War College. You belonged to the Department of Defense, the Pentagon, and the chain of command.

Commander Ryan Evans was temporarily on loan to an army joint-operational counterintelligence unit comprised of intel specialists from the army, the navy, and the air force. As a unit they fed and bled intelligence data from satellite surveillance, human intel assets, electronic taps, and military intelligence. Pieces of data came from every corner of the intelligence spectrum, funneled down to a direct point. *Bottom line, up top,* as command liked to say.

Most of the time verifying and assessing intel was like looking at a circuit board through a telescope. Or like trying to open a tin of canned food with a tuba. But every now and then, intel was just that. Intelligence. *Discovery.*

Ryan was an analyst, borrowed from the navy to serve with the army. He read reports, examined evidence, and poured more reports up the chain than the Pentagon could read. Nothing short of a human sieve. But in the end he was just one small piece on this game board called war. End of story.

Or on this particular day, the beginning of a story.

Advanced game theory, tactics, terrain, numbers, percentages—this was how Ryan had always viewed the world, even before he'd made the decision to pursue a career in the navy. The last two years in-theater had convinced him that a career in accounting might have been the wiser choice, but he wasn't one to complain or reconsider the sixteen years' investment of his life. Particularly not when he was only three months from the end of his final tour.

To be fair, his position in the military was enviable when compared to the duty of many others. Rather than entrench or advance with infantry, most of his days were spent at a desk, reviewing orders, sifting through the work of the twenty people working under him, intercepting and decoding every scrap of information gathered in a net of assets cast over a much broader region than most could possibly guess. Between satellite photos, electronic interception, UAV footage, and hard, boots-on-sand reports, the flood of information passing through his office on any given day would bury a man who couldn't view the world from a distance. Where others obsessed over each twig and leaf, Ryan kept a watchful eye on the entire forest, so to speak, searching for an enemy hidden beneath the leaves. Patterns and trends.

But today command had decided that he should move to a different quadrant of his sector to take a closer look. A raid in a small village ten miles east of Fallujah had netted what might or might not be a treasure trove of information. They called it *Sensitive Site Exploitation*. He still wasn't entirely clear on why the general had decided that he should take a closer look at the bunker complex—in person—particularly in a region not yet assessed for equally unknown threats. But Ryan wasn't one to question orders. Information, certainly, but not the decisions of his superiors.

Eight AM and it was already over a hundred degrees in the shade.

He slapped the swinging door that led into the intel room open and sidestepped Jamil, a twenty-one-year-old whiz kid who, like Ryan at his age, had a unique knack for pulling needles out of haystacks, as they sometimes referred to sifting through intel.

"They're waiting outside with the convoy, sir."

"Tell them I'm on my way. You get the report on the Iranian border breaches down to General Mitchell?"

"Last night, as promised."

He dipped his head. "Carry on."

Ryan surveyed the thirty-by-seventy room, a metal Quonset hut that had been loaded with enough electronic equipment and communication cells to keep any civilian blinking for a full minute. If it happened in the Middle East, it went through this room. At the moment a dozen regulars hovered over their stations, mostly monitoring feeds rolling down their monitors. The sound of laser printers provided a constant hum, white noise that had followed Ryan most of his adult life.

Lieutenant Gassler approached, cracking his neck. "We have a new batch of intel coming from the south; you sure you don't want me to take this hike?"

The general had left that call up to him, but he'd kept behind his desk in the office adjacent this hall far too long. A day trip out into the desert now and then could clear the cobwebs. Not that his intelligence was clouded.

"It'll do me good. You got this covered?"

"Like a lid."

Ryan turned back toward the door. "Back by sunset, then."

"Keep your head low."

He left the Quonset without acknowledging the advice. Bad luck.

THE TIRES OF the armored Humvee roared on the pavement beneath Ryan's feet. He'd sat in silence for the last ten minutes as they sped west along Highway 10 toward Fallujah.

"Three klicks to the turnoff," the driver, a corporal from Virginia, announced. "You okay back there, sir?"

Ryan shifted his body armor to ease an itch on his left breastbone. "Fine. Air would be nice."

The enlisted man next to him, Staff Sergeant Tony Santinas, chuckled. "You think this is bad, sir? Try sitting in this hotbox for eight hours at *five* miles an hour. Welcome to the army."

Ryan wiped a bead of sweat from his brow. "I can only imagine."

They followed a lead Humvee and were trailed by a third, moving a good eighty miles an hour. A fast target made a hard target. On the highway speed meant security. It also turned the Humvee into a mobile blast furnace, crushing through hot air upwards of a hundred and twenty degrees. Thankfully, the reinforced windows were cracked only enough to allow good circulation—like windchill, when fast moving, the hot air somewhat exacerbated the heat.

Ryan stared past the sergeant at the desert. Heat waves rose off the flat desert ground on either side. That the Arabs had managed to bring life out of this desolate land served as a testament to their resourcefulness. While most Americans would shrivel up and blow away with the first dust storm, the Iraqis had thrived. It was no wonder the Babylonians had once ruled the world.

A caravan of five huge oil tankers thundered past them, headed back toward Baghdad from Amman, Jordan.

"This your first tour, Tony?"

"Yes, sir." The staff sergeant shot him a nervous look. Big, blotchy freckles covered a sharp, crooked nose. A skinny kid who looked not a day over twenty-one.

"Where you from?" Ryan asked.

The driver interrupted, speaking over his shoulder, "Lead vehicle is turning off. It's gonna get dusty. Hold tight. This will get bumpy."

Roils of dust billowed from the tires of the lead vehicle as it exited the main highway, still moving fast. The burnt-out husk of a large transport vehicle with Arab markings lay on its side in the sand. No signs of civilization. The village in question, a collection of mud huts built around a deepwater well called Al Musib, lay eight miles north.

The sergeant shifted his grip on the M16 in his hands, checked his magazine and safety without looking, eyes peeled at the desert. At nothing. But if there was one thing the American forces had learned, it was that nothing could become something in a big hurry out here in this wasteland.

The driver took the corner at full speed, hanging back just far enough to stay clear of the dust from the lead vehicle. The tires' roar gave way to a cushioned whooshing sound. Eerily quiet.

"I grew up in Pennsylvania," Tony said, answering Ryan's question. "But I live in South Carolina now."

"Married?"

"Yes, sir."

"You miss her?"

Tony dug out a photograph and handed it to Ryan. "Betty," he said.

The picture showed an average-looking blond woman on the heavy side, with big hair that was out of fashion in most parts of the country. Her nose was pudgy and the teeth behind her smile could have used a year in braces. On second look, a very average woman. Maybe even homely.

The sergeant stuck another picture under his nose. A newborn baby, grinning toothless. Ryan glanced up at the freckled, redheaded sergeant who made no attempt to hide his pride.

"Cute, huh?"

These few bits of information spread out before him

were enough for Ryan's trained, calculating mind to fill in the man's life. Tony had grown up in a small town, near a coal mine, perhaps, where his selection of suitable mates had been limited to a couple dozen, of which only two or three had expressed any interest in him. Discarding any adolescent fantasy of a whirlwind romance with Jessica Alba, he'd entertained a life with Betty who, although neither pretty nor rich enough to afford braces, had a good heart and, more important, had opened that heart to him. Eager for love from a woman, he'd quickly convinced himself that Betty was the best woman for him. That he loved her, which he did, of course.

The baby's conception had come first. Then the wedding.

Now a proud father, Tony equated mother with child and genuinely loved both. Being separated from them only intensified his feelings, absence making his heart grow the fonder.

"She's a doll," Ryan said. He wasn't given to emotion, being the more calculating type, but a strange surge of empathy tugged at him. Or was it something else?

He sat there in the back of the Humvee, bouncing slightly as the vehicle sped over the sandy road, gripped by the sudden realization that he wasn't so much empathetic for the snapshot he'd assigned to this man's life but rather was trying to ignore a tinge of guilt.

Guilt because he had long ago given up on his own child and wife. He'd justified his decision to leave them for long stretches at a time, but in all truth he couldn't be absolutely sure if he'd left them or fled them. At the very least he'd fled Celine, his wife.

Bethany was another story. Collateral damage, the

unavoidable fallout from his and Celine's admittedly distant relationship. He loved Bethany, he most certainly did, but circumstances had forced him to miss most of her life.

Not forced, really. Circumstances had caused him to miss most of her life due to his choice to serve. And that choice had reaped resentment from her.

Ryan realized that the sergeant was holding his hand out, waiting for the picture of his wife back. He set the photograph in the man's hand. "Nice."

"You have any kids?"

"Yes. Same as you, one daughter, though she's a bit older. Sixteen. Her name's Bethany."

"Sucks, don't it?" Tony carefully slipped his two pictures back into the wallet he'd taken them from. "Being over here."

"Yes."

Unlike Tony here, who had nothing to live for but a wife and child back home, Ryan had chosen a far more complicated path. Not that he didn't care for Celine and Bethany—in some ways he missed them terribly. But sacrifices had to be made.

For him that sacrifice had been made when he'd made the decision to accept a post in Saudi Arabia ten years ago despite his wife's refusal to accompany him. He was the best at what he did, and his work in Saudi Arabia had saved more lives than anyone could know.

He'd returned to San Antonio, where they'd lived at the time, and became immediately aware that for all their efforts to put up a good front, he and Celine could not be as close as they had once been. She couldn't understand his world and he had no interest in being a socialite.

Nevertheless, he'd remained at his post in San Antonio for two years before accepting another overseas post, this time in Turkey.

By the time he'd shipped out for Iraq, his relationship with Celine existed solely for the sake of their mutual commitment to marriage and family. If Ryan wasn't able to provide his wife with the kind of intimacy and personal friendship she desired, he would at least provide her with his loyalty as husband, protector, and provider.

Generals didn't have to be in love with their troops to be good generals. Truthfully, he didn't miss Celine. Bethany, on the other hand . . .

The thought stalled him for a moment.

"You think it's worth it, sir?"

"Depends. You have a job to do, right? Mission first, men second, everything else comes in third."

The man stared out the dusty window. "I just never thought about what it would cost them, you know?" He shook his head. "A kid changes everything. God, I miss her."

"She'll be there when you get back."

His guilt came from not sharing the same kind of ardor in the mind of this young sergeant who longed to be home with his wife and daughter more than anything else in life at the moment.

Then again, Ryan *did* love his wife and daughter in a far more important way. Not a love demonstrated in gushing words or heart-wrenching desire, but by loyalty and steadfastness for not only them but for his country, for the world. The cost of separation was an acceptable sacrifice for such a noble and worthwhile calling.

Still, seeing a man like Tony here, filled with eagerness to return to his very average-looking wife, had awakened that hidden sense of guilt.

Interesting.

"I know it's hard, Tony, but what you give up today will come back one day. You have to believe that. We're not the first to pay the price."

"Price for what, sir?"

"For freedom."

"Is that what we're doing here?"

He was briefly tempted to tell the sergeant to check his loyalty, but he doubted Tony had a bone of disloyalty in his body. He was simply a young man stretched between loyalties.

He shifted his body armor to ease that itch by his left breastbone again. Last time he'd worn full combat gear had been over a month ago. Ryan asked, "How many soldiers asked that same question during the Civil War? Or the Revolutionary War?"

"I was thinking more along the lines of Vietnam," Tony said.

"Sure, Vietnam. But it's hard to see the forest when you're in the trees. History will one day get us far away enough from this mess to tell us what we did here. Until then you won't do yourself any favors by second-guessing your mission. Make sense?"

"Yes, sir, it does. But it doesn't make it any easier, if you don't mind me—"

Whomp!

"Crap!" The driver, who had been fixated on the convoy's tracks, slammed on the brakes. "Crap, down, down, *down*!"

Ahead, the road was shrouded by dust—from the lead vehicle's wheels or from the detonation, Ryan couldn't tell. But there was no mistaking that sound. Either a rocket-propelled grenade or an antitank mine—he didn't have the field experience to know which was which any longer.

"Get on the fifty!" the driver screamed. "RPG, RPG, incoming fi—"

Whomp!

This time behind them.

"Move, move!" Tony yelled. "We're sitting targets!"

That they were under assault was not a matter of question. The driver slammed his foot on the accelerator. "Hold on, we're going through."

The Humvee surged forward into the boiling sand and smoke. Ryan instinctively crouched as much as the back of the seat in front of him allowed him to, but he kept his eyes ahead, where a cloud of dust and smoke now plumed skyward.

The driver keyed his radio and veered to his right using one hand to drive. "Convoy Echo-One, this is Three, come back. What the heck's going on?"

The radio crackled static.

"Crap." Into the radio again. "Convoy Echo-One . . . this is Three. Caboose, you got me?" Over his shoulder, to the sergeant, "Get up in the fifty, Tony!"

"I can't see anything!"

Still nothing from either the lead vehicle or the one trailing them.

The dust directly in front of them cleared enough to reveal a plume of black smoke boiling to the sky ahead. Orange fire licked at the hot desert air.

"Crap, hold on, hold on!"

The Humvee swerved a wide right, then hooked to the left in a tight U-turn. Ryan grabbed the door handle to keep himself from plowing into the sergeant, who was plastered against his window. Most vehicles would have tipped with such a sharp turn, but the army's workhorse loaded with nearly a half ton of armor wasn't easy to roll on flat ground.

Odd how different minds work in moments of sudden, catastrophic stress. Ryan's tended to retreat into itself, baring the cold calculation that had served it so well in his intelligence training. He had no clue how to extricate them from the present crisis, but he could analyze the attack better than most chess players leaning over the board on a cool summer day.

One: They were taking enemy fire, a combination of shoulder-fired RPGs and machine-gun fire now slamming into the armor like pneumatic hammers.

Two: Both the lead vehicle and the Humvee that had brought up the rear had likely taken direct hits.

Three: The absence of radio chatter likely meant that—

The glass next to the driver imploded. Blood sprayed across the far window. The Humvee swerved off the road, into a short ditch, and slammed into the far embankment.

Four: The driver of the second vehicle, the one in which Ryan was riding, had been killed, and the Humvee had plowed into a ditch, where it would be hit at any moment with an RPG.

Silence settled around him with the ticks of a hot engine.

Ryan lunged over the seat, grabbed the radio, and spoke quickly into the mic. "Home Run, this is Echo-One

Actual, on convoy to Fallujah. We're taking heavy fire, anti-armor, small weapons. All vehicles down, I repeat, all three Humvees are out, over."

A moment's hesitation, then the calm, efficient response of a dispatcher all too familiar with similar calls. "Hold tight, Echo-One, we are clearing close air support, and medevac en route. ETA seventeen minutes. What's your sitrep, over?"

"Assuming all personnel are KIA. My Humvee is sideways in a ditch, four klicks north of the highway. You can't miss the smoke."

"Roger. Hold tight."

It occurred to him that he'd heard nothing from Tony. He spun back, saw the soldier slumped in his seat, one hand gripping his M16, the other stretched toward the canopy, as if still reaching up to deploy the M2 .50 caliber machine gun, topside. No blood that he could see. Could be a nonvisible wound from shrapnel, could be the impact had knocked him out.

"Sergeant!" Ryan slapped the man's face several times, got nothing, and quickly relieved him of his weapon. Images of flames crackling through the cabin pushed him to the brink of panic. He took a deep breath.

This is no different. Just another mission. One step at a time.

Never mind that this particular mission didn't involve a pencil or a computer, it was still just one step at a time.

Ryan reached over the driver's corpse, took the modular radio from the console, grabbed his door handle, cranked it open, and rolled to the sand, relieved to be free of the coffin. He lunged back into the Humvee, grabbed the sergeant by his belt, and dragged him out. The soldier landed on the ground and groaned.

Still, no more gunfire. Their objective was now simple. Stay quiet, stay down, stay alive. Survive, watch, wait for the helicopters. Air support was now the only link to survival for either of them. Rising smoke from the wreckages would be visible from a long way off.

"Where are we?" Tony had come to.

"We were hit," Ryan whispered, scanning the desert for any sign of the enemy. Unlikely. They'd perfected the art of hitting and running, knowing that when the Apaches showed up, any attempt at fight or flight was doomed to failure. Insurgents with the skill to remain hidden in a flat desert (likely under the sand) and take out three Humvees definitely had the brains to bug out so they could fight another day.

"We have support coming," he said, turning back.

Something black, like a sledgehammer or a rifle butt, slammed into Ryan's forehead. Pain shot down his spine and he fought to hang on to something, anything.

Another blow landed, and only now did his calculating mind wonder if it was a bullet rather than a sledgehammer or a rifle butt that had struck his head.

2

BETHANY EVANS SCANNED through her Hotmail account, looking for a callback from her agent at Tripton, the modeling agency she'd signed with three months earlier. The jobs had been fairly small—mostly clothing catalogs, everything from StyleWear to Sears. Two television spots, including working as an extra: toning her body for a Gold's Gym ad and one of three high school babes to kiss a guy in the lip gloss piece for Severe Lip Service—a rather funky brand name, if anyone was asking her.

This time it was a *cover*. A clothing catalog cover for *Youth Nation*. Assuming that she got it, which her agent, Stevie Barton, had all but guaranteed, over five million buyers who received the fall catalog would see *her* face.

"Is it there?" Patty asked.

Bethany shifted her cell to the other ear. "Hold on. Good *night*, can you believe the junk that gets through these days?"

"Whatever. It's probably all the huge fashion magazines throwing free products at you to get you into their stuff."

"Gimme a break."

"Seriously, you know that's what happens. You make it and they start to send you free stuff. Like football players getting free shoes, that kind of thing."

"I'm a model, Patty. One in a thousand faces in a million magazines. We're not talking Angelina Jolie here."

"Where do you think she started? I swear, Beth, you gotta get me in there. I still can't believe all this is happening to you. You're going to be freaking famous!"

Bethany's hand paused over the mouse. Famous? The word had an odd ring to it. She'd never agreed to her mother's urging to take a few modeling classes and build her portfolio out of any desire to be famous. She was only sixteen years old, for heaven's sake!

Famous.

She wasn't even sure what that word meant anymore. It wasn't like she was going to Hollywood or taking up singing lessons any time soon. She was simply making her way on her own, as her mother put it. Making good on what was given her. Which just happened to be decent looks, a pretty smile on a body that looked eighteen, albeit a *short* eighteen.

"Don't say that," she said.

"Whatever. You're gonna be freaking famous and everyone knows it."

"Shut up! I'm serious, Patty. I'm going to be a doctor, not some face everyone can . . ."

She caught her breath as the email scrolled into view. *From the desk of Stevie Barton. The Tripton Agency. Austin, Texas.*

Patty noted her pause. "What? You got it, didn't you?"

"Hold on."

She double-clicked on the email and read it quickly.

Bethany—
   Congratulations, sweetie! You got it. They want you in New York in three weeks for the photo shoot. One week, $20,000 as discussed. You're going to be the poster child for Youth Nation *this fall. This is just the beginning. Call me.*

Stevie.

Bethany blinked. Heat drained from her face as the realization of what this could mean settled over her. Perhaps she'd been just a tad too quick to dismiss a life of stardom. She nearly dropped her cell phone.

"You got it?" Patty demanded.

"I . . ." Bethany couldn't help herself now. She squealed. And despite her loathing of little girls who jumped up and down with their fists clenched, she did just that. Squealing like a little girl.

Patty's voice squealed over the line with her. "I knew it, I knew it, I freaking knew it! Read it to me."

Sitting back down, out of breath and feeling slightly ashamed of her display of emotion (thank God no one had seen her), Bethany read the email to Patty.

"Uh-huh, just the freaking beginning, what did I freaking tell you?"

"Is everything *freaking* with you?"

"Heck yeah! Now it is. And I'm going with you."

"To New York?"

"Where else? Broadway, baby."

The complexities that might result from this small

trip to New York to become the next poster child for *Youth Nation* began to present themselves to Bethany. For starters, it was now late August and school started next week. School meant cheerleading, and she'd landed leader on the varsity squad. Leader had to make every practice; the rules were clear and Coach Carter wasn't the kind to bend them for a magazine cover.

"When is homecoming this year?" she asked.

The phone was silent.

"Second week in September?"

"I think you're right. That's not good." Patty clearly understood the importance of the issue, should it arise. But her appreciation for all things pop culture, not the least of which was fame, outweighed her appreciation for leading two thousand red-blooded, Texas-bred teenage boys in a cheer while wearing a miniskirt—though it had to be a close call.

"Forget homecoming. You're going to be famous."

Predictable.

"I'll call you back."

"Hold on, hold on! Where are you going?"

"I've got to tell my mother."

Bethany hung up and flew down the stairs two at a time, spun around the railing at the bottom, and ran for the kitchen. She slid to a stop in stocking feet and faced her mother, who was on the phone.

"Mom—"

Her mother's hand flew up, palm demanding silence as she bore down on her own conversation.

"I got it!"

Her mother snapped her fingers and pointed at her face, scowling. Her way of saying, *Shut your mouth; can't you see I'm on the phone?*

Of course I can, Celine. Can't you see that your daughter has something more important to say than anything you're gossiping about at the moment?

She didn't say it, of course. Instead she crossed her arms and drilled her mother with a stare that Celine hated with a passion.

"They're letting him out? He's only been locked up for two years." Celine walked to the far side of the kitchen to avoid the heat of Bethany's stare. Bethany stepped around the counter and waited, ignoring a quick glare.

"What about all the evidence? Surely they can't just set him free on a technicality. You nailed that freak."

Her mother was talking to Burton Welsh, the district attorney. Now there was an interesting thread in her convoluted web of relationships. How Celine managed to work her way into the lives of such powerful people never ceased to amaze Bethany. Celine should have been a politician.

She'd met the DA during his investigation of the BoneMan after the killer had abducted a girl from Bethany's high school, Saint Michael's Academy, where Celine served on the PTA board. The rest was history, as they said.

Bethany slid to her right so that her mother could see her.

"What does this mean for you?" her mother asked, turning her back again. She had to be nearing the limits of her tolerance.

In a softer voice now, "It'll be fine, Burt. Don't let them back you down." A pause. "I have to go, I'm sorry. My daughter seems to think that the sky is falling." She offered a short, forced chuckle. "I will. Good-bye."

She clicked off and turned quickly, waving her cell phone. "How many times do I have to tell you how rude that is? Was I on the phone when you crashed in here?"

"I got it."

"I don't care what you got, you're not the only one who lives in this house. We share space, you and I. That means you respect my space and I pay for yours, and we all know how expensive that can be. I swear, the next time you pull a stunt like that, I'm cutting you off. You hear me?"

Bethany felt her face grow hot. Her mother could be such a child at times, a condition that had grown far worse over this last year, while her father was off killing people in Iraq. At times like this Bethany wasn't sure whom she resented more.

"Are you done?"

"I don't know, are you?"

It was too much. She lost interest in sharing what might very well be the most important news in her short life with this woman who called herself a mother.

"Aren't you forgetting something?" Bethany asked.

"What?"

"In this space of ours, as you call it, you're the parent. I'm the daughter. So act your age."

Her mother blinked, but she always blinked to show shock, even though she was rarely truly shocked. It was like role-playing, all a part of what made Celine the manipulating monster she'd slowly become.

"How dare you speak to me that way? I'm your mother!"

Bethany felt a knot building in her throat. "And I'm your daughter."

They faced each other in silence, Celine with drawn

lips, Bethany trying to hold back a torrent of repressed feelings about what she summarily thought of as her abandonment.

Her mother was here, but never here for *her*. Always off chasing herself through a string of relationships with men, slaving to keep herself from adding a pound of unwanted fat, regretting every day she lived because it brought her one day closer to forty.

Her father wasn't self-absorbed. He simply wasn't. His abandonment of them both hadn't become apparent to her until she'd grown old enough to piece it all together. He was clueless about both Celine's unfaithfulness and Bethany's need for a father. She would settle for her mother's selfishness over her father's ignorance most any day.

Most. At the moment her mother's complete failure to be a mother was pushing Bethany to the brink.

Her mother finally set the phone on the counter and turned her eyes away. "What's so urgent, you little narcissist?"

"Forget it." Bethany turned and walked out of the kitchen, eyes misted and blurry. At times like this hate wouldn't be the wrong word to express her feelings. She hated her mother for being her mother and she hated her father for not being there to rescue her from her mother.

"So what, you're just going to walk away now?" her mother snapped, following her. "Get back here."

Bethany kept walking.

"Look, I'm sorry. Is that what you want to hear? This is hard for all of us, you know. You think trying to be a parent alone is easy? You aren't the only one Ryan left. Forgive me if I'm not perfect all the time."

More manipulation, built on truths, used at the right moment to get the desired response. But Bethany had a hard time empathizing with her mother's incessant talk of being deserted by her man, particularly when she replaced him with other men, which she had no difficulty doing. If anything, her father's absence was a convenience for Celine, for her game.

It was Bethany, not her mother, who'd been abandoned.

Her mother suddenly gasped behind her. "You got the cover?"

Bethany stopped.

"You got the cover of *Youth Nation*, didn't you?" The coldness in her mother's tone had melted away.

Bethany took a deep breath and pushed back her anger. "Yes."

Her mother's feet quickly padded across the wood floor. "I'm so proud of you, angel."

Celine's hand touched her shoulder but Bethany pulled back. "Don't call me that. You know I hate it."

"Oh, get over yourself." Celine hugged her.

Her father used to call Bethany "angel" when she was a young child. But in his leaving, he'd treated her like anything but an angel and she resented the name. That her mother would choose the term at a time like this was criminal. Welcome to Mother's world.

When Celine pulled back, her eyes were bright, oblivious to her painful jab. "Why didn't you tell me? When did you find out? That's wonderful news!"

Bethany didn't bother answering the questions; they were placeholders, not notes of interest.

"How much are they paying?"

"Twenty thousand. They want me in New York in three weeks for a photo shoot."

Wonder filled her mother's eyes. "I am so proud of you."

And for all of her antics, Bethany knew she meant it. This was why she would stay loyal to her mother.

"So you really think I should do this, huh?"

"Are you kidding? This is fantastic! Don't you worry; I'll be with you every step of the way. We'll go to New York and we'll have a hoot. There's no way you can waste this opportunity."

"I might miss homecoming."

Bethany could see the wheels turning behind her mother's eyes. Not missing a beat, she said, "Don't you worry, leave the coach to me." She headed back toward the kitchen. "You just stick with me, Bethany. We play our cards right, we'll rule the world. Which is more than I can say for the lame duck who calls himself your father."

There was a time when Bethany would have objected with a comment about how he was still her father, but she'd forgotten how she'd felt back then. She might not agree with the way her mother had conducted herself these past few years while Ryan was off playing war, but she found herself wondering what it would be like to have a different father. One who cared enough to participate in her life. Maybe that would have been the best solution for all of them.

Her mind flashed back to her mother's phone conversation. "What was that Burt Welsh was saying?"

Her mother glanced back, as if undecided about telling. But she did.

"Some craziness about the BoneMan being released from prison."

3

THE VOICE ECHOED around the edges of his consciousness, like a speaker in a murmuring crowd whose words rose above the cacophony to be heard, if only barely.

"Wake . . . wake . . ."

An image of waves crashing to shore while Ryan and his younger brother, Pete, stood with their wakeboards, ready to rush into the receding waters, joined the voice. Pete had been killed in a car crash ten years or so ago—had it really been so long?

Maybe he was dead.

"Wake up. Wake up!"

Something struck his cheek and the sting jerked him away from the murmuring crowd into a lonely, dark place.

"Wake up!"

Another hard slap chased away the darkness. The horizon turned red and he heard himself groan.

"Yes? Yes, you're going to finally join us?"

His memory of the firefight lit up his mind like a bomb blast. The Humvees had been hit . . . he'd survived . . . the staff sergeant had survived . . . he'd been struck and knocked unconscious . . .

He was alive and in the presence of someone who spoke with a heavy Arab accent.

"Open your eyes."

His eyelids fluttered open to see a dimly lit room. The details fell into his mind; simple facts that painted a picture that could only be interpreted in its entirety. No conclusion yet, no need to rush to judgment. Bad intel got more soldiers killed than bullets.

Concrete walls. An old wood door. No windows. A metal table on his right, stacked with papers. He was seated in a chair and his hands were bound behind him. One dim bulb hung overhead, shrouded by a green metal shade. An empty corkboard hung on the wall directly ahead of him.

Three Arab men dressed in dirty tan slacks and shirts stood in the room. Two of them leaned against the wall and cradled AK-47s. The third, presumably the speaker, paced directly in front of Ryan, one hand resting on his holstered pistol, the other limp by his side.

So then he had been taken captive by what appeared to be three insurgents or terrorists who held him either deep within a building, judging by the lack of windows, or underground, a more likely scenario.

Ryan shifted his arms, heard the chains around his wrists more than he felt them, and settled. To say that he was concerned would have been a gross understatement, but he refused to allow fear to gain any foothold.

He was alive, which was far better than the fate the

others had suffered. Or was it? They would either torture
him for what information he could give them, a thought
that he shoved away, or they would use him as a political
tool and eventually kill him.

The man who'd slapped him leaned close enough for
him to head-butt—clearly he'd been born a fighter rather
than a thinker. Ryan was a man of considerable size,
weighing in at a hundred and ninety pounds, give or take,
standing at just six feet, and the navy kept him fit, but he'd
never struck or taken a blow in his life.

"Can you hear me?"

The man's breath smelled like clean dirt. Like most
Middle Easterners, he valued cleanliness far more than
your typical westerner—even here in the desert, assuming
he hadn't been out long enough to have been driven to a
city, the man would take care to bathe each day. Ryan could
still smell the soap on him.

He tried to speak but nothing came from his parched
mouth, so he cleared his throat and tried again.

"Yes."

"Good." He closed the distance so that his nose came
within inches of Ryan's. He wore a beard and red-
checkered headdress, which placed him firmly in the
camp of what most hastily called extremists. But the
Middle Eastern psyche wasn't so easy to categorize.
There were dozens of ideologies, each with its own long
history, each with its own complaints, all with an under-
standable perspective, if you looked at the world through
the right lenses.

"You may call me Kahlid. And until I know your true
name, I will call you Kent. You're a race of Supermans,
you Americans, aren't you?"

One of the men behind him murmured in Arabic, "And we are the Lex Luthor." The other chuckled.

If they didn't know his name or rank, they wouldn't know that he spoke a fair amount of Arabic.

Kahlid, clearly not his real name, pulled back and placed both hands behind his back. "If you're wondering, the rest of your friends are dead. We were able to escort you away from the scene before the helicopters arrived. You're now alone here with us, for us to use as we see fit. Does this bother you?"

Ryan answered honestly, "Yes."

"Good. Then I don't mind telling you that we have the full intention of bothering you even more. Much more, I would say, judging by your relative lack of concern."

The man's impeccable grasp of the English language, spoken without a hint of a British accent, meant he'd probably studied at an Ivy League school in the States. Harvard or Stanford, perhaps. The education wasn't surprising, but the fact that such a valuable man would be involved in a simple hit-and-run outside of Fallujah was highly unusual.

Which could only mean that their mission hadn't been designed as a simple hit-and-run.

A slight smirk crossed Kahlid's face. "What are you, Kent? Hmm? An intelligence officer? Special Forces? Hmm? Why do your eyes show no fear? Or perhaps you are stupid. Unfamiliar with the methods we use to press back the butchers who have invaded our land."

Ryan found some encouragement in the man's assessment even though he knew he was being manipulated.

"You are here for a purpose, Kent. You are our poster child and with you we will send a message to the world.

To do that we will need to break you. Because our mission is so critical, we will use any and all means to break you. If you're as intelligent as you appear, you know we've already begun. Do you know this?"

"Yes."

"Good. This bunker is thirty feet beneath the ground, too far from any housing for your spies to notice any coming or going. No one will find you, no one will hear your screams. You should be wishing we'd pointed the RPG at your Humvee instead, yes?"

"The thought had crossed my mind."

"Well then. You can say more than 'yes.' Do you mind telling me, Kent, why you are here in my country?"

Ryan hesitated, considering his options. He could clam up and hasten the inevitable smashing of bones or electrocution or a myriad of other techniques perfected in these deserts. Or he could engage them, hoping to stall them while he looked for alternatives. He opted for the latter.

"I'm following orders," he said.

"Yes, I'm sure you are. As am I. In the end does it really matter which of us does a better job? Will lives be saved? Freedom won?"

"I don't know."

The man paced back and forth now, hands still behind his back, like an interrogator from an old World War II movie.

"Then let me help you *know* a few things. Assume for a moment that you are God. That this is really all about you and your children." He motioned to the outer wall as he spoke. "Can you think in terms of God, or are you an atheist like so many of your countrymen?"

"Yes."

"Yes you are an atheist, or yes you believe in God?"

"I believe in God."

"And you believe he loves his children. All of his children."

"Yes."

"Well then, tell me, if you can, how God feels when he looks down and sees this war of yours."

"Assuming God feels anything, I'm sure war bothers him."

"If you were God, Kent, how would you feel? Please try to stay in character."

Ryan glanced around the room. The only way out was through the wood door, but that hardly discouraged him. He was shackled in place—there would be no escape from this hole. All he had was his mind, and he had to keep it active.

"Focus, please."

Ryan looked back at his interrogator. "I suppose I would feel disturbed."

"Why? Why would you feel disturbed? Because your children were being killed?"

"Yes." But he didn't feel any emotional connection with the man's point.

"So then, like me, on at least one level, you are saddened by this war."

"Yes. But also like you, I'm bound by my duty to those who have my loyalty."

"Your loyalty is to man, not God?"

"God hasn't issued any orders lately," Ryan said.

"And if he did, would you follow them, or would you follow the orders given to you by man?"

Ryan didn't respond. He knew where the man was

headed, but his approach was meaningless because, unlike many Muslims who believed they were following
God in political matters, his own belief in God was far
too distant to consider in the same thought.

"In truth, everything that happens here in the desert
leads back to God," Kahlid said. "But I can see you don't
follow God the way I do. As I thought. So I'm not going
to bother manipulating you with an appeal to his will. I'll
have to follow our original plan and attempt to test your
own will. Is that okay with you?"

"Not really, no."

"You're honest, I like that. We're going to find out just
how honest you are." He nodded at the man closest to the
door, who pulled open the latch, spoke quietly to someone outside, and disappeared into a dark hall. A tunnel.

"It may take us a few days, that's up to you, but eventually you will see the world the way we see it."

The soldier returned with a camera case and a tripod.
He latched the door and began setting it up.

"We're going to film you so that we can show the world
what we have learned here today. I hope you don't object.
It's the truth we want, nothing more. We don't care about
your rank and serial number; you'll gladly give us that
before we're done. We're more interested in your heart. In
God's heart, assuming you're still in character."

A thin chill snaked down Ryan's spine. The interrogation was taking a turn that, for all of its similarities to the
hundreds of cases he'd been exposed to during his career,
felt profoundly different, beginning with the choice of
Kahlid's language.

He looked at his interrogator, who was now smiling.

"You don't have enough footage of American soldiers condemning the war?"

"We do, yes. And we won't need any more from you."

Then what?

An unnerving quiet settled over them as the soldier with the camera carefully set up the tripod, mounted the Panasonic, inserted a tape, and plugged the unit into an extension cord.

"We have enough gasoline to run the generator for three days. If it takes longer, we will refill the tanks. But it's not gasoline that I'm concerned with running out of." He glanced at the cameraman, who was looking through the lens. "Are we set?"

The man nodded.

"Turn it on."

A red light was the only indicator that the camera was live.

Kahlid crossed to the table, scooped up a stack of papers and a handful of tacks, and then stepped over to the corkboard. He began to pin 8½ x 11 inch sheets of photocopied images up on the board in a neat row.

Pictures of collapsed buildings, chunks of concrete immediately recognizable as the handiwork of explosives. The photographs had been taken on the ground, some slightly blurred, as if the photographer had taken them in haste.

He'd seen volumes of war images, enough to deaden his mind to all but the worst. But there was something about the presentation of these pictures that he found disturbing.

Then he saw it: hardly distinguishable from the chunks of rubble, broken and twisted limbs. The evidence of bodies that had been trapped and crushed under the weight of the crumbling building.

Kahlid went calmly about the business of pinning more photographs on the wall, one at a time, until he had twelve of them in two rows of six each. The last eight were close-ups, showing a dusty arm thrust out from the space between several large blocks. A very thin, small hand that was attached to a boy or girl younger than ten, hidden under tons of stone. Three different pictures of this arm, broken above the child's elbow, hanging limp, dusty but not bloody.

Ryan now saw limbs between the cracks in the rubble. All children, noticed only upon a second look, then noticed singularly, as if the mounds of broken building didn't even exist. His stomach turned.

Kahlid turned around and stepped aside. "Do you recognize these, Kent?"

Did he? No, he didn't think so.

"Mr. Kent?"

"Umm . . . no. No, I don't."

"Of course you don't. Your pictures come from high in the sky, where your collateral damage is safely hidden from the public eye."

Kahlid took a deep breath. His lip quivered.

"I, on the other hand, do recognize these photographs because I took them. If you look carefully you will see my daughter's arm in the third photograph from the left at the bottom. The next two are also Sophie. And the next one is of my son's leg."

The man's eyes narrowed almost imperceptibly, then he stepped to his right. "They were seven and nine when your bombs fell from the sky and crushed the apartment next to the one I'd sent my wife and four children to for safekeeping. They all died that day. Their bones were broken and crushed. It is hard for me to imagine the pain they must have felt."

Ryan didn't know how to respond to this man's obvious heartache.

"I'm going to leave you with these pictures for a while, Kent. I want you to stare at my children. At God's children, lying broken on the ground, and I want you to feel their pain . . . the way God feels pain. And when you have done that, I will return and we can go to the next step. Fair enough?"

For the first time since waking, Ryan felt completely out of his element.

Kahlid dipped his head and left the room, followed by the others. Ryan sat alone under the steady gaze of the camera's red blinking light and the handiwork of collateral damage.

4

RICKI VALENTINE SAT with her right leg crossed over her left, slowly swinging her foot as she studied Mort Kracker's brooding gray eyes. A crew cut topped the Assistant Director in Charge's large square head, giving him the appearance of a softer, kinder version of Frankenstein, sans scars.

The conversation in the room had stalled. If the defense attorney's latest filing with the court bore up under judicial scrutiny, Phil Switzer, aka BoneMan, could very well be walking the streets two weeks from now and all eyes would be on the DA who'd put him behind bars.

Burton Welsh, the man who now served as Austin's district attorney in large part *because* of his highly touted prosecution of BoneMan two years prior, stared at them from his perch against the windowsill, one hand across his waist, the other stroking up his chin, as though scratching at a thought.

Welsh might be on the bubble here, but Ricki had been the FBI's lead investigator in the case. She, more than the DA, had been responsible for BoneMan's capture and conviction. There would be more than enough scrutiny to go around if the folder on the chief's desk contained the truth.

"So?" Welsh demanded.

"So"—Kracker glanced between them—"we have us a problem."

Although not directly responsible for the investigation, Mort Kracker's oversight of the case wouldn't be dismissed. Not to mention the well-known fact that Kracker had essentially fed the case to Burt Welsh, whose relationship with him extended all the way back to UT School of Law.

Here, in this room, sat the three law enforcement professionals who may very well have put an innocent man behind bars; even worse, they had possibly left a serial killer to take more victims, always careful to cover his tracks.

"You're not actually suggesting you believe this load of crap," Welsh said, shoving a thick finger at the wall. "That man is as guilty as a pregnant nun. That's why we prosecuted; that's why he's serving time."

He crossed the room and towered over Ricki. "You led the investigation; the file on him is a foot thick."

Uncomfortable under his shadow, Ricki stood. Welsh wore a tailored blue suit that hid his muscled frame well, but at six foot three, there was no hiding his power. Standing a mere five feet two if she stretched, Ricki felt like a mouse next to him.

She walked toward the window he'd vacated. "And you know as well as I do that the blood samples from the last victim connected the evidence and sealed the case."

Kracker put his elbows on his desk. "Which they say was contrived. Defense says that they can prove it came from the same sample taken to run him through VICAP, and that we broke the chain of evidence. Like I said, we have a problem."

"Assuming this evidence of theirs pans out," Welsh said. He took a seat in the chair Ricki had left. "Either way, Switzer's as guilty as sin."

Ricki nodded. "Probably. But that doesn't help us in appellate court. Double jeopardy—he can't be tried for the same crime twice. Unless and *until* we find another victim to link to the case, we're stuck."

"I understand the legal problem," Welsh shot back. "But if you think I'm just going to sit by and wait for him to take another victim before I do anything, you don't know me. When news of this leaks, the city will go nuts."

The BoneMan, so dubbed by Ricki for his MO of killing his victims by breaking their bones without breaking their skin, had left a total of seven victims behind, all in plain sight, all in quiet Texas neighborhoods, from El Paso to Austin, where he'd taken his last two before being caught.

Assuming the man they'd put away really *was* BoneMan.

"I'm not saying we have the wrong man," Ricki said. "I'm simply pointing out the challenge we're facing."

Welsh exposed his true concern. "I don't need to restate what this means to me, Mort. Personally."

"We all have both professional and personal stakes in this case," Mort returned. "That doesn't change the challenge Ricki's addressing."

"Don't patronize me." He took a breath. "There's more

at stake here than BoneMan and his victims. I'm trying
to run a city. The last thing the city needs is more fear-
mongering over a case like this. The media will sensation-
alize and speculate for millions of people who don't think
for themselves. Next thing you know, schools will close
and people will be hiding in their homes. Like happened
in DC, with the sniper."

"I thought the mayor ran the city," Ricki said. "Does
he know yet?"

The man shot her an angry glare.

Easy, Ricki.

"Of course he knows. I have his full support."

"Support for what?"

"Don't be so naïve. We have to shut this down. For all
of our sakes, for the sake of the city, for the sake of justice
on behalf of millions, not just one man."

Ricki wasn't sure she understood him correctly.
She'd always thought of Welsh as a bull, stomping to run
over anyone who stepped into his ring, but she'd never
pegged him as one to subvert the laws he'd been elected
to uphold.

Her boss leaned back in his chair and cast a furtive
glance at her. "I don't think any of us disagree that we
need to deal with this in an appropriate manner," he said
carefully. "We have over two thousand man-hours logged
on a case to bring a criminal to justice; no one's suggesting we just let him walk. But we're facing evidence here
that undermines our position. We can't just ignore it."

Welsh slammed his palm on the chair's arm. "Then
find me *more* evidence!"

Ricki thought about asking him what he meant by *find*.
But she held her tongue.

"There has to be something we can use to nail this shut. Another blood sample, maybe overlooked by the lab, DNA evidence that was overlooked because we had what we needed. Anything!"

Her boss spread his palms. "Ricki?"

Her mind quickly rehearsed the details of the case she'd lived and breathed two years earlier.

BoneMan's first victim had been found in El Paso, Texas. Seventeen-year-old Susan Carter, who'd gone missing after going out for milk on a Tuesday night, had finally turned up in an abandoned barn. The police had immediately asked the FBI for assistance and Ricki had been the federal agent assigned to the case.

The image of Susan's bruised and broken body staked to the ground in a circle of candles had haunted Ricki's nights for a year. Though she'd been missing for a week, post-mortem evidence from blood pooling, edema, and decomposition revealed that she'd been dead less than thirty-six hours when they'd found her. The evidence response team from the Dallas field office revealed a dim reflection of Susan's ordeal during the four days she'd spent with her captor.

The killer had gone to great lengths to break the victim's bones, one at a time, without so much as scratching the skin, likely beginning with her fingers and working his way to larger bones over a period of days. The only blood found at the scene had come from rope burns at her wrists and ankles.

No evidence of sexual assault. No bodily secretions that didn't belong to the victim. No hair, no fiber, no prints.

They took castings of tire tracks where a vehicle had

been parked and of boot impressions left, apparently without any effort to conceal them. The hemp rope was a common variety, as were the tent stakes used to pin the body down. So the killer shopped at True Value and paid in cash. Nothing traceable.

Lab analysis later told them that they were likely looking for a Ford F-150 truck, based on the position and depth of the tire impressions, but half the county drove similar trucks. The size-thirteen boots were made by Brahma and were as common in Texas as tumbleweed.

They had a male killer who weighed roughly a hundred and seventy to two hundred pounds, wore Brahma boots, and drove a Ford F-150 pickup. Helpful, but by no means isolating. In the Republic of Texas, *everybody* wore boots and drove trucks and could sing "Dixie" from memory.

Although the motivation wasn't clear, Ricki had been the first to suggest that they were looking at a twisted kind of crucifixion taken from the Roman tradition of breaking the bones of those they crucified to speed their death. Either way, they knew they were looking for an acutely psychotic individual who found some kind of justice or deviant satisfaction in going to such great lengths without a clear cause. Motive? Rage rather than pleasure was his reason for what appeared to be a ritualistic killing. The killer was new to VICAP, and his profile presented an entirely new case study in motivation. Not sexual, but predatory. Not bloody, but extremely violent. It was a murder of detailed planning, and there was nothing on the Web to profile this level of intensity with an unclear motive.

Thirty-nine days later, BoneMan's second victim

was found in Lubbock, Texas, roughly three hundred miles northeast of his first victim. This time in an apartment building. He was on the move. A traveling salesman with an alter ego or a deeply antisocial sense of self?

Another girl, Heather Newlander, thirteen years old. No tire or boot prints this time, but the execution had occurred in precisely the same manner as before. Now they had a transient serial killer.

The news had picked up on the story and worry began to spread. A murderer, now being called BoneMan, was at large in Texas.

The third victim had been found in Abilene, Texas, roughly one hundred and fifty miles southeast of Lubbock, two months later. Photographs of young Eileen Ronders's broken body found their way to the press. In the space of twenty-four hours the BoneMan became national news and horror began to take root in Texas.

They now had three dead young women on a clear path headed east toward the larger cities in Texas. On the television screen the maps looked as though they were plotting a black plague methodically working its way east. A monster of the most sinister kind, out of the FBI's reach, breaking the bones of the Republic of Texas's most innocent children.

An exaggeration of course, but in Ricki's way of thinking, not by much.

The fourth victim had been found in Mansfield, near Fort Worth. The fifth in Waco, south.

The last two in Austin, Texas. Brandi Lewis, a nineteen-year-old grocery clerk who worked at the H-E-B on the corner of Highway 71 and Bee Cave Road, and

Linda Owens, a fourteen-year-old high school freshman who attended Saint Michael's Catholic Academy.

Austin had reacted as it should have: With outrage. With fear. With a cry for the mayor, the governor, the FBI, the police, anybody and everybody to do something. Anything, just stop this madness.

Standing in Kracker's office now, mind spinning over the past, Ricki wondered if the district attorney hadn't done just that. Anything. Or more to the point, planted the one drop of blood they'd found in Linda Owens's hair as a means to take the one suspect they all suspected off the streets.

Ricki had built her case methodically, in the same manner she'd built a dozen other cases during her ten years with the FBI. She'd already garnered a strong reputation in the bureau as a motivated investigator who did not know how to quit.

But the BoneMan case had worn her to a thread. Welsh was right; they had a file full of evidence that pointed to Phil Switzer, but only the blood was definitive. Only the blood placed him at the scene—of only the *last* victim. And now the sample was being challenged.

Switzer had first shown up on Ricki's radar when police had responded to neighbors' complaints of odors emanating from his mobile home in Waco. There they found a forty-seven-year-old male who lived alone in a house full of cats, six of which he'd strangled. Disturbing, but by no means a connection to the BoneMan.

The fact that he drove a 1978 Ford F-150 with Bridgestone tires matching the tread they'd found at three of BoneMan's crime scenes was more interesting to

Ricki. The fact that Switzer also wore size-thirteen boots that matched the impressions of those left at the crime scenes was enough to move him to the top of the FBI's suspect list.

A complete search of his mobile home turned up the man's penchant for Bibles and pictures of his mother, who'd passed away one year earlier. All the evidence matched the BoneMan's new FBI psychological profile on VICAP.

But they had no direct evidence of Phil Switzer's movements over the previous year. Further complicating the matter was the fact that Switzer was a deaf-mute who refused to cooperate with any form of interrogation. Ricki had persuaded local law enforcement to back away from any prosecution for his animal cruelty and ordered twenty-four-hour surveillance.

On the day that Linda Owens was killed, the surveillance on Switzer had failed, for reasons still unclear. Sloppy police work. An agent negligent on a camera system. But when a drop of blood had been found in the victim's hair, probable cause had forced Switzer to give the FBI a sample of his blood.

Six hours later they had the match. The blood sample taken from Phil Switzer matched the drop of blood found on the victim.

They had found BoneMan.

Four months later a jury of twelve convicted Phil Switzer on one count of first-degree murder and sentenced him to death.

"Any ideas?" Kracker asked, prodding her from her recollection.

She shook her head. "Except for the blood . . ."

This wasn't what Welsh wanted to hear. "Come on, you can't possibly be telling me—"

"The rest is all circumstantial, you know that as well as I do," she snapped, letting her frustration with his insistence break through.

The DA stood and paced to the oak bookcase on the far wall, hands on hips. "We took a serial killer off the streets. The murders stopped when we put him away. The whole world knows we got the right guy." He turned back and stared at both of them. "And now you're telling me we can't pull together any evidence to keep him where he belongs?"

"You're the prosecutor, you tell us," Kracker said.

"I am telling you. I need evidence, and I need it in the next two weeks."

"We have closed the case, Burt."

"Then open it. Focus on the other murders. I need enough to convince the judge to let me hold Switzer as a person of interest while we build another case. You're the FBI, so it's a federal case now. Yes, they got an appeal, so let's get enough on this guy to obtain a stay of appeal from the judge. Double jeopardy is only on his side if he gets an acquittal. Let's not give him that chance."

In a common-sense way what the DA was suggesting made perfect sense, but they all knew that legal proceedings didn't necessarily follow common sense. He was asking for the impossible.

Ricki asked the question that none of them seemed eager to put on the table. "And what if we really did put the wrong man behind bars?"

"We didn't."

"Even worse, what if the blood really was planted by

someone on our team? Switzer's attorneys are hinting at a
lawsuit that could do some damage."

The DA's steady look said it all. *Bingo. And we can't
let that happen.*

"I think we all understand the situation," Kracker said.
"Let's reopen the case, Ricki."

5

KAHLID'S DECISION TO leave Ryan alone with a camera and twelve pictures of broken limbs worked both against Ryan and for him.

Against him in that the photographs were disturbing.

For him in that Kahlid's intentions gave his mind something to consider. A puzzle to piece together. A string of new dots to connect with the picture he was already forming. Data to process with the absorption and care that he'd trained his mind to apply when confronted with disconnected pieces of information.

The camera's purpose was obviously to record his every reaction on tape and transmit those reactions real-time to a monitor now being watched by Kahlid himself. In addition, the camera was meant to keep Ryan on guard. Like any organ, the mind could only function so long before tiring, and remaining on guard would hasten that exhaustion. An obvious intention on Kahlid's part.

Less obvious were the photographs of the broken children. Again, the mystery of them was undoubtedly designed to wear on his mind as much as the horror they presented.

It was unlikely that Kahlid had any idea what Ryan's occupation was, but he'd scored one small victory because Ryan couldn't help but to set his mind on overdrive in an attempt to understand the mystery put before him.

What did Kahlid, who had been very thoughtful in this abduction, hope to gain by making this particular choice? Beyond pointing out the obvious connection between the U.S. military bombing Iraq and the unfortunate collateral damage resulting from war, Kahlid had little to gain. He surely could have found a far more manipulative incentive than this attempt to disturb him with pictures, however gruesome they were.

Which meant that Ryan was missing something. Kahlid had more up his sleeve. He was manipulating Ryan in a subversive way. There was more meaning here. Much more meaning.

Ryan slouched in the chair with his arms shackled behind him, searching his mind for answers. He left no stone unturned, no possibility unconsidered, no thread unexplored. But the answer eluded him.

Unless there was no answer, the possibility of which only added to his mental gymnastics.

The light overhead flickered once; otherwise the only movement in the room came from the blinking camera light and his own periodic shifting to keep blood flowing to his extremities.

An hour went by. Two hours. Three. He began to lose track of time. Also part of Kahlid's plan.

Most humans gave up on unsolved puzzles within a matter of minutes. Those who purchased and played games like Myst could contemplate a single puzzle for twenty or thirty minutes before growing bored with the lack of progress and pulling out the cheat sheet.

The best code breakers could spend days or weeks on a single challenge and remain engaged. But the conundrum facing Ryan contained an element that shifted the balance in his mind. He was staring at images that began to disturb him, not for the mystery in them but for the brutality in them. Not being an emotional man, he found his reaction awkward.

The more he studied what he could see of the victims, the more he felt sucked into their plight. Unlike the thousands of similar photos he'd scanned since coming to the desert, he had time with these images.

Instead of using his mind to understand Kahlid's purpose in leaving him alone with the images, he began to analyze the puzzle in each broken body like he imagined a forensic scientist might.

How had the building collapsed? A nearby hit or a direct hit? Did the victims fall to the bottom before the falling concrete blocks? Which bones had been broken first? How much abuse could a human body sustain? How many breaks could one human being suffer before dying from internal bleeding? How long had the children lived?

Wearing him down was Kahlid's objective, he knew that much. And he was succeeding on that level. But there was more. There had to be.

At some point Ryan woke without realizing he'd fallen asleep. Pain flared in his back and right shoulder and he tried to ease it by shifting to his left. The camera still winked red. The photographs still hung on the wall. His BDU trousers were wet from his own urine.

Nothing else had changed.

Ryan sat in the chair for yet another long time before the latch finally clacked and the door swung open. Kahlid walked in bearing a bottle of Evian water and some yellow rice cakes. He shut the door behind him, studied Ryan with dark but gentle eyes, and then crossed to him.

Without a word he opened the bottle, pressed it to Ryan's lips, and fed him like a mother might feed her child. Ryan sucked down the liquid, surprised at his thirst.

Kahlid withdrew the bottle and set it on the table next to the rice cakes. "There's a bucket in the corner. I will remove your chains so that you can relieve yourself and stretch your bones. If you attempt to escape, I will put a bullet through your thigh. Do you understand?"

Ryan blinked.

Kahlid rounded his chair, unfastened the shackles, and helped him to his feet. His joints felt like fire and it took him half a minute to loosen the stiffness. Hobbling over to a lone bucket and roll of toilet paper in the back corner, he glanced around his prison, but there was nothing new to see. Just the lone chair, the table, the camera, and the photographs.

He used the bucket and walked back to the chair. The locks on the chains were made by Master Lock.

"Go ahead, stretch, get your blood flowing. I need you to be exhausted, but not in pain to the point of indifference."

Ryan's mind began to spin again. Kahlid could hardly utter a word without complicating matters for him. Navy Intelligence could use a man like him.

"That's enough. Please"—his captor motioned to the chair—"sit."

Thirty seconds later Ryan was back in chains, staring at Kahlid. It occurred to him that the brief reprieve had worked against him. Chained again, he felt a surge of hopelessness that wouldn't have been as acute without the reminder of freedom.

All expected techniques, and effective.

"According to your uniform, you are an officer," Kahlid said. "Not that it matters. You have extraordinary control of your mind. You don't express emotion very well. You might even be emotionally repressed. Worse, you might even be proud of yourself for not succumbing to my blatant attempts to affect your emotions. What you don't know is that this will only work against you."

Again, expected.

A slight, nearly sympathetic smile crossed Kahlid's mouth. "You're in intelligence, aren't you? G-2? Again, just a guess. Tell me, how would you judge the effectiveness of my methods to break you thus far?"

No harm in engaging the man on this level. "You're good. Predictable at times and unorthodox at the same time. But I don't think you understand me very well. We both know that I'm already dead. None of this matters to me. Yes, it would be nice to die quickly, but we both know that you won't allow that. So I'm left with no option but to suffer whatever you have in mind for a matter of hours, days, or weeks and then die."

"So calculating. Arabs are far more passionate than Americans are, I think. Everything makes so much sense in your perfect world, doesn't it? Now you've come over here to show us poor Arabs how to enter your perfect world."

Ryan didn't think a rebuttal would help matters.

The man's shoulders sagged and he frowned. "Okay then, you leave me without a choice. We will play our game. But you must know one thing before I tell you what my intentions are. Many would say that I am insane. What I'm about to do will be heralded as inhuman by my own brothers. But you give me no choice."

"Like I said, I'm already dead," Ryan said.

"Yes." Kahlid looked at the pictures. "And so are they. Killed by Satan himself, whom you don't seem to care about, because you don't believe in God."

Kahlid swiveled to him, and Ryan saw the change in his eyes immediately. Something in his mind had shifted.

"Do you know how many women and children your war on our country has killed? Do you have any notion at all of how many thousands of innocent victims the Great Satan has left dead in my country?"

A small voice whispered a warning in Ryan's mind, but he couldn't make it out.

"They all die; they die, they are butchered by your bombs and your missiles and it's all so clinical and distant—you don't feel the pain because it's so far away and because you don't understand the wailing of the mothers and fathers and of God himself when you kill the children!"

He spat the words with bitterness.

"So now"—he paused, taking a deep breath through his nostrils and closing his eyes—"you are going to help me bring the pain of our loss to all the mothers and fathers of your country."

Ryan's eyes snapped open.

"Do you understand yet?"

The man thrust his finger back at the photographs. "If Satan had killed a few children on the streets of any town in your country, horror would settle in the hearts of millions. Ted Bundy kills a few dozen women and the press screams foul, foul, foul. Your Beltway Killer shoots a handful of people on the streets of your capital and the country cries out with outrage!"

Kahlid blinked. "But Satan comes here and kills thousands of women and children and not a single tear is shed. And I tell myself, I have to turn the thousands into one. If they can see just one die, they will understand our pain."

"This is madness," Ryan said.

The man's nostrils flared. "Bring him in!"

The door swung open and a shirtless young man, perhaps fifteen, walked in, wearing an expression that looked part confused, part curious.

"Ahmed." Kahlid smiled at the boy. "Come here, Ahmed."

The boy walked over to Kahlid tentatively, eyes wide at the sight before him.

Kahlid put his hand on the youth's shoulder. "Don't worry, he doesn't speak a word of English. Which is good, because if he knew that I was going to kill him the way my own son was killed—that I was going to crush his bones—he would cause quite a scene."

Nausea swept through Ryan's gut.

"I don't have a building to drop on him, so I'm going to break his bones with a hammer. To be more accurate, *you're* going to break his bones. You will kill him, just as you killed my wife and my child one year ago to this day. No one cried because no one saw. So you will do it again, and this time we will put it on film."

He wouldn't kill, of course. How could they force him to kill? But the mere suggestion of it made his mind swim.

"Don't be ridiculous," was all he could manage.

"You can save this child a fate that neither of us would wish upon him," Kahlid said. "You're wearing a wedding band; tell us where your wife and children live. I have some friends in your country who are waiting for my call. They will go to your home, kill your wife and your child on camera so that the whole world will know how painful even one lost child can be. Look into the camera and tell us to execute your child and I will spare this one."

Ryan's mind refused to process his thoughts logically for a few beats. What was he being asked to do? Surely they . . . Surely this man didn't . . .

Then the game altered in his mind and he knew that he wasn't the only one who would die here in this room. They would use empathetic pain to break him. Survivor guilt and self-loathing, meant to crush his will.

The ease with which he made his decision surprised even him. It was as if a steel wall had gone up in his mind, shutting off all but his stoic resolve. If it came down to it and this man was not bluffing, then he would have to accept the death of this boy, however monstrous it seemed. The alternative was simply an impossibility.

"You'll only make them hate you more," he said.

"I don't think so. Americans have a great capacity for forgiveness once they understand a man's pain. Their problem is that they don't understand our pain."

He wasn't bluffing, was he? The man actually intended to go through with this.

"I will leave Ahmed with you for six hours. Then I will return and kill him, unless you are willing to sacrifice your child's life for his. And then"—a tear formed on the edge of Kahlid's eyes and slipped down his cheek—"then we will bring in the second one. A girl named Miriam. You've killed thousands, but I beg of you, don't make me kill even one more."

6

THE ATMOSPHERE AT Truluck's steak and seafood restaurant in downtown Austin reminded Bethany of success, with all the clinking silverware and wineglasses, the murmur of important people reviewing what they'd accomplished this day and planning the next. The fact that the district attorney, Burt Welsh, had joined her and her mother, two days after her selection to be on the cover of *Youth Nation,* only solidified the impression.

Problem was, she was quite sure she didn't belong.

Everywhere she looked, waiters in white aprons served customers heaping plates of broiled lobster tails and crab legs while a piano player filled the dimly lit room with music.

"A toast?" The DA held up his wineglass with an infectious grin.

Her mother lifted her glass and Bethany followed suit, raising her own, never mind that it was Dr Pepper.

"To the next cover girl of *Youth Nation,*" the DA said.

"To the most wonderful daughter a mother could ever hope for," Celine chimed in, beaming.

Her mother was certainly in her element. Bethany smiled graciously. "Thank you."

They clinked their glasses and took sips.

"I have to say, I've been around the block a few times, and I admit I have an eye for those bound for glory. You, young lady, are one such person, I could see it the moment you walked in tonight."

What did you say to that?

The DA continued before she could say anything. "Like mother, like daughter."

Her mother's eyes sparkled with pride. "Thank you, Burt."

It was the first time Bethany had actually met the DA, and thinking of him by his name seemed strange to her. Her mother, on the other hand, wasn't nearly so reserved. Only a blind man wouldn't see the chemistry between them. Didn't they care that half the restaurant probably recognized the DA and was wondering at this very moment why he was sitting at a table with a married woman and her daughter, with more than food on his mind?

"Thank you," she said.

They talked about the upcoming trip to New York and the modeling business while they waited for their food. She was surprised to learn that the DA—Burt, he insisted she call him—that Burt Welsh had modeled himself once, while attending law school at the University of Texas. He'd quit when they'd asked him to do an underwear shoot.

Honestly, she wasn't quite sure what to make of the man. He certainly had the look of a model, with large square shoulders and a closely shaved jaw, but she found him oddly repulsive. A perfect fit for her mother maybe, with his compelling, confident demeanor, but that didn't make him God's gift to all women.

They'd come to celebrate; when Celine suggested they take up the DA's offer to take them to dinner, she'd agreed. Clearly something was going on between them; maybe it was time to meet this man her mother spent so much time on the phone with.

But half an hour in Burt's company reminded her why she didn't think she could stomach the modeling business as more than a passing gig.

She began to regret her decision to let him join them. It was fine for her mother, who deserved some love in her life—her father had failed miserably on that front. But that didn't mean Bethany had to like the man who was sharing her mother's bed when it suited them.

In fact, sitting here with him in the lap of luxury, Bethany felt oddly sick. Here the rich partook of the spoils of their wealth, but in Bethany's world girls were cutting their skin with razor blades to escape the emotional pain that haunted them.

She'd even thought about cutting herself a time or two, if for no other reason than to see what so many saw in it. She knew the reasoning, of course: better to control the pain inflicted by yourself than the pain dumped on you by your circumstances.

Bethany blinked. Here she was thinking about razor blades while her mother and Welsh were toasting life. There was irony. She decided to bring them into her world.

"I've decided that I don't want to pursue modeling beyond this job," she said and sat back to hear their response.

Her mother dismissed her with a slight flip of her hand. "Oh, don't be ridiculous."

"Why would you say that?" Burt asked, swirling the red wine in his glass.

"I just don't think I could stomach all the superficiality that comes with it. What do people really know about models anyway?"

"What do you mean, angel? It's not a marriage; it's a job. A job that could lead to acting, Hollywood. This is just the beginning. What happened to all those calls with your agent, was that all just for grins?"

The DA tipped his glass at Celine. "Your mother has a point. This could be just the beginning of something much bigger. Cover at your age? That's pretty impressive."

"Hollywood stars are the same thing. I walk around school and already they look at me like I'm some kind of monkey in a zoo. They don't know a thing about me."

Her mother's mouth gaped in a show of shock. "How could you be so ungrateful? Every last girl in that school would kill to be you right now. You just want to throw that away because you don't have a deep, meaningful relationship with every boy in the hall?"

Now this was more like Mother. Bethany had to admit that she wasn't entirely ready to throw out modeling just yet, but her claim was at least partly true. Maybe even mostly true.

"I'm just saying"—she picked at the bread on her plate—"it bothers me."

Her mother offered Burt a condescending grin. "She's sixteen going on twenty-one with a degree in philosophy. *Everything* about life bothers her when it suits her. Nothing is really meaningful. Our little existentialist in the making. But that doesn't mean she doesn't love to shake her butt in front of a thousand boys at football games, now does it?"

A raised brow from Burt. He seemed to be enjoying the shift in conversation.

"So I play the game; you taught me that, Mother, didn't you? Play all the angles, use your assets to take all you can from life. Just because I've decided to try things your way doesn't mean I have to like it or give my life to it the way you have."

"My, my." Burt's eyes were bright with interest, and she thought his grin was more one of fascination than embarrassment. "You're quite intelligent."

"For what? A bimbo on a cover? I think you may have made my point."

"No, for a sixteen-year-old."

"Too smart for her own britches, if you ask me," Mother said.

Bethany decided to take it one step further, aware that she might be purposefully throwing a few stones into their perfect little love affair.

"I love you, Mother, and I will learn whatever you have to teach me. But don't expect me to live the same life you live, hopping around from party to party, man to man, looking to fill the hole in your soul with social fluff."

Both Celine and the DA sat frozen in place. She might as well have dropped a stun grenade. But her mother recovered quickly; it was a skill she'd long ago perfected.

She uttered a short chuckle and lifted her glass. "I'm sorry you feel that way, Bethany. But don't take your own search for significance out on me. I wasn't the one who left."

Touché. She hated it when Mother played the father card. Bethany wasn't sure how to respond.

"She's never forgiven him," Celine said to Burt. "Sorry you have to hear all of this, I had no idea—"

"Don't be sorry, I think this is entirely appropriate," Burt said, folding his fingers together in front of his chin. "We all have a cross to bear. So tell me, Bethany, what's it like having a Naval Intelligence officer as a father?"

She resented the question and considered telling him that she wasn't in the market for a counselor, particularly one who was sleeping with her mother. She wasn't looking for a father, either, just in case he was getting any ideas.

On second thought, maybe she should clear a few things up.

"I'm not looking for a father, if that's what you mean."

"No. No, that's not what I meant. I meant exactly what I said. What's it like to have a Naval Intelligence officer as a father?"

"What is this, cross-examination?"

He laughed and Mother joined him, relieved by the break in tension. "It's what I do, I suppose. You're right, you should drop the modeling thing like I did and pursue a career in law or politics." He lifted his water glass. "Here's to you, kid."

After a moment, Mother pushed the point. "So tell him, Bethany. What's it like?"

"I wouldn't know, actually. I don't remember having a father who was a Naval Intelligence officer. I used to think I should feel bad about that, but I really don't know what it's like to have a father. Ryan's never been home.

He feels more like a statue in my life. An ATM in the corner of our house."

"Well, that's an interesting way of putting it," Mother said.

"You don't feel any loyalty to him?"

"Maybe I'm not being clear. I don't like Ryan. I might even hate him. Like I said, I used to feel guilty about that, but I've come to realize that my father left us long ago for another wife. The worst part is that he's too stupid to see that. I'm sure that he's a good enough person in his own way, but I can't think of him as my father, and I don't blame my mother for looking for another husband."

There. Was that what you wanted to hear? They weren't laughing.

The waiter stepped in and placed hot butter and crab forks next to each plate.

"Everything to your satisfaction, sir?"

"It's fine, Robert. Thank you."

He dipped his head. "Your food will be right up."

The waiter left.

"Aren't you a little concerned about what people will think, seeing you in public like this?" Bethany asked.

"Doing what? Having dinner with a mother and her daughter?"

"Please. Half the waiters in the joint probably know you're sleeping together. You can see it a mile away."

"Bethany," her mother scolded, flushing red.

"You don't think so?"

"You may be right," Burt said. "Did I say you should consider a career in law?"

"Too many charlatans."

"Present company excluded, I hope."

Bethany didn't respond to the unspoken request. But as long as she was clearing the air, she might as well clear it all.

"I don't know you that well, Mr. Welsh, but if my mother loves you, that's fine by me. Not that you need my permission."

"No. But I appreciate both your candor and approval."

"You're welcome."

"Are you sure you're only sixteen?"

Bethany arched her eyebrow. "You never know, in this happy little family of ours. For all I know I'm really fourteen or eighteen and adopted."

Her mother chuckled.

"Well, for the record, your honor, I think I like this happy little family. Very much."

A cart loaded with cracked Alaskan king crab legs and three large lobsters rolled up to their table.

Bethany still wasn't sure how much she liked Mr. DA Burton Welsh, but she liked him more now than she had ten minutes earlier.

7

THE BOY SAT in a chair opposite Ryan, staring at the wall with round eyes that had long ago stopped crying. Their captors had tied his hands behind his back and his ankles were strapped to the chair legs with nylon fishing line. Sweat had washed away the long lines that tears had etched down his cheeks.

The camera winked red. Kahlid's pictures peered at Ryan over the boy's shoulder.

This was the situation.

But this didn't even modestly describe the situation, because the real situation resided in their minds. In Kahlid's mind, in the youth's mind, in Ryan's mind.

Above all else, Ryan knew that he could not allow his mind to break. If Kahlid managed to shape his responses, Ryan knew he would do whatever the man wanted, which in this case would likely mean the death of his wife and daughter.

The manner with which Kahlid meant to break his mind was clear enough. What kind of man could stand by and watch innocent victims being killed on his account without suffering terrible anguish? The pressure of such horror would eventually break him.

But the only way to save Ahmed was to offer up his own wife and child.

The similarity between this particular situation and war was inescapable. Kahlid was right, innocent victims were allowed to die in war for the greater good of the campaign. To slay the dragon you had to kill a few bunnies who got in the way. Collateral damage. You could try to say the innocents weren't truly innocent, but in the end they were daughters and sons and wives and they *were* innocent.

Innocent like Ahmed.

The only difference between the quivering Arab strapped to the chair before Ryan and the innocents who'd been killed by shrapnel from a bomb dropped on a building was that one was face-to-face, and one was distant.

Kahlid meant to make it all personal to Ryan and through his camera to the world.

It was an impossible conundrum. But Ryan had long ago learned that every code could be broken. Every game could be beaten. Even the impossible ones. He'd given his life to this one objective. He'd saved a thousand lives by doing what very few could do or were willing to do. This was what he knew.

And he knew that the only hope he had of beating this game was to shut down his emotions entirely so that he could focus on the challenge at hand. Doing so with Ahmed weeping in the chair had been a monumental hurdle, but Ryan had managed for the most part.

The fact that Kahlid had left a clock on the table this

time didn't help. The ticking was a constant reminder that they were in a time lock.

He glanced at the small white alarm clock and saw that three hours had passed. Three to go.

"What's going to happen?" the boy asked in Arabic for the hundredth time.

Ryan looked at him without expression. If the boy learned that he could speak his language, he would continue as he had for the first half hour, begging for some explanation, asking for his mother, explaining that he was only going out to get wood as his father had asked him to.

None of this was useful information and only weakened Ryan's resolve to guard his mind.

He closed his eyes and centered his thoughts once again, stepping through the facets of this challenge as he had so many times already.

One: Kahlid's entire game was built upon the belief that if presented with an edited video of an American officer begging that his wife and daughter die to save the lives of Iraqi children, some of whom were seen broken on the floor, the American public would cry out in outrage and demand that such senseless killing of children be stopped, regardless of whose side it was on. And Ryan thought he had a point. Especially if the video included images of his wife and child being killed. They would be furious at the terrorist, but his point would be made in spades.

Two: To accomplish his mission, Kahlid must coerce an American soldier into the position of making such a plea by presenting him with precisely the kind of threat he'd chosen.

Three: The game assumed that Ryan actually cared

whether or not the children died as much as he cared whether his wife or child died.

Four: The game required him to play. If he was incapacitated or killed, he would do Kahlid no good. A dead man could not make a plea on videotape.

Five: The game depended on a camera. The one now eyeing them.

Six: The game depended on whether or not he cared that his wife died.

Ryan stopped to consider this matter again, since it had presented itself to his mind twice now. The fact was, he really wasn't sure that his loyalty to this one woman was any greater than his loyalty to the American people. Or his loyalty to Ahmed. Especially if Ahmed was joined by another child. A girl named Miriam.

The six primary concerns he'd laid out in his mind represented a total of twenty-seven independent variables, and he'd dwelt on each from every conceivable angle already, but he reapplied himself to some of the more obvious solutions to his conundrum now.

The most obvious solution was to change Kahlid's mind. Highly unlikely, but in this game of wits, Ryan could play a few cards of his own and at the very least stall the man. Naturally he would try.

He could try to escape. Again, not likely, but he'd considered a dozen possibilities, all of which depended mostly on luck, but he wasn't exactly brimming with optimism.

He could try to remove himself from the equation by either killing himself or by being killed. In an escape attempt perhaps. It would require some ingenuity and some luck, but he would do it if needed.

He could simply offer up Celine.

Again, the thought stopped him cold.

His mind drifted back to the eighteen years since his marriage to Celine. She'd waltzed into the computer department at Office Depot, one year out of high school, and accepted his help in choosing a new laptop for a job she was taking with an ad agency. The job turned out to be a telemarketing scam that she had quit two weeks later.

The spark ignited between them in Office Depot turned into a whirlwind romance and marriage four months later. Admittedly, the worst mistake he'd ever made.

Within weeks Ryan realized that he'd married an uncommonly needy woman who quickly turned her lack of fulfillment into the belief that having a baby would satisfy her. Unable to have a child due to a botched abortion when she was eighteen, she insisted they adopt. Ryan had agreed, perhaps one of the *best* choices he'd made in his eighteen years of marriage.

Bethany had entered their lives one year later, and Ryan had never drawn any distinction between her and a daughter they might have had through birth.

Bethany he would never jeopardize for any reason. This he knew. This he refused to even consider, regardless of the reasoning behind it. Maybe it was true that he'd abandoned her when she needed him the most, but he was still her father and he still loved her as a father loved his child. How could a father give up his daughter?

But Celine . . .

No. No, he could never live with himself.

Then again, who said he had to live with himself? What if giving up Celine, assuming Kahlid would agree, actually saved Bethany as well as Ahmed?

But no. He couldn't.

Then what?

Then he had to stop wasting time considering options that were impossibilities for him and focus on those that might be viable solutions, however unlikely.

A new thought presented itself to him. What was the true worth of one child?

He opened his eyes and studied Ahmed, who was watching him. His coal black hair was ruffled, and peach fuzz extended down from his sideburns in the earliest showings of facial hair. He wore stained tan shorts, probably one of only a few he owned.

His green T-shirt had an image of Arnold Schwarzenegger wearing dark glasses, with the word *Terminator* beneath it.

He closed his eyes and shut out the image. Was his life worth more than this one boy's life? How could you assign worth to human life?

Kahlid was doing all of this because he'd lost a boy like Ahmed and he believed that the only way to save many more like him was to sacrifice this one. He believed that this was the will of God.

Now Kahlid wanted Ryan to play God. So then, assuming there was a God who made such choices, what would God do? Sacrifice one child?

Save Ahmed.

The thoughts began to run together. Dizziness swept over him and his world turned black. What if he couldn't beat this game? What if there was no way to win?

His heart rate suddenly increased and his breathing thickened in the telltale sign of a panic attack. Ryan sucked deep through his nose and blew the air out slowly several times. This was not good. He had to get a grip, clear his mind, and apply himself to the three options that made the most sense.

Manipulation.

Escape.

Suicide.

THE DOOR SWUNG open four minutes after the six-hour mark and Kahlid walked in with the two men who'd first confronted him in this prison. They had towels, a dozen or more, rolled up. And a sledgehammer.

Ryan's world faded for the second time in the last six hours. Blood coursed through his veins, pumped by a heavy beat. His chest tightened to restrict his breathing, and his eyes, though open, stopped seeing for a moment.

He'd suffered panic attacks once in Turkey for no outwardly good reason at all. The doctor had said they might be related to diet.

Everything in him suddenly wanted to scream out in rage. But giving in at this point would only undermine any chance he had of beating Kahlid at his own game.

Slowly his vision returned.

The boy was chattering through tears. Three words drummed through Ryan's mind: Manipulation. Escape. Suicide. In that order, if possible.

"I'll make you a deal," he said.

"I've already offered a deal. It's the only one I'll consider."

"Did I say my deal was different than yours?"

The man cracked his neck slowly. "You are not in a

position to be clever, Kent. By now you've considered every possible outcome of this scenario and you realize that the only option that makes sense is for you to do as I say. That is my only deal."

"Then I'll agree to your deal. I'll give you the name and address of my wife."

Kahlid arched his brow. "Really? To save this one boy?"

"Isn't that what you wanted?"

He would give an entirely false address, of course, one that he knew didn't exist. A street in San Antonio that he knew ended in the 1200 block. Celine and Bethany had moved to Austin when he'd shipped out for this last tour. He didn't want Kahlid anywhere near them.

"No, I said wife and child. Not wife."

The demand was unexpected and Ryan hesitated. And in that hesitation he knew that he'd made a critical mistake. He'd just informed the man that he indeed had a child.

Kahlid smiled. "Thank you. I was hoping you had a child. And I need both."

"If I give you one I'm giving you both, aren't I?"

Kahlid walked behind the boy, ripped gray duct tape off a roll, and strapped it around his quivering lips, eyes on Ryan.

"I'm tempted to let you hear him scream, but I don't think I could stand it."

"I'll give them to you!" Ryan snapped, losing himself.

"Emotion. That's good, Kent. Because I need more than just the name and address of your wife and daughter . . . it is a daughter, isn't it?"

"None of your business." His fingers were shaking now.

"Better." He nodded at the men, who came over and knelt down on either side of the boy. "I need you to look into the camera, give your true name and your rank, and then beg that I kill your wife and daughter for the sake of this child. I need the world to see it all."

"I'll give you their names and—"

"Now, Kent. What is your real name?"

His world started to dim again, and he began to shake. It was involuntary and he made no effort to still himself. He had to keep the man talking.

"Okay. You win. You sick pig. Captain Frank Barnes."

"Address?"

"1400 Houston Way."

"City?"

"San Antonio, Texas."

Kahlid withdrew a radio from his pocket and spoke the address into the mouthpiece.

The men forced the boy to kneel beside the metal chair, positioning his forearm over the edge.

Nausea swept through Ryan's gut. His mind quickly ran through his remaining options.

Escape was out of the question at this moment.

Suicide would take too much time now, assuming he could really go through with it.

The radio crackled. Soon. Only seconds had passed. They'd planned this down to the last detail.

"The address doesn't exist," a voice said in Arabic.

"Please . . . okay. Just give me a minute!" Ryan cried the words without intending to yield to emotion.

"Watch! I want you to watch what you have done. You can't hide your head in the sand like the rest of your country! Watch what your decision does!"

"Please . . ."

Kahlid shifted his eyes to one of his men. "Break his bones."

Something snapped in Ryan's mind. He could feel it break loose and fall away like curtains dropping to the stage.

The chains that held him gave him a mere six inches of play, but he didn't care about that. He had to do something, anything. So he lunged forward with all of his strength, screaming a wordless protest.

His backside barely cleared the seat before the chains stopped him.

He heard the boy screaming through his tape. And above the scream he heard the sound.

It was only a soft *pop* of bone breaking within flesh, but it was a sound that would haunt even the coldest heart.

The pop chased Ryan into darkness and he slumped into unconsciousness.

WHEN RYAN'S MIND drifted back into the dim light, the first thing he discovered was that the metal chair that had been occupied by the boy Ahmed was empty. He looked left and right and saw no one.

So then he'd imagined it? A flash of relief was immediately followed by reason.

No. He'd heard the pop. Kahlid had simply removed the boy. In what condition, Ryan refused to consider.

An overwhelming sense of remorse flooded his mind. Remorse for the boy, Ahmed, yes. But even more, remorse for his own daughter. For Bethany.

He now knew with very little uncertainty that at the end

of this ordeal, Bethany would be either dead or fatherless, and he was surprised by the pain he felt at the latter possibility. Not because he feared death; and in truth he was dead. But because now he realized that Bethany already was fatherless.

He'd abandoned her already.

What had he been thinking?

And Celine? Yes, his wife as well! How could he blame her for needing love if her own husband wasn't close to love her?

Suicide was his only option now. He had no choice but to take his own life and end this madness. It was the only way to save his family and any more children like Ahmed, whom the butcher named Kahlid put before him.

Something else had changed. His arms.

Ryan looked down and blinked. They'd bound his arms in towels and strapped them tightly to the sides of the chair. His first thought was that they intended to break *his* bones.

But then he saw that they had taped his legs to the chair as well. They had immobilized him. Crude but effective means to keep him from cutting his wrists on the chains.

They'd put him on suicide watch.

A knot formed in Ryan's gut. Kahlid knew his psychology. He'd trapped Ryan in a predicament that could not end with an escape into his own death.

A soft whimper sounded behind him. He twisted his head around and saw two things that etched a bitter chill down his neck. The first was Ahmed's dead, badly bruised, and twisted body on the floor just behind his chair.

The second was a teenaged girl hog-tied in the back corner, staring at him with brown eyes through long stringy hair.

Miriam.

Dear God. Dear God, forgive me . . .

8

RICKI VALENTINE SLOWLY paced along the two tables on which she'd carefully organized the reams of reports and photographs from BoneMan's files. Laid out in seven columns, one for each case, in the order they'd been investigated. A map of Texas faced her from the wall behind the tables, showing the path of death BoneMan had carved from El Paso to Austin.

Four days had passed since Kracker asked her to dive back into the case that had consumed her two years earlier, and she'd spent half of that time pacing. Running her hand along the table, examining each piece of data, each field report, each photograph, with the intent of extracting even a whiff of evidence they'd missed before.

Her task was a simple one: Keep Switzer behind bars, because they all knew that Switzer was BoneMan. Save the DA. Prevent a killer from breaking another bone.

Convince the evidence to tell her something new.

But the evidence wasn't cooperating.

Mark Resner, her partner on the case, leaned against his

desk ten feet to her left, sleeves of his white shirt rolled up, tapping a pencil on his palm as he watched her.

"The lioness stalks," he said quietly.

She looked at him and saw that he was smiling.

"Is that what I am? I feel a bit more like a snake at the moment."

"Now there's an image."

"Snaking through all this slimy mess."

"Give it a break, Ricki. We've both been over it a hundred times; there's nothing new on that table."

She shifted her gaze to the black picture window. They were three stories up, facing a large brick building that cut out the city's night lights. Her reflection stared back. Haunting. Her black hair was absorbed by the night, leaving only a face with brown eyes gazing at her.

To think that the fate of BoneMan was held in the grasp of this petite thirty-five-year-old woman. An odd thought.

"Mind closing the blinds?"

Mark walked to the window and lowered the white blinds.

It was more than just BoneMan's fate. It was the fate of other victims, should BoneMan strike again. Of the DA, should Switzer go free. The people when the realization that the killer who'd terrorized Texas was not behind bars.

"I think you're right, Mark," she said, turning her attention back to the stacks of files. "There's nothing new here." She walked to the end of the table, picked up one file marked Blood Lab, and headed back the way she'd come, drumming her fingers on the file.

"I can't help but thinking . . ." But she wasn't sure quite how to put it.

The thought had run circles through her mind all afternoon and into the evening, but she'd refused to give it much attention, because her task was to find *new* evidence, not rehash old.

"Blood?" Mark asked, eyeing the file. "The blood work's been verified in three separate lab workups."

"I know, Switzer's blood, both samples apparently from the original sample."

"But not conclusive."

"Not conclusive in our way of thinking. But the margin of error is so small, we both know the judge will probably allow the new evidence and declare a mistrial. That's why we're here."

"But . . ." Mark said expectantly.

Ricki took a deep breath and eased to the middle of the room, eyes on the table all the way. She stopped, held out the blood file, and released it.

The manila file landed on the carpet with a soft *plop*.

Ricki put her hands on her hips and nodded at the table. "What do you see?"

Mark joined her and stared at the stacks, the map, all that was BoneMan in the FBI files.

"You're saying Switzer isn't BoneMan?" he said. "I know how it looks, but—"

"No, Mark. Just tell me what you see. What do you know about the files on that table?"

"They meticulously detail BoneMan's work in seven murders. Crime scene investigation reports, lab work, evidence gathered and analyzed, interviews, behavior profiles, photographs. You want me to go on?"

"You see BoneMan."

"I see BoneMan."

"Do you see Switzer? Just what's on the table, do you see Switzer?"

"I think I do, yes."

"Well, I'm not sure I do, Mark." She paced to her right, propping one arm on the other, turning the silver cross on her breastbone absently. "Standing back, two years after the fact, if I really do pull out the blood work, I just can't say for sure that the killer on that table is the man we have behind bars."

"Well, that'll go over. The killings stopped."

"Wouldn't you stop the killings if you learned that they had blamed your work on someone else?"

"Not if I were a serial killer, I wouldn't. You know killers like BoneMan feed off the game. He would find the opportunity to show off his handiwork irresistible, particularly after the public had sighed in relief at his supposed capture."

"So it would seem. But pysch profiles are only educated guesses. They're hypotheses about criminals. Isn't it at least a possibility that BoneMan, a killer who isn't necessarily taking pleasure in his killing, is smarter? Having killed seven, the number of completion in many religious circles, he's fulfilled his obligation to God *and* gotten away with it. Or maybe he's still killing but burying the bodies, waiting for the day to go public again."

"Possible. But with the weight of evidence—"

"Take away the blood"—she walked over to the table, lifted a thick file, and tossed it on the carpet—"take away the psychobabble. Now what do you see?"

"This isn't new territory, Ricki. We thought we had the right guy before the blood turned up."

"Just follow me. Do you see Switzer on the table now? Separating out the psych and blood?"

"He's white, hundred and ninety pounds, size thirteen—all things we know about BoneMan."

"So are a couple hundred thousand other Americans."

"There's also his refusal to deny."

"Not an admission."

"Dead cats—"

"Not dead girls."

"No alibi for any of the murders."

"Not exactly a Polaroid of him leaning over the bodies."

He frowned, but there was a sparkle in his blue eyes. She'd dated the blond-haired agent from Mississippi long before the BoneMan case, but they'd decided that a romance would only complicate their relationship in the office. He'd since married Gertrude, a pretty brunette from his hometown, Biloxi.

Ricki had drifted in and out of a dozen casual relationships over the past ten years, but not too many guys were strong enough to handle an "agent with tunnel vision," as Mark put it. She was admittedly preoccupied. Not that she didn't want a serious relationship; she just wasn't the type to go hunting for a man unless he'd committed a federal offense and deserved to spend the rest of his time behind bars.

Not the best of bedmates.

"You really buy all that?" he said.

"I'm just saying." Ricki walked up to him, turned to face the table, and crossed her arms. "We're not necessarily looking at Phil Switzer. We may be. We may not be."

"You think that's the way a jury would see it?"

"Depends on the attorney. But I think the judge will see it that way."

"So you think we have the wrong man. The DA's gonna convince the mayor to throw you a party."

"I'm not saying we *do* have the wrong man, Mark. I'm saying that we can't be sure, not without the blood evidence. And if we can't be sure that BoneMan is behind bars, we might want to consider the fact that he's still out there."

He said nothing to that.

"If he is, we still have a lot of work in front of us."

Mark crossed to his desk and sat. "I don't know, Ricki. I think you're wrong about this one. And unless we get another dead body, I think the rest of the world will agree with me."

"You willing to take that risk? Another victim?"

"Come on, Ricki, this is me. Of course not. Please don't tell me you're going to pitch this to Kracker. You know how tight he is with the DA. They'll crucify you, going out on a whim like this."

"I don't know what I'm going to do yet."

"Don't do it. If you do, I'm not backing you."

She studied him for a moment, then crossed to her chair, plucked her purse from the corner, and walked for the door.

"You're right about one thing, Mark. There's nothing new on this table. It's all on the floor."

9

"I WOULD LIKE to go back to the cell, before you escaped and were picked up by the helicopter."

Ryan's mind swam back to the hazy rescue, the hot desert, the helicopter's flashing lights, the disbelief that he had actually survived the incident.

"Can I get you some more water, Captain? A Coke?"

Ryan stared at the civilian psychiatrist from command that the joint task force had assigned to debrief him. He'd met the man once before. A gray-haired doctor who had kind blue eyes behind thin spectacles and an understanding smile.

The doctor's eyes shifted down to look at Ryan's hands, which were resting on either side of a microphone on the table before him. His right hand was shaking. Like an old man suffering from the onset of Parkinson's disease.

Ryan stared at the hand and tried unsuccessfully to stop the quiver. He removed both hands and set them on his lap beneath the table.

"Captain?"

The psychiatrist's name was Dr. Newman, a civil-service mental health professional deployed with the U.S. Army. Seven days had passed since Ryan's rescue, and each had brought a brighter day with more clarity, but his mind still buzzed and his hands still shook.

"Yes?"

Ryan glanced at the woman beside him, a staff counselor named Julie Stewart, who had visited him twice a day at the 28th Combat Support Hospital in Baghdad over the last week. He alone knew the full details of what had happened in the desert, but today, that would all change. He was finally going to speak.

"Would you like more water?"

"Yes, that would be nice, thank you."

Newman nodded at one of the MPs at the back of the sparsely furnished room. There were just these two tables facing each other; glass louvered windows facing another hot but oddly quiet day in Iraq.

At times they looked at him as if he was too unstable, but when he'd pressed them earlier, they'd agreed that he was perfectly capable now. The last seven days had been touch and go, admittedly, but he had woken this morning feeling fresh and ready to get back to work.

He had to pass this debriefing and psych evaluation, and shaking hands not withstanding, he would demonstrate that he was just fine. And then he could get back to his post.

A hand reached over his shoulder and placed a bottle of water in front of him.

"Thank you," he said. But he left the water for now.

"I realize this is difficult," Newman was saying. "But the more we can get from you now, the less likely command will want more later. I'm sure you understand."

"Yes."

"It's also important that we cover various aspects of the incident so that we can properly evaluate you."

"Yes. That's fine, go ahead."

"Okay," Newman looked over at the laptop Julie was typing into. "Where were we?"

"The girl named Miriam," Julie said. Her eyes flittered over the screen, caught Ryan's, and dropped immediately back down.

Newman turned back to the yellow pad before him and drew a line with his pen. "Yes, of course. And just so I'm clear, at this point the camera is still recording you?"

"Yes."

"The images of the broken children are still on the wall—"

"Collateral damage," Ryan corrected.

"The children that Kahlid equated with collateral damage in Iraq. Women and children."

"His children, yes."

"Yes."

Newman lifted his blue eyes and peered over his wire-framed spectacles. "The boy named Ahmed is dead on the floor behind you, killed in a similar manner, that is, his bones broken, crushed."

"Yes."

"Miriam is tied up in the corner."

"Yes."

"At this point you were seriously considering suicide as the only way to save the victims without giving them what they wanted."

Ryan hesitated, trying to determine if his admission would in any way undermine their evaluation of his psychological soundness. But his mind was buzzing and he knew that his best course was to simply tell them what had happened as calmly as he could.

"Yes."

"But they had effectively removed that possibility by restraining your arms to the chair."

He gave them a nod.

"Please speak into the microphone, Captain. We need the audio."

"Yes." He leaned forward and said it again, this time in a clear voice. "Yes, that is correct."

"Tell us what happened next," the psychiatrist said, setting his pen down.

Ryan spoke in a steady voice, determined to appear as calculated and reasonable a possible.

"They left me in the room with the girl for six hours. Then they came back in and killed the girl."

"Can you describe that for me?"

Ryan felt nauseated. Clearly an attempt to analyze his psychological response to the situation.

"It was just like the boy," he said.

"You said you heard the boy's bones break and then you fell unconscious. Did you lose consciousness again when they killed the girl?"

A painful knot rose up his throat and for a moment he thought he might actually throw up.

"No."

Newman looked at him for a moment, then spoke in a soft voice. "I need you to tell me what you saw and heard, Captain. I realize—"

"They killed her," he snapped. Then forcing back his emotion as best he could, "Isn't that enough?"

The doctor calmly picked up his pen, made a note on his pad, and set the pen back down. "I think I'm going to recommend that we give you a little more time before we continue. For your sake."

They were here to decide his fate, they all knew that. The military could be brutally efficient when it needed to be. Newman was simply extending Ryan the courtesy of more rest to improve the likelihood that whatever fate was decided during the evaluation would be consistent with both the military's objectives and Ryan's desires.

But Ryan didn't think he could put up with another day in the hospital, lying on white sheets like a decomposing corpse. He needed something to pull him out of this no-man's-land he'd entered.

"No, I'm sorry, it's just . . ." He reached for the bottle and saw his left hand shake as it gripped the plastic, and regretted the decision. But he couldn't draw attention to it by withdrawing his hand, so he lifted the bottle, took a short sip, set it down, and put his hand back in his lap, where it continued to shake.

It's wrong, Ryan. You can't do this.

"I'll be fine," he said. "Watching someone die is a hard thing."

"During this time what was Kahlid doing?" Sweat had dotted the doctor's forehead. He had been exposed to atrocities, but this one had to be near the top of the list.

"He stood by the door, watching me."

"He didn't say anything? No reaction from him?"

"No, he didn't say anything. But there were tears on his face."

"Did this surprise you? To see such an emotional reaction from such a brutal man?"

"The whole game was an emotional reaction on his part," Ryan said. "He believes we've butchered a thousand children with no less brutality."

The doctor nodded as if he understood, but Ryan doubted he could.

"It's hard to even imagine how you must have felt in that room, Captain."

It was a question. "How would you feel?"

"Tell me how you felt."

The urge to throw up returned and Ryan had to swallow for fear that he would. The emotions that haunted him would slowly pass. In the meantime he had to accept and deal with them as best he could. As he had when they'd killed Miriam.

"I couldn't give in to him, you understand. His objective was to break me. The only thing I could do at that point was to break him."

"So you sat there while they were killing Miriam and did what?"

"Nothing."

"You closed your eyes," the doctor said.

"Yes."

"But you felt nothing?"

"I had no choice."

"You were able to shut off your emotions?"

"I don't know. All I know is that Kahlid was weeping and I wasn't."

Julie's eyes kept flashing him glances over her screen. He wasn't sure if she wanted to strangle him or cry for him.

"Tell us what happened next."

"They brought in a third victim. Another boy. Kahlid

called me a heartless pig when I refused to do what he wanted."

"You were absolutely convinced that if you'd given him your wife's name and address, he would have carried out his threat?"

"Yes."

"Go on."

"Three hours later they came in and killed the boy."

"Three?"

"Kahlid shortened the time frame."

"He killed him the same way?"

"Yes."

"Did you watch this time?"

"No."

"Did Kahlid react visibly?"

"He left the room this time."

"I see. And you? What was your reaction this time?"

"This time . . . this time I passed out."

"So it would be fair to say that your efforts at controlling your emotions were not entirely successful."

"Not entirely, no. But I couldn't react the way he wanted me to react. You do understand that. My wife and my daughter . . ." The fist of sorrow that rose into his throat at the mention of his daughter prohibited him from continuing.

"Take your time, Captain."

It occurred to him that his attempts to show them his restraint might be misguided. He didn't want to appear inhuman, did he? This wasn't the game, after all. The game had ended a week ago.

Or had it?

"My daughter's life was at stake. I'm sure you understand."

"Did they bring in a fourth child?"

"A male. A little older than the others."

"They killed him?"

"Yes."

"And who won this little game between you and Kahlid this time?"

The question hit Ryan like a battering ram to his chest. This man was reducing his torment to the consequence of a little game of chicken played between two stubborn bullies?

Ryan shifted his gaze to a large photograph of the president on the wall behind Newman and answered in a tight but otherwise reasonably settled voice. "Neither of us won. The boy died."

His legs began to quiver, barely. He moved them and they stilled for a brief moment, but then started again.

"This is the fourth body they laid on the floor behind your chair?"

"No. They put those two on the floor to my left."

Julie's fingers stopped moving on the keyboard and she closed her eyes for a moment.

"How long did this go on, Captain?" the psychiatrist asked.

He tried to tell them. But his mouth wasn't doing what his brain was telling it to do.

Instead it was telling him that he was now living a lie, sitting here in perfect control, playing the game most respected by him and all of his peers, calm as any naval officer was expected to be, regardless of what happened. He'd maintained the façade without breaking.

But now his mind was telling him it couldn't keep up the charade any longer. The fact was, he couldn't possibly continue life as he had once known it. Everything had changed with the breaking of the first bone.

No matter how Ryan tried to tell himself that he could go on, deep inside where he refused to hear himself, he knew that a part of him had died when Ahmed, the first innocent Arab boy, had died.

He had no interest in judging war, but for him, it had to be over. No more. The death of the innocent had collapsed his entire world.

The psychiatrist seemed content to wait for him.

Ryan tried to tell them again, but his mouth still wasn't cooperating. It occurred to him then that he might be losing control of himself. Right here in front of them. His legs shook as if they were in a blender.

He made one last desperate attempt to force his body into submission, but the wall of control he'd erected suddenly crumbled and he could not stop the tidal wave that had been slowly building behind it.

His whole body began to quake, from head to foot. His chair rattled beneath him. And even now he tried . . . tried to stop it, just *stop* the emotion that was tearing his chest in two.

He lifted his trembling hands from his lap and set them on the table but they only made the table shake. The water bottle toppled over and he pulled his hands back.

The psychiatrist was watching him without emotion; Julie had stopped typing and was staring. And Ryan was facing them in silence, shaking like an earthquake.

Despite his turmoil he'd at least managed to spare himself the embarrassment of dumping the pain on the table for all of them to see. The raw agony he'd felt at sitting there in the chair while they . . .

A ball of emotion rolled up his chest and filled his throat.

Dear God. Dear God.

Tears blurred his vision and a sharp sting spread over the bridge of his nose as he fought to hold them back.

But God . . . God, why? Why children?

He could not stop his face from twisting. Though he clenched his jaws tightly, he could not hold back the cry that was already forcing its way past his throat, filling his mouth.

And then Ryan began to sob, body shaking, eyes streaming tears.

He tried to explain something to them. He tried to tell them he was sorry for this momentary lapse in control; that it would just be a minute and they could finish up. He tried to say that it was the children, the children, all the children lying on the concrete around him, broken . . .

"I'm sorry. I'm sorry." He tried to make them understand but all he could do was sob these words, just barely, breath catching, chest jerking.

"I'm sorry. I'm sorry."

"Doctor, please."

The two words from Julie swept over him like a balm. She was trying to get him to stop this. The subject was failing miserably. He'd exposed himself and made an utter fool of himself.

"Doctor?"

Ryan sucked deep, stilled the sobs with a hard sniff, and spoke. "No." He was still shaking but the pain in his throat has lessened and he could speak.

"No, it's okay. Let me finish. I have to finish."

"I don't think he's in any condition—"

"Seven," he said.

They stared at him.

"Seven. They killed seven."

"I think we should take a break, Captain," Newman said. "You've been through a very difficult time and you need some rest."

"No, no I don't!" He was still shaking but the worst of it had passed. "They killed seven innocent bystanders!" he cried. "I can't do this. I can't pretend any longer. I . . . I was in the room with them, you see? I can't do this!"

"Easy, Captain. You've been through—"

"No. No, you weren't there! He was right, we have no right to kill innocent women and children! I can't do this!"

"Captain . . ."

"I tried to kill myself! I tried to swallow my tongue, I tried to choke myself by twisting my head, I tried, but . . ." Ryan knew now that something profound had changed in him. It had taken days to break through, but sitting here telling them all that had happened, he couldn't deny the shift in him any longer.

If Kahlid hadn't accomplished his objective of changing America's mind by personalizing the collateral damage, he had succeeded in altering Ryan's mind.

"Try to stay calm, Captain," the psychiatrist was saying. "We can stop at any time if—"

"I kept passing out until I finally managed to rub the skin on my wrists raw on the towel."

Newman's eyes dropped to the bandages around his wrists. He nodded, understanding that Ryan wanted to get all of this out. To purge himself of the horror through confession.

"When he came in and saw the blood soaking through

the towel and me slumped in the chair he thought I might have succeeded. I hadn't, but he had to stop the bleeding."

"He was alone?"

"One other guard was with him, and when he undid the towels to stop the bleeding, that's when I attacked. He thought I was unconscious and Kahlid was screaming at the guard, telling him that if I died it would all be wasted."

Ryan sat there in the chair still trembling, letting it all out in a long rush.

"I grabbed Kahlid by his hair and I bit him on his face, his nose. My ankles were still taped to the legs, but they'd removed the chains when they'd strapped my arms to the chair. He was screaming and I lunged forward with his face between my teeth. The chair broke. I don't know what all happened, because I only wanted to hurt them as much as I could before they killed me. But they didn't want me dead, that was the thing . . . that was why the guard didn't shoot me when I was over Kahlid. He tried to pull me off but he didn't try to kill me and he couldn't use his gun because Kahlid was right there under me. Hollering."

The tremors in his legs had passed. His hands were calming and had stilled almost completely when he folded them on the table.

"You killed Kahlid?"

"I think so. He went totally limp. But I wasn't really thinking. I managed to knock the guard out with my elbow when he grabbed my shoulder. It was a mess, I was screaming, hitting, biting . . . I think my elbow slammed him back into the concrete wall, where he collapsed. I realized I could escape. So I grabbed a knife from the guard's belt, cut the boy's rope—"

"They had another victim alive in the room?"

"Yes, they'd come in to break his bones. But I set him free."

"And?"

"And then I took Kahlid's radio and ran. There were no other guards that I saw, I don't know why . . . maybe they were in another part of the bunker or had gone for gas, I don't know."

"None of the doors were locked?"

"Yes, they were bolted. But I was on the inside and I opened them."

Doctor Newman settled in his chair. "How long did you run before you called in on the radio?"

"I don't remember. I had to get far enough away so that if they intercepted my transmission, they wouldn't have the time to track me down before the helicopter came for me."

They sat in a protracted silence. His breakdown here in front of them could only lead to one conclusion, and thinking of it now, Ryan was filled with the same terrible urge that had haunted him as he'd sat in the dungeon and had also followed him to the hospital.

He was a father. He'd convinced himself that he could continue his duties because it was what he did. But he couldn't do them without being a father.

And now he wasn't sure he wanted to do his duties. Setting duty aside, he was left with only one desire. To be a father.

To rush home and hold Bethany tight. To sweep Celine off her feet and kiss her and beg her forgiveness. They hadn't let him call home yet, not before a full debriefing, but now . . . now . . .

"I want to go home," he said, and a fresh flood of tears silently filled his eyes.

"You'll need more rest."

"I really want to go home. I can rest at home."

"I think we both know that you're suffering from post-traumatic stress disorder. These things don't pass over-night. You've expressed some emotion here today, but you're going to feel survivor guilt, guilt over feeling re-lieved that you escaped, and anger as well. Maybe a lot of anger."

"I'm begging you. Please, I need to go home. I just need to . . . I have a daughter and a wife." The tears snaked down his cheeks. "Please."

After a moment of thought, Newman nodded. He scrawled something on the sheet in front of him.

"I think you're right, Captain. Command will want to review your statement. They may have more ques-tions, but I'm going to recommend that you be put on an extended leave with ongoing psychiatric treatment and evaluation CONUS."

"When will I be able to go home?"

"If all goes well, you'll be home with your wife and daughter in a week, Captain. Fair enough?"

Ryan wiped the tears off his cheek. "I want to call my wife."

"I think that can be arranged. Let's give command one day to look this over and we'll arrange a call."

"Thank you. Thank you, I would like that very much."

10

THE SEED THAT had taken root in Ryan's mind after he'd lowered his guard in the psychiatrist's debriefing had grown throughout the day and as he slept that night, until only one thought filled his mind when he awoke the next morning.

Bethany. Celine. He had to call Celine and tell her everything. Then he had to get out. Out of the desert. Out of the war.

He was no longer fit to serve in this war.

The shakes had all but vanished upon his return to the hospital—he felt as stable as he had since his return. Not a thing wrong with his mind that he could discern. He'd gone into the debriefing thinking of it as yet one more game to beat so that he could get back to being who he was, and he'd come out realizing that he was no longer who he was.

Ryan sprinkled sugar on a slice of grapefruit and placed it into his mouth. Normally he would have avoided the pink fruit because of the harsh taste the skin left in his mouth. But today he sucked the sweet nectar alongside the bitter white flesh and found the contrast refreshing.

He took a bite of toast, looked up, and stared at the empty bed beside him. They'd removed the soldier who'd died there last night. Corporal Bill Townley from Utah who had been in-country only six days when an antipersonnel mine had removed both of his legs. Bill had told Ryan his story, explaining that he was going home to his wife and two children as soon as they could move him.

The white bedsheets had been changed and folded back with perfect lines, waiting for the next patient.

Perfect lines, like Ryan. For most of his life he'd been the stoic computer in the corner, accepting input, then calculating, parsing, breaking down data before spitting it back out in the form of a report to be acted upon by others. A fine machine, highly praised for its efficiency. He had saved lives and won freedom and been a model to follow.

But that was the old him. In some ways he was a new man. The old version of himself had died in Kahlid's basement along with seven children. The new version of himself had been resurrected yesterday as he endured the psychiatric evaluation.

He couldn't possibly thank Doctor Newman enough.

Now realizing that he wasn't who he thought he was, he was left with the mind-boggling task of figuring out who he really was, only a part of which he truly understood.

The part about his role as a father.

For the first time in many years Ryan thought he might actually be feeling love again. Real love, based on a feeling of great adoration, not simply the dull demands of duty.

He loved Bethany, the kind of love that made men do irrational things. In all honesty, he didn't love Celine, but he was
eager to learn how. Neither knew what he'd been through
this past week, naturally. It was information of a sensitive
nature that he would be allowed to speak about only when
they'd finished their preliminary investigation and then only
if they deemed it appropriate, which they would.

The outer door squealed and swung open. Julie walked
in, smiling, black shoes clacking on the polished linoleum
floor with each step. She'd said ten; it was only nine.

Ryan pushed his tray aside, swung his legs to the floor,
and stood. She ignored the other patients who watched her
walk. Most had physical wounds far worse than Ryan's
superficial cuts, and he felt guilty for having taken up one
of the forty-eight beds in this ward. But he supposed their
decision to keep him under observation as he rested his
damaged mind had been justified at the debriefing. Either
way, he couldn't wait to leave the room for good.

"Good morning, Ryan," Julie said, stepping up to him.
"I see you're ready."

"Yes, ma'am."

"That's good, because we're early. We called your
wife earlier to locate her and were informed that she has
a pressing engagement this evening at eight PM central
time, one she seemed unwilling to break. Texas is ten
hours behind us—that would be ten in the morning, an
hour from now. So we made arrangements for her to be
home now."

"You . . . but you didn't tell her anything?"

"No. Just that it was important that you speak with her.
As you requested we'll let you break the news. Your wife
hasn't heard a word."

He'd rehearsed his words a dozen times through the night and had decided that he would start with an explanation of his ordeal before expressing his new outlook on both her and Bethany. She would dismiss any words of graciousness and love as so much more surface talk, the kind he offered her when the occasion fit. In order for her to understand that Ryan had changed, really changed, he would have to give her a glimpse into the pain he'd felt first.

And Bethany . . . angel . . .

He hoped she would embrace him the way he wanted her to. The way he needed her to.

"Okay," he said, stepping past her.

He held back to let her pass and followed her from the ward to the phone room set up outside the hospital command center. "So command's okay with it, then?"

"The phone call? Yes."

"My going home."

"Oh, right. Based on Dr. Newman's recommendation, yes. He wants to see you for a follow-up at ten, after your call."

"When? When can I go home?"

"If he clears you, three days."

The ball of relief that rolled down his spine should have hardly surprised him, but he wasn't acclimated to this new version of himself just yet. His gratitude must have been obvious, because Julie smiled.

"It must be nice."

"What must be nice?"

"Being so loved. I'm jealous."

"Really?"

She cocked her eyebrow. "Not of your wife specifically,

I didn't mean it like that. But yes, really. I can tell you love your wife and daughter very much. It must be nice."

"It hasn't always been like this," was all he could think to say.

"War changes us all, Captain. Just be thankful you're going home in one piece."

How perfectly true.

They entered a room with cubicles set up along both walls, roughly half of which were occupied by soldiers, sailors, marines, and airmen calling home for one reason or another. Julie led him to one of several at the far end, where he would have at least a modicum of privacy.

"You have half an hour, Captain." She smiled and turned to leave him.

"Were you the one who spoke to my wife?"

"I was," she said, turning. "Don't worry, she's waiting by the phone."

"Thank you, Julie."

She seemed slightly amused. "You're welcome, Ryan."

He eased into the metal chair, picked up the black phone receiver, and dialed the country code, the area code, and then the Austin number. The phone rang six times before going to voice mail. Celine's chirpy prerecorded voice greeted him.

You've reached the home of Celine and Bethany Evans. Call our cells or leave a message. Beeeeeep.

"Hello?" She wasn't picking up. "Celine?" When no once answered, he told the machine he'd try again and hung up.

Ryan jerked his head around to see Julie glance back as she exited out the far side. She had said home, not cell. To be sure, he quickly dialed Celine's cell phone.

Her buoyant message—*call me back if you insist*—reminded him of just how independent Celine had become over the years. Which was fine, except that she'd become so because she wasn't able to depend on him.

Frantic now, Ryan stabbed in the home number again. Transposed the last two numbers. Swore and started over.

The day was hot and he was sweating, but neither accounted for the faint ring in his ears.

"Hello, Celine."

She answered. For a moment Ryan was too overcome by thankfulness to respond.

"Hello?"

"Celine?"

"Is this Ryan?"

"Yes . . . yes, hello, Celine." The phone trembled in his hand but it quickly stilled when he placed his elbow on the desk. "It's Ryan, honey."

"I was on the other line when you called, sorry about that. It's been a while, hasn't it? What, a month now since your last call?"

"A month?" Had it been so long? "Yes, well . . . that's not good. I—"

"A lot's happened in this last month," she said. "Bethany got a cover from *Youth Nation*."

"She did? A cover?"

"Please tell me you know what a cover is, Ryan."

He shifted his back toward the rest of the room. He had no idea what she was talking about. An organization called *Youth Nation* had offered Bethany a position, perhaps, he really couldn't guess.

"Celine—"

"She's modeling, you remember that much?"

"Modeling? She . . . she's going to be on the cover of a magazine?"

"*Youth Nation*, a clothing catalog for teenagers."

"Wow. Wow." He couldn't think of what else to say to this news, so he said it again. "Wow."

"You might want to call and tell her yourself."

"I'll call her right away. Maybe I can tell her. I mean, tell her . . ." Emotion flooded his chest, cutting him off. He leaned his forehead on one hand and gripped the phone with the other, choked by his own remorse.

"On second thought, maybe it would be best if you didn't."

What? What was she saying? He refused to reason through any answers to the question.

"Celine." Where did he begin? "Celine, honey, there's something I have to tell you. Something happened to me this week."

"Hold on." The line clicked off for a few moments before she was back. "Sorry. Just Janie and her stupid cats' shedding. Never mind."

"Who's Janie?"

Celine didn't respond right away.

There was something in that silence that spoke with greater volume than anything she'd yet said. *You don't even know my friends*. But that's why he was calling. He was going to make all of that good.

"Celine . . . I was taken by—"

"Why are we doing this, Ryan?" she asked in a lower voice.

"That's what I'm trying to say. They . . . I was on a mission—"

"Please, Ryan. Be quiet for just a second. You're rambling."

What was she doing? Ryan's face flushed with heat. What was she doing? He had to get to the point.

"I'm coming home, Celine."

"I can't do this any"—she stopped and then pushed for clarification—"what do you mean, 'coming home'?"

"I mean I'm coming *home*. That's what I've been trying to tell you. The convoy I was in was hit, and I was taken by some insurgents. It wasn't very . . . it was hard."

"When?"

"A week ago."

She hesitated.

"Sorry. You okay?"

"Yes. I am now."

"They hurt you?"

"No." He decided then that he would hold back any details that might make this rough on her. They needed a clean slate, not emotional turmoil over the past.

"I'm fine. Scary there for a bit but it all panned out. It made me remember, you know." When she didn't respond, he added, "Remember who I am."

"Tough to be an American these days."

"No, I mean who I am there. A husband. A father."

She went silent.

"I know we haven't been on the best terms, Celine, but I would like to change that."

Still nothing from her. She wasn't buying it.

"Celine, I'm coming home."

"It's too late," she said.

"What do you mean, too late? It's never too late."

"When are you coming back?"

"They said three days. Maybe five days before I reach Austin."

"You can't do this," she said softly. "Not now." And he knew in that moment that she was in love with someone else. He knew from her tone, from a long sordid history of affairs, it was his job to know and he did know. But he felt no anger toward her. Only pity. For both of them.

"Celine, please, you don't understand. I . . . things have changed."

"Well, they've changed here too, Ryan," she said with more strength now. She was realizing that his coming home would threaten whatever life she'd built up around herself in Austin. "You can't just waltz in here as if nothing's changed."

"You're right, you're so right. I . . ." He grasped for the words to tell her, but it was all bottled up by years of silence. So he said the one thing most rehearsed since his debriefing yesterday.

"I love you, Celine."

"No." Her voice cut through his veins. "You just can't come begging on your knees after all this time. And the truth is, Ryan, I'm not sure I want us to be together any longer. I know that may sound cruel at a time like this, and I'm sorry for what you've been through, but we have to face the truth about each other."

"You don't know what I've been through."

"And you don't know what I've been through for all of these years. I don't think you love me. In fact I'm sure of it. I don't even think you like me."

"Celine, please, you can't say that!" But she could.

"The fact is, you've never really wanted to be with me."

And he knew that she was really saying she didn't love

him, that she didn't want to be with him, but by putting it on his shoulders she was absolving herself of any guilt in her admission.

Ryan sat back in his metal chair, gut punched. It was going all wrong. She didn't understand. Once she understood, she would change her mind. He'd brought this on himself, now he had to work his way through it. He couldn't really blame her.

"I'm coming home, Celine. Please, I'll be home in five days. We'll talk then; I can explain everything. We'll work this out, okay?"

"You don't understand, Ryan. I don't want to work this out. Are you listening to me?"

"Bethany—"

"Don't even talk about Bethany! You left her a long time ago."

His world swam. She *couldn't* understand.

"It's over," Celine said. "You have to understand that, Ryan. This time it's finished. I want a divorce."

He finally found his breath. "Please . . . please, Celine, you don't understand."

"I understand that I can be loved by someone who actually loves me with more than just a paycheck."

Her words were like blades, and Ryan tried to accept the pain they brought him. He'd beat Kahlid, hadn't he? He would beat Celine.

He would win back her love.

He would win back Bethany's love.

"Good-bye, Ryan."

Thoughts of his daughter brought with them a searing pain that began to shut down his mind. The shakes were returning, and that couldn't be a good thing, not here in front of all these officers. He had to gain some control of himself.

He would win back Bethany's love if it was the last thing he did.

It occurred to him that the phone was silent.

"Celine?"

But Celine had hung up.

11

PATTY RHODES STOOD taller than Bethany by several inches, all skin and bones and legs. Gangly, she called herself, and although Bethany always shut up her rants of self-pity, she didn't disagree. Not that Patty was ugly by a long shot. She was just developing. Braces, long stringy brown hair, a few hard-fought pimples, no chest—what could she say? Not ugly at all, but not the girl she wanted to be.

That would be Bethany, the girl with straight teeth, long flowing hair, and skin as clear as the day she turned six. Oddly enough, Bethany didn't really want to be Bethany.

They walked down Barton Creek Boulevard toward the Saint Michael's campus around the next bend, Patty with a copy of *Youth Nation* stuck in her face.

"You're going to fall over, reading that trash," Bethany said.

Patty flipped a page. "You know, not all the girls in here look like they belong. Check her out." She shoved the page at Bethany just long enough for her to see a quite plain blonde dressed in a red T-shirt, but then the catalog was in front of Patty's face again. "I suppose so all of us lowlifes can identify and buy the clothes, huh?"

"Give me a break," Bethany said. "It's all stupid anyway." She stuck out her hand, and Patty plopped the catalog into her palm with a sigh.

"Yeah, well, anytime you want me to join you in stupid New York, just say the word. Stevie ask you out for homecoming yet?"

"Fat chance. I'm not going this year."

"What? Don't be an idiot."

"Serious."

Her friend frowned, no doubt burdened by the complications faced by any sixteen-year-old these days.

"You honestly don't see it?" Bethany asked. "All this stupidness?"

"What stupidness? I don't see what the big deal is, and you're starting to annoy me with all your stupidness talk. Okay, you're freaking out with the realization that you're going to be famous. You got guys hitting on you in the halls, you got freaking New York calling you every day, you have a mother who gives a rip. Wow, so tough. Hard life there. So you're freaking out because it's all so stupid. Well, forgive me for not getting it."

The mother bit stuck in Bethany's head. Patty's father had left her and her sister when they were much younger and her mother had gone off the deep end. She'd gotten all the money she needed, enough to send them to private school and live in the neighborhood, but left alone, she'd drowned herself in alcohol.

"You're right, I should be thankful. And I suppose I am. I mean, you see me turning the cover down? But like . . . it's all pretty shallow, you have to admit, Patty. I don't know, it's not like I need the money. I don't want the attention."

"The guys?"

She felt her face flush. "Okay, so I don't mind that."

"So quit fooling yourself. You're just playing it to the hilt."

"Please."

"Okay, so Broadway Bethany would never do that, I get it. But you do like having all those boys watch you strut your stuff across the campus headed to theology class, don't you kid me, baby."

Her mention of the class derailed Bethany's train of thought. Theo class and *Youth Nation* had a lot in common, actually. Both sold fantasy based on something larger than life.

"Call me Sister Bethany," she said.

"Even better. They could dress you up like a nun for the front-cover shoot."

"Dreams of the afterlife, enter if you dare." Bethany snapped her fingers and hit a few beats. The words from one of Brianna's singles rolled off her tongue. "Sister, sister, what you doing tonight?"

"Makin' love until the morning light," Patty sang, joining her friend in a slinky but surprisingly supple move. "Bring it on, baby!"

They laughed and turned into the back parking lot.

Bethany dropped the bomb then, while Patty was distracted by her own sexiness. "You really wanna go with?"

"To homecoming?"

"To New York."

Patty gasped and pulled up hard. "You serious?"

"They said I could—"

But Patty didn't need to hear more to know that Bethany was dead serious. She uttered a short shriek, then shoved her hand over her mouth and glanced around to see if anyone had seen her in her moment of uncoolness.

"Sorry." She promptly forgot her blown cover. "Serious."

Bethany gave her a grin.

"When? This is so cool. You think they'll let me, you know"—she batted her eyes—"show my stuff?"

"I doubt that's what they had in mind."

"But it's me, right? You're taking me."

"You think I'd take"—she thought better of mentioning any names that might come back on her—"who else?"

"That's freakin' awesome, girl!"

"On one condition."

"'Course."

"You don't tell anyone until we leave."

"What? No basking in the glory?"

"And you quit all this stupidness about being famous. Just play cool."

"Coolness. I swear."

Bono began to sing "Beautiful Day" on her iPhone. Mother's ringtone. Bethany tapped the screen and angled for the main entrance.

"Hello, Mother."

"Hello, angel. You're headed back from lunch?" Their rental house was close enough to the school for Bethany to sneak off for lunch now and then, as Patty and she'd just done.

"He called?"

"No. But I talked to his base commander, and he's in

the country. I asked Burt to come over for dinner tonight. You okay with that?"

Bethany had learned about Ryan's call five days earlier and been confronted with the prospect of his immediate return. Something about him having a change of heart, Mother had said. He needed a break from the war. He'd had a close call, that's all she knew. But she had to agree with Celine: too little too late.

Ryan represented everything that was wrong with life. It had come to Bethany in a moment of clarity as she showered the next morning. Her father was a false hope.

He occupied the place of savior, but he'd failed miserably as savior and, although he wasn't a terrible person, he wasn't what he stood for, not at all.

He wasn't lover to Celine or father to her. As such he was a kind of enemy. Celine needed someone close to her during this time, when she felt threatened by that enemy.

"Of course," she said. "What time?"

"Six o'clock. You walking home tonight?"

"Why not; another five minutes of exercise never hurt."

"I thought we'd make chili."

"Sounds good. Don't worry, Mom. He might be a deadbeat, but he won't hurt us."

"You don't know that."

"He's not the kind."

"I'd feel better with Burt there, just the same."

One small benefit of Ryan's sudden announcement that he was coming home was that she and Mother were on the same side of an issue for once. Bethany thought she could grow used to the feeling.

"What if he comes this afternoon?" she asked.

"I don't plan on being there. You have practice till six, right?"

"Right."

Her mother paused. "I'm going through with it this time, Bethany. If he shows up, I'm going to tell him."

"I think you should. Don't worry, Mother. Go make a call to one of your friends or something. Take your mind off it."

"See you tonight."

She hung up thinking it might be nice to see the DA again. He was a snake; even *Mother* could see his shiny scales. But Celine was attracted to snakes, and at least this particular one was well-behaved, caring, and successful. More important, her mother seemed crazy about him.

"She's going through with the divorce?" Patty said.

And with those words Bethany's world darkened, as if her friend had flipped a switch. It was the word *divorce,* she thought. It suddenly reminded her just how pointless all of this nonsense about New York really was.

All the cool clothes in the world didn't cover up a black heart. For a passing moment Bethany hated herself for going along with Celine's dreams for a modeling career. Did her mother think fancy dinners and trips to New York could make up for her and Ryan's own sickness?

For that matter, the whole world was sick, Bethany included.

Seeing her darkening mood, Patty shrugged. "It's not like he's around anyway, right?"

"Right."

But none of it felt right.

Despite the fact that she was the envy of half the school,

Bethany felt as low as she could remember feeling. Which in and of itself was a pretty sick thing.

FEW PEOPLE UNDERSTOOD how much of the best investigative work depended on intuition. There was the patience required to sift though mounds of data or to sit for hours in a car, waiting for something to happen. There was the eye for detail to ascertain which minutiae were askew, what oddity or normality was out of place. There was the logic required to string together dots on a graph to form a meaningful picture. Intuition could point you to where none of the other evidence pointed. Evidence became the case. Sometimes, intuition was the voice that whispered a suggestion or two when all else failed.

After eight days back on the case, intuition was telling Ricki Valentine that her failure to produce new evidence that would implicate Phil Switzer in the BoneMan case wasn't necessarily a bad thing. But she knew by the tone in his voice that her boss, Mort Kracker, wasn't a happy camper.

She nodded at Derek Johnson, a junior investigator she'd worked with a couple of times, and knocked on Kracker's door.

"Come in."

Ricki stepped in and closed the door. "Afternoon, sir."

"Have a seat, Agent Valentine."

She sat and crossed her legs. Kracker sat behind his big oak desk facing her with his large, square head. She could swear someone had taken a cricket bat to the man's forehead when he was a kid. They'd missed his bulbous nose but flattened the top of his head proper.

Kracker set his elbows on the desk and folded his hands together to form a large teepee. "The ruling just came down from the judge," he said.

Ricki's heart skipped a beat. "Already."

"Exactly."

Meaning a quick decision meant a definite decision in a case that felt anything but definite to both of them.

"And?"

Kracker put a large hand on a sheet of paper and slid it next to a neatly stacked pile on his meticulously arranged desk. "He threw the whole thing out."

Ricki blinked. She'd half expected this to happen. It wrenched her gut to hear that the case she'd spent over a year on was just tossed out because of a judicial hearing on the evidence. The possibility of planted lab specimens.

"Switzer's going free," Kracker said.

"When?"

"Now. He'll be out before nightfall."

Ricki nodded. She wasn't sure what kind of reaction he expected, but judging by his steady gaze, he wasn't pleased. A few foul words appropriately expressing her rage at such a terrible turn of events might serve her career well. But she wasn't feeling enough rage to work up the words.

"You look crushed," he said.

"I'm tired. Just tired."

"You don't look tired. You look . . . fine."

"I'm not."

"Good. Neither am I. We just had our faces rubbed in it, in case you hadn't figured it out."

"That I'm okay with," Ricki said. "What bothers me

more is that BoneMan is free. Whether or not Switzer's guilty."

He nodded once, very slowly.

She added to her assessment. "Unless, by chance, he just happened to get picked up for another crime."

Kracker's lips formed a meaty frown. "I'm receiving some pressure to take you off the case. I hope you can understand that."

"I can, sir. The public has to be fed someone, why not me?"

"This isn't about appeasing the public. It's about your failure to put or keep the right man behind bars."

"Then reassign me. Put someone better on the case. Some junior agent who knows more about BoneMan than I do. Heck, tell the whole city that they can now sleep easy because the one agent who is best equipped to nail BoneMan to the wall has been removed from the case so the FBI can save face."

"I wouldn't put it so succinctly, but I see you get the point."

"And I suppose the DA would love you for it."

"I wouldn't know; I haven't talked to him since I heard."

"I thought you two shared all your secrets."

He went on without a hint of offense. "We work closely, yes. It's better that way. And one way or another, we're going to get to the bottom of this case. The only question right now is whether we do that with you or without you."

Ricki stood and walked to the window, hands on hips, aware of her black skirt hanging delicately just above her knees, her black power heels that looked too prissy, too refined. At times like this she wouldn't mind being a foot taller and six inches broader in the shoulders. A few extra parts in the right places wouldn't hurt either.

She faced Kracker. "Your call, obviously. But you know that it'll take any other investigator a month, best case scenario, to settle on the same understanding I have of this case."

"*What* understanding, Ricki? What exactly do you know?"

"For starters, there is a better than even chance that we do have the wrong guy," she snapped, pointing out the window at some imaginary suspect. "The evidence fits, yes, and with the blood dangling in front of us we made sure of that. But the evidence also fits a thousand other men walking the streets. Don't tell me you're sure we have the right man."

"I didn't say we did. But yes, I believe we do."

"There's two ways you can approach this. You can either spin your wheels, scouring the evidence from one of the three cases we didn't try Switzer for so we wouldn't get hammered by double jeopardy—be my guest. Or you can assume that BoneMan's out there, snickering at all the foolishness in the papers. At the very least, let me lead a new investigation. Let me pick up where I left off two years ago."

"Pick up where? You don't have another body."

"No." She crossed her arms. "But I have some new thoughts."

His brow arched.

"Just thoughts, that's all they are now."

He waited.

"Okay." Ricki paced back and forth in front of him.

"The last thing I was working on before the blood evidence surfaced was a standard military-issue KA-BAR knife we found in the barn at El Paso and another at the murder scene on Fourth Street. The first one couldn't be linked directly to the El Paso case, but we were quite sure the second knife had been used to sever one of the cords that held the girl."

"The evidence proved useless."

"Yes, at the time it did because we honed in on Switzer and found no connections between him and the knives or the military. Could have been anyone who picked them up at any army surplus store, right?"

"Go on."

"Assuming that Switzer's not our man, I'm left wondering what kind of military man might have killed seven women in the space of six months and then disappeared."

"And?"

"And I can't help thinking its someone who isn't killing in Texas because he's *not in* Texas."

"Because he's been deployed for the last two years."

"It's a thought." Ricki shrugged. "We don't know. The point is, until we get off Switzer and start looking at other possibilities, we'll never ask the right questions. I should be talking to the military instead of trying to get permission to do my job. My only priority should be to stop him before he kills again."

"Assuming he hasn't." Kracker blew out some air. "Now you have me talking like you."

"If I'm wrong? What's the downside?"

They both knew there was none.

Kracker spread his huge hands on the desk and padded

the surface with thick fingers. "Okay, Valentine. Go chase this ghost. But if the evidence even sniffs Switzer's way, I want to know about it."

She started toward the door. "You should know that one of the threads I have to track back to the source is the blood evidence."

"No, Ricki, I don't believe I do know that."

"Someone planted the blood, sir. I need to know who."

"You're *assuming* that someone planted the evidence."

"I'm assuming that Switzer's not the guy, which means someone set him up. Knowing who did could lead us—"

"Leave it alone, Valentine. If someone from inside this office planted evidence, I'll deal with it. But that's my call, not yours. I don't want you sniffing around my operation, you got that?"

Ricki lifted both hands in a sign of surrender. "Got it. No sniffing around our beloved FBI. I swear it."

She pulled the door open.

"Or the DA's office," Kracker said.

But she was already walking down the hall and was in no mood to ask for any clarification.

12

RYAN HANDED THE cabdriver two twenties and stepped out onto Barton Creek Boulevard. The bold numbers on the mailbox read 1300, which was the address Celine and Bethany had moved to after his last deployment. This was it.

Six days had passed since he'd first realized how desperately he needed to rush home and embrace his wife, and this was it.

Austin was hot in August, but not uncomfortably so, not after two years in the desert, where temperatures regularly ran in the hundred-and-twenty-degree range during the hot season. A light breeze cooled the sweat on his neck. Crickets . . .

He had missed the crickets. The constant chirping of insects hidden in the dense foliage that bordered the large lot.

Ryan stepped up to the edge of a driveway that sloped down to a large white house all but hidden from the road. The Mediterranean architecture featured a large carport that fed into the glassed twin doors.

Home.

The thought faded as quickly as it had entered his mind. In reality the house below didn't look anything like home. He'd tried to contact Celine a dozen times since arriving in the United States—on her cell phone, which he knew she carried with her at all times. She'd ignored the calls.

Not a problem, she was just frightened. Confused. By now, she probably knew at least some of the details of his breakdown and it had brought to her mind the first time he'd broken down, during basic training. But as soon as she realized how profoundly he'd been affected in the desert, her confusion would fall away. If there was one thing Ryan did particularly well, it was understanding the human psyche and response. The inner workings of the mind.

That's why Ryan was here, to show Celine that his own mind had changed. That he finally could see it all so clearly.

A car's horn blared behind him, and he glanced after the black Mercedes that had objected, hardly noticing.

He returned his eyes to the house. This was why he was here. To make all things right. To show his remorse. To beg their forgiveness. God help him, please help him.

Ryan walked down the drive. His heart hammered and the crickets sang, but his feet moved in silence, stealing their way back into a world he'd snuck out of many years ago. He wasn't foolish enough to think that there wouldn't be some challenges in reconciling with Celine and Bethany, but he would lie himself down at their feet if he had to.

He would never use another angry word with Celine.

He would buy her whatever she wanted no matter what it cost him.

He would make her breakfast in bed and wash the clothes and smile at her lovingly from across the room. And roses, he would fill her world with roses, enough red and pink roses to make the neighbors think he'd lost his mind, which he just might have.

As for Bethany . . . He'd silently cried his way through a numb existence these last six days, walking to the cafeteria, sitting through four separate debriefings, lying in bed late at night, boarding the airplane, staring out the window as the sea passed far below, disembarking the AC-130 with his seabag over his shoulder, talking to the psychiatrist at Bethesda Naval Hospital, and while flying home to Austin, where he'd had the courtesy to rent a hotel room.

Here now, thinking again of Bethany, tears stung his eyes and he blinked, telling himself that he wouldn't allow emotion to muddy the waters once he stepped inside.

The thought stopped him two feet from the door. *No, Ryan, avoiding emotion has been your downfall. Show them, show them how you feel.*

But he'd decided he wouldn't seek their sympathy. The details of his abduction in Iraq could not play a part in winning them back. He'd lost them before the incident, of his own doing or lack of doing. He would win them back on his own merit.

Ryan stepped up and rang the doorbell with an unsteady hand.

Celine's voice called from deep in the house. "Door's open, angel!"

Bethany. She thought he was Bethany.

"It's me," he called in a croaking voice.

"We're in the kitchen!"

Two thoughts crashed his mind. *We* meant Bethany was with her. They were in the kitchen, waiting for him. She'd called *him* angel, the term of endearment she'd once used for him, now reserved for Bethany.

Broadsided by his good fortune, Ryan slipped in and closed the door quietly behind him. Celine chuckled in the kitchen. "No, chocolate, you idiot. It gives the chili a bite. Trust me, you'll like it."

He stood on the mat just inside the front door, allowing her voice to wash away his fear. If he could just stand here for a while and listen to his wife speak to his daughter about something so ordinary as how to cook chili.

Celine continued to speak, explaining how the chocolate worked. Ryan hadn't even been aware that she'd taken up cooking as a hobby.

He walked through the living room to the brightly lit kitchen, thinking with each step that he must stay with his speech, exactly as he'd rehearsed, no variance. And he had to get it all out before she could respond.

He stepped into the arched entry and stood in his plaid shirt, hands by his sides. Celine was leaning over the stove with the ladle in one hand, the other cupped below the spoon as she blew on the food as if preparing to sample a small taste.

Below her the chili bubbled.

"Hello, Celine."

Her blue eyes snapped up and she froze.

Ryan wanted to rush up to her and sweep her off her feet, but he knew he couldn't just barge into her life, not without her full acceptance. He'd been the one to abandon her. Now he would pay whatever price was due him as he won her back.

"I'm sorry, I tried to call."

She slowly lowered her ladle.

Now. He had to say it now, before she could fully react.
Where's Bethany?

But he had to say this quickly, so he did. "I'm so sorry.
I beg your forgiveness. It's been my fault, all of it. I'm
the one to blame. I've been a fool for leaving. Will you
please, please, just please take me back?"

It wasn't exactly the way he'd planned it. She was still
frozen over the chili. Why was she so surprised? She'd
just called to him. And where was Bethany?

"Who let you in?" Celine said.

"I . . ."

Her eyes darted to his left, and Ryan knew then that
he might have misjudged things. He followed her line of
sight to a man standing by the table. A large man with
dark hair slicked back from a sloping forehead, watching him casually, one hand in his black dress slacks, the
other on the wood table. A dish towel hung over his right
shoulder.

"Ryan, meet Burt Welsh," Celine snapped. "Burt,
Ryan."

Where was Bethany? He glanced around the room.

Burt crossed the room, placed one arm around Celine's
waist, and drilled Ryan with a firm glare.

"Where's Bethany?"

Celine's jaw muscles bunched. "Please, Ryan. This is
the wrong time. Don't make this more difficult than it already is for us."

He lifted his hands, stunned. "No, that's not it. You don't
understand, I was wrong. I was . . . I should . . . I've come
back. . . ."

"Don't tell me I don't understand. We've been here before. This time it's over. I want you to leave."

"That was fifteen years ago. I haven't had a single episode since."

"Is that so? You may have only gone AWOL for a week, but as far as I was concerned, you never did come back. It's over. Leave this house, and for goodness' sake, don't drag Bethany into this. I won't allow you to hurt her any more than you have."

The words rushed him like a battering ram that slammed into his gut and took his breath away. He tried to form words, to tell her that he would never hurt Bethany. That he'd come to make things right.

All he could manage was, "No."

"I think she was pretty clear, Ryan," Burt said. "Get out of here or I'll throw you out. Is that clear enough?"

"I . . ." He couldn't move. "This is *my* home."

"Mother?"

Ryan spun at the sound of Bethany's voice. She stood in the living room wearing jeans and a Nike T-shirt that read *Warriors*. He saw the similarities to the fourteen-year-old he'd last hugged good-bye two years earlier, but the person who gaped at him was hardly that little girl.

She had grown into a young woman. This was Bethany, the beautiful baby he and Celine had adopted sixteen years ago. His daughter.

He loved her more than even he could possibly have realized.

For a long moment Bethany only stared at him. Ryan couldn't find words for them. Not for Celine or for the man she'd befriended, and certainly not for Bethany.

"Hello, angel," he said.

"I'm not your angel, Ryan," she said, glancing at Celine through the door.

"Bethany . . ."

What could he say? She hadn't come to his defense. The poor girl had been poisoned against him.

"Please . . ."

"I've had to lie awake at night for years hearing Celine cry herself to sleep," Bethany said. "That doesn't change with a snap of your fingers."

"Just go, Ryan," Celine said. "Please don't make this more difficult than it already is."

The room began to spin around him. He'd anticipated some challenges, but this. They were murdering him!

As if to make the point absolutely certain, the big man, Burt, walked up to him, smelling of aftershave. "Look, Ryan, I think they've made it clear. People can only put up with so much, you know what I mean?"

Ryan hesitated one moment, torn by indecision. But he'd been here before, in similar games, facing long odds, determined to crack the code. And he knew that the only way to win was to outsmart them.

So he spun from them, walked past Bethany, out the door and up the driveway, all the while telling himself that it was okay, it was going to be okay. Tomorrow.

He would make it all right tomorrow.

RYAN SPENT THE night in the Super 8 Motel at the corner of Highway 290 and Lamar, sinking into the realization that none of the structure he'd surrounded himself with in the navy could aid him in this world. Logic, though useful, couldn't compel any more authority.

This was a matter of the heart. He simply had to convince Bethany and Celine that he wasn't the same man they'd once known. And even then, he hadn't been a terrible man, not altogether terrible. He was guilty of ignoring them, but not because of evil in his heart—his heart had always been good.

Either way, he had to convince them, which was a matter of the heart. But convincing them ultimately came back around to logic and reason. He had to figure out how to convince them, a task that his mind, however stressed in the face of such rejection, was uniquely qualified to tackle.

In the early hours, while the rest of Austin slept, he came to the conclusion that in order to persuade Celine and Bethany of his worthiness, he had to first remove the primary obstacle to the flow of communication between him and them.

The man named Burt Welsh who smelled like aftershave. Ryan lay in the waning morning hours, ignored the ache in his heart, and dreamed of dealing with Burt.

He rose at seven o'clock, showered, dressed in blue slacks and a white shirt, and took advantage of the free continental breakfast on the lobby floor. At seven forty-five he caught a cab that delivered him to the John Henry Faulk Central Library on Guadalupe.

"Give me twenty minutes. If I'm not back, keep the change." He left the driver with thirty dollars and entered the library.

Burt Welsh turned out to be someone Ryan thought he might be able to reason with. An attorney. In fact, the district attorney for Travis County.

Ryan stared at the file that Google had dug up, and

the sliver of hope that he'd stubbornly clung to through the night hours grew. Not only would finding Burt be a relatively simple task, but talking sense into him would be easier than trying to reason with a less educated man. At the very least, an attorney who held such a public position would be forced to go through the motions of considering reason.

His mind returned to the image of Bethany, standing like a queen, regarding him with bright eyes. At the very least, Burt would understand the deep longing he had to reestablish a relationship with his daughter.

Ryan quickly scrolled down a newspaper article about the man's election, and his eyes stopped on two words bolded as a link.

BoneMan.

He scanned the paragraph in which the link was embedded. Apparently Burt Welsh owed his election as district attorney in large part to his success in prosecuting Phil Switzer, aka BoneMan, who had allegedly killed seven young women by breaking their bones without breaking skin, although he had been convicted on only one count of homicide.

The last victim had been a girl who'd attended Saint Michael's Academy. It didn't take any genius to guess that Celine had met Burt there, at Bethany's school, while Ryan was off saving the world.

Ryan shut his eyes and grasped for a thread of hope. He had to explain himself to this man. Surely Welsh would understand once he understood the way Ryan's own heart had been broken in the desert.

He printed the page, folded it neatly, slipped it into his pocket, and walked out of the library.

The Travis County Administration Building, in which the district attorney worked, was on 11th Street, a couple dozen blocks farther up Guadalupe. He paid the cab, passed under a Texas flag on his right and an American flag on his left, and entered through the glass doors.

It took him only a few minutes to locate the lobby outside Burt's office on the third floor. He intended to calmly wait the man out if necessary—the man would eventually come to his office—with any luck, today.

Above all, remain calm. Like a ghost in the corner as he waited for the man to show. The last thing he could afford now was a physical breakdown in full view of the staff.

"May I help you?"

The receptionist sat behind a cherrywood desk, peering up at him over pencil-thin glasses. Brooke Silverstein, according to the gold plate next to the green lamp.

"Um . . . yes. Yes, I'm here to see the district attorney."

"Do you have an appointment?"

"I do, yes. Not on the books, but he's expecting me. We weren't entirely clear on the time. Is he in?"

"Your name?"

"Tell him it's Ryan Evans." Then he added to impress her more than him, "Captain, Navy Intelligence. It's critical I speak to him."

Brook's eyes flared just enough for him to know he'd risen from the ranks of *How-do-I-ditch-this-guy* to *Hmm-interesting*.

"Please have a seat, sir."

She picked up the phone as he backed into one of four stuffed chairs set around reading lamps. Her lips were moving. She glanced at the third unmarked door to her right, then peered at him over her glasses.

In that look Ryan saw dismissal. She was getting an earful, no doubt. *Keep that maniac out of my office. Call security. Whatever you do, do not let him near me in public.*

Calm, yes. And he would remain perfectly calm. But he would not waste this opportunity to play his hand. Welsh was an obstacle who had to be confronted and convinced.

Rather than sitting, Ryan reversed his direction and walked briskly toward the third unmarked door.

"Sir? Please wait in—you're not authorized to go in there!" Brook's tone confirmed his guess.

He twisted the knob, shoved the door wide, saw Burt behind a desk inside, and quickly locked himself in with the man.

"Just a word, sir."

Burt was on the phone, no doubt with his secretary. He set the receiver in its cradle and stood. Dressed in a black suit with shirt collar opened just enough to reveal his well-muscled chest, Burt Welsh looked even more imposing than Ryan remembered.

A fist pounded on the door. "Sir?"

"Give us a moment," he called out.

"Thank you, this won't take long."

"I hope not," Burt said, steely eyes locked on Ryan. "You're already on very thin ice."

"I'm just trying to get your attention. Surely I deserve that. You're sleeping with my wife."

"Am I? I was at Celine's home because she feared for her life."

The comment was unexpected. Welsh was posturing. He had to be.

"Celine tells me you've had a rough couple of weeks,"

the district attorney said, stepping forward, hand in one pocket, "but the fact of the matter is, your wife wants a divorce. You've never cared before, I suggest you not care now. This has nothing to do with you. Go back to your desk at the navy, become an admiral or whatever, catch some terrorists, do whatever you want. Just stay away from Celine and Bethany."

It took all of Ryan's concentration to keep from shaking.

"She . . . she doesn't understand."

"Understand what? That you're a loser?"

"What happened to me," Ryan managed. "You have to let me explain myself, at least to my daughter. Please, you have to understand what I've been through. I was taken by insurgents and forced to watch some terrible things. I'm not the same person I was when I left."

"But you did leave, didn't you? That was your choice. Just like leaving my office now before I throw you out is your choice."

"The man who took me compared the United States to a serial killer," Ryan said. "Ted Bundy. Didn't you prosecute Phil Switzer? The BoneMan?"

Welsh stilled.

"The killer who played games with me, who killed all those children in the underground chamber they kept me in, said he was only doing what BoneMan did. That I was like BoneMan. That I was BoneMan. That we were all like BoneMan."

That got the man's attention. Actually, Kahlid had used Ted Bundy as an example, not BoneMan, but they were essentially the same, and the use of BoneMan would have far more connection with the district attorney.

"You put BoneMan behind bars. So you know what it was like for all the mothers and fathers of the women he killed. Please," he begged softly, "please don't take my daughter away from me."

"I didn't stop BoneMan," the district attorney said. "Phil Switzer was released from prison this morning."

Ryan didn't care at the moment. He took a step closer to the man. "I'll do whatever you want, just help me repair the damage I've done with Bethany."

"I love them, Ryan. I love them both and I'd just as soon see you disappear forever than have you hurt them again. Now if you know what's best for you, you'll turn around, leave this office, sign the papers when they come to you, and find a way to get yourself back to Iraq, where you can do some good."

Ryan could feel the waves of heat rolling down his neck. But he maintained perfect control because he knew he must.

He stepped over to the wall, removed the painting of the large brown stallion, walked to the window that overlooked 11th Street, and slammed the picture against the glass. The frame shattered and he dropped the torn horse on the floor. It was all a bit juvenile, he realized. But he couldn't come up with any good alternatives.

When he turned around he saw that Burt had turned to watch him but otherwise hadn't moved.

"Sorry. I'm just trying to get your attention."

Without so much as a nod of acknowledgment, the man who intended to take his wife and daughter calmly turned his back and pressed a button on his phone.

"Brooke, please have security come to my office immediately. And call the police—"

It was as far as Burt got, because as he spoke, Ryan crossed the carpet behind him, grabbed him by the back of his white collar, and with more strength than he knew he had, pulled the man off his feet. The phone clattered to the desk and Burt grunted as his back slammed onto the floor.

Ryan stood over him, legs spread on either side of his head.

"Sorry. Sorry, but you aren't listening to me." He was breathing heavily both from emotion and exertion. Burt was a big man.

The man cursed and started to lift his head. Only then did it occur to Ryan that he'd made an unrecoverable mistake. In a moment of panic he'd done the one thing that would almost assuredly make this man an enemy for life.

And now Burt, a much bigger man, was going to rise to his feet and maim him.

Ryan dropped his knee into the man's chest, slamming him back onto the carpet. He shifted his leg so that his shin pushed hard into Burt's throat. The larger man grabbed his leg and tried to jerk it off, but Ryan had the full advantage of leverage on his side. He might not be a marine, but that didn't mean he didn't know how to kill a man without a weapon. And for the briefest moments, Ryan wanted nothing more than to end this man's life.

Knuckles pounded the door again, this time with a demand that the door be opened immediately.

Ryan lowered his face and spoke in a low, biting tone, "She's my daughter."

"Open this door!" *Crash!* The frame splintered under the weight of an assault.

Reason reclaimed Ryan then, while the DA was thrashing under him, face now red as a beet. He rolled off and came to his feet just as the door flew open.

"Hold up!" A security officer had his sidearm out and trained on Ryan.

He lifted both hands. "Easy. Just talking."

"Put your hands on your head!"

Reason had reclaimed his mind, but reasonable courses of action had yet to present themselves. "He's sleeping with my wife."

"Hands on your head!"

Three security officers faced him in a semicircle, eyes bright as if they'd just busted a terrorist in the act of blowing up the Travis County Administration Building. But he was only a man who'd learned how much he really did love his daughter. This was a mission of love, not of terror.

"Put your hands on your head before I blow your head off!" the guard screamed.

"He's stealing my daughter," Ryan said and put his hands on his head.

13

RICKI VALENTINE PULLED up to the Super 8 Motel, parked her car in a visitor's space near the entrance, and made her way to the elevator.

Room 312, Evans had said. She pushed the call button and waited for the elevator car.

She'd spent the three days that had passed since Kracker had authorized her to open a new investigation conducting interviews of all those linked in even the most limited ways to the last victim, Linda Owens, on whom someone had supposedly planted blood as evidence. At least that's the way she was viewing the blood evidence—everything she did was predicated on the assumption that Switzer really was the wrong man, which could only mean the blood had been planted.

Although they'd conducted a full investigation of Linda Owens's murder, the interviews had come to a screeching halt when the lab had matched the blood sample found in Linda Owens's hair to their primary suspect at the time, Phil Switzer. There was still a string of possible links between the victim and those who knew her at school, which hadn't been fully explored.

But that wasn't the reason Ricki was here this Friday afternoon. It was this business about Burt Welsh, who had somehow managed to tangle with a naval officer whose wife he'd become friendly with. No concern of Ricki's. But according to Welsh, Ryan Evans had made some unusual claims that linked him to BoneMan in the Iraqi desert. That made Ryan Ricki's business, if only until she made sense of these claims.

Ricki had already spent fifteen minutes on the phone with Celine Evans and half an hour at a Starbucks with Bethany Evans, his sixteen-year-old daughter who, interestingly enough, now attended the same school, Saint Michael's Catholic Academy, that the last victim had. She'd learned more than she wanted to know about their family.

Nothing of note regarding BoneMan.

The bell rang and the elevator door slid open. Ricki stepped in and patiently waited for the car to grind its way up three stories.

Ryan Evans. She'd done her homework on the man after Kracker had asked her to check him out. One of the navy's best, from everything she could gather. His commanding officer had nothing but the highest praise for the captain's work in Naval Intelligence, most of which was classified. But his record in the military wasn't classified. By all accounts, Ryan Evans had the kind of character that men like Welsh couldn't touch.

The kind of backbone that would lead a man to barge into the DA's office two days ago and accuse him of sleeping with his wife.

The idea of Burt Welsh on the floor with a knee in his throat—you had to at least grin. The DA hadn't pressed criminal charges, but what he had done was probably worse.

She stepped up to #312 and knocked.

The man who opened the door looked like he hadn't set foot in the sunlight or the shower in a week. Ryan Evans was dressed in jeans and a white T-shirt, no shoes, at least a few days' growth on his face, his short brown hair disheveled and dirty. A big man with a naturally strong physique.

He stared at her out of a dark room with brown lost-puppy eyes. "Yes?"

"Ryan Evans?"

"Yes. Oh . . . FBI?"

She stuck out her hand. "Agent Ricki Valentine. You mind if I come in?"

His grip was limp, but he dutifully shook her hand before politely stepping aside.

"Whew, this place could use some air." She crossed to the drawn drapes. "Do you mind?"

"No, no, go ahead. Actually, maybe it would be better to turn the lights on."

She withdrew her hand from the cord. "Sure. Yes, light. At least that much."

He flipped on the overhead light. One of the two queen beds wasn't made up. The orange floral on the bedspreads matched well with two impressionistic prints on the wall, typical of so many hotel rooms. Someone had cut a deal with someone to turn virtually all budget-priced hotels into one of five common models, the orange floral variety being the most common.

"Mind if I sit?"

"Sure." He crossed to a small table with an empty ice bucket and pulled out the chair for her. A regular gentleman.

She set her wallet (the black snakeskin one that was large enough to be called a purse) on the table and sat. "Thank you."

Ryan sat on the bed and folded one leg under the other. "You're welcome."

"As I told you on the phone, this shouldn't take long; just a few questions. You've heard about the BoneMan case, I take it."

"It's all over the news."

Ricki glanced at the muted television playing CNN. "Of course. By the looks of it, you have all the time in the world to watch the news these days."

He just looked at her.

"When was the last time you left this room, Captain?"

"I've been in the country for just over a week. I'm still getting my bearings."

"I have to admit, I'm not accustomed to interviewing an intelligence officer who spends his time reading between the lines." She crossed her legs and folded both hands over her knee. "So why don't we skip the cute stuff and get right down to the issue?"

"That would be fine."

"Are you always such a gentleman?"

"Excuse me?"

"I'm here for two reasons, Ryan. Can I call you Ryan?"

"Yes."

She nodded. "First of all there's this business of your assault on the DA after you discovered his relationship with your wife. Frankly, your reaction seemed entirely reasonable to me. Unfortunately, it didn't help your case any. I've been asked by the DA to give you this."

She withdrew an envelope from her purse and handed it to him. "You can read it later. It's a restraining order that prohibits you from stepping within one mile of your wife, your daughter, or Burton Welsh. Seeing as how Welsh is the DA around these parts, I would stick to the terms of this order without compromise. He's agreed not to press charges for that little stunt you pulled because he'd rather not deal with this in the press. But he made it quite clear that any violation of this order will land you behind bars."

The man blinked. "One mile?"

He looked completely stunned. The police had released him from custody two days earlier with strict orders not to move from the motel, and it looked like he'd abided by their terms. But his good behavior clearly hadn't earned him what he was hoping for.

"One mile?" he asked again, standing slowly. "That's . . . What about Bethany?"

"You might want to consider leaving town."

He stared for a moment, incredulous, then sank back on the bed and shifted his stricken gaze past her.

"I'm sorry, Captain. There's nothing I can do."

"They have no idea what it was like. I . . . I watched them die."

"Watched who die?"

Ryan stood and paced to the window, then back. "This can't be happening. This just can't be happening."

Ricki felt oddly moved by the sight of this man's angst. He clearly loved his daughter in particular and was over-wrought at the thought of being kept away from her.

But she was here because the DA claimed that the captain had hinted at a connection with the BoneMan in the desert. She turned to her objective.

"I understand that you were confronted by a party in Iraq who compared you to the BoneMan."

He cast her a side glance but kept pacing, eyes fixed on the carpet as if the fibers at his feet held the answer to his dilemma.

"You may know that I was the lead investigator on the case against BoneMan two years ago," she continued. "With Switzer officially exonerated and free, I'm revisiting the case. Your daughter, Bethany, goes to school at Saint Michael's Academy, the same school the last victim attended."

He nodded absently.

"It's interesting, to say the least, that you ran into the case in the desert, an ocean away from here. Any details of the encounter would be appreciated."

"It's classified," Ryan said, then immediately returned to the pressing issue at hand. "She can visit me though, right? How long will this last? Surely they can't expect me to just . . . not see my own daughter."

He was too distracted by his own loss to focus on his ordeal in the desert, Ricki thought, swiveling the leg that hung over her knee. She felt overdressed here in her black heels and skirt; the only way to draw out useful information was to appear completely comfortable with him.

She stepped out of her heels, crossed to the curtain, and crossed her arms, leaning back on the darkened window. "I can see you love your daughter very much. This must be very difficult."

He stopped and looked up at her, and she could see

immediately that Ryan Evans wasn't going to clear his mind to accommodate her need for information any time soon. He stared at her with those puppy eyes.

Tears appeared, then snaked down his cheeks. His hands balled into fists and he began to shake, just a little at first, but the tremor overtook his body from head to foot.

And all the while he stared at Ricki.

His breakdown was so unexpected, so riddled with anguish, that Ricki didn't have time to prepare for the sudden emotion that swept over her. This was more than a husband who'd just discovered that his wife was leaving him. Something else was eating away at Ryan Evans.

She had to say something in the face of such pain. Do something, anything. "I'm so sorry," she said.

He caught himself and steadied his hands. Blinked away the tears. "Sorry. Sorry . . ."

"It's quite all right; you've been through a lot."

"I didn't know . . . I didn't know that she felt like this. What could I do? I tried, I tried. I thought I was doing the right thing for my country, for her, for Celine. I was sacrificing everything for what I knew how to do."

"Ryan, I—"

"Where did I go wrong?"

"This doesn't mean—"

"They have to give me another try."

"I'm sorry. . . ." Ricki had wept with mothers whose daughters had been broken up by a horrible monster. She'd stayed awake through the night, seething with anger at the kind of human being who could prey on the innocent with such savagery. She'd held a dead baby in the aftermath of spousal abuse that had gone way too far. The horror haunted her always.

But there was something different about the sight before her. Fresh tears filled his eyes and he turned away.

"Ryan . . ."

What could she say? She stood and crossed to him. Gently rubbed his shoulder and lowered her voice. "Ryan, please, it's okay." A knot filled her throat.

She had come to interrogate a sailor who might be able to shed a glimmer of light on a killer who'd broken bones and instead she found a father with a broken heart.

Someone pounded on the door.

Ricki stepped around the bed and walked to the door. A maid stood in the hall. "Will you be checking out today?"

"We'll call the front desk," Ricki said. "Give us a minute?"

"Take your time."

"Thank you."

When she shut the door and turned around, she saw that Ryan was lying on the bed, face buried in the pillow. The bottoms of his white socks were dirty, and his right pant leg was hitched up so that she could see his calf. What was she to do, sit by him and comfort him?

She had to bring this scene back to earth so that she could do what she'd come to do. If that meant helping him make a little more sense of his world, so be it.

Ricki slid one of the chairs closer to the bed and sat facing him. "I'm really sorry for all of this, Ryan. But you have to get a hold of yourself and make some decisions. You can't keep yourself cooped up in this dingy motel forever. It all looks bad now, I know, but bad times have a way of passing. Right?"

He lay still, back slowly rising and falling with each breath.

"I'm sure your daughter loves you very much. Teenagers are terrible at knowing how to express themselves."

Her mind bounced back to her own youth, a time when her father, then a cop, had been killed in a motorcycle accident. He'd never been one for words of encouragement and he'd recorded his regret in a journal that her mother had found after his death.

The memory of reading those two pages from his computer had been seared into her mind for all time. She'd sat there in silence, alone in the house a full month after his funeral, and wept uncontrollably for the first time since his death.

I swear I'd kill the man who laid a hand on Ricki. And at times I feel like I deserve no more. I've been such a bad father. Dear God, I hate myself.

The pain had haunted her for years, and sitting here next to another broken father, the memory threatened to tear her apart again.

She spoke very softly. "Listen to me, Ryan. I know what it's like. She loves you. She has to; every daughter loves her father. It's hard at times, but in the end they feel different."

He didn't react.

"I spoke to your wife and daughter this morning. She seems like a reasonable woman. And your daughter's angry; none of this makes any sense to her. You have to admit, your reactions have been a bit erratic. But she's only sixteen; in time she'll forgive whatever stands between you."

Captain Ryan Evans suddenly rolled off the bed and stood on the far side, looking disoriented for a moment before fixing her in his sight. His behavior was strange, she thought, even for a distraught man. She didn't know much about him, but his commanding officer had made one thing very clear: Captain Evans had a unique and very intelligent mind. What she would give to know what was going through that mind now.

"BoneMan?" he asked, crossing to the room to the television and flipping it off. "BoneMan, or whatever you would like to call him, was only doing what he felt needed to be done, Agent Valentine. He followed his instincts, just like we did when we bombed Iraq to smithereens. That's what I learned in the desert from BoneMan's work. Beyond that, I'm afraid it's all classified."

He stood calm and thoughtful, as if the father in him had flipped a switch and become the captain.

"I'm sorry, there's nothing I can tell you that will help you."

"Seven girls lost their lives to a sadistic killer who may be out there right now, stalking an eighth. And you say you can't help me?"

"I'm saying that nothing I have to say will help you stop the man, assuming he's still active."

"You of all people should know what it means to make sure BoneMan never kills again."

For a moment she thought he might yell at her. But if the impulse tempted him, he covered it well.

"Unless you don't realize that Muslim fundamentalists think of us as no better than the BoneMan, I have nothing to add to your profile of the man," he said.

"What happened to you in the desert, Captain Ryan?"

"A group of insurgents tried to take out my convoy in retaliation for the coalition forces bombing Iraqi women and children. Before I escaped they made it clear that I was no better than BoneMan. So while there is a very loose connection between your investigation and myself, it will hardly deliver you new evidence to solve the case. I'm sorry for your frustration, Agent Valentine, but I'm useless to you. Really."

He was probably right, but the ease with which the man righted himself and faced her with such a reasoned conclusion struck her as uncanny.

She studied him for a moment, then rose, withdrew her card from her purse, and set in on the table.

"I'm sorry for your troubles, Captain Evans. It sounds like you've had a rough few weeks. If I think we need it, we'll get a subpoena that will allow you to tell me what happened in the desert. In the meantime, if you wouldn't mind keeping me apprised of your movements?"

He nodded once.

"Are you headed back any time soon?"

"No. I'll be stateside for a while."

"End of tour?"

"Something like that."

She wondered about that.

"Word of advice, Ryan. I really would steer clear of Burton Welsh. He can be an animal if he gets backed into a corner. You picked the wrong guy to drop your knee into."

"I understand."

"I was serious when I said you might want to get out of town."

"Yes."

She picked up her heels. "You have my card. Call me."

"Yes," he said.

But she doubted he would.

14

Two Months Later

HE WENT BY the name Alvin Finch, not because that was his real name, although it was, but because he went by the name Alvin Finch.

Some called him BoneMan.

Some called him by other names, depending on where he was or what he was doing, none of which he found interesting enough to think about when he was alone in the place of complete peace and fear, as he was now. That wonderful, terrible state when heaven and hell collided here, in his mind.

After almost two years of peaceful nights, resting in the full knowledge that he'd executed and survived his crusade without so much as one scratch to his lily-white skin, Alvin had begun to grow restless.

His mission had always been painfully clear. On the one hand he was punishing fathers, all fathers, because all fathers were the fathers of lies. None knew how to truly love their daughters the way he could.

On the other hand, Alvin was looking for the perfect daughter who would love him with complete devotion, the way he loved himself. Unable to find such a daughter, he'd killed all of the girls, satisfied that he was at least punishing the fathers.

Then the authorities had blamed another man for his mission and he'd taken a sabbatical, always knowing that he would resume his quest at the right time.

But his growing restlessness had turned to the place of complete peace and fear three weeks ago when he'd made the one discovery that would now haunt him until he either possessed a daughter or died.

Alvin Finch opened the red robe he'd been wearing all morning and watched it fall around his feet in a heap. The new him, thinner by twenty pounds as a result of rigorous exercise, prompted by the incessant news of how the country was growing fatter by the day, stood naked in the full-length bathroom mirror. His brilliant blue eyes stared lovingly at himself, beautiful next to his white skin. They were his window into heaven itself, reminding him often of his angelic nature. Short-cropped blond hair hugged his skull, easier to keep clean that way.

He trimmed his hair every morning. Included in his routine were a shave of his neck, chin, and cheeks, as well as the plucking of any stray hairs from his nostrils, ears, and eyebrows. Above the neck he was as neatly groomed as was humanly possible.

Below the neck, he was perfect. Absolutely exquisite.

The FBI's physical profile published in the papers had been nearly perfect, but he'd expected nothing less. He'd run the full stats on white men who weighed roughly a hundred and ninety pounds, stood six feet, wore size-thirteen shoes, and drove pickups, and found similar redneck males to be numerous.

Satan.

BoneMan, Alvin Finch, and Satan—these were the three names that awakened the place of peace and fear in his mind. His names.

The odd thing about hell was that it contained a piece of heaven, or at the very least what felt like heaven. Peace was there, in the place of perfect fear. Or to be more precise, his peace was found in their perfect fear. This alone was Alvin Finch's piece of heaven on earth.

Alvin Finch had milky white skin, nearly perfect in every conceivable way. Soft and subtle like a young woman's, but smoother because he allowed no hair growth, preferring to shave and wax regularly, and because he'd always applied lotion, ever since his mother had given him his first jar of the white Noxzema skin lotion over thirty years earlier.

There were two things that Alvin loved; three that he cherished. He loved unblemished skin because it made all things perfect on the outside. He loved butterflies because they had perfect skin.

He loved soap, lots and lots of soap.

Alvin stepped into the shower, took his time, using six liquid ounces of unscented soap to lather his entire body four times between rinses. He washed his hair three times, as was his custom when he was in the place of peace and fear, as he was now. When the hot water in his one-hundred-gallon tank ran lukewarm, he shut it off and dried himself before stepping onto the tile floor.

Steam had blanketed the mirrors and he wanted to see his clean, smooth skin again, so he wiped the glass with a fresh towel and then used a hair dryer to clear the mirror of all moisture.

He studied his image again, paying special attention to his white belly, which, no matter how many sit-ups he did, persisted in showing a small roll of fat. So-called love handles. But otherwise he was quite pleased.

He took one of the blue jars of Noxzema from the vanity, dipped four fingers deep into the cream, and smeared the luxurious balm over both hands as he watched himself in the mirror. His skin bristled with excitement as he smoothed it on, starting at his chest, working down until he softened his ankles and the soles of his feet.

Fully moisturized, he next clipped his toenails as he did every day, taking his time to clear the slightest trace of toe jam from under each nail. Using a tissue, he swept up the clippings, rolled them into a ball, and flushed them down the toilet.

Satisfied that he was clean, he dressed in a pair of loose cargo pants and slipped into a brown plaid button-down shirt. In El Paso and other parts west, he'd worn a hat, but here in the city he found that whatever impression the community had of itself, very few people actually wore hats. They wore work boots and cargo pants and brown plaid, buttoned shirts.

Alvin stepped into his bedroom and stopped next to the bed. He never opened the blinds, preferring table lamps to the bright sun, which damaged the skin. Now both bedside lamps were off, but he could still see the faces on the wall peering, and he paused to let them stare at him.

The photographs on his wall numbered well over a hundred now, all faces of younger girls and teenagers, all staring at the camera lens, all without a single pimple or blemish.

All had all been candidates at one time or another. Potential daughters. Alvin required a daughter, this was his one obsession. A perfect daughter who could love him the way he deserved to be loved. Not sexually, of course. Only sick men stooped so low. They, more than flies and mosquitoes, deserved to be crushed.

His method was simple: upon searching the world for the candidates who might make him a perfect daughter, he selected only the very best.

From the very best candidates, he had taken those very few who, after considerable clandestine examination, appeared both accessible and worthy of his standards. Seven. He'd taken seven, and under pressure none had measured up.

Confronted by their failure, he'd killed all seven. Once having been exposed to him, they simply could not live. But more than this, he knew that he deserved at least some pleasure for all of his hassle.

Their bones had to be broken, one by one, until their internal bleeding eventually forced them to give up the ghost.

He'd marked the photographs of the seven he'd killed with a small red dot in the upper right-hand corner. Although none was qualified any longer, he enjoyed their stares and he now considered removing his shirt.

The new daughter's face filled his mind, and he turned from the wall of fakes. Alvin was a reasonable man, fully able to control his needs, even the need for a daughter, and when the police had pinned his victims on another man, he'd decided to take an extended break.

But three weeks ago his hiatus had been dramatically interrupted by a single photograph, like a flash grenade that had been dropped into his world. Welsh, that pretender of the worst sort, had reopened the case after they'd released Phil Switzer.

Naturally, Alvin had taken a new interest in their every move. He'd learned a great deal, not the least regarding a man who'd claimed to have tangled with a killer tied to the BoneMan in Iraq. A Captain Ryan Evans, who seemed to have lost his head in the incident. A father.

But that was only a fraction of what Alvin had learned. Ryan Evans was no ordinary father. He was the father of a most extraordinary daughter who no more belonged in Ryan's heart, mind, or house than did a devil.

Within the day of stumbling across the girl, Alvin knew that his hiatus was over. He had found the girl who would love him as a father, and no amount of restraint could dissuade him.

He walked to the head of his bed, lifted his pillow, and withdrew the photograph. This girl would be Alvin Finch's daughter. Nothing else mattered now besides this stunning creature staring back at him from the 5 x 7 inch glossy photograph in his right hand. He would take her and he would crush any imposter who called himself her father and he would either win her devotion or he would kill her.

Alvin tucked the photograph back under his pillow and left the room, stilling a tremor in his hands.

The living room was dark although it was day outside the apartment. He switched on the lamp beside his computer and saw that it was just past noon. The trip would take an hour and a half and he would need to arrive when the sun was down. There was no rush. He'd waited over two years; he would wait another hour.

There were two things Alvin hated. Nay, three that were an abomination to him. He hated humans. He especially hated ugly skanks with perfect, beautiful faces and skin.

He hated mothers and fathers.

Mothers because he hated his own mother who'd made him the way he was and although he cherished himself he also hated himself.

Fathers because they were all pretenders who could not love their daughters the way he would. The way his mother should have loved him.

If Alvin had his way, he would line up all the mothers and fathers in the world and break their bones to teach them a lesson.

Alvin made himself a cheese sandwich and ate it slowly with a large glass of cold milk. He'd been in this particular apartment for just under two months but he'd paid the lease for a full six months, explaining to the landlord that he traveled often and didn't want to make the mistake of missing a rent check.

He wasn't sure how long he would be gone when he left tomorrow. A week, a month, maybe longer. What he did know was that all the waiting would soon be over. All his preparations at each location, the trailer, the truck, the manner in which he would abduct his next victim.

Alvin washed the last of the cheese sandwich down, rinsed out the glass, and checked the front door to make sure it was locked. Then he walked once around the dark apartment, making sure that everything was in order before stepping out the back door and descending to the garage.

He'd sold the Ford truck two years earlier, when they'd

pinned his work on Phil Switzer, who didn't have the brains to eat a bowl of cereal without spilling milk down his chin much less kill seven women without breaking their skin. The Ford F-150 parked in the garage now was a blue king cab, identical to the one he'd used before. They should know that the father was back, taking his daughter from under their noses. Nothing would make the statement as much as the tires on this truck and his boot impressions.

It took Alvin an hour and forty-five minutes to reach the outskirts of the city. He parked in an H-E-B grocery parking lot at the corner of Highway 71 and Bee Cave Road, lay down on his side, and tried to rest.

But the anticipation was too great and he spent the next two hours fighting off chills of excitement rather than sleep. This particular trip was only a dry run, but he took his dry runs very seriously. If all went well, he would return tomorrow and execute the mission flawlessly. He'd learned a few things in the military that came in very handy now, planning being the most important of them all.

At six o'clock he went into the store and purchased two lemons, a box of prepared sushi, and two liters of Mug root beer.

The sun slowly sank into the western horizon, and unwilling to wait another hour, Alvin started up the Ford and headed down Highway 71 toward Southwest Parkway. By the time he pulled onto Barton Creek Boulevard, he was tingling with anticipation.

And by the time he'd parked the truck and hiked into his position near the house, where he had a clear view of the girl's bedroom, he was covered in sweat. He'd learned long ago that applying lotion to sweaty skin was nasty business that turned one into a fish. So he withdrew the towel he'd brought in his knapsack, carefully removed his shirt, applied some lotion to his cooling skin, and feeling refreshed, shrugged back into his shirt.

Now he could settle down and wait until midnight before walking up to the window to peer inside.

He'd been watching the house ever since he'd decided he must take her, three weeks ago. The fact that the district attorney, Burt Welsh, was evidently making a play for Bethany's whore mother was a pleasant surprise that would complicate Alvin's plans but only in the best of ways.

The fact that still another man claimed to be her father was even more compelling. The time had come. This was it; he knew this was it in his very bones.

There were two things that excited BoneMan more than he could possibly express with mere words; nay, three things that sent shivers up his spine.

A young girl's cries for mercy.

Noxzema skin lotion.

The sound of bones breaking beneath skin.

15

"GOOD." FATHER HORTENSE smiled and sipped his tea. The man reminded Ryan of Tevye from *Fiddler on the Roof*, a thick man who always dressed in black with a heavy beard that he enjoyed stroking as he contemplated life.

"Very good, Ryan. I think we could call that a breakthrough."

"Yes, sir."

The last sixty days had perhaps been the most difficult months in his life—a long, dark tunnel without a light to guide him other than his weekly visits with Father Hortense who, in addition to being a priest, was also a board-certified psychiatrist. Under the rather unique circumstances the navy had agreed to give Hortense full supervisory authority over Ryan's case, including all recommendations as to how his career may or may not continue with the navy.

To Ryan, Hortense was God. The puppet master. Which would make him the puppet.

"And the lapses in time?"

They were seated in a Starbucks on University Parks Drive in Waco, three blocks from the apartment that Ryan had rented after moving out of the Super 8 in Austin. The coffee shop was the priest's idea, a way to get Ryan out of his dark world and into general circulation, as he put it.

"Better," Ryan said. He picked up his black coffee and motioned with it. "I still have the nightmares and time gets away from me, but I'm doing better this week. Much better."

"Good. Time is a magnificent healer and you are the recipient of her best intentions."

"Time, yes. Thank God for Father Time."

"Not just time, of course. I think you're coming to terms with the divorce through careful thought and grace. Those are the backbone of any strong character. No one can accuse you of having a weak character."

"So you've said."

"You disagree?"

Ryan leaned back and crossed his legs. They sat outside in a corner, beyond the hearing of the next group. A black BMW on its way to the drive-through slid past, driven by a gray-haired man in a green polo shirt.

And who was this man? What kinds of challenges had he faced in life? To all who saw him from a distance he appeared like one more successful man quietly enjoying the fruits of life, not unlike Ryan. But like Ryan, was he really a man torn by life's most cruel circumstances? Divorce? A failed business? A wayward child? Insomnia?

"Ryan?"

"Hmm? Yes, I'm sorry, do I disagree? What was the question again? I'm sorry, I was drifting."

"That's fine. I was asking if you thought you had a weak character."

"I suppose that depends on when you ask me. I've had some pretty weak days these last couple months."

"And a weaker character may have never recovered from them. Few men have endured the kind of ordeal you faced in the desert, not to mention the divorce."

The air grew silent around Ryan, despite the roar of cars nearby.

"All told, I'm surprised you've done so well."

"Tell that to the man who stole my wife."

Father Hortense chuckled and Ryan smiled with him. "The man you assaulted."

"I hardly assaulted him. During the darkest times I wish I had."

"Ah, yes, the time of deep, dark despairing."

He'd made one final plea to Celine following his interview with FBI agent Valentine, during which he'd learned that he would be legally restrained from seeing Bethany. But then his now ex-wife (it was hard to believe she was no longer his wife, that the laws of Texas allowed for such a hasty divorce) had handed the phone to Bethany, who'd hung up on him.

He'd fled Austin. An hour and a half north was as far and as near as he dared. He'd taken the furnished apartment, dutifully stocked up on food, mostly the nonperishable kind, and shut himself in.

Hortense, who'd been assigned to him without his knowledge, had tracked him down and found him in his dungeon. He'd been so concerned for him those first two weeks that he'd come by every other day to open the curtains and haul him from bed. Thinking back now, Ryan was hard-pressed not to think of the change in him since as anything short of a genuine breakthrough.

"Was Kahlid insane?"

Father Hortense frowned. "Either insane or blinded by rage."

"Or simply destroyed by sorrow," Ryan said. "As strange as it sounds, I think I understand Kahlid."

He'd never made the admission, and he did so now at the risk of sounding like he might be regressing. On the other hand, this kind of honesty was anything but a sign of regression. Hortense, like all psychiatrists, thrived on complete honesty.

"Tell me how you understand him."

"Those first few weeks"—a college student talking into an iPhone walked by and Ryan waited for him to pass—"those first few weeks the horror of war haunted me; I couldn't shake the feeling."

"So you've said. And I can understand how it's led you this new conviction of yours to turn away from war. God knows the shedding of innocent blood is a terrible business no matter where or how it's done. But that's exactly what Kahlid did. Shed innocent blood to make a point. That was his own kind of war. You're saying you understand that?"

"He was driven to do exactly what he accused us of doing, taking innocent lives for a cause that"—Ryan stopped, shaking his head at the memory—"God, I could never do that. Not now."

"So you understand what Kahlid did but you could never do it yourself. I would say that's healthy."

Ryan nodded absently. "Funny how it all begins to fade over time. I don't think I will ever be able to go back into the field again, but those first few weeks . . . it was so raw then. I came back hating war. I looked at every teenager walking down the road differently. What Kahlid did shook me to my core, Father. I'm not sure I could hurt a fly now."

"But it doesn't feel as raw and you feel like it still should feel raw. You're saying you're suffering from guilt for not feeling as bothered as you were in the weeks after—"

"Not guilty. Just curious. When you step away from it all, you lose perspective. Like the rest of the country."

"Then that begs another question," Father Hortense said. "You think the war is wrong?"

"The war, I can't say. Killing innocent life, yes. And abandoning children is as bad as killing them."

The priest grunted. "Now there's the real issue for you, isn't it? It's not just that you've found a heart for the inno-cent, it's that you're suffering guilt for failing as a father to your own daughter."

Yes. Ryan didn't say it, but they both knew it was true.

"Shall we head back?"

They stood and walked down the sidewalk toward his apartment complex.

"You didn't fail, of course," Hortense said.

"No, Father, I didn't fail." They'd been over this a dozen times. "But I did."

"No more than half the fathers in this country."

"Yes, as you've been so willing to point out. And I'm not saying it doesn't help. Millions, hundreds of millions of children grow up without a father nearby. In whole cul-tures, fathers are less accessible to their children than in ours. During the times of the patriarchs, times of war, the birth of our nation, I get it. But to be rejected by your own daughter . . ."

They walked in silence for a few moments.

"It was a painful experience."

"One that you'll live with for the balance of your life," the father said. "But you're finding yourself again. And that's the important thing."

"Yes, I suppose so."

"The fact that you can talk so freely about all of this is sign enough."

Ryan nodded. A smile crept across his mouth with the memory of young Bethany, age seven, pronouncing that he was smarter than the president because the president couldn't read people's minds while he could—speaking of her mind, of course.

"Have you considered our last discussion?" the father asked.

"I have."

Hortense had suggested the possibility of his returning to work on a limited schedule, stateside. Temporary duty, or TDY, as the military called it. Getting his mind into familiar territory could well speed his full recovery.

"And?"

"I think you might be right. As long as I can insulate myself from certain duties. I don't think I can stare at pictures of casualties."

"That can be arranged on my orders."

The thought of reclaiming the life he knew so well in the navy was comforting. "I'm assuming it'll take a couple weeks to line things up."

"A few weeks, yes. Think of it as an extension of your ongoing therapy."

Ryan took a deep breath through his nose, smelling the fresh scent of grass, churned up by the mower giving the park to their right one last mow before winter.

"As long as it's not in Austin . . ."

"San Antonio. You'd need to move back, of course."

"Another few weeks, why not? I've never been crazy about Waco, anyway."

"You'd be back under the command structure with the CO. Another psychiatrist would be assigned, but it might be for the best."

Ryan found the thought unnerving. "Maybe."

They dropped the subject and talked about college football, a favorite of Father Hortense. He'd suggested taking Ryan to two different UT games but the thought of traveling to Austin was far too much to consider during those dark days. He'd never been a big football fan anyway. And those crowds . . . they were enough to make him shudder.

Today, however, he might take the father up on a similar offer.

And if he just happened to run across Burton Welsh or Celine? Or, God forbid, Bethany?

The thought made his belly churn.

Father Hortense accompanied him up the stairs to his apartment on the second floor. "Let me make the calls and get the paperwork going."

He'd waited until this moment to pull the envelope out of his pocket. "Father, I was wondering if you could do me a favor. I know this is a lot to ask, but—"

"Bethany?"

He held the unmarked envelope out and nodded. "Yes."

"You know I can't."

"The court order, I know. But if you could just, I don't know, drop it off at her school, get the janitor to slip it into her locker . . . anything. This would mean a lot."

Father Hortense took the hand that held the envelope into both of his own. "Look, I know how badly you want to reach out to her and explain yourself, and I believe you'll get that opportunity. But it's too soon. It would also defy the court's order. If Bethany or your ex-wife reports this kind of direct communication from you—"

"It won't *be* from me!"

"The letter's from—"

"Picture, not letter."

Hortense frowned and glanced at the envelope, considering.

Ryan explained while he still had the chance. "It's just a picture, not a single written word. A picture of Bethany and myself at her ninth birthday party. There'd be no proof that it came from me."

"What can you hope in return from her?"

He pressed the envelope into the priest's hand and lowered his arms. "Just knowing that I'm not out of her mind. It's my way of putting this all behind me. If I know that she has something to remember me by, something that she will know came from me, something that tells her I'm thinking of her . . . it's all I can ask."

"And you'll put this behind you?"

"I think I can, yes. Seriously, I just need something symbolic like this to . . . you know, take the next step."

"Somehow I doubt you'll be stepping beyond your own daughter."

"But it makes sense, you have to agree. I need a marker

like this, a signpost, anything that tells me I've done what I can."

Father Hortense eyed the white envelope. "I guess I can see that."

"And I don't think a picture counts as the court's understanding of written communication."

"Okay. I'm actually going to Austin for a meeting this afternoon. I suppose I could swing by Saint Michael's Academy."

"Thank you, Father." He took the man's hand and shook it aggressively. "Thank you so much. Really, you have no idea what this means to me."

Hortense took the envelope and slipped it into his coat pocket. "Okay. See you next week."

Ryan nodded, feeling positively relieved. "Next week."

16

ALVIN FINCH HAD spent the day showering and applying cream and remaining calm in the face of the coming night. The waiting was always like this before he broke their bones. But this time it was different.

Two years of delayed gratification had quietly built up his need, far beyond his capacity to understand it now that he'd made his decision. How a human mind could desire anything with such compulsion mystified him. He'd always been aware of his own superiority to the masses that fed, like sheep, on society's self-indulgent grasses. Now it seemed that he'd become like his own victims, though he was able to beat back his raw craving for personal satisfaction.

On the other hand, he was above them all, as their lord and master. He was their Satan, come in sheep's clothing, walking among them daily without so much as raising an eyebrow.

This time was also different because this time he had other plans.

At four o'clock Alvin, who was also BoneMan, left his apartment, climbed into the blue Ford F-150 pickup, headed out onto I-35, and drove south toward Austin.

There was one thing Alvin despised, nay, two he resented more than death itself. Writers and journalists of all stripes, because they knew far less than their words suggested.

Mini Cooper automobiles, because they looked like ladybugs. He disliked bugs because bugs seemed to be attracted to Noxzema lotion for the nutrients it provided them, and he hated women, which made ladybugs a pretty nasty combination.

It took Alvin nearly three hours to fight his way through traffic and reach the H-E-B on Highway 71 and Bee Cave Road, but he'd allowed for any such delay, so although he found the crowded roads to his disliking, he was able to make the trip without too much frustration.

Once again he tried to rest by lying down on the seat. Once again the wait proved fitful because of his eagerness. Once again he walked into the store and purchased two lemons, one pack of prepared sushi, and two liters of Mug brand root beer.

It was dark by the time Alvin finally took up his position in the trees near the back of the house, where he dried his sweat and applied lotion.

"I DON'T THINK you understand what I'm saying, Mother. You're the one who got me into this, so why the resistance now?"

"Why? You're sixteen years old and you want to run off to New York and you wonder why I, your mother, who loves Austin, thank you very much, suggest that maybe, just maybe you're being a bit impulsive?"

"Something like that, yes. I was under the impression that you wanted me to pursue a career in modeling."

Celine plucked the square white box of beef and broccoli off the table and marched to the waste bin into which she summarily dumped the half-eaten takeout. "You can be such a snob, but you know that, don't you?"

Mother rounded the counter and made a show of wiping down the tile with a dish towel, but the kitchen was spotless from lack of use. "I can't believe you would dump this on me now of all times. I finally find someone I love, and you know very well he can't move out of Austin, even if he wanted to, and you do what? Dump something like this on me."

Bethany set her chopsticks into the box of noodles, crossed her arms, and sat back, fully aware of precisely what her mother was saying.

Before taking her trip to New York for the *Youth Nation* photo shoot, Bethany had honestly entertained doubts about her interest in pursuing a career in the camera's eye. All five of the shoots prior to New York had been hot and tedious affairs that made her feel more like a slab of meat than an honored guest.

But the cover shoot in New York had showed her a completely new side of the business. She'd been treated like royalty from the moment she, Celine, and Patty had set foot in *Youth Nation*'s reception room, beginning with the large bouquet of flowers and Henri, the masseur who had met her.

Each step she'd taken in the building had been followed by an assistant, whose sole purpose was to see to her comfort, whether that meant emptying the room of the countless persons fussing over her so that she could have a moment or getting her a soda.

They'd stayed in a very luxurious suite in the Waldorf and ordered whatever they liked from room service and over the course of the week, they'd seen four Broadway shows, including both *The Lion King* and *Wicked*.

Naturally, she was smart enough to look past all the trappings, however enjoyable they were. In fact, she found them just a bit over-the-top. These weren't why she'd decided that she loved New York.

But something else had happened in New York that she couldn't easily put aside. For the first time she could remember, Bethany had seen herself not as Celine's daughter, in a never-ending struggle for control, or even as her mother's peer, jockeying for position in a constantly changing environment, but as herself, apart from Celine.

She, not Celine, had been the center of attention, and apart from a few fits of frustration, Celine had been forced to step back and keep her mouth shut.

For the first time her mother's opinions hardly mattered. Bethany's makeup and hair, and the clothes she wore, the food she ate, even the way she talked—none of it was any of her mother's business, a point made very clear on day one. Celine and Patty were welcome to watch. Quietly.

What at first felt uncomfortable to Bethany soon turned to relief and by the end of the week, she'd grown so pleased with her ability to cope in this environment without her mother's hawking that she began to plot ways to return.

"You're only sixteen, for the love of God!" Mother snapped. "Don't let all of this attention get to your head."

"I'm who you always wanted me to be, Mother. I wasn't the one who chose this life. Everything I am is because of you. And who I am, not to mention my agent, tells me that I would be much better off in New York. I have two other covers waiting in the wings; a whole string of smaller shoots, but I can't very well fly to New York every weekend for photo shoots."

"They said they could work around you! Why are you insisting on all of this? Moving to New York is out of the question. I'm getting married here!"

"Yes, of course, we would hate to interrupt your precious life for the sake of your daughter, wouldn't we? Never have, why start now?"

"You can't possibly think that I would actually even consider giving up a relationship with Burt so that you can run off to New York."

"No, but you could send me to the New York Institute for College Preparation. They have a boarding program."

Her mother looked as if she'd been slapped. "Boarding school? Who's going to pay for that?"

"I will."

"Don't be ridiculous."

But Bethany knew that the idea was already taking root in her mother's head. She would put on a good show of resistance while secretly cheering the solution to her last barrier to freedom. With Bethany out of the house, Celine could do as she pleased, when she pleased.

"We both know you owe me this," she said, pushing her chair back. She left the takeout on the table and walked to the counter.

"I don't owe you a thing. You're attending a private

school, you're on the cover of *Youth Nation,* I've always given you everything you wanted. You're spoiled rotten!"

"You married a man who deserted us and you didn't have the guts to set things straight. You dragged me around the country, forcing me to leave old friends and find new ones. I don't belong anywhere, my friends are about as shallow as they come, I don't have a father worth spitting at, I have nothing! I followed you stupidly because I was just a kid who had no choice. But I know better now. I'm not denying you your relationship with this new fling; I don't see why you should deny me what I want."

Hearing herself say it all, Bethany felt even more compelled to leave this city and make a new start, this time with people who valued her beyond their obligations.

She'd even been deserted by those who did have an obligation.

Slowly Celine's stare softened. "You're overreacting," she said.

To what? Bethany didn't ask the question because suddenly she felt quite emotional about her own predicament.

"You're hurt."

"Obviously."

"By him," Mother said, clenching her jaw. "By that freak who ran off. I hate him."

"Don't blame this all on your husband—"

"Ex-husband."

"He may be a loser, but you've never cared much either."

"How can you say that?"

"You know how I can say it, Mother. You're just playing; you're absolving the guilt you already have for wanting me out of your hair for good."

The moment Bethany thought it, she became convinced it was true. Which only made her predicament worse. She was hated by both father and mother. New York really was her only option.

"You want me to go, don't you?"

Celine hesitated, confirming her suspicion. She crossed to the cupboard and withdrew a red wineglass.

"I don't know, Bethany. You sit here and talk like this and I just don't know what to think. Maybe it would be best."

The final confirmation sliced into Bethany's chest with surprising pain. "My own blood doesn't want me," she said. "I hate you, Mother. I hate you as much as I hate my father."

Celine spun and threw the glass in the sink, where it shattered. "You insolent little cow! You're not even our blood."

Bethany blinked. "What do you mean?"

"You . . . you're adopted."

Her heart stopped. Tears sprang to her eyes. *Adopted*?

"What do you mean?"

"I mean we took you in when you were a baby. I can't have children." Celine's upper lip was trembling. "See what you've forced me to tell you?"

It now all made perfect sense to Bethany. Why her father had left. Why Celine had never shown her any affection. She wasn't even their child!

But she didn't know what to do with this information. She felt completely lost and vulnerable, staring across the island at Celine, whose glassy eyes signaled her regret for what she'd said. She turned away and poured herself another glass of red wine.

The woman who had been her mother up until a moment ago was right. Bethany was only sixteen, and no sixteen-year-old should have to face this kind of life.

How could it be that with all the cars and clothes and houses they had, they didn't have the most basic of all human needs? They didn't have each other.

Celine now had Burt Welsh.

Bethany had nothing.

"Thank you for sharing, Celine. I think I'll go to bed now, if it's all right with you."

"Don't try to manipulate me," her ex-mother said in a low, biting tone. "I may not be your mother by birth, but I still changed your diapers."

"Is that what I smell? Hmm, and here I thought it was coming from your mouth."

The phone rang, and Celine stepped to the phone on light feet. She saw the caller ID, cast one glare at Bethany, and then turned away.

"Hello, Burt."

All smiles. She was already done with her daughter and in the arms of her lover.

Bethany grabbed her book bag and headed upstairs, furious at the woman. She plopped her junk on the bed and sat down in front of her iMac. A quick scan of her email showed nothing interesting; a link to the New York boarding school revealed nothing new.

No new texts. No voice mail; no escape of any kind. Saint Michael's, cheerleading, her friends, this house, even her so-called modeling career—it all felt like an empty cell to her. She was in a prison of her parents' making.

Celine's shrill laugh rang through the house.

Tears stung Bethany's eyes again, and now she sat

back, crossed her arms, and allowed herself to cry silently. Adopted? What did that make her? A daughter, but Celine's daughter, not really.

No, she was the daughter of some other mother who'd dumped her. Some other father who'd deposited her into a pod until she could be dumped on a woman who needed an obedient little blob to make her feel significant and powerful.

But there was a problem, see? That little blob had grown up and now they had to decide what to do with it. Well, why not just dump it out again? Someone else will pick it up.

She knew she was oversimplifying the matter, but not by too much, right?

Bethany sat back in her chair, lost in thoughts of utter worthlessness, and the longer she considered her predicament, the more useless she felt. She picked up the scissors that lay on her desk and eyed the razor edge. They were the kind you could buy at any Walmart, with orange handles, made from aluminum.

Sharp. What would Celine think if she were to carve up this pretty little body? There would be an interesting cover for a magazine.

The moment she thought it, Bethany closed her eyes and scolded herself.

But girls did this, right? They cut themselves. And why not? Why not make a statement to yourself that you were what mattered, not everyone's opinion of you? You could do what you wanted. You had the power.

If you couldn't beat the world, you could join it on your own terms. Not on a magazine cover, but with a pair of scissors and your own skin.

She lifted her arm. Pressed the sharp edge on the back of her wrist and drew a thin line across the flesh. Didn't really hurt.

So what could be so wrong with just cutting her skin a little? Just a thin red line across her arm. It was her body, she could punish it as she saw fit, right?

Bethany pushed harder and pulled just a little. Not too far, just enough to—

A sharp pain streaked up her arm. She uttered a small gasp and lifted the blade, revealing a thin red line that swelled with blood.

She'd cut herself. Half an inch or maybe an inch. Okay, so maybe that was stupid.

She flung the scissors at her desk and pressed her finger against the small cut. Still, she'd made her own statement. Tomorrow she would tell anyone who asked that she'd scraped her arm on the trunk or something. And as stupid as it was, it did feel just a bit deserved.

Bethany sighed and began to surf, hardly caring where her screen took her.

She downloaded a new song by the band Red and another from Breaking Benjamin's new album. Patty tried to contact her twice but she ignored both texts.

Finally, at eleven, she pulled on her plaid flannel pajama bottoms, lay down on her bed, curled up in a ball, and fell asleep.

THE NEIGHBORHOOD WAS quiet at one o'clock in the morning, when Alvin Finch walked along the tree line that skirted a large yard behind the house.

The two dogs on the property to the south were dead

already. He'd learned the hard way that dogs had a sixth sense when it came to strangers after dusk. He'd killed the German shepherd that had barked on his approach to the first victim in El Paso, but caught unprepared, he'd resorted to a bat over the animal's skull, not an ideal distraction in the heat of a taking. Tonight he wouldn't be bothered by any such interruption.

The house they were renting had a pool that snugged up to a sliding glass door at the back, but this would not be his point of entry. There were two bedrooms that shared a bathroom upstairs, both with balconies. The family used the first room for storage and odd projects. The girl slept in the second bedroom.

Pulling on his black leather gloves, Alvin walked to the side of the house, lifted the metal ladder that they stored behind the heat exchanger, and carefully rested it against the balcony railing. With one last glance along the trees, not because he needed to but because he wanted to, he mounted the ladder and climbed up the rungs.

The evergreens hid the neighbors from the house, and him from the neighbors. Privacy was a wonderful thing.

Careful not to shake the balcony, he hefted himself over the railing and set himself on the wood flooring. He'd chosen a night without a moon, but the clouds could not be controlled, and for the moment what starlight there was would show his form to any careful observer.

He'd been on this balcony twice in the last week. Nothing had changed.

There were two things that BoneMan loathed. Nay, three. He loathed dogs that barked in the night. He loathed the man who'd tried to stop him. And he loathed the mother cow asleep on the floor beneath them.

From his right pocket Alvin retrieved a diamond-tipped glass cutter attached by a thin cable to a suction cup. He pressed the cup against the glass on the sliding door, oiled the diamond tip from a small tube in his shirt pocket, and ran the cutter in a circle. The slight scraping sound might wake someone in the storage room, but this didn't concern him. His subject's room was insulated by a bathroom and two walls.

It took him fifteen minutes to cut a five-inch-diameter hole through both panes in the glass door. Pocketing the cutter, he reached in and unlatched the lock. With a gentle nudge the door slid open and Alvin slipped inside the house.

He'd studied each room of the house on his numerous visits, and a quick glance now told him that all was precisely as he'd expected. Boxes piled on the left and a folding table set up on the right.

The anticipation coursing through his veins was now so intense that it brought a small shiver with it. He stood safely in the dark and considered the turmoil he was about to cause.

Welsh, who'd swaggered under his boast of throwing BoneMan behind bars where he belonged, would wake up tomorrow and learn that not only was BoneMan back, but that he'd taken the daughter he would make his own.

The enormity of this taking was enough to give Alvin decidedly more pleasure than he'd felt with the last victim, and he took his time now to relish the accomplishment.

The silence stretched and he stood perfectly still, satisfied by this slice of heaven on earth. The daughter asleep in the next room, the mother dreaming of Welsh below them.

BoneMan standing in the dark—their lord and master had come to take their souls. When he could wait no longer, Alvin withdrew the syringe from his left pocket and walked into the girl's room.

His subject was lying in a ball. He studied her dark form for a moment, then stepped along one side of her bed and positioned the needle just over her neck.

He thrust the 22-gauge needle into her jugular vein and shoved the plunger home. She jerked and cried out into his gloved hand—they always did—but the girl also managed to twist and stare up at him with wide eyes.

The drug was a tranquilizer of his own creation. One part sterile saline, two parts pentobarbital, two parts chlorpromazine, all adding up to nine cc's of tranquility. The jugular vein pumped it through the heart and then on to the rest of the vascular system, quickly shutting the brain off by sealing the gates between the central nervous system and the peripheral nervous system. She fought for less than ten seconds before her voluntary muscles ceased all function and she lay still.

Satisfied that his subject was now subdued, Alvin left the room and headed downstairs and across the house, moving quickly on the balls of his feet. He withdrew the second syringe as he entered the mother's room. She, like the daughter, slept on her side, with her back toward him.

Alvin slid a ski mask over his head, crossed the room, and slid the needle into her jugular vein, making no attempt to still her sudden cry of horror.

The relaxant froze her throat muscles first, then the rest of her body when it entered her spinal column. She lay on the bed staring up at him, fully conscious but unable to move more than the muscles required to breath, and then only barely. Soon, she would hallucinate, then sleep, with her saliva glands excreting onto her pillow.

His fourth subject had died from an overdose before he could finish his task with her. He would not make the mistake again.

"Tell him this is payback," he whispered hoarsely and broke her left forefinger as if it were a pretzel. The soft pop had the sound of justice, but only a whisper of it. She deserved so much more. He considered breaking her wrist but held off. There would be plenty of time for justice later.

Alvin slung the woman over his shoulder and took her out the back as if she were a bag of rocks. He set her on the ground next to the pool, and her head struck the concrete with a wet thump when she toppled to her side.

The rope was where he'd left it, by the barbeque. He tied her ankles and her wrists behind her back, then lifted her by her clothes and dropped her on the air mattress, as planned.

She would float on the water, staring up at the night sky, immobilized for a few more hours before her ability to move finally returned. By then, Alvin would have retrieved the camper and driven to his first stop.

With any luck, Welsh would feel the need for an early breakfast with her, as he had on two occasions since Alvin had been watching the house.

Without wasting another minute, he hurried back upstairs, threw the daughter over his right shoulder, and walked out the front door.

17

RYAN ROSE EARLY the morning after his weekly session with Father Hortense, feeling more refreshed than he'd felt since his abduction in Iraq. More important, he thought, free from distraction; his mind was working again. He could even reflect on his mental state with reasonable accuracy.

At eight o'clock he made himself breakfast for the first time since he'd been in the apartment. He toasted two slices of whole-wheat bread, placed sliced avocado on each slice, then sat down at his table to enjoy the food with a tall glass of milk.

In hindsight his experience these last few months made perfect sense to him. Having passed through the valley of death and climbed up the mountain beyond, looking back provided an interesting view. This is what had happened.

One: He'd been forced into a situation beyond his control and had faced a horror that even now sent a chill down his spine.

Two: He'd managed to escape but only after watching

children die, in part because of his refusal to sacrifice his own wife and daughter.

Three: His experience had fundamentally altered his view of his own daughter, Bethany, and the senselessness of abusing innocent life.

Four: After a week of holding as strong as he could in the base hospital, he'd suffered an emotional break for which the navy had put him on an extended leave.

Five: Rushing home to repair his relationship with Celine and Bethany, he'd discovered that he was too late. The damage done to Bethany had understandably blinded her to any reconciliation, and Celine had found love in the arms of another man.

Six: Still suffering from the emotional break, Ryan had lost his calm and assaulted that man, which did nothing but give them all grounds to legally exclude him from their lives with a restraining order.

Ryan stared absently at the blue sky, framed by the window to his right, as he bit off a corner of avocado and toast from the second slice.

Seven: It had taken him two full months to climb out of the hopelessness that had consumed him after their complete rejection of him, but last evening, in a time of deep reflection, he'd finally broken completely free of the emotional bonds that had ripped the life from him.

He was almost whole. A changed man to be sure, but able to function again.

Father Hortense had called him at six o'clock last evening and told him that he'd given the envelope to Bethany, who'd pulled out the photograph, stared at it a moment, then handed it back, asking him who the man in the picture was. She brushed past him without another word.

His daughter had summarily dismissed him.

His ex-wife was in love with another man.

So, then. He had done what he could do. A month ago he would have crawled back in and lost himself to one of the blackouts that were his mind's way of seeking peace. But now his mind was stable enough to consider it all in a calculated balance.

He would always love his daughter, of course. But the problem was no longer his. He had to get back to his own life. He would make sure that Bethany never hurt for money and get back to living.

He'd decided then that he would travel to San Antonio this very day and begin to look for suitable housing for his move.

Ryan rinsed out the glass, placed it in the dishwasher, and pulled out the keys to the Toyota Camry he'd purchased a week earlier. Silver, decent gas mileage, plenty of power for his tastes.

He left the University apartments and headed south on I-35. Heavy construction on either side of the highway could have bothered him; in his agitated state of hypersensitivity it certainly would have. But today, calm and calculated as he was, he hardly noticed.

It took him four hours to reach San Antonio because he decided to take a side trip through the Hill Country on Highway 281 and come into the city from the west. Late October had brought cooler temperatures, and in the wake of heavy late-summer rains the rolling hills were brilliant green beneath a blue sky.

He knew then, thinking about the landscape around him, that he really was finding himself again. On several occasions he wished he had a cell phone so that he could call up Father Hortense and inform him that he had turned the corner, more so than they had realized even yesterday, but he didn't have another cell phone yet.

San Antonio was pretty much the way he remembered it. He headed to the east side and took his time driving through neighborhoods near Fort Sam Houston. Knowing that he wouldn't be staying long if he did come, he looked for monthly rentals—common in this area. He didn't really care how nice the neighborhood was; he would be going it alone this time.

It was seven o'clock that evening before Ryan Evans pulled the Toyota Camry into the parking lot of the Howard Johnson off I-35, checked in for one night, and retired to his room to watch a pay-per-view movie, something he hadn't done in over two years.

He fell asleep in the first ten minutes.

RYAN WOKE TO a housekeeping call at his door the next morning. He pulled his sheets off and informed the maid that he wasn't ready.

Ten o'clock? He'd slept as though dead.

Standing and stretching, he felt an unusual calm. Sunlight flooded the room when he ripped open the green curtains. A new day awaited and there was no way it could disappoint him; he'd already lived through the worst life could bring his way.

Not even death, he thought. He'd faced death and no longer feared it.

He spent the next two hours taking a long, luxuriously hot shower and relishing each bite of his bacon-and-eggs breakfast at the Denny's next to the hotel. He finished his fourth cup of coffee, paid the cashier sixteen dollars and an extra five for tip, then headed back out to his Toyota Camry.

Two nearby apartment complexes were to his liking and he took applications from both and told the managers he'd be in touch. No hurry, but both had several vacancies that they were eager to fill immediately.

The drive back to Waco was uneventful, except for the driving rhythm, which provided for an excellent environment to think clearly now that he was once again capable. Celine was in the hands and arms of another man.

Bethany was growing into a young woman with a bright future who would thrive in this self-indulgent landscape called North America.

He, on the other hand, was an outsider, with neither lover nor bright future in a place he was neither needed nor wanted.

The thought did pain him some, but he was now healthy enough to understand that some emotion was good, so long as it didn't interfere with sound reasoning.

His apartment off University was no worse off for sitting vacant for two days. He flipped the lights on, tossed his keys on the counter, and took another shower. Few realized the benefits of raising one's skin temperature roughly an hour before sleep through a hot shower. The body compensated by slowing itself down to cool, and this often resulted in drowsiness and sound sleep.

He pulled on a pair of gray sweats and a black Nike T-shirt, then sat down to scan the cable feeds. Nothing jumped out at him. Unless the terrorists had knocked over another tower, he wasn't interested in the news. The evening soaps, as he called them, no better. He settled on the Science Channel, which was running a program on how technology was changing forensics and crime scene investigation. CSI.

This he found utterly fascinating. But when the show ended fifty minutes later, it was followed by a less interesting program about the building of the *Titanic*.

Feeling drowsy from his hot shower, Ryan clicked the TV off, poured himself a glass of water, and headed off to bed.

He'd pulled back the covers and was about to climb under the cool sheets when it occurred to him that he hadn't checked the answering machine for messages. He'd gone days and even a week without checking the messages, something that Hortense had chided him for.

Not that it would matter at ten in the evening. He would check the machine when he woke.

Ryan slid into bed and sighed deeply. He'd slept a lot over the past two months but those times of lapsed consciousness had been a mental retreat from reality. The sleep his body demanded now came from a healthy, even overactive mind.

The next morning came too soon for his tastes, thanks to the shrill ring of his phone. He rolled from the bed and lurched for the kitchen, noting that it was already a quarter past eight. But the phone stopped ringing while he was still in the living room.

Time to get up anyway.

Whoever it was didn't bother to leave a message. He walked into the kitchen, started the coffeemaker, and filled the pot with filtered water. The little red light on the answering machine was blinking.

So he did have a message?

He looked closer. *4 messages.*

Four? He'd received maybe a total of five messages since taking the apartment. Setting the pot he was filling back in the sink, he wiped his hands and pushed the playback button.

The first message was from a gravely concerned Father Hortense. "Please, Ryan, if you're there, pick up the phone. It's urgent I talk to you." A small stretch of silence. "Check the news. Call me as soon as you can."

The news? He'd never heard Hortense speak with such urgency.

Ryan let the machine run, a second message from Father Hortense, demanding he call him immediately. He hurried into the living room and tuned to CNN.

Football scores.

FOX was no better, some story about a bear that had taken a swipe at a photographer who—

Headline News. Sports again. But the headlines ran across the bottom in a ticker tape.

REBELS STRIKE MILITARY BASE IN SOMALIA, KILLING 34 U.S. TROOPS . . .

STOCK MARKET GAINS 312 POINTS ON NEWS OF HOUSING REBOUND . . .

KILLER KNOWN AS BONEMAN TAKES ANOTHER VICTIM AFTER TWO-YEAR HIATUS . . .

CHINA . . .

But Ryan's mind was locked on the story that had just rolled off the screen. The BoneMan had struck again. Either because the man they'd released from prison had indeed been BoneMan or because the killer no longer wanted to hide behind the wrong man.

Father Hortense was calling him to talk it through with him so that he wouldn't overreact.

He let out some air. Hortense didn't realize just how far Ryan had progressed these last few days. He not only cared very little about this whole BoneMan connection to his torture in the desert but he had released the guilt that had kept him bound to the experience.

He'd let Bethany go.

Headline News was talking about Michael Jackson. Ryan watched for a minute, waiting for the ticker tape to roll back around to news of the BoneMan, just in case he'd missed something.

The third message was from Hortense, yet again, left yesterday afternoon. Same thing. He would have to call the man back and set his mind to rest.

There it was again, rolling across the bottom: *Killer known . . .*

The fourth answering machine message began to play, a soft, low voice from the kitchen. "Hello, Father. I have the girl you think is your daughter."

Ryan spun his head in the direction of the kitchen.

The voice continued after a brief pause. "Her name is Bethany and she is mine now. It took you seven days to make her, now I'm giving you as much time to save her. If you think you can catch her, follow me where the crows fly, alone, Father."

Click.

18

FOR WHAT FELT like several minutes but could only have been a few seconds, Ryan found that he could not move. He just stood in his living room, arms spread slightly by his sides, eyes peeled at the kitchen, mouth gaping. Frozen like a stone pillar in the dead of winter.

The photographs that Kahlid had pinned to the wall filled his mind. The sound of Ahmed's breaking bones.

BoneMan had Bethany. The knowledge felt distant, only vaguely relevant because it couldn't be true, not in its entirety. He was missing something. A mistake had been made. It defied all reason.

Ryan had allowed other children to suffer to protect his own daughter. This wasn't Kahlid because he'd killed the man. And yet by escaping Kahlid he'd still condemned his own daughter? BoneMan had stumbled upon the story, maybe talked to Burton Welsh after Ryan had rubbed the BoneMan in his face for effect.

Was it possible that he'd actually attracted the BoneMan's attention?

His heart pounded like a steam piston. His mouth felt like it had been stuffed with powder; waves of heat rolled over him, but he was fully aware and fully in control, because he knew that his mind was in a delicate place and could be thrown back into disorder, driven by irrational emotion. He had to stay calm!

Ryan's eyes jerked to the television screen. The woman anchoring *Headline News* was now talking next to bold letters that read BONEMAN STRIKES AGAIN. A photograph stared at him from beneath the letters.

A beautiful, smiling young woman with flowing brown hair and bright blue eyes who looked nineteen, not sixteen. Bethany.

Ryan knew that he was losing control before the shakes came, but he was powerless to stop them. He felt as if a giant hand had reached down his throat and ripped out his heart and, now hollowed, his chest was reacting violently with the rest of his body before dropping into a pile, dead.

But he didn't drop dead and was no longer only shaking. He was sprinting. Racing into the kitchen, stabbing at the play button, fighting a full-tilt panic.

Father Hortense's voice came on, asking him to—He erased the message, and the next, and the next, and then BoneMan's voice crackled over the machine's tiny speakers.

"Hello, Father. I have the girl you think is your daughter. Her name is Bethany and she is mine now. It took you seven days to make her, now I'm giving you as much time to save her. If you think you can catch her, follow me where the crows fly, alone, Father."

He slammed his fist down on the machine and screamed.

"Mail box empty," the device announced.

He had to think. . . .

Think, think!

Stay calm, Ryan. Just stay calm.

Come and get me, Father.

Ryan grabbed the phone and punched in Celine's cell number, pacing as it rang.

"Come on, Celine. Please pick up."

"Leave a message," her cheery voice announced.

He quickly entered the home phone, missed a digit, retried, and hit the connect button.

This time it was Bethany, and Ryan's world blurred at the sound of his daughter's voice. "Hello, you know the drill. If you want me, call me. If you want Celine, call Celine. Don't bother with this machine, no one checks it."

Click.

"Celine?" His voice sounded frantic. "Celine, for God's sake, pick up the phone!"

Silence.

"Celine?"

But she wasn't answering. He stood breathing hard for a moment, then tried all the numbers that might connect him with someone, anyone, who could tell him what was going on. He had to know why? When? How long had she been gone? Had they found her?

He frantically spun through the handful of contacts that might connect him to Celine. Her cell again, the home phone again, the DA's office, which connected him to another voice mail.

Why hadn't Celine contacted him?

He tried the priest's line, but again, no live connection.

The apartment walls felt like they were closing in on him, toppling over, pushed from the outside to crush him.

Did the FBI know about the seven days BoneMan had given them? Or was it just him? Had this been a private challenge only for his ears?

Angel, my angel, dear God please, please don't let her be hurt.

But he knew that it was too late. No matter what the outcome now, Bethany, his sweet little girl who was the very essence of his life, would be scarred for life.

He had to know what was happening!

Ryan snatched up his car keys, ripped the answering machine from the wall, and ran from the apartment.

It took him an hour, most of it doing ninety miles an hour in a cool, steady sweat, to reach Capitol of Texas Highway. Another twenty minutes to reach Celine's neighborhood, all of it regretting that he didn't have a cell phone yet.

The moment Ryan pulled up to Celine's house, he knew that BoneMan had taken Bethany from this house. A squad car sat in the driveway, along with two unmarked sedans—likely FBI. Yellow tape cordoned off the sidewalk that ran around the house to the backyard.

Rather than march in through the front door and demand answers as he'd intended all along, he parked his Camry on the street and angled around the house toward the backyard.

Only then did the restraining order occur to him, but the thought did little more than slow him down. Clearly, a restraining order meant nothing in the face of what had happened.

He stumbled forward, legs wobbling beneath him like Twizzlers. An extension ladder rose from the ground to the upper balcony, where it rested against white railing in need of a fresh coat of paint.

Ryan pulled up hard, locked down by the sight. A slight breeze was blowing lazily through the trees. Behind him, car tires rolled past on Barton Creek Boulevard. High overhead a jet roared as it clawed higher.

But none of the sounds swirling around Ryan were as pronounced as the stillness of the ladder BoneMan had used to access his daughter's bedroom.

It was the stillness of utter emptiness and it hit Ryan's chest with enough force to rob him of breath for several long beats of his heart. The crime scene had already been processed a full day after the crime. The yellow tape served as a reminder that forensics investigators had been and gone and enough time had passed for any trail to have gone cold.

He felt himself guided by an innate need to know. To the foot of the ladder. Up the metal rungs, one step at a time.

His gut and his heart and his mind were all staging a full-scale revolt, demanding he get off the ladder, away from the vicinity of the taking, to protect himself from the agonizing images that flooded his mind.

His daughter screaming into duct tape as her wide eyes searched for meaning.

Daddy!

Daddy, Daddy, please!

How he managed to hoist himself over the railing he wasn't sure, because by the time he reached the top of the ladder, he was a limp mess. He stood on the balcony facing drawn blinds, now regretting his decision to climb the ladder. He couldn't possibly go inside!

But he had to. He had to know what his daughter had felt and seen when BoneMan had come.

Pushing back a dreadful ache, he tried the door, found

it open, and slid it wide. The room inside was a storage room, not the bedroom. Bethany's bed was in the next one over.

Her white sheets were tucked in at the bottom, otherwise strewn about as if ripped from her and left to lie half off the bed. He could still see the indentation of her head in the pillow.

This was his first time in her room since his return, and he hated himself for it. If he could have even one day back, he would deny every court authority known to man to make his love evident to his daughter.

He'd buy her a car. A room full of roses. He'd fly her to Dubai and put her up in a suite that cost four grand a night and demand the staff bring her anything she wanted without the slightest thought of cost.

He would fall to his knees and beg her forgiveness and tell her how much he loved her.

Seven days, as of yesterday, when the message had been left. That left just over six days.

Ryan turned from the room, wiped his eyes, set his jaw, and walked downstairs.

They were in the living room; he could hear them before he saw them.

"Every hour you delay is one more he's got."

"We need more."

"Then get more. You have Celine's testimony, that's enough to bring him in. For God's sake, we don't have time to sit around on this."

Ryan stopped in the doorway and looked at them. Burton Welsh, the man whom he'd attacked, tall, cleanly shaven. The smell of aftershave had to be his.

Ricki Valentine, the FBI agent who'd interrogated him

in the hotel two months earlier. The small woman with a big heart.

Celine, dressed in a green flowered dress, pacing, nursing a bandaged forefinger at the end of her slung arm.

He tried to say something but his voice suddenly felt inadequate. He didn't belong here; he belonged out where BoneMan wanted him, bartering for his daughter's life.

"Ryan?"

Ricki Valentine had seen him. They all turned to look at him, and he wanted to run because he knew that even now the effects of that empty bed upstairs were haunting his sanity.

But there was nothing to do. He couldn't turn and run because that would only make him the object of their search rather than BoneMan. He couldn't say anything to them because there was nothing to say that made sense to him.

He could only stand there and return their stares.

"Well, speak of the devil," the DA said. "What are you doing here?"

The FBI agent shot him an angry glare and closed half the distance between them. "I'm sorry, Captain, I'm sure this is very upsetting."

"Why didn't anyone call me?" he asked.

"Get him out of here." Celine glared at him like a wolf standing off a bear. "Get him out!"

"Celine?" Something was wrong. He'd come with news, but . . .

And then he understood. The DA had been talking about him when he'd walked up. Welsh wanted to bring him in for questioning.

Rage flared up his back. "What's going on?" he demanded.

"For starters, you're in violation of the court's order," Welsh snapped.

Ryan's last restraint was severed. "My daughter has been kidnapped!" He thundered the last word, face flushed and hot. "And no one even bothered to call me?"

"I'm sorry, Captain," Ricki said. "I know these aren't ideal circumstances for you, but we have to be careful."

Celine had taken several steps backwards, where she stood against the couch, trembling. "What are you doing, Ryan?"

"Don't stand there shaking as if I was the one who broke your finger. Our daughter's out there!"

"Why didn't you tell Agent Valentine the truth about your association with the BoneMan in Iraq, Captain?" Welsh asked, head tilted down slightly.

"I . . . What association? It's classified. I don't see what that has to do with—"

"You just happen to come out of the desert spinning tales of your nightmares about the BoneMan and now he takes your daughter as his next victim after a two-year absence? Forgive me if it doesn't all seem just a bit much."

The man was accusing him? "He . . . Serial killers! He was comparing us to serial killers. I said BoneMan for effect. Why did you tell the media about my claims? That's how he found me!"

"Is that right?" Clearly the man didn't believe a word he said.

Ryan turned to the Ricki. "What about you?"

She shrugged. "There are a lot of questions that need answering."

Ryan turned on Celine, furious and unable to hide his anger. "How could you think this?"

But her eyes were fired with fear and he knew that something very definite had convinced her that he might present a danger to her.

"You just, what, left the alarm off so that he could walk in here and take my daughter!?"

"I'm waiting for your full file, Ryan," Welsh said. "But I really don't need to see it to know that the BoneMan killings just happen to line up with the dates you were between tours."

"Don't be asinine! That's pure coincidence."

"Is it? And when you broke Celine's finger, you told her to tell me it was payback. Is that what all of this is, Captain? Payback for your own bitterness?"

A uniformed police officer had presented himself in the doorway leading to the kitchen, blocking any escape. Surely they didn't really think he was the BoneMan!

"If you've read my file, then you know I was a victim of torture, not the torturer. You're wasting time while he's out there with my daughter."

"It must have been hard, watching all those children die," Welsh said. "I can understand why you snapped."

"That is irrelevant!" He was breathing hard. "We only have six days to find him—"

Ricki's right eyebrow arched. "Six days? Care to elaborate?"

"He called me. He said that it took the father seven days to create her and now he was going to give me seven days to save her."

"Really?" Welsh smirked. "He just *happened* to call you?"

So that was it, then. Between Celine's harrowing experience the night of the kidnapping during which BoneMan had broken her finger and Ryan's experience in the desert, the DA was ready to pin the abduction on him.

A jealous father suffering from PTSD, caving in to his true nature by taking his own daughter.

He looked at Ricki. "You buy this?"

"Like I said, there're some questions that need answering. Do you mind telling us where you were two nights ago?"

"Home. Asleep."

"Alone?"

Something else occurred to him. BoneMan had issued him a personal challenge. Bethany's life hung in the balance of *his* choices now. And looking in the DA's eyes, there was little doubt that the man had no intention of letting Ryan walk from this room a free man to make any choice at all.

He stared at Welsh and saw him for what he was, an obstacle to saving his daughter's life.

"Alone? No, actually, I was with some good friends who stayed over after a night of poker. I'm sure they wouldn't mind if you called them."

"We will. Father Hortense tells me you've been pretty much a hermit these last two months. Hard to imagine you having a whole passel of close friends."

Both doors were now blocked. Where the second cop had come from, Ryan didn't know, but he was hemmed in.

"None of this should be that difficult to settle," Ricki said. "You say he called you?"

"Yes." Ryan nodded and eased closer to the kitchen entryway. "He left me a message."

"Where's the message?"

Erased, he almost said.

"At home."

The urge to panic was now fully grown and biting its way out of his chest. He had to get out!

Follow me where the crows fly alone. As in, where the crow flies by itself.

Or was it *Follow me where the crows fly, alone?* As in, come by yourself.

Either way, he had to get out and he had to get out now!

"Then you don't mind going with me to get it," the agent said.

"It's . . . I live in Waco now."

"Then we should get started."

The DA stepped forward. "I'm sorry, Agent Valentine, I can't allow you to take this man out of my custody." He nodded at the cop behind Ryan. "He'll have to tell you where it is. I'm sure you can appreciate my concern, but—"

Ryan threw himself backwards into the cop. His back was met by a startled shove, precisely the reaction he'd hoped for. He ducked and spun while the cop's hands were still up, blocking his charge.

The forty-five semiauto slid out of the man's holster like butter. And then Ryan was by the wall, gun up, trained on the cop who guarded the front door.

"Gun on the floor, gun on the floor, now! You too, Agent Valentine!"

The man glanced at the DA, then slowly complied.

Ricki eyed him. "This is no way to save your daughter, Ryan."

"You, Agent, know nothing about me or my daughter. Put your gun on the floor and kick it over to me. Now!"

She slipped a nine-millimeter out of her shoulder holster, slowly set it on the floor, and kicked it over.

Ryan grabbed the gun and stuffed it behind his belt. He motioned to both cops and nodded at the wall. "Against the wall. All of you."

Welsh cursed bitterly.

"Get. Against. The wall!" Ryan shouted.

The man reluctantly stepped up to the wall next to Celine, who was whimpering. They stood five abreast now, facing the wall.

"On your knees."

Ricki began to protest, but Ryan told her to save her breath.

The room quieted while Ryan spun through his options. Beyond this point he hadn't considered any elaborate plans. He knew that he had to find Bethany, he knew that he would do anything and everything in his power for even one chance to stop BoneMan. If need be he would gladly sacrifice his or any of these five lives for Bethany's life.

The thought stopped him behind them. Would he?

But he couldn't think straight enough to answer the question. He backed to the front door.

"Stay there," he said. "Just stay there."

Then he slipped out and ran for his car.

19

THE EARTH FILLED her nostrils, a damp, cool smell that might mean she was in a pit or a grave or a root cellar somewhere. But Bethany couldn't see. A blindfold prevented the light from reaching her eyes, assuming there was light.

She was alone, she was pretty sure of that. Tied to the metal post behind her so she could only slump over for rest with some pain to her shoulders and back. He'd come and gone several times, but mostly he was gone. And when he was with her, he said nothing aloud.

He'd whispered in her ear several times, telling her that she was beautiful and the perfect lamb to take away the sin of the world.

He untied her once and led her to a commode to do her business.

Bethany wasn't sure how much time had passed, a day at least, enough time so that the initial terror of her abduction had passed, replaced by a dull anguish, a certainty of the inevitable pain awaiting her.

She'd been taken by the BoneMan. Her mother's new lover had brought BoneMan upon them and it was only a matter of time before he began to break her bones.

A slight medicinal odor lingered from BoneMan's last visit, hours earlier. He'd wiped lotion on her face and neck and quietly rubbed it in. She couldn't shake the thought of a butcher marinating his choice cut before lowering it over the flame.

But she'd held her tongue and he whispered something in her ear then that gave her the first narrow thread of hope she'd been able to grasp since he'd taken her.

"You're much braver than the rest."

It was the tone of his voice more than the words that made her think he had just shown a weakness. He respected her courage. Even seemed taken aback by it.

And true, the images from horror movies of victims trembling in their own waste did not fit here, not with her, at least not now that she was thinking clearly again.

Bethany remembered opening her eyes in her bedroom the moment before the dark figure over her shoved the needle into her neck. Twisting to stare into the eyes of a tall stranger with a strong, fleshy, pale face and blue eyes. The drug had immobilized her almost immediately and the next time she dragged herself into a conscious state she'd found herself bound up and gagged on the floor of a pickup truck.

She'd panicked and thrashed about, screaming raw through the gag, and a boot or a bat had silenced her with a single hard blow to her temple.

The next time she'd come to she was here, sitting on this concrete floor strapped to the pipe behind her. The gag had been removed and she'd screamed for help for

an hour before finally concluding that anyone as meticulous and accomplished as the BoneMan had surely
thought of that.

She leaned back and rubbed her head against the pipe,
attempting to dislodge the blindfold again, to no avail.
Her neck ached, as if it had been broken, which she knew
was an impossibility.

A shudder passed through her bones. The truth was,
fear had stalked her like a lion and no matter how strong
she pretended to be, it was eating her raw.

The argument she'd had with Celine about moving to
New York sat at the edge of her mind, a ridiculous little
lump of history that felt so distant now, she couldn't be
sure it had really happened. The very idea of modeling in
New York now struck her as an obscene joke. However
irrational it might seem, she put the blame for BoneMan
on Ryan as much as on Burt. Both men, both lousy father
figures, both offering a false sense of security.

She ground her jaw and groaned. If only she could see.
Anger flared through her gut, her chest, and her face, and
she suddenly wanted to scream. So she did. She screamed
her frustration at the darkness that surrounded her.

Pointless, she realized, and closed her jaw.

Her knees.

The thought stopped her cold.

She could remove her blindfold with her knees, couldn't
she? Why hadn't she thought of that before?

She folded her legs and leaned over her knees. Her
forehead made contact easily enough, and it was only a
matter of seconds before she was able to push the blindfold up over her eyes.

Dim light filtered into a large concrete room from

several cracks in the ceiling corners. A wooden door was shut, twenty feet away. Several ammo boxes sat on a table to her right. A folding chair. A metal bed with a thin gray mattress sat unused against the far wall.

She was underground, she guessed, in a bunker or basement.

She stared at the bed, wishing she could lie and rest while she waited. But then a new thought occurred to her, one that was mixed up with the sounds of James Caan having his legs broken while he lay in bed in that movie *Misery*.

She swallowed hard and tried to relax. Her blue plaid flannel pajama bottom was smudged but not ripped. She wore a white T-shirt that was surprisingly clean. Bethany stared at her bare feet.

The problem with the character in *Misery*, as with so many characters in horror movies, was that they didn't think clearly. Bethany could understand why, seated here, strapped to a metal pole in a cement basement, waiting for BoneMan's return.

But she would not allow herself to give in to her emotions the way all of those other girls probably had so that he could send them straight to hell in a bucket of broken bones.

She would engage him, work his respect, draw him out, and if she could—if she found even the slightest opportunity to do so—she would bash his skull in and send *him* straight to hell.

That was one side of it. The other side of it was that she was finally getting what was coming to her. A bit extreme, but her whole life had been a bit extreme. What goes around comes around and this was life coming around. One day in New York, the next day in a lunatic's basement.

She was having some difficulty piecing together exactly why she deserved to be in this place, but she wasn't stupid enough to deny that in the end life was cruel and didn't pay attention to what was fair.

Bethany sat back and let out a long breath. No, no, that was ridiculous. She no more deserved this than she deserved to be abandoned by her father. If only he'd been there . . .

She closed her eyes and clenched her jaw. *Stay calm, Bethany. It'll work out. It'll all work out.*

RICKI VALENTINE HAD seen her share of type A raging bulls, but Burt Welsh had the unique ability to make even the twenty percent of those in society who were type A cringe.

She should know; she was a type A, and she felt as uncomfortable around the DA as a kitten in a cactus patch. Not that she had any trouble telling him what she thought, only that she had trouble believing that he cared one iota what she thought.

He leaned over a desk in the downtown police station, running down a list of demands on the phone with the chief of police and mayor. The DA had little business running an investigation, and of course Welsh would insist that he was doing no such thing. But he might as well be—the local authorities ate out of his hand when he asked them to.

To be fair, the BoneMan case was now as much a political and social issue as a matter of the law. The whole city was neck deep in fear because Burton Welsh had put the wrong man behind bars and the right man had just taken another high school student.

Ricki sat back against the desk and watched, judging, thinking.

"Every road, Bill. I don't care if it's a dirt road that leads to a vineyard off 183; I want a hundred-mile noose around this city. . . . Then get more men!"

He spun to Ricki. "Where are those agents from Dallas?" he demanded.

"On their way. This is a thinking game, not a pissing match."

Welsh glared at her. "I'll call you right back, Bill. Fine." He set the phone down and walked up to her.

"Whatever this attitude is, lose it. You might be FBI, you might be the freaking Secret Service or the NSA. You might be whoever you like, but we just got handed a gift, Agent Valentine. How he managed to get out of Barton Creek before we could stop him, I don't know, but I'm not going to let him slip through our fingers again. Either get on board, or run along home."

One of these days she would have to slap the man just to see his reaction.

She nodded. "Are you done?"

"For now."

"Fine." She stood and faced the room. A dozen officers, agents, and detectives assigned to the joint task force were working over their desks or speaking quietly into phones. Ricki clapped her hands.

"Okay people, listen up. The FBI is still taking the lead on this, but the task force's mission has not changed."

The room quickly stilled as the officers turned their attention toward her. Mark Resner eyed her from where he stood by a large wall map, working with two detectives on plotting a network of blockades.

"He's been out there for"—she glanced at her watch—"an hour and ten minutes, which puts him within sixty miles of Barton Creek without traffic. We have an all-points bulletin on the Toyota Camry. Over two hundred uniformed officers are now actively engaged in the search. We have eyes in the air, four helicopters searching four grids. As of ten minutes ago, all four major affiliates went live on the air with photographs of Mr. Ryan Evans. By now half the city knows what BoneMan looks like. But we still don't have the slightest idea what happened to him. I hope I'm not the only one who sees this as a unique challenge."

She had their attention now, all of them.

"I've eaten, slept, and breathed BoneMan. His disappearing into thin air shouldn't come as a surprise. There's a reason he's remained at large."

"You're sure this is the guy?" a Detective Richardson asked.

"He's the guy," Welsh said.

Ricki nodded. "Everything we have points to him, yes."

"Someone once said the same about Phil Switzer."

Welsh turned on the man. "We have a witness with a broken finger this time. He spoke to her before he snapped her bone. Then he took her daughter. This is the first time we have a live witness. Ryan Evans is BoneMan."

"That is the assumption we are all working under at this time," Ricki said. "Naval Intelligence. Been through some pretty nasty stuff. He's reportedly suffering from severe post-traumatic stress disorder; I wouldn't put anything past him."

Captain Bradley, who headed the city's Special Weapons teams, shifted on his polished black boots. "What are the rules of engagement?"

"Use all necessary force to apprehend. Do not terminate. Corner him, but do not shoot unless fired upon. Use of nonlethal force is authorized. He's got a hostage out there, people. Our top priority right now is to bring his daughter back alive."

The mention of his daughter brought stillness to the room.

"Sick freak," someone muttered.

Something about the connection between Ryan Evans and BoneMan's latest victim, Bethany Evans, struck Ricki as disjointed. She'd sat with the man in his hotel room for an hour, watching him come apart at the seams over the prospect of losing his daughter. An obsessed man, broken by the war, she'd assumed.

Or a man broken long ago when he was a much younger man, when he was in basic training and suffered his first snap.

When the drugs administered by BoneMan had worn off, Celine had screamed until the neighbors found her floating in the pool. She'd been hysterical for several hours and hadn't made any connection to the possibility that the man who'd taken her daughter might actually be Ryan until this morning; the reason for her demand that Valentine and Welsh meet her at the house.

Even to Ricki the idea had first seemed preposterous. But the more she considered the killer's profile, the easier it became to match Ryan with that profile.

He had a history of breaking under intense stress that extended beyond his trauma in the desert.

The string of murders had ended at about the same time he'd been deployed for his second tour in the Middle East, just coincidently the same time that Phil Switzer had been arrested.

He'd come out of Iraq after supposedly encountering a kind of BoneMan in the desert, which could easily be a fabrication built upon his own obsession.

Ryan's unusual intelligence might account for the cleverness that BoneMan had exhibited in each of his murders. And his falling out with Celine and Bethany provided the motivation for this most recent assault.

There was more, and all of it pointed to the man who'd held them at gunpoint this morning before fleeing.

All of it except for the love she'd seen in the eyes of the man who'd fallen apart in his hotel room two months ago.

Then again, Ricki knew how easily eyes could lie.

One thing was certain: if Ryan was indeed BoneMan as they now suspected, he was one twisted and very shrewd adversary. Enough to send a chill down her back now, as she paced in front of the joint task force.

"That's right," she said softly. "One very sick puppy. So tell your men to keep their guard up. He's scary sick. In all likelihood, he doesn't even know what he's doing."

Burton Welsh stepped up. "We can't let him out of this city."

"Please, sir, have a seat." She looked him over, satisfied by the twitch in his cheek. "The reason he hasn't crossed our paths in the last hour is because he hasn't left the city. And if he's as smart as I think he is, he won't leave till it's dark. We're going to leave roadblocks in place on the seven primary thoroughfares leaving the city." She nodded at her partner. "Mark?"

He turned to the wall map and pointed out the roads.

"Good. We have two more helicopters en route from Dallas as we speak. When they arrive, they'll join the four we have in the air now and monitor the tributaries that funnel into these seven routes. In the meantime I want you to pull all of your cars off all these other roadblocks you're setting up and begin a full sweep of the city itself."

She could almost feel the DA's face heat up. "The FBI is posting a $50,000 reward for information leading to the capture of Ryan Evans. Please circulate the news as aggressively as possible. I'm open to any and all suggestions. It's no secret that we missed this guy once; no one wants to miss him again. Any questions?"

The deputy chief was already on his phone, quietly speaking orders. She didn't give the rest of them time to consider her request for more than a few seconds.

"Good."

Ricki grabbed her cell phone and strode toward the door.

"Where are you going?" Welsh demanded.

"To Waco, Mr. Attorney. I'm going to take a look under Ryan Evans's sheets, if you don't mind."

20

THE VALUE OF leaning on the power of understanding and wisdom in a world ripped apart by schoolyard bullies and third-world tyrants had first become saving knowledge to Ryan when he was in the sixth grade.

He'd always been a bit of a nerd, admittedly so even at twelve. And Bobby Knutz had always gone out of his way to make sure he didn't forget it. Ribbing and an occasional beating on the playground had been a part of Ryan's life as long as he could remember. But Bobby Knutz and those he ran with were simply taller and thicker.

Thing of it was, any idiot in the school could see that Bobby didn't exactly come from a home brimming with goodwill and covetous treasures. His father was an unemployed drunk and his mother didn't make enough as a waitress to keep Bobby in much better than rags. Muscle, it occurred to young Ryan, didn't pay.

Intelligence, on the other hand, like that exhibited by professors and all those who worked in office buildings, did pay. He began a very purposeful and quietly successful retreat away from the impulsive, macho, pubescent world of the American teenage scene then, determining instead to excel in the more rewarding pursuit of knowledge.

Ryan had torn up less than a mile of Barton Creek Boulevard after fleeing Celine's house when his good sense returned and announced in no uncertain terms that if he didn't settle down and think like he'd never thought before, he was going to the clinker. And if he was going to the clinker, Bethany was going to the grave.

It was that simple.

In a strange way he'd been thrown into the same situation in which Kahlid had found himself in the desert. Like the father in the Middle East, Ryan was reacting out of love for his child. He could never do what Kahlid had done, killing innocents for the sake of others.

The thought made him shiver. Dear God, help him. For the first time since seeing what he'd seen in the desert, Ryan's mind was able to comprehend Kahlid's anguish at losing his child.

War was hell, quite literally. And Ryan was now in a war, wasn't he? This was no different. The only difference was that having suffered as he had in Iraq, he would be unwilling to sacrifice any innocent blood. Period. He just could not go there.

He grabbed a lungful of air, then another, and slowed down. Nothing like a speeding Toyota Camry to draw attention.

His mind, however, did not slow. To understand that he was in a pickle required only a very little bit of intelligence, the amount that graced the minds of America's upper half, including him.

He had just held his wife, two police officers, the district attorney, and the FBI special agent in charge of the BoneMan case at gunpoint. And he'd done so after being asked if he might be the BoneMan. A ludicrous suggestion, of course, but one that was now undoubtedly all but assured in their minds.

Having held these five individuals at gunpoint, he'd fled the scene, an act of complete desperation because he, like they, surely knew that he couldn't get away. Yet he'd fled anyway, having walked directly into a trap.

To make matters worse, he'd made it perfectly clear that he had special knowledge of the case, knowledge only BoneMan should have.

But none of these particulars were as disturbing to Ryan as the one that flogged his mind as he tried to harness its calculating prowess, fleeing down Barton Creek Boulevard, sixty seconds after leaving Celine and company against the wall: Bethany was with BoneMan.

Think, Ryan. He took another deep, cleansing breath. *Think.*

Okay. He had to ditch the car. They would be all over Bee Cave Road and Southwest Parkway, the two primary roads that fed the vicinity, and Southwest Parkway was a wide-open thoroughfare with little traffic—not the best road to blend in on.

He whipped the Camry around and tore back the other way, past the house, relieved to see that they weren't climbing into their cars to chase him down. No, they were too smart for that. More likely on the phone, getting choppers in the air, locking down the surrounding streets.

Ryan turned right on Lost Creek Boulevard and took the twisting road through two valleys before jerking the car into Lost Creek Country Club's private drive.

He rolled into the parking lot, stopped between a black Mercedes and a BMW M6, and turned off the ignition.

The motor clicked softly.

Now what?

Now two things: One, he had to avoid being taken into custody at all costs. Two, he had to find BoneMan. To do either he had to remain perfectly calm and reasoned.

The second objective was one that had eluded the law—there was no reason to think that he could succeed where they had failed. Except that BoneMan had engaged Ryan directly, maybe even wanted him to find his daughter. If the law got too close before Ryan found them, they would be gone. Which meant he couldn't help the FBI find BoneMan.

He had to find BoneMan on his own.

Ryan looked at his hands, trembling on the steering wheel. See, now his mind had retreated into reason, but his body wasn't keeping up, not since his breakdown in the desert.

He placed both hands on his lap.

BoneMan's words echoed through his mind. "Where the crows fly." What the oblique reference could possibly mean was beyond him, but then so was every cipher at first glance.

Or was it a simple riddle? For that matter, it could be a straightforward clue. Either way he'd broken it down a dozen times on the drive down to Austin, and he did it again now, knowing that meticulous repetition was the key to breaking all codes.

He lingered on the whole message. A chopper beat the air far above him, but he ignored it. There was no way they could see through the massive birch under which he'd parked.

From a dozen feet, BoneMan's message was plain. *I've taken your daughter and I want you to see if you can find her. If you can't do so in seven days, I'm going to kill her.*

Her name is Bethany. Bethany, from the Hebrew Beth, meaning *My God is a vow* or *the vow of God.* Bethany is a living reminder of God's perfection in creation.

It took you seven days to make her. It took God seven days to create this vow called life.

Now I'm giving you as much time to save her. But now God's perfect vow is in trouble and she is in my control because I, not God, have her. I will give you seven days to save her.

Follow me where the crows fly, alone, Father.

Follow me . . . I want you to come, not the FBI or the police.

Where the crows fly . . . Where black birds called crows congregate. Where people who remind me of crows congregate.

Or was it more metaphorical? Where crows fly, meaning in the mind, or up high, in the open . . .

In the open. In the air. Where everyone can see you. Follow me where I can see you. I will find you.

Ryan let the thoughts circulate, like crows, taking whatever path they liked, however jerky or abstract. A full twenty minutes passed, and he decided that it was enough.

He walked up to the clubhouse and stepped around to the side, where two vans sat next to a large protected garbage receptacle. He'd intended on taking one of the vans either by hotwiring it or by acquiring the keys inside, but he now saw that the closest used a magnetic logo.

He peeled the large Lost Creek Country Club placard off and slipped behind the vehicle. Working with his utility knife, he quickly unscrewed the license plate and returned to the Camry.

It took Ryan only a few more minutes to make the switch with his own car and pull out of the parking lot. He now drove a club car with a club license plate, not enough to escape scrutiny for long, but it would slow them.

Half an hour had passed since his altercation with Celine and company. None of this would get him any closer to finding Bethany, but for the sake of his own sanity he'd set aside the objective for the moment. He had to get past whatever net they were spreading before he took BoneMan up on his challenge.

In the open. On the air. As the crow flies.

He couldn't be sure it was what BoneMan wanted, but until or unless a better idea presented itself to him, he would run with the assumption.

Ryan drove the Camry to Lost Creek Clubhouse and parked it on one of the upper lots, where it would likely remain inconspicuous for some time. The main resort rose from the golf course a hundred yards farther down and, taking the answering machine with him, he walked to the hotel without concern of being spotted as anyone other than just one more golfer who'd come to take on the world-class course.

The authorities were much farther out by now—they would never suspect that he was still within a mile or two of Celine's house.

But BoneMan wasn't here, in this mile or two, he was sure of that.

It took him a half hour to find the right car, a black

Ford Taurus that looked as if it had been parked for at least a few days. He was forced to break the side window to gain access, but fortunately this was Texas—he hardly needed a window to keep out the cold.

Ten minutes later he rolled out of Lost Creek and turned south on Bee Cave Road. He took 360 north to Westlake Plaza, where he once again took his place in a parking lot, just another black car in a sea of similar cars.

Satisfied that he was safe for some hours, Ryan sunk low in his seat, eyed the radio tower at the lot's south end, and focused his mind on the problem at hand.

RYAN HAD FIRST seen the towers two months earlier on his way out of town—an intelligence officer obsessed with communication tended to notice things like antennae. KRQZ FM 106.5 had particularly sexy towers. Not that it mattered. Once he made his statement, every audio source in southern Texas would be rebroadcasting it.

The hours ticked by slowly as he waited for the day to pass. Once he stepped out they would have a fix on him—he had to wait for darkness to cover his escape.

So he sat low and he listened to the radio and he waited.

It was strange to hear his name over the car's sound system, particularly as the man now identified as being armed, dangerous, and under suspicion of being BoneMan.

He ran through the dial, surprised at the extent of the coverage. Ryan Evans was described as an embittered combat veteran potentially suffering from mental disorders. An estranged father of the victim and a hostile ex-husband who'd broken into the administration building two months earlier and physically assaulted the district attorney.

They were offering $50,000 for information that led to his arrest.

Hearing the reports, Ryan wasn't sure that he *wasn't* some kind of crazed lunatic who had gone off the deep end. They seemed to know him better than he knew himself. It was all enough to lure him back into a state of complete despair.

But he couldn't allow despair to cloud his judgment, not now. He was in the middle of breaking the code of his life, a challenge of wits with stakes that made those in the desert seem like child's play in his way of thinking.

By midafternoon the authorities had publicly launched the largest manhunt in recent Austin history. By all reports the face of Ryan Evans was plastered all over the Internet and on all of the newscasts. Hotlines were already flooded with tips.

And yet here he sat, in the corner of a parking lot, lost and alone.

They were now looking for a silver Camry with Lost Creek Country Club logos on the sides, they said. By morning it might be a black Taurus, but by then, if all went well, he would be across the state.

Dusk fell at seven that evening, and as the sky began to grow gray, Ryan began to sweat. Contrary to the endless speculation on the airwaves, he wasn't as bloodthirsty or ruthless as they'd painted him. Thoughts of committing the smallest crime turned him weak.

But there was one facet of their characterization that rang true and was perhaps even understated. Ryan was desperate. He was a desperate father who would do whatever it took to find and save his daughter. The fact that he'd managed to temper that desperation through great effort did not keep him from sweating as the time approached.

Satisfied that there was enough darkness to aid his flight, Ryan shoved the gun behind his belt, exited the Taurus, and walked up to the glass door that read KRQZ FM 106.5, THE SEXY SIDE OF COUNTRY.

He paused with his hand on the door, took a deep breath, and walked in.

The long, curved reception desk was empty after hours, his first break, and God knew he needed as many breaks as he could get. He walked straight to the hallway door and pushed his way past it.

A wide, darkened hall lined by several large picture windows that peered into studios ran into the building. No one had seen him so far, no one around that he could see.

And then that changed with the emergence of a man and woman, who pushed open one of the doors and turned up the hall toward him.

"No, but what I am saying is that *American Idol* is finished if they don't completely change up their presentation," the woman dressed in khaki slacks and a pink top said. "Call it burnout. I know I'm a victim."

Her friend lifted his eyes and stared at Ryan. "Not disagreeing. But you gotta admit Seacrest is the real star in . . ."

And then his eyes went wide, and Ryan knew he'd been recognized. He lifted his hand and strode forward.

"Excuse me. Excuse me, you guys know where the manager is?"

"It's him!" The young man had red hair piled in curls atop his head, a thin guy who was more frame then flesh, and his round blue eyes bugged like balls from his boney head.

They both stopped and stared.

Ryan withdrew the gun but he held it low, in a non-threatening manner, so as not to frighten them.

"I just need to use—"

The pink-shirted woman screamed, and Ryan knew it was all over. He lifted the gun and shoved it at both of them. "Fine, if you insist. But please, keep your mouths shut." He glanced through one of the picture windows as he passed. A darkened, unused studio.

Back on the pair. "How many people are working here tonight?"

"You're him," the man said, swallowing with the help of a pronounced Adam's apple.

"How many?"

"Just three of us."

"Where's the other one?"

"In the studio."

"Okay, that's good." He stopped two yards from them and held the gun awkwardly. "If you've been watching the news, you know that I'm unstable, right?"

She nodded.

"So you don't want to do anything stupid, like scream or try to warn your friend. I'm not going to hurt you; I only want to use your equipment."

They thought he was the BoneMan, he realized. BoneMan was standing in their hall, waving a gun at them. They were too shocked to respond.

"What's your friend's name?"

"Brent," the redhead squeaked.

"Anyone else due in tonight?"

"No."

"So . . . we should be alone for a while."

"Please," the girl whispered.

He waved the gun. "Take me to Brent."

They both turned as if walking on pins and retraced their steps down the hall toward the door they'd just passed through.

Their friend was a younger man with long black hair who wore headphones and was bopping his head to music when they stepped inside the studio.

Ryan locked the door and pulled the blinds that covered the window.

"Whoa!" The dark-haired hippie turned and spotted his gun. "What the—"

"Shut up, Brent." He waved the gun at a bank of chairs along the wall. "Sit, all of you."

But they just stared at him.

"Sit!" he yelled. "You think I'm just playing around here? Now sit your asses in those chairs and . . . just sit!"

They hurried to the chairs like frantic geese and sat. Brent's headphones where still in place, and the cord was stretched across the room.

Ryan walked up to him, plucked the headgear from his head, and tossed it on the floor.

"Now, I'm going to make this really simple. I need your help. If you help me, I won't break your fingers and toes and maybe your . . . ankles." Dear God, he wasn't sounding like the BoneMan, certainly not the likes of Kahlid. He steeled his jaw.

"I need to send out a message and then I need to get away before the authorities swarm this place. You need to help me, okay?"

They stared at him with round eyes.

Ryan snapped his fingers. "Do I start breaking fingers, or are you going to snap out of it?"

"We'll do anything," the girl pleaded. "Please, please don't hurt us."

"I won't. Just don't . . . mess things up. I can transmit live from here, right?"

"Yes," the redhead said.

"How many frequencies can you broadcast on?" He glanced at the hippie kid.

"Legally?"

"No. How many?"

"Seven."

"Then I want to send a message out on all seven frequencies."

"You can't do them all at once. We don't have the equipment for that."

"How many can you do at once?"

"One."

"Fine. But I want what I say to be picked up and broadcast on every news channel and station in this city. I want you to supply the feed to them all, you got that? Just leak it out."

"Leak what out?"

"What I have to say."

"What you have to say to who?"

"To BoneMan."

"Are . . . aren't you BoneMan?" Brent asked.

"Well, that depends. Maybe there are two of us. I'm not the one that has my daughter, now am I? I need to get him a message and for that, I need your help. If I fail, he's going to kill my daughter."

They stared at him, clueless.

"Just tell me you'll help me. I need your help."

Sweat snaked down Ryan's cheeks. This was taking too long.

Then again, no one but these three knew he was in this building. They were looking for him on the roads, not in radio stations.

Ryan lowered the gun, momentarily swamped by deep sadness. He couldn't do this. How could he stand here and pretend to be strong in the face of such impossible odds while his daughter lay in a bag somewhere, crying in fear.

The image turned his vision black for a moment and he yelled at the three young station workers. He didn't yell anything specifically, just a roar of outrage directed at the BoneMan and whatever demonic entity had possessed him to visit such pain upon him. Was this the price for having ignored his daughter for sixteen years? What this the price for all fathers who had forgotten how precious their daughters were?

If so, this price was too great for any grievance.

And what kind of creature from hell would take it upon himself to extract such a cruel price?

Ryan realized he was breathing hard, but he didn't have the strength to bring himself back into full control.

He glared at the three workers, who looked as though they realized their worst fears were going to happen after all. For a moment the BoneMan had seemed quite lucid, but then he'd lost it and began snapping their bones right there in the studio.

He walked around the equipment, sat hard in the chair before the microphone, and set his gun on the desk. He dropped his head into his hands and began to cry.

He knew that he was taking a terrible risk by not training the gun on them, but he just couldn't stop the sorrow that rolled over him. He felt so hopeless, so dark, so powerless to affect the inevitable outcome he knew awaited his daughter.

BoneMan would break her bones.

Ryan lifted his head and picked up the gun. The three workers were still staring at him.

"Sorry." He sniffed and stood. "Sorry, I just don't know what I'm going to do. They think I'm the BoneMan, but I'm not. He has my daughter and he wants me to find her. No one believes that, but that doesn't get me off the hook. Have . . . have you seen pictures of my daughter?"

Brent nodded. "Bethany?"

"Bethany." Saying her name brought a quiver to his lips. "Tell me how to turn this equipment on, Brent."

He lifted his hands.

"Just tell me from there."

"It's a playlist now. Just hit the third red switch on the top, the one that says Live Audio."

He saw it. "That's it?"

"You activate the microphone by pressing the A button next to it."

Ryan nodded. "And that's it?"

"Do that and you're live, yes."

Ryan sat down, gun propped up in his right hand. He eyed the three, flipped the red switch, and pressed the A button.

One last look at Brent, who nodded.

And then Ryan spoke over the airwaves for BoneMan to hear.

"BoneMan, this is Ryan Evans. You have my daughter and I accept your challenge. I will follow you as you've requested and I will save my daughter. You hear me? I'm doing what you wanted me to do. I'm doing it for the whole world to hear, and so now I have the power. You're in check, my friend. It's your move. The only question now is whether you can find me before they do."

He paused, considering the words he'd spoken.

"You've taken the daughters before. I know your work. I sat with the children for three days and I heard their bones break. Now take the father. You know that's what you need, to destroy the father."

The foam cover on the mic touched his lip. He lowered his voice and delivered his final set of instructions.

"I'll be waiting where they make their home, BoneMan. Find me before they shoot me out of the sky."

He reached up and flipped the switch.

To Brent: "You're sure that went out."

"It went out."

Ryan stood. "How many people would you say heard that?"

"On a Wednesday night? A couple hundred thousand."

"Then the police are probably already on their way here. You make sure this gets picked up, or I'm going to pay you another visit, you hear?"

"I hear."

Ryan gave them one parting glance as he walked for the door. Then he pulled the door open, stepped into the hall, and sprinted for the front door.

He checked the outer door before exiting the building—no police. Not yet, but that would change in a matter of minutes. The black Taurus sat undisturbed under the tree where he'd left it.

He crossed the parking lot, slid behind the wheel, and piloted the car out of the lot and onto Westlake Drive.

Two police cruisers screamed up Capitol of Texas Highway as he headed south. He'd missed them by less than a minute, but in the dark, driving a black sedan, a minute was all he needed.

It took Ryan half an hour to clear the southwestern outskirts of Austin, headed west on Highway 290. He had a long drive ahead of him, a long time to think things through. But there was nothing more to be thought of.

He'd made his play and he'd made it right or he'd made it wrong.

If he'd made it right, he would wait at the Crow's Nest as indicated by his broadcast and BoneMan would find him, hopefully before the authorities tracked down the stolen Taurus.

If he'd misjudged BoneMan, however, he would wait at the Crow's Nest in vain without having the luxury of leaving, just in case BoneMan did finally show.

He'd made his play; now it was BoneMan's turn.

21

BETHANY WAS AWAKENED by the squeal of a metal door opening slowly. It was either that or a cry from her own throat, like the last time. She'd woken crying but so disoriented that she didn't realize the squeals filling the room were hers until a fly had lighted on her lower lip. The moment she clamped her mouth shut, the sounds ended.

But this time she wasn't crying. This time she'd heard a door open; she could swear it. BoneMan, assuming that was really who had taken her, had finally come to pay her another visit.

She blinked in the dim light and peered ahead at the door.

Open. It was open, wasn't it? Her heart pounded through thin ribs.

"Hello?"

She'd managed to dislodge the blindfold a long time ago, maybe more than a day ago. But it hadn't given her any peace of mind. She knew nothing more than she'd known three days earlier, when she'd first woken in this concrete basement.

The squeal came again, distant but very distinct. Bethany sat up and strained for a better view out through the open door. The hall outside probably led to other rooms, a whole system of rooms for all she knew, and at least one of those rooms had a rusted metal door that was now being opened.

Or . . . or the hall ended in a concrete staircase that rose to the outer world and someone had just opened the door that welcomed freedom.

"Hello?"

"Shhhhhh . . ."

An involuntary shiver ran through her bones. Someone had just hushed her!

"Who's there?" she whispered.

"Shhhhh . . ."

It was the first human sound Bethany had heard in over a day and it filled her with enough hope to send her pulse flying.

"Talk to me," she said. "Who are you?"

"Shh, shh, shh, shhhhhh."

She wasn't sure if she should be terrified or encouraged. But now fully to her senses, she realized that the voice couldn't belong to another prisoner or someone who'd come to rescue her. They would have said something to that effect by now.

Instead all she was getting was this hushing. *Shhhhh . . .*

She took a deep breath and calmed herself. Her emotions had ridden a track that dipped and turned and thrust her to the highest peak before sending her plummeting into a deep valley. And all of that in total isolation without a single other human being there to help her take the journey.

She'd cried, she'd wept.

She'd screamed, she'd yelled at the wall until she was hoarse.

She'd begged. She'd argued. She'd cussed and sworn and called the darkness every name her mind could conjure up.

She'd slept and she'd cried again, but above all she'd slowly come to the realization that she was already dead. If the authorities hadn't found her yet, they probably wouldn't find her, ever, at least not until BoneMan wanted her found.

Bethany pressed her teeth together and steadied a tremor that swept through her jaw. If no one was coming to save her, then her life hung in the balance of her ability to affect whoever had taken her.

But to affect him, she had to be able to talk to this stranger who'd taken her from her bed. The image of his white face staring with brilliant blue eyes haunted her, but now she wanted to see him, to engage him. Anything but this solitude and not knowing.

"You're BoneMan, aren't you? You're going to break my bones because you hate me. Or you hate my mother and father. Or you're just a mental case and you're doing this without even knowing why you're doing it. Either way, I think I get it because I hate my mother and father too . . ."

A shadow crossed the hall just beyond the door.

"I was hoping we could talk. Before you broke my bones."

A hand reached from the shadows, gripped the door handle, and slowly pulled it closed.

"Fine, be that way," Bethany said.

The door closed.

Feet walked away. After a moment a distant door clanked shut and she was back in her solitude.

Only then did she realize that something had changed. Her hands were by her sides, freed. Her captor had come in while she was sleeping and freed her?

She scrambled to her feet but fell under her own weight before she could get both legs under herself. Her head throbbed and her back flared with pain, but she felt buoyant, full of hope, as light as a feather.

She pushed herself up and stood in the middle of the room, steadying herself as best she could. The commode sat in the corner and she managed to make use of it without soiling herself. Relieving her bladder had never been quite so satisfying.

She tested the door and found it locked, as expected. Apart from the commode and the door handle, the only object in the room was the metal bed. A simple spring frame with a thin mattress.

Light filtered in from the cracks in the corner. If she got her mouth up there and screamed, someone walking past might hear. But somehow she doubted the man who'd done all of this would be so careless.

She walked around the room slowly once, then sat on the bed. The springs creaked softly, then silence returned to the room.

So . . . her bones didn't ache for the moment. What did it matter, they would soon feel all the pain they could stand.

She lay down and put both feet on the bed. The concrete ceiling was etched in old, dead vines. A lizard scampered across, eyeing her with a cocked head.

There would be no escape. He'd set her free in preparation for the next step. Her only hope was to understand him and to help him achieve what he wanted. He was looking for something. Gratification of some kind, justice—he had a mission, a task he felt he needed to accomplish.

Bethany was now the means to something very important to him. She had to discover what that was and help him achieve it while remaining alive.

She lifted her arm and stared at the thin red line on the back of her wrist where she'd cut herself that night. Seeing it now, she felt like vomiting. In a small way, as small as this cut, she did understand him.

BoneMan was only a more advanced version of her.

Bethany lowered her arm and shook.

THE SITUATION ROOM at the FBI's Austin bureau had grown vacant in Ricki's way of thinking. Agents still milled about wall maps and spoke urgently into phones, treating each and every lead with as much attention as they'd been trained to do. Files were strewn about the tables and desks, sleeves were rolled up, half-eaten boxes of takeout Chinese sat here and there—all the signs of the last forty-eight hours, which had worn them all to a frazzle.

But it was all for nothing. Vacant. There hadn't been one solid lead on BoneMan's whereabouts since he'd made his plea on the airwaves two days earlier and then walked out of their lives.

Ricki had spent an hour with Brent Styles, Vicki Sandburg, and Paul John, the three staff members at the country station Ryan had chosen to deliver his message to the world. Clearly, in Ryan's mind, he wasn't BoneMan.

In fact, listening to them explain the fifteen-minute ordeal, one would think that Ryan was a sympathetic character in all of this. Ricki had brushed the thoughts aside and focused on the one overriding objective they all had, regardless of Ryan's guilt or innocence in the abduction of his daughter.

Either way, he was a fugitive who had to be located and brought to justice.

The door opened and Mark walked in with Father Hortense, the psychiatrist who'd been treating Ryan on the navy's orders. Ricki sighed and cut across the room to Mark's office. She followed them in and eased the door shut behind.

"Thank you for coming, Doctor. Or should I call you Father?"

"Either is fine." He sat in one of the side chairs and crossed his legs.

"I know we went over all this on the phone, but seeing as how we're not exactly banging down the door of progress, I wanted to get your thoughts on the tape."

"Like I said, no problem. The navy has instructed me to cooperate fully, given the PR disaster this could end up being for them. I'll do what I can."

Ricki glanced at Mark, who plopped down on his desk. "Nothing?" she asked.

He was in charge of communication with the various state and city agents that had joined the search in force over the last two days.

"Nada."

She frowned and eyed the priest. "Par for the course.

Your patient is proving to be quite the resourceful vaga-
bond, Father."

"Does that surprise you? He was trained in intelligence
and counterintel. They pay him to outwit and outguess his
opponents at every turn in the road. You've seen his file.
Captain Evans is one of the best."

"Evidently. I'm sure you've heard this," she said,
crossing to a playback machine on the credenza. "You've
had to have been dead not to have heard it over these past
couple days. But I want you to listen to him carefully before I ask you a few questions. Fair enough?"

"Sure."

She pressed the play button. A hissing preceded his
voice.

> *BoneMan, this is Ryan Evans. You have my daugh-
> ter and I accept your challenge. I will follow you as
> you've requested and I will save my daughter. You
> hear me? I'm doing what you wanted me to do. I'm
> doing it for the whole world to hear, and so now I
> have the power. You're in check, my friend. It's your
> move. The only question now is whether you can find
> me before they do.*

She pressed the pause button. "The prevailing wisdom
is that he's speaking to himself, Doctor. What do you
think?"

Hortense stared out the window, momentarily lost in
his thoughts.

"It's possible. Classic case of multiple personalities.
Fractured by a traumatic event. He wouldn't have been a
multiple before the most recent experience in the desert,
naturally . . ."

"You mean he would have known what he was doing two years ago as BoneMan and carried that knowledge with him when he was deployed to Iraq this last time."

"Yes. If he fractured, it would have been in the desert. He no longer remembers that he was BoneMan."

"And so now he's playing both parts, abductor and father. He's essentially playing a game with himself."

"It's possible, yes. I told you as much on the phone."

"Right. As the therapist in charge, you probably know Ryan better than anyone. When you hear his voice on the tape, what conclusion do you draw? I just want your gut reaction, Father."

Hortense's soft brown eyes flickered. "Hard to say, agent."

"If you were to guess. If his daughter's life depended on your guess."

"Then no."

"No as in he's faking it, or no as in he's not BoneMan?"

"No as in he's neither faking it nor BoneMan," Hortense said.

She let his statement stand for a few seconds.

"We have a lot of evidence that suggests he took his daughter, Father," Mark said.

The psychiatrist nodded at the machine. "Play the rest."

Ricki depressed the pause button to disengage it.

You've taken the daughters before. I know your work. I sat with the children for three days and I heard their bones break. Now take the father. You know that's what you need, to destroy the father.

Then:

I'll be waiting where they make their home, Bone-
Man. Find me before they shoot me out of the sky.

"Understand, MPD is anything but a precise diagnosis,
and I can understand the temptation to pin it on Ryan—it
would answer plenty of questions. But the man I treated
was a distraught father who was just coming to grips with
the realization that his failure as a father wasn't solely
his responsibility. He never once broke from that persona
while I was treating him. What I hear on this tape is the
same man, pushed into regression by the discovery that
his daughter whom he loves more than his own life is now
in the hands of a killer. He is a desperate man, capable of
only God knows what, but I don't think he's fractured."

"Welsh is gonna love that," Mark muttered.

"It's just my opinion," Hortense said. "I'm sure you
could find other professionals to disagree. And with more
evidence, I myself might change my opinion."

"But if you are right," Ricki said, "then this is all a
crime of passion, not something that he planned."

"No, he did plan it. But men like Ryan Evans don't
need a lot of time to plan. They think well on their feet.
I would say that what you have here is one very desperate father who is playing along with the killer for his
daughter's sake."

"And this last statement?"

"Where they make their home?" he said, repeating
the tape.

"Mean anything to you?"

"No. Clearly the killer has been in contact with him."

"He claimed the killer left him a message, but we found
no answering machine in his apartment."

"Really? I left him messages all the time."

"Then he took it with him."

An FBI evidence response team had spent six hours tossing the entire apartment and found nothing of earth-shattering import. The lab had confirmed numerous interesting details that filled out his profile as a meat eater who loved Lucky Charms and coffee, wore Armani Exchange boxers, changed his sheets frequently, and read books on foreign politics for pleasure. But nothing in the apartment had led them any closer to understanding the man who'd kidnapped his own daughter after brutally killing seven young women as BoneMan.

"The machine holds the killer's voice," Hortense said. "His only tangible connection to the person who holds his daughter. I would take it as well."

"Where would you go?" she asked. "If you were Ryan?"

"That's an impossible question. Depends who *they* are. Where they make their homes. A home or lair somewhere, home to more than one, but who. The victims?"

"Did you ever talk about flying?"

"What?"

She shrugged. " 'Before they shoot me out of the air.' I know it's grasping, but that's all we have now."

"Birds?" Hortense said.

"What birds?"

But he just shrugged.

Ricki stood and crossed to the window. "Anything else comes to mind, I'm sure you'll contact us, Father."

"Of course."

"And if he calls you . . ."

"You'll be the first to know."

She turned back. "You may be the only person he trusts."

"You may be right."

"And you, do you trust him, Father?"

He thought about that for a moment, then frowned. "I trust that he will do whatever love demands he do for the sake of his daughter."

"Well, he's running out of time."

"Why do you say that?"

"He said the killer gave him seven days. He's down to four days."

22

ALVIN FINCH DISLIKED two things about the human condition; he truly despised three. Their love of pleasure. Their love of knowledge. Their love of life that was devoid of both pleasure and knowledge.

He'd seen a bumper sticker once that claimed life wasn't measured by the number of breaths one took but by the moments that took one's breath away. It was one of those sayings that impressed average humans because, however much they hoped they believed it, they simply couldn't. In reality they were too fearful of death to consider living any moment of life in a manner that might even harm, much less kill.

In fact, the only humans who risked death for the sake of living, truly living, were those who had lost their minds and did stupid things like jump out of airplanes or off high-spanning bridges with rubber bands attached to their legs.

Alvin had provided those in Texas with a string of moments that quite literally took their breath away, both on a very intimate level and on a social level. Instead of thanking him for exposing such beautiful moments of life, they'd set out to hunt him down and erase him from their petty little world.

Ryan Evans, on the other hand, was proving to be a human being who was willing to explore death for the sake of living well, and this fact disturbed Alvin Finch.

He would flush out the man's true nature as an imposter soon enough, of course. He would humiliate this traitor and send him away yelping with his tail tucked between his legs. He would destroy the man's resolve to play father. He would rip out his heart and shove it so far down his throat that he would die from constipation.

Killing the man outright was tempting, and the time for that would come, but not before he convinced the man to wholly reject Bethany first. So that Alvin could truly be her father.

The only way to truly be a daughter's father was to win her heart, regardless of who contributed the seed. And the only way to truly win a daughter's heart was to help her reject any other father she blindly accepted as her own so that she could be free to love Alvin as much as he loved himself.

Thinking these thoughts, he fought a terrible temptation to turn around and rush back to the daughter. He'd spent days watching her through the cracks, studying her every move, resisting only with great effort the temptation to rush in and persuade her to love him.

This time was different. This time he had to deal a decisive and final blow to any living soul who would pretend to be her father.

Alvin slowed the Ford F-150 pickup down as he

approached the sign along Highway 166 that read CROW'S
NEST RANCH, 2 MILES. Gravel crunched under the tires
like popcorn.

He'd heard the message on the radio seventeen hours
after Evans had delivered it. He would have heard it sooner
because he did like to follow the authorities' general progress on the case each time he took a girl, but he'd been
preoccupied with securing the site with Bethany, which
explained his delay.

The moment he heard the challenge his heart had begun
to beat strong. He understood where Evans was immediately. A place called Crow's Nest.

Crows made their homes in crow's nests, and Evans,
an intelligence officer who was accustomed to speaking
in code, was telling him that he would wait for him at a
place called Crow's Nest.

An intelligent man would choose a location unlikely
to be visited by authorities or a steady stream of patrons,
which eliminated the seven restaurants in Texas that in-
corporated Crow's Nest in their names.

He dismissed two small bed-and-breakfasts as well.

The Crow's Nest Ranch was the only place in Texas
that Alvin would have chosen to wait, if the shoe was on
the other foot. Not only was Evans courageous, he was
highly intelligent.

The Internet brochure for Crow's Nest Ranch claimed
that it was a secluded camping retreat eighteen miles
west of Fort Davis, four hundred and thirty miles directly
west of Austin. Rugged, only for the discriminating trav-
eler who wanted to commune with nature in the most
positive way. Evergreens grew from a parched landscape
that rose to the mesas surrounding the isolated camping

retreat, which offered some cabins as well as RV spots and dry camping.

Alvin drove past the self-service payment box and the cabin near the entrance that announced a manager lived inside and wound past the three motor homes that were parked at the hookups. He knew that all F-150 pickups were suspect now that he'd struck again, but there were far too many of them to raise suspicion every time one drove by. He felt reasonably safe.

A man wearing a blue plaid shirt and a brown cowboy hat walked with his head down. Anyone who came to Crow's Nest Ranch was probably looking to escape the hustle and bustle of the city. It was an almost perfect hiding spot.

Perhaps he would bring the next girl here, to this remote getaway nestled in the trees eighteen miles away from the closest town. But there wouldn't be a next girl, because he had finally and fully found his daughter in Bethany, he was sure of it.

He pulled the truck onto a dirt road that wound around the campground to a ravine along the north side. Taking the binoculars, he exited the truck, checked to make sure he was alone, and headed up into the trees to his right.

A large outcropping of rock hid the campsite that Evans had chosen, but from his vantage point above the grounds, Alvin could see him and his car, laid out bare like a dog.

He wiggled in behind a pile of boulders, brought the binoculars to his eyes, and scanned the campsite below. He acquired the man's form, seated in the dirt, with his back against a tree, slumped over, bored out of his skull.

The black Ford Taurus was parked behind some trees in precisely the same spot Alvin had found it yesterday.

By all appearances, the man had not moved a muscle in the last twenty-four hours. He'd raced here after delivering his message and then waited like an obedient father, out of options.

Alvin set the binoculars down and folded his hands. A lizard scattered some pebbles behind him. A faint breeze cooled his neck. The boulders provided some shade here. He wondered how many hikers had found their way to this precise spot. Likely very few. In fact, he might be the first human to touch this soil.

He wasn't able to shower regularly during a taking, and this time, because he'd agreed to extend the father seven full days, he was concerned that his skin might begin to smell.

Protected as he was from the elements, hidden behind the rocks, he stripped off his shirt, set it next to the binoculars, and then loosened his belt. He pulled out the travel-sized bottle of Noxzema lotion and set it next to the shirt, then he lowered the cotton dungarees and pulled his boxer shorts down to his ankles.

Now he stood naked except for his boots, his underwear and his pants around his lower legs. Not ideal, but it would have to do.

Alvin wiped a generous portion of Noxzema on his right palm and began to apply, beginning at the back of his neck and working his way down over his unblemished chest. He could feel the beginnings of stubble growing around his nipples, and this bothered him some, but it couldn't be helped.

There was one thing that bothered Alvin, two things that drove him insane. The smell of body odor after three days without a bath. And cologne.

The medicinal smell of camphor associated with Noxzema, however, was the incense of the gods.

He used the contents of half the bottle to smoothe his skin from his neck down to his ankles. At one point a small ladybug had lighted on his naked hip, and he'd flattened it with a loud smack.

A quick check through the binoculars assured him that Evans hadn't heard the strike. He'd used a stick to scrape the remnants of the bug from his skin before resuming the application of Noxzema between his legs and behind his knees, all the way to his ankles.

Satisfied that he was clean, Alvin dressed, then looked at his subject again.

No movement. Was he sleeping?

He was tempted to go down and talk to the man. Why not? He couldn't afford to be seen yet, naturally. But why avoid the pleasure of talking to the man instead of leaving the note in his car as he'd planned?

Alvin took his time, letting the idea grow slowly inside of him until he didn't think he could delay much longer. He thought about reapplying, but the desire to hear the fear in Evans's voice was so great that he couldn't even concentrate on thoughts of reapplying, however enjoyable such thoughts might be.

Yes, why not? It was time to talk to Ryan Evans.

HE'D DONE EVERYTHING he could think to do, which was precisely what BoneMan wanted him to do, Ryan thought. But none of this made the task at hand easy or even manageable.

He'd kept telling himself as he'd driven west two

nights earlier that he was doing the right thing, that he hadn't lost his mind, that he was making the kind of move that would give him the highest likelihood of recovering his daughter alive.

That with each mile the Taurus rolled west, his daughter drew closer, although he felt sure he was leaving her behind, hidden in a hole somewhere. He wanted to be close to her bedroom, he wanted to walk around her room and touch her photographs and schoolbooks.

He'd pushed the speed limit as much as he dared and pulled into the campground early the next morning after a five-hour drive. Driving through the darkened camp, following the bright twin beams from the headlamps, he'd suspected that he'd made a mistake. And when he'd finally guided the car under a large pine and turned off the engine, the silence had crushed him with the fierce certainty of utter failure.

He'd sat unmoving in the car until dawn broke. But the rising sun had brought nothing except for more silence.

He'd walked around the camp, relieved to see that he was one of only three campers in the entire ranch. Then he'd climbed to the highest point behind his small clearing and scanned the horizon for most of the day.

All the while he replayed his message, begging the BoneMan to come. Surely he'd heard. Ryan had kept up with the radio coverage of his incursion into the country station, and he'd taken hope in the fact that anyone who turned on a radio in Texas now knew of his challenge.

You've taken the daughters before. I know your work. I sat with the children for three days and I heard their bones break. Now take the father. You know that's what you need, to destroy the father.

I'll be waiting where they make their home, BoneMan. Find me before they shoot me out of the sky.

But what if BoneMan didn't take him up on his challenge? Or what if the man was less intelligent than Ryan had assumed? What if he was in a gully even now, scratching his head, wondering what Ryan had meant when he said he would be where they made their homes?

Then again, BoneMan's choice of the crow could hardly be the product of an uneducated man. Throughout history the crow had been identified with the messenger of God, whether for good or for evil.

In India, for example, in the Mahabharata, the messengers of death were drawn as crows. The Celts, the Japanese, and the Chinese all identified the crow as a good omen from God. Whether good or evil, the black bird was identified with the forces of creation and destruction wherever it was found.

BoneMan saw himself as a messenger to society, flying high for all to see, and he wanted Ryan, the father of his latest victim, to join him. Ryan had gone one step further by calling BoneMan to find him at the Crow's Nest.

He'd managed to fall into an exhausted sleep the second night, but when he woke the next morning to the sound of birds chirping in the nearby trees, a depression he didn't think possible had swallowed him.

There was nothing to do but wait. An agonizing wait that consisted not of hours or minutes but of seconds. Each one ticking off slowly. He'd listened to the radio to get the latest news on the case, but there was no news.

Bethany was gone. BoneMan was gone. Ryan Evans was gone.

He'd chanced a quick stop at a gas station halfway across the state and paid cash for several loaves of bread and lunch meat, but he'd lost his appetite and had to force himself to eat after a day of fasting.

There was nothing to apply his mind to. No course of action to take. No puzzle to solve. He sat on the ground with his back to the big tree and prayed to God, the same mantra, over and over.

Please, help her be safe. Keep her alive. Just keep her alive. I'm sorry.

He tried to remember what he was sorry for but after a while even this began to fade. Yes, he'd failed Bethany. Perhaps if he'd been in the house that night, the killer would have thought twice. Perhaps if he'd been a loving father, the killer wouldn't have chosen Bethany in the first place.

Perhaps if he'd slept by the front door with a shotgun cocked in his elbow, ready to blow the head off of any demented maniac who dared step one foot in his home . . .

He spent some of the time imagining how he might kill BoneMan. He might put a gun in his mouth and pull the trigger. He might hit him in the face until it became bloody and lifeless. He might jab him in the eyes with a sharp stick, then shove the stick up into his brain. He might take a rock and crush his head.

He thought about how he would rescue Bethany. About how she would rush into his arms and weep into his neck. About how he would sweep in with a shotgun, end BoneMan's life with a load of buckshot, then pluck his daughter from the jaws of death.

Mostly, he imagined how he would crush the man who dared cost his daughter one night of sleep. The thoughts made him wear his jaw tired from all the grinding.

But after hours of contemplating the manner in which he could kill BoneMan and save his daughter, he was left with only himself. Alone. Useless. Seated in the hot sun.

Hopeless.

The desperation that had sent Kahlid on a mission to kill children to save many more children. It was a sickness, and Ryan began to wonder if he'd been infected with it.

ALVIN FINCH WALKED up the hill fifty yards, then cut to his right, working his way around so that he could come up behind Evans without being seen. His heart was beating in his chest like a fist, and he began to sweat—something he hadn't counted on so soon after applying the lotion.

It took him twenty minutes to position himself directly behind some boulders to the rear of the man, who still had not moved. If the man surprised him and tried something foolish, he would use the gun in this pocket, but with the daughter safely stowed, Evans couldn't risk anything stupid.

"Do not turn around, Ryan Evans," he said.

The man jerked upright, but he did not turn around.

"That's good. Just stay where you are. Don't try to stand up. Just stay seated."

The man was stiff like a board. Alvin would prefer to see his eyes, but he couldn't risk showing his own face yet.

"You're a smart man, Mr. Evans. It worked. You called

to me and now here I am. That's pretty good if you think about it. Pretty amazing, isn't it?"

But after two days of sitting in fear and trepidation, the poor man couldn't get his vocal cords going.

"Say something," Alvin said.

"Yes," the man said.

He sounded pretty rational, after all.

"You know who I am?"

"Yes."

"Do you think you're me, like they say?"

The man hesitated, as if seriously considering this possibility. Could it be true? Alvin thought about it for a moment then decided that anything was possible.

"No," the man said.

"I agree. But they are right about one thing. I have your daughter and I am going to break her bones. Unless—"

"I'll do anything."

"I've been watching your daughter through the cracks in the wall and I think I'm going to have some challenges breaking her arms without breaking her skin; it's so frail you know. So soft. She looks like she's never had to work a day in her life."

The man said nothing, but his body was now trembling.

It was such a strange and wonderful sight.

Alvin peered out at the shaking man and let him quake for a while.

"If you bring me the father of lies, I'll give her back to you. I've given you some directions on this note that I'm going to leave back here. You either have the stomach for this or you don't, so I'm only going to give you until morning. Bring me the father of lies and I can show you how to break his bones. Or do you already know how to do that?"

The man didn't respond.

Alvin set the folded blue note on the rock and backed away silently.

It took him only five minutes to reach his truck and another two before he was on the gravel road again, cutting a line due south to the place of hiding. The father had spoken back there as he retreated, but Alvin didn't hear him, nor did he care. He was on his way now. Back to the hole.

Back to daughter.

23

THE JOY THAT swept through Ryan at the sound of that voice was like cool water to parched lips in a cracked, barren wasteland. It was soft but perfectly clear. Like the voice of an angel. There could be no mistake. BoneMan had come! Everything Ryan had prayed for, all of his waiting, the hours of hopelessness, they'd all delivered him BoneMan, and he nearly shouted out in his thankfulness.

The many ways he'd considered killing BoneMan flooded his mind at once now. The breaking, crushing, shooting, slashing—all of it at once to make sure that the voice behind him was truly dead.

He became aware that he was trembling. The air remained silent for some time and he just sat there, shaking. Then the man spoke again.

"If you bring me the father of lies, I'll give her back to you. I've given you some directions on this note that I'm going to leave back here. You either have the stomach for this or you don't, so I'm only going to give you until morning. Bring me the father of lies and I can show you how to break his bones. Or do you already know how to do that?"

Father of lies . . . father of lies . . . Ryan didn't have to look at a blue note to know who the father of lies was.

"Yes," he said.

There was no response.

"Hello?"

Still nothing.

The man had left! Ryan turned around and stared at an outcropping of rock ten yards behind the tree against which he'd been leaning. There on the closest rock that rose three feet lay a folded slip of blue paper. His heart rose into his throat, thinking of the man, standing right there just a moment ago.

He stood slowly. Then bounded up to the rock, ripped the note off the surface, and ran for the black Taurus.

He slid behind the wheel, slammed the door closed, and unfolded the quartered note with quaking hands.

BoneMan's handwriting. Scrawled in block letters.

FATHER OF LIES.
MENARD–7 MILES SOUTH
WEST–2 MILES
BENEATH THE CROWS
I'LL BE WATCHING, FATHER.

He sat, staring at the piece of paper for a full minute, maybe two minutes, maybe five minutes, in part because he knew what he was expected to do now, in part because he wanted to give BoneMan as much time as he needed to get away.

The man was on foot, making his way back to his vehicle. What if Ryan ran into him? This wasn't the kind of
man who would turn over the location of his daughter just
because he'd been caught red-handed.

And this location on the blue slip of paper wasn't where
he'd find his daughter, he knew that. BoneMan would be
watching and would bring her in only if and when Ryan
complied with his demands.

He fired the car and backed it hastily over a bush before whipping it in a dusty circle and angling down the
dirt path that led out of Crow's Nest Ranch.

No sign of any other vehicle. Good. He didn't need any
attention. He certainly didn't need the involvement of any
authority beyond what BoneMan was demanding.

Ryan pulled up to the highway and looked first left,
then right. No cars.

He glanced at the round clock on the dash. Ten minutes
past noon. It would be dark in seven hours.

He shoved the accelerator to the floorboards, shot out onto
the blacktop, lined the car up between the yellow dashes and
the white edge, and took the Taurus up to ninety. Out here
west of Fort Davis, cops would be scarce—not so as he
closed in on Austin, where he was still public enemy number
one. There were only so many roads leading into Austin, and
the FBI would be waiting on all of them, with arms open
wide, waiting for BoneMan to rush into their trap.

He had to make good time while he could. After three
days of stillness the rush of the wind sounded like the
voice of God, roaring out of the sky to save this one.

Texas was dry this time of year, a near desert. He kept
his head down and gripped the wheel tightly and sped into
their arms. But he had no intention of giving himself up,

not now when he finally had at his means the way to save Bethany.

An hour passed before he thought to slow down, and then only when he passed a cop going the other direction. Evidently Texas cops didn't pull over cars doing ninety.

Ryan breathed a prayer of gratitude, slowed to eighty, and flew east. A storm was coming, the radio said. Black clouds boiled on the horizon.

He fixed his eyes on the road ahead and took the car back up to eighty-five.

What are you doing, Ryan? You can't do this!

The horror of what BoneMan was asking of him suddenly struck him.

You can't do this . . .

But what choice did he have? BoneMan had Bethany!

A CRACK OF thunder rattled the phone booth. Ryan instinctively kept his head low as large raindrops pelted the glass. Storm clouds had cut off the sun early, hastening nightfall, but there was still an hour of dim light before blackness settled over the Hill Country. The phone in his hand was ringing on the other end. He pressed it closer to his ear so that he could hear better.

Rivers of water distorted his view of the western horizon. *Pick up, Father. Please pick up.*

If the drive had been only three hours, he would have been able to get it done before his conscience had the time to consider the moral implications of what lay ahead. Ignorance was bliss, but hours of time and thought had shattered that bliss.

Slowly the horror of what he was about to do swallowed him until he found that he had to make a preemptive confession, not for his sake, but for Bethany's sake, should it all go terribly wrong.

"Hello?"

The father's voice crackled on the line.

"Hello?"

"Father?"

A long beat.

"Ryan . . ."

"Listen to me, Father. You have to listen to me. I know I'm AWOL and I know the FBI's made contact with you. The CO's probably climbing down your throat—"

"Slow down, Ryan. I can hardly hear you. Take a deep breath."

He took a deep breath through his nostrils, then blew out slowly. He was playing a dangerous game, calling Hortense.

"Can I still talk to you, Father? I need someone to talk to."

"Of course you can. But you have to know that command is climbing all over me. They're cooperating fully with the FBI. This is a publicity disaster for them."

"I need some time. I'm going after my daughter and I need you to give me some time. If you call the FBI and tell them about this call, she could die."

Father Hortense didn't respond.

"Do you understand what I'm saying? Her life's in my hands and now her life will be in your hands."

"We can help you, Ryan. You can't take this all on your shoulders."

"I talked to him, Father. He found me and he talked to

me. And now I'm going to do something that no one will understand. But I need you to understand, Father."

"What are you going to do?"

Yes, Ryan, what are you going to do?

He stared out at the rain streaming over the glass, like tears from heaven. A knot formed in his throat and for a moment he thought he might join God and begin to cry.

"God's done many things that have been misunderstood, right?"

"Ryan—"

"He's destroyed whole nations to save those he loves, isn't that what he did? Nineveh?"

"He spared Nineveh."

"Jericho?"

"Please, Ryan. I don't like the sound of this. It is critical that you turn yourself in. No good can come of this."

"How far would you go to save your daughter, Father?"

"Half the state is out there looking for you because they believe that you're the one playing the devil here. You are not God, Ryan. You're one man and you've broken the law."

"This is no different than what we do in any war, Father. Collateral damage is a part of what we do to achieve justice. Setting the captive free comes at a cost."

"That sounds like a desperate attempt at justification."

"Am I wrong?"

"No one will understand that kind of logic!"

"What I'm going to do, I'm going to do for my daughter's sake. And if you don't give me some time then both me and my daughter will be killed."

"Ryan, you listen to me—"

"I don't want to do this, Father." Ryan's throat constricted and he had to swallow to continue his confession. "You know me, this is the last thing I would do, I was there, I'm not up for this, but I have no choice!"

Father Hortense waited a few seconds before responding. Finally, he was listening.

"Think about what you are doing, Ryan. God spare you if you become BoneMan."

Ryan knew what he meant and it didn't help him. He'd been a fool to place the call.

"If you report this call, Bethany and I will both die."

"How much time do you need?" the priest finally asked.

"A few hours."

"Maybe."

"I need a yes."

"Then yes. I will give you a few hours, and then I will call the FBI."

"Tell them to look seven miles south of Menard. He'll be watching. I need till first light. If they come before morning, we'll all die."

The line remained quiet.

"Father, promise me."

"What are you going to do, Ryan?"

Ryan hung up.

24

RYAN DROVE INTO Austin under cover of darkness, thankful for the hard rain, which alone might have been responsible for the ease with which he drove to his destination undetected.

The black Taurus had surely been reported stolen by now, but no one had publicly connected the car to him. Even if they were looking for it, on a dark stormy night it suited him.

He knew his destination precisely because he'd been there twice before, two months earlier, before the restraining order had forced him out of town. The gated community sat on the west side of Austin, in a neighborhood called Spanish Oaks. He was surprised that the construction code he'd acquired earlier still worked. Either way, he would have simply followed another car past the gate.

He parked under a tree a full block from the large white colonial and slid down in his seat to wait. Rain pelted the roof and windshield, a thunderous cacophony that smothered the sound of passing tires on the wet pavement. Not that it mattered; he had committed himself. The time for careful planning and meticulous execution was now far past.

The rain was on his side. The brashness of what he was about to attempt was on his side. Speed was on his side. His gun was on his side.

Time was against him. Sanity was against him. The law was against him. Reason was against him. Morality was against him.

He could do nothing but sit low and urge his mind to shout over the voices of caution that kept filling his mind.

The rain had eased enough by ten o'clock to give him full view of the Cadillac that pulled into the driveway and disappeared behind a rolling garage door. Ryan waited another two hours before he shouted down the last warning barking in his head, fired the Taurus, and pulled up to the sidewalk that led up to the front door.

He withdrew his pistol, disengaged the safety, and stepped out into the drizzling rain.

Without bothering to look to his right or to his left, he walked up to the front door and tried it. Locked, naturally. He pulled his collar up, hunched his shoulders, and shoved the metal stock of the gun through the door panel.

The glass broke and crashed to the floor inside. Rain muted the sound, but not entirely. He reached in, twisted the dead bolt, and pulled the door open to the sound of a loud beep that accompanied a countdown to the alarm.

Ryan cut to his right where a large door looked like it might lead to a bedroom. But it turned out to be a darkened study.

The alarm's warning began to speed up. At any moment it would begin to blare.

Dripping on the large tiles, he ducked into a second hallway and this time was greeted by a large atrium that led to an entire wing. His rubber soles squealed with each step now, but the sudden wailing of the alarm on all sides shattered any thought of creeping in unnoticed.

He spun into the master bedroom just as the form on the four-poster bed rose from its slumber. The man was too stunned to react properly, and Ryan moved in while he still had the full advantage.

He shoved the gun barrel in the man's face, grabbed his collar, and jerked him from the bed.

"Shut up!" The man hadn't uttered a peep, but he said it anyway. Again. Because it covered the shame he felt. "Shut up!"

The gun's barrel had already split Welsh's lip but he found his voice and began to deliver the expected protest. "What in God's name—"

Ryan hit him upside the head. "I said shut *up*."

He dragged the district attorney around and shoved him forward, out into his own living room, where the sound of the shrill alarm was nearly deafening. "Outside, if you want to live."

The man wore thin cotton pajamas but his feet were bare. He stumbled through the front door, pushed by Ryan, but pulled up when the rain hit him.

"In the car!"

The man stood in a crouch, as if unsure what to do, so Ryan helped him out. He kicked the man with his heel in the small of his back. "Move!"

He moved, grunting with pain.

"In the car."

Burt Welsh was still reeling from the suddenness of

the attack, but he was a big man and he wouldn't just take such a violation lying down for long. Not without Ryan's help.

The man piled into the passenger seat, cursing bitterly now. Not the sign of humility and cooperation that Ryan was looking for.

He reached in, grabbed the larger man by his black hair, tugged his head out of the car door, and slammed the gun on his temple with as much force as he could manage, working in the tight space.

The DA slumped, unconscious. Ryan shoved him in, slammed the door after him, and raced around the car.

He'd succeeded thus far because of his urgency, not through any finesse, and he made no attempt at it now. He whipped the car through a tight turn and flew through streets running like rivers.

Beside him, the father of lies' pajama-clad form leaned against the door. He'd known from the first mention of the term that BoneMan had been very careful in his selection of Bethany. This was far more than retaliation for the district attorney's bravado in swearing to bring him to justice.

BoneMan knew that both he and Ryan agreed on at least one thing: Welsh was a pretender who had no claim to Bethany. He was the father of lies, and of all those BoneMan could have asked him to take, Ryan felt less conflicted about taking this one.

He had to slow down at the exit gate and wait for it to open, but he was already on Highway 71 before the first cop car flew by and peeled into Spanish Oaks.

The DA began to moan, and Ryan leaned over to give him another blow to the head. He simply could not allow the man to give him any trouble in the middle of his flight from the city.

Going northeast on 71 and then directly east on 29, the trip to Menard would take about two hours if he moved quickly.

Ryan moved. He cleared the city limits in under ten minutes and took the car up to eighty again. Now a nearly frantic urgency consumed him to get the man he'd abducted into whatever hole in the ground that BoneMan had prepared for them. He didn't know what awaited them, only that it would involve breaking Welsh's bones, and for the time being he refused to think through what that might entail.

The man stirred again thirty minutes east of Austin. The human head could only take so much trauma, and having been knocked out twice, the DA's head wasn't a good candidate for surviving yet another blow to the head.

"Whad . . ." the man was slurring, "whad . . . whad . . ." His head wobbled on his neck as he tried to climb back into consciousness.

Ryan rested the gun across his waist, trained on the man's chest. "Don't give me an excuse to shoot you. Dead or alive, that's what he asked for, and I'd just as soon it be dead."

Not true, but the only way Ryan could go through with this was to play his part without compromise. He'd set aside his emotions for the time being and if he did allow any to resurface, they'd best be anger rather than a sudden pang of guilt.

The man eyed him curiously, eyes taking in the gun as if he wasn't sure it was real.

"What's . . . what's the meaning of this?"

"Are you going to make me hit you again?"

The DA studied the road ahead for a moment. His abduction was coming back into focus, Ryan thought. The man was a bull and would not make for an easy prisoner.

As if to confirm his suspicions, Welsh frowned. "Now you've done it. Now you've really gone and done it."

This was a revelation that either gave the man courage or was meant to frighten Ryan. But the fact that he had "gone and done it" was no news at all.

"Do you have any idea how many officers are out looking for me now?"

"More than were looking for me? It doesn't matter, they won't find either of us until morning."

"And then what?"

"And then the FBI will follow the directions I left for them. They'll find us."

The man didn't seem capable of digesting this frank admission. He blinked repeatedly in the darkness.

"You're giving yourself up?"

"Not yet."

"What are you going to do? You'll never get away with this—"

"Do you see any cops? I think I just did get away with it."

"They'll find us. I'm the district attorney—"

"Do you love her?"

"What?"

"Do you love Bethany?"

"That's what this about? You're throwing your life away because I'm sleeping with Celine?"

"Do you love them?"

It took the man a while to form his answer, and when

he did he spoke in a low, rushed voice. "I swear I'll never touch them again. Just let me go. I won't press charges, I won't say a thing—"

Ryan hit the man on his temple again. The DA collapsed in a limp heap on the front seat.

He pulled out the blue note and wedged it into the seam above the radio.

FATHER OF LIES.
MENARD–7 MILES SOUTH
WEST–2 MILES
BENEATH THE CROWS
I'LL BE WATCHING, FATHER.

Highway 29 intersected Highway 83 just south of Menard, and they made the junction at just past two in the morning. The two-lane roads were deserted and the rain had long ago tapered off to hardly more than a mist.

Ryan turned right on Highway 83, away from the tiny town of Menard, Texas, and headed south into the darkness.

No streetlights out here. No stars to light the sodden ground. Just his headlights, and as he approached the seven-mile marker headed south, he felt conspicuous, so he turned off the headlights as well.

Now he rolled along the asphalt in a quiet darkness that he found even more disturbing. He turned up the radio. The soft, melodic voice of Karen Carpenter singing "Bless the Beasts and the Children" sliced the silence.

He scanned the fields on either side. The man who they called BoneMan had Bethany out here in a hole somewhere, but no one driving by would ever guess it. The world didn't like to look at the dark underside very often. But that didn't change the ugliness; it only ensured that those who perpetuated the ugliness were left alone to kill and maim and rape.

The melancholic sounds of the Carpenters suddenly struck him as obscene and he turned off the radio and drove on in silence.

He stopped the Ford Taurus at the seven-mile marker. A dirt road headed directly east into the field on his right. The green sign that hung at a slight angle said it was called Landers Lane. He could just see the white letters by the light of a moon that was now trying to gleam past the breaking storm clouds.

Ryan held the car at the intersection for a few long breaths. He wiped his palms on his pants and looked over at Burton Welsh, the man who'd seduced his wife while he was in the desert.

The gravel under his rubber tires popped as he turned and rolled down Landers Lane. Cornstalks rose on either side. The road veered left—south—and he followed it with one eye on the odometer. But there was no need because the huge switching station rose from the earth at about the right distance, and Ryan knew immediately that he'd arrived.

The crows would perch themselves on the high-voltage lines that ran into the switching station. And under these lines somewhere there was a room. An old storage room that had sat unused for a long time while it waited to be occupied this night.

Then he saw it, a board on the fence that surrounded the switching station. A crudely marked red arrow pointed to the right, where a large mound of gravel stood against the dark sky.

He angled the car for the hill and saw that the ground dipped into a large pit beyond. This was a switching station, but it was also an old gravel pit. Or a mining pit.

The storage facility was built into the side of the hill. He could see that it sat closed on the face of the concrete, and on this wood door was the rough outline of a bird.

A crow.

RICKI VALENTINE JERKED upright with dreams of a sunny day in Saint John, Virgin Islands, still ambling through her head. She'd spent two weeks there after the apprehension of Phil Switzer, basking in the careless sun as far from the hot Texas summer as possible. She spent the time wandering the beach and visiting small establishments that catered to tourists by selling over-priced trinkets and water-sporting opportunities, and all the while her mind had returned to the BoneMan only a few times. Amazing how a change of geography could jar the mind out of its deep, dark trenches.

The clock on her nightstand read 2:43 AM in large red letters. Her phone was still chirping. She wasn't in the Caribbean now and BoneMan wasn't behind bars.

"Hello?"

Mark sounded like he'd been up for a while. "Sorry for the hour, Ricki. We have a development. Burton Welsh's house was broken into and he seems to be missing."

The data swirled through her mind.

"Seems to be?"

"Well, he lives alone and the neighbors say he has a

habit of coming and going at all hours, so the police can't be sure he isn't shacked up somewhere else."

"But?"

"But his door shows signs of forced entry and his bed was slept in. His car's still in the garage."

Ricki stood from the bed. "So he was taken. When was this?"

"Almost three hours—"

"What?" She hurried to the bathroom, flipping on lights as she went. "You're just now being told?"

"Evidently the man was a bit of a womanizer and someone down at the department has been sitting on a theory that this is woman trouble, nothing more. You go public only to learn that Welsh left with a jilted lover and . . . well, you get the picture. He's an elected official."

"Okay, text me the address. I'm on my way."

"You gotta hand it to the guy, he's got a set."

That he did. If this was Ryan Evans, and Ryan Evans was indeed the killer, he'd come back to take the man whom he perceived as being the spoiler of his family. BoneMan had never taken male victims that they knew about, but the circumstances provided the perfect opportunity.

There was a kind of ironic beauty to it, Ricki thought. And then she scolded herself for such a crude thought.

"He's breaking his own pattern and escalating. You realize what this means, Mark."

"That the daughter is still alive."

"That's right. He's involving Welsh. We find Welsh, we find the girl. No obvious leads."

"A police cruiser remembers a black Ford sedan on Highway 71 as he responded to the call. Not too many cars on the road at that time."

A black Ford Taurus had been flagged as stolen and put into the search grid along with another hundred possible vehicles Evans could have used for his escape.

"Nothing else?" She pulled on her jeans, cradling the phone between her shoulder and ear.

"They're running prints from the door now. Nothing else."

"Find that Taurus. Flood the airwaves with it. Anyone who drives a dark-colored Ford Taurus gets pulled over."

"They're on it. We could use some light; he couldn't have picked a better night."

"We may not have the time to wait for light."

25

RYAN SAT IN the car as it ticked, cooling still after a full fifteen minutes of sitting in the quarry. Beside him, Welsh was still slumped up against the window, dead to the world. The clouds had just started to break up, allowing starlight to cast a cool glow over the barren depression into which he'd driven. The hum of high voltage from the nearby wires reached past the sealed car.

And ahead there, on the side of the hill, that concrete wall with a painted door. Other than the one arrow on the fence and this crow on the door, there was no sign of BoneMan.

But he was watching. Just as sure as he'd watched Ryan sitting under the tree at the Crow's Nest Ranch, he was watching now, from the cracks between the boards in the door. From behind one of the boulders that lay around the quarry or from the rim above them.

He stared at the door, fixed to the seat like a skeleton long robbed of life. Bethany was either behind the door or she was not.

If she was behind it, then BoneMan intended for them both to face their greatest fears in the hours to come.

If she wasn't behind the door, then he would be forced to face his greatest fear, which was that his daughter was still in the killer's grasp somewhere, and Ryan would be left to do whatever BoneMan required in order to rescue his daughter.

For this reason Ryan found himself immobilized as he stared at the door.

And for what lay ahead of him pertaining to the DA. However guilty Welsh was of countless sins, he was not deserving of what lay ahead any more than the children in the desert were deserving of Kahlid's hammer.

On the other hand, Ryan didn't necessarily have to kill the man. Not yet. There had to be another way.

The thoughts ran in circles, but they did not bring any relief. These facts remained: The night was quiet. The night was dark. A captive man lay to his right. The wooden door was shut.

He had to enter that door and do what BoneMan demanded before morning.

Ryan pushed his door open and blinked at the obscenely loud buzz that cut through the air. He collected himself, then stepped out onto the gravel.

If there was any moment in his life he'd been born for, it was this one. No ordinary man could shut down his emotions and do what must be done the way he could. Hadn't he proved that?

So then he would simply move through this situation in a cold, calculating fashion, without lingering long enough on any moment to allow his nervous system time to react with those chemicals that spawned emotion.

This wasn't about him or, for that matter, about the man who'd sworn to uphold the law, his captive, Burton Welsh.

This night was about Bethany.

Ryan took one very deep breath, crossed in front of the car, and opened the passenger door. No longer supported, Welsh's body slipped halfway out. His hands dangled onto the gravel—by all appearances, lifeless.

Ryan checked his carotid for a pulse, found one, and took both of his hands in his. He tugged the man out of the car and managed another ten feet before the man's weight became too much to manage without slipping.

Removing his belt, he tied Welsh's arms behind his back as tightly as he could manage. It took only a few sharp slaps on the man's cheek to rouse him.

Another minute before the man was coherent enough to get his feet under his weight and stand, and Ryan took advantage of the time to shove a paper towel he retrieved from the car into his mouth.

The man made a feeble attempt to protest, but one poke of the gun barrel in his ear shut him up.

"Move."

The man lumbered forward, up to what Ryan now thought of as a toolshed. It could have been built to house fuses or some other high-voltage parts that were best kept cool underground, or it could have been used to store machinery necessary to operate the quarry back in the day.

None of this mattered to Ryan, but he drew some comfort from the fact that he was able to think clearly enough to make simple deductions. The last thing he should do was react impulsively to whatever greeted him beyond that door.

That unlocked door.

He reached around Welsh, keeping the gun on his neck, and pulled the door open. Orange light from an oil lamp that hung in the middle of the room spilled out.

So then BoneMan had been here. Or was still here.

He used the barrel to propel Welsh into the room ahead of him, then closed the door behind them.

They stood in a room, perhaps twenty feet square, poured from concrete, with three large timbers to support a wood ceiling. The lantern hung from a hook on the center beam.

One glance around the room told Ryan that neither BoneMan nor Bethany was in this place, and he nearly ran back out to search the hillside for another door, another room, anyplace in which they might be hiding.

But there were drawings on the walls and these drawings made the purpose of his invitation here clear. BoneMan had used to chalk to draw dozens of medical diagrams showing the human skeleton. Large circles served as insets that magnified the form's bones, marking joints and specific points on each.

Instructions were written by each inset, detailing the correct amount of force to use so the bone wouldn't break with enough force to cut through the skin.

Along one wall sat a metal-framed bed. And on the bed lay several piles of four-by-four wooden blocks. A neatly folded stack of towels and several coils of string had been set at the head of the bed.

Atop them lay a large sledgehammer and vise grips.

At first Welsh just stared, as did Ryan. But when the meaning of what this room might hold for him formed in Welsh's mind, he protested with a wide-eyed grunt.

He bolted across the room before Ryan could stop him and spun back, tugging at the hasty restraints that held his arms behind his back.

"Stop it!" Ryan pointed the gun at his head, but Welsh showed no signs that he intended to stop anything. He was now yelling into the makeshift muzzle, attempting to spit it out.

"Stop it, I'll shoot!"

But Ryan knew that he couldn't shoot because the largest letters on the wall made this fact painfully clear.

> *Break his skin and he's no use to me.*
> *Break all of his bones and she goes free.*
> *Father.*

The complete absurdity of his predicament struck Ryan broadside for a moment. That he was seriously considering following BoneMan's instructions felt at once sickening and compulsory. He wouldn't kill Welsh. He wouldn't do what Kahlid had done in the desert, no matter what was at stake. He couldn't kill an innocent man even if it meant saving his daughter.

Or could he?

Because he couldn't *not* save his daughter! He couldn't not do whatever was humanly possible to keep Bethany from death. If he stopped now, Bethany would die, he was certain of it. And so, though he knew he would not, could not kill this man, he could not stop now. Not yet.

A way would come. A ram from the thicket to spare the innocent man. The FBI, BoneMan himself, Ryan's own death—anything to spare him from abandoning his daughter, no matter what the cost.

Ryan did what he knew best to do. He shut down the emotion and kept the gun trained on the DA.

Welsh didn't appear concerned that he might take a bullet. He jumped up on the bed and kept pulling at his arms.

He'd chewed up the paper towel enough to spit most of it out and now his voice howled through the storage room.

He tried to protest with cries, but it sounded more like a wounded wolf baying straight from its throat. The sound more than the fear that Welsh might actually escape pushed Ryan into immediate action.

He leapt for the man.

Welsh had the high ground and he feigned first to his right, then to his left. Ryan jumped in both directions, following him with the gun.

Welsh suddenly tore free from the belt. Now Ryan faced a moose who had the strength to clobber him if it were not for the fact that he'd already taken several very hard knocks to the head.

Then again, raw adrenaline returned all of his strength to him. He clamped his mouth shut and made a break to his right.

His foot caught on one of the metal bedposts and he tumbled through the air—and all Ryan could think was *He's going to cut himself. He's going to break his skin!*

But the man caught himself on a desperately extended foot and staggered upright. He carried his full momentum forward and shot toward the front door like a battering ram.

Now panicked himself, Ryan took chase. He cut the man's angle of flight and reached him just as Welsh's hand reached the door.

Even as Ryan swung he knew that he would probably break the man's skin at the back of his head, but he had no choice, and there was a distinct possibility that BoneMan had meant for him not to break the skin of the bones he broke, which did not include the head.

Thunk!

The gun's butt landed a sickening blow, and Welsh collapsed like a rock.

Ryan stood over him, panting, victorious. But the moment passed almost immediately as his purpose here returned. He was now required to strap the large man at his feet to the blocks of wood on the bed, wrap his bones in the towels, and then break his bones using the sledgehammer.

Welsh moaned. So quickly?

Ryan grabbed one of his legs and dragged the man over to the bed. Working quickly, he set the blocks of wood on the floor, clearing space for Welsh. He hoisted first the man's upper torso, then his legs up onto the bed, then, using rope from the coils, he tied his arms and legs to the four posts.

He stuffed the chewed-up clumps of paper towel into the man's mouth as Welsh began to stir.

Ryan stood back, satisfied that he'd secured his victim to the bed. Above Welsh, the detailed drawings flickered by the lamp's flames. And at the head of the bed the sledgehammer and vise grips waited.

For the first time Ryan was confronted with the task that was now upon him. He'd driven to Austin and taken the father of lies and returned him to this underground chamber prepared by BoneMan, and he'd done it all with near-perfect execution, ignoring all but what was necessary for him to complete his task.

Now he had to break the man's bones. And Ryan was now sure he could not go through with it.

And he was sure that he must.

AUSTIN WAS STILL in a dead sleep at four AM, when Ricki stepped past Burton Welsh's front door and looked at the night. Behind her, bright lights aided a full evidence response team that was dusting for more prints, gathering data on the carpet imprints, photographing the rain residue left by a pair of shoes that had come out of the weather earlier in the night, presumably the killer's. They were still waiting on the results from three sets of prints lifted from the dead bolt an hour earlier and rushed to the lab.

Mort Kracker joined her on the tile landing and pushed aside his long raincoat to shove his hands into his pants pockets. The streets were still wet, but the sky had stopped dumping water on the town and the moon edged broken clouds. By morning the sky would be blue.

"Any word from the lab?" Kracker asked.

"Any minute."

He nodded, frowning. Not too often he would be found on a crime scene at four in the morning, but the kidnapping of the DA wasn't exactly a common occurrence. A bulletin had already been circulated to the networks—the FBI now believed that the BoneMan had forcibly abducted Austin DA Burton Welsh from his home in the Spanish Oaks subdivision, west of Austin. New evidence suggested that the perpetrator may have been driving a black Ford Taurus and was last seen headed south on Highway 71.

"The town's going to explode in the morning," Ricki said.

"That is the hope. The more eyes we have, the more likely we'll catch a break."

She nodded. "Something doesn't sit right."

"Nothing like stating the obvious."

"No, I mean with Ryan Evans."

"We'll know soon enough," her boss said in his deep baritone voice.

"No . . . not whether this was Evans but whether this is the same killer involved in the seven cases we investigated two years ago."

"I would have thought this moves us closer to that possibility, not farther away."

"Except that this isn't BoneMan's style. He wouldn't leave his fingerprints on the dead bolt. He wouldn't have slopped in with wet feet. BoneMan is a precise, classically calculating serial killer. This"—she nodded at the broken glass—"this is a crime of passion."

"Isn't that the point with MPD? Different personalities?"

"Personalities, maybe. But methods as well?"

"Now you're splitting hairs, Valentine. Look, I'm no expert on MPD, not sure how much I even accept it all, but I know enough to conclude that it's messed up. As in not neat. This isn't a precise science. All the evidence we have now points to Ryan being involved on some level. We haven't been able to establish a single alibi for him in any of the cases; he had the opportunity, the motive, and now, if we're right, he's taken the district attorney."

"And you are right," Mark said, coming up behind

them. "The lab just confirmed that one set of prints matches VICAP's file on Captain Ryan Evans."

She'd expected nothing else, but the finality of it gave her one less thing to worry about.

"We haven't established an alibi in part because we haven't been able to interview the suspect," she said, pushing the issue with Kracker. "All the evidence we have is circumstantial."

"Until now."

She nodded. He had a point. "Until now."

"Whether Evans is the BoneMan we investigated two years ago or some nutcase who snapped in the desert and is now imitating those who broke him hardly matters right now. What does matter is that he took Welsh and probably took his daughter. Our first priority is to bring them both back alive. Looks to me like he's getting sloppy. Let's hope and pray he's left a trail we can follow this time."

Ricki's phone vibrated in her pocket. She pulled it out, saw that the priest was on the line. He'd heard already?

She stepped over to the railing and accepted the call. "Father Hortense. You're up early."

"I have a message," he said. His voice was tight and low, and she knew immediately that BoneMan had made contact.

She turned and made eye contact with Kracker. "What did he say?"

"He told me to tell you he was going after the father of lies," Hortense said.

"He *asked* you to make this call?"

"And he insisted that no one look for him until first light. BoneMan will be watching, and if anyone comes before morning, they'll all die. He said to look seven miles south of Menard."

The phone against her ear fell silent.

"Did he tell you who the father of lies was?"

"No. I assumed he meant BoneMan."

"Ryan Evans took Burton Welsh from his home a couple of hours ago, Father. I think he just told us where he took him."

"He's a desperate man," Hortense said. "I strongly suggest you hold back till first light."

26

"STOP IT! STOP moving. I can't do this with you jerking all around like this!"

The district attorney stared up at him with bulging round eyes and screamed into the strip of cloth Ryan had torn from his shirt and stuffed into his mouth. He couldn't hear what the man was trying to say, but he didn't need any auditory confirmation of what was already painful obvious.

Welsh didn't like what was happening to him.

It had taken Ryan a full hour to prepare the man, in part because handling a two-hundred-pound piece of protesting muscle wasn't an easy task; in part because Ryan had to retreat into himself often in search of calm and reasoning, which to this point he'd done with only partial success by shutting down his emotions.

He kept telling himself that he wouldn't kill the DA. He *couldn't*. He wouldn't. But he couldn't stop.

If he was God, perhaps he could swoop out of the sky and save Bethany without hurting a soul. But he wasn't

God. He kept telling himself that this was a war between him and BoneMan and the prize was his daughter.

Welsh was collateral damage.

But he couldn't kill the man. He wouldn't.

And he couldn't not save Bethany.

Once having secured the man spread-eagle to the metal bedposts using the nylon rope, Ryan had decided that he could no longer afford to knock him out with blows to the head. He wasn't a doctor, but he had been exposed to hundreds of cases involving various forms of forced inter- rogation and he knew that there was a limit to how much blunt-force trauma the human brain could take before it suddenly turned itself off.

The drawings on the wall provided step-by-step in- structions on how BoneMan intended for him to proceed. There were apparently two hundred and six bones in the adult human body—three hundred and fifty in a child, but many fused together as the child grew.

The bones were divided into the two primary systems, the axial skeleton, or trunk, and the appendicular skel- eton, or limbs. The former was of no concern to Ryan. His task was to break portions of the appendicular skeleton.

Of the two hundred and six bones in human body, fifty- two made up the feet and fifty-four made up the hands, placing over half of all bones in hands and feet. The smallest of all bones was the stirrup in the inner ear, the largest, the femur, or thigh bone.

BoneMan had drawn a full human skeleton on the back wall, arms spread wide on what appeared to be a crude cross. He'd labeled all the major bones, starting with the skull and working down. The maxilla, the mandible to form a jaw. Vertebrae, clavicles, scapulae, ribs forming the upper torso. Pelvis and sacrum forming the hips. And that was it except for the limbs.

The arms, legs, hands, and feet were covered in much greater detail. These seemed to be BoneMan's fixation.

Start here with pliers he'd written in chalk, then he'd drawn a long arrow to the skeleton's front teeth.

Then here and he'd drawn another arrow to an inset that magnified the right hand.

Ask him to stay calm or it will hurt more. It will be easier after he passes out.

Then, break wrist first, as it's most painful. Scaphoid fracture.

There was also a detailed drawing that showed how to break the thumb so as to collapse the hand, but leaving the victim with continued mobility in the rest of the hand, thus BoneMan's insistence that he begin with the scaphoid fracture.

Ryan had repeatedly tried to gain Welsh's cooperation so that he could snap off his front teeth, but getting him to open his jaw proved almost impossible, and he'd given up after several attempts.

Instead, he focused on the wrists. The breaking of teeth was too barbaric. Then again, breaking any bone was barbaric.

As was war, he told himself. As was any war in which any innocent man died. This was no different. No different. That's what he told himself as he struggled to keep his emotions in check, his mind on the task, his daughter's face in mind.

Refusing to break Welsh's bones was tantamount to killing his daughter.

Unfortunately the wrist bones weren't proving to be

much easier than the teeth. Leverage was important because, pound for pound, human bone was the strongest natural substance known to man. Stronger than steel, four times stronger than reinforced concrete, thanks to a mineral called calcium phosphate and a protein called collagen. The pressure required to break healthy bone was far greater than most people realized.

Evidently, as BoneMan pointed out on the wall, the human skeleton was designed to transfer shock distally to proximal skeletal structures. A direct blow to the palms is actually transferred up the arm and is more likely to break the collarbone than the wrist. The body seemed to know that a broken collarbone heals much more easily than a broken wrist. Thus, he must not use the sledge to break the scaphoid, or he might just end up breaking the collarbone. He needed to break it with leverage.

And if one didn't apply just the right amount of pressure at the right angle when applying leverage, he was more likely to break the radius bone, which would complicate any subsequent fracture of the wrist bones because, as BoneMan put it, your leverage will be shot.

Ryan stepped back and tried to calm the jitter in his hands. He'd stripped the man of all but his boxer shorts and then strapped his right arm down on two blocks of wood with a six-inch gap between them.

The gap was important, the notes claimed. Too wide a gap, and the bones would separate when broken and tear the skin. Too narrow, and the sledgehammer wouldn't be able to snap the bone.

Burton Welsh lay shaking and spent, having wasted the majority of his energy by thrashing against his restraints over the last hour. A heavy coat of sweat covered his heaving chest and belly. He closed his eyes and began to sob into the cloth. The man's closely shaven neck was lined with thin trails of dirt; his neatly trimmed hair soaked and plastered to his skull now. Clear snot ran from both of his nostrils.

The only way Ryan managed thus far was to keep an image of Bethany at the forefront of his consciousness. He made no attempt to foster anger or bitterness toward this man for trying to step into his role as father and husband. He simply held this man's life next to the life of his daughter and chose to sacrifice him over Bethany.

He would simply do what was needed to reclaim his daughter. No compromise. No hesitation.

Yet he was hesitating.

The idea of following the drawings on the wall was one thing, but as he'd learned in the last half hour, manually contorting another man's arm until the wrist snapped was an entirely different thing.

Kahlid had possessed the strength to snap innocent bones for what he perceived to be the salvation of many mothers and daughters in his country.

Likewise, Ryan possessed the strength to fracture Burton Welsh's scaphoid bone, but he was having trouble summoning that strength.

Worse, he was finding it more and more difficult to remember why breaking the man's scaphoid was the only way to save his daughter from a similar fate.

Yes, of course . . . in exchange for breaking the man's bones, not necessarily killing him, BoneMan would extend his daughter's life. It was a very simple proposition.

Orange light from the lamp silently flickered on the concrete walls, illuminating the numerous drawings, obviously made with great care over the course of at least several hours.

BoneMan was a decent artist.

Outside, the sun was inexorably climbing toward the horizon. The FBI would be coming. And if they arrived before Ryan had complied with BoneMan's demands, Bethany would suffer more than she already had.

His own arms and hands dripped with sweat. He wiped them on one of the towels, then wiped his face and his neck so that he wouldn't drip over the man when he resumed the position the drawings instructed him to take if he wanted to fracture the scaphoid cleanly.

Ryan dropped his right knee on the back of Welsh's forearm and grabbed a foot-long dowel that he'd taped to the man's palm, as instructed.

Welsh began to sob loudly, even before any pressure had been applied. He struggled against the arm restraints, but what little strength he still had proved no match for Ryan's knee.

He twisted the dowel so that most of the force that came from bending the hand back would be concentrated on the scaphoid.

Then he pulled back with as much strength as he could summon.

For an extended moment the man's muscle and connective tissue and bone demonstrated why this particular part of the body was so difficult to break, however small.

Ryan's own resolve began to break before the bone did. No matter what reason he brought to bear on the situation, the experience of brutally violating an innocent man in this manner brought with it a severe case of revulsion.

Nausea rolled up his stomach and chest and for a brief moment he was sure he would throw up.

Pop.

A bone in the wrist snapped and now Welsh began to scream bloody murder. Ryan released the wood dowel and staggered off the man. He'd broken his wrist?

Welsh stopped screaming and lay still. He'd fainted.

Ryan's heart crashed in his chest, pumping blood through his neck and ears like a massive hydraulic piston, and his hands shook at his sides, and the flame licked at the walls, but otherwise the room lay perfectly still.

He'd broken the man's bone. And now he should break his fingers and both of his arms and both of his legs as instructed by the drawings. He should do it now, while the man was out.

He already had the man's right arm wrapped in towels, bridging the gap between two blocks of wood. He should break it.

How would BoneMan know? He hadn't seen any closed-circuit camera. There was no indication that he was being watched from a hole in the concrete; he'd examined the walls already. Up to this point he'd trusted that his adversary would know, but now that he'd taken this step and actually broken Welsh's bone, he dearly hoped BoneMan wouldn't let him down!

The sun would soon rise. Father Hortense had made the call. It had been a mistake to tell him, but one now out of his control.

He leapt over to the wall and hefted the heavy sledgehammer.

A ring cut through the room. The ring of a phone.

He released the hammer and dropped to his knees. The

cell phone had been taped to the underside of the bed's metal springs. He reached under, tore at the tape, and ripped it free.

Shoved the receiver to his ear, still on his knees.

"Hello?"

"Hello, Father. How are we doing?"

Ryan tried to stand but couldn't, so he sank to one leg.

"Is he unconscious?"

Ryan glanced around, wondering if he was being watched. "Yes."

"You please me," the man said. "I wasn't sure you had what it took. Did you enjoy it?"

"I . . . where are you? What am I supposed to do?"

"I thought I made that clear. Are you losing focus?" He could hear the man's steady breathing. "Perhaps I could . . . help you focus."

"No. No, that's not necessary. I'm focused."

"When you're finished breaking ten of his bones like the drawings show, I want you to leave him there and re-turn to the place of the crows. If you've been a good fa-ther, I'll bring you in and let you see Bethany. Would you like that?"

"Yes." Rage, the kind of bitter rage that wipes away all reason, clouded his mind.

"Then you'd best be hurrying. She's waiting for you. Remember, seven days. I'm going to do it Sunday at dawn."

"I . . . I can't kill him. I can't do this."

Silence.

"You can't make me do this!" he cried.

When BoneMan spoke his voice had softened and he sounded tired, even exhausted.

"I'm sorry."

Click.

"No, wait! Wait, I didn't mean—"

But the line was dead.

Ryan sat with the phone pressed to his ear for a full thirty seconds without being able to muster the strength to move. He knew he'd just crossed a line but he couldn't bring himself to consider the cost of his mistake.

He slowly pushed himself to his feet, set the cell phone on the bed, picked up the sledgehammer, and approached Burton Welsh's unconscious form.

"FORTY MILES WEST of your current location." The radio crackled in Ricki's lap. She couldn't see the helicopter that relayed the information to them because the sky was still dark despite a graying line on the western horizon. The clock read 6:07 AM.

"We have a dark-colored sedan, I repeat we can see a dark-colored sedan parked at the bottom of a small quarry near the switching station in question."

A pause.

"Do you want us to go in and take a look?"

Ricki lifted the transmitter and keyed the talk button. "No, hold on that." To Mark who was driving: "How long?"

"Twenty-five minutes."

"Make it fifteen."

"I'm not sure the old Buick will do more than a hundred."

She switched back to the radio. "I need you to stay back. Copy that? I don't want anyone on the ground to know they've been spotted."

"Copy that. But if they're outside, they've already heard us."

282 TED DEKKER

"Then back off. Get out of there."

"Roger that."

She set the radio back down, studied the graying sky dead ahead. A farmhouse sat in predawn slumber off the road. She remembered a similar country house, peaceful and sleeping, ten years earlier. Approaching the house you could see nothing out of place, certainly nothing that indicated the kind of tragedy hidden by the four white walls of the Heath homestead. Inside they'd found four dead bodies, two of whom were the parents of the seventeen-year-old daughter who'd agreed to help her manipulative boyfriend kill her family because they had forbidden her to see him.

It happened. It happened all around the country, all the time. Typically not as dramatic as the Heath slayings, but signs of society's evils just the same. Bruised faces, strung out druggies, torn hearts . . .

On January 1, 2008, for the first time in history, a full one percent of all Americans were locked behind bars (one in every 99.1 persons, to be precise). The number had shocked those who took the time to consider its magnitude because America did a wonderful job of hiding its ugly underbelly.

No one wanted to look at the common evils of society. Very few were willing to put aside their own pursuit of happiness long enough to consider the effects of greed and jealousy around them. From what she'd seen, humans were essentially troubled. For every one behind bars, another ten deserved to be behind bars, but that would put one in ten Americans behind bars.

So what do you do? You focus on the big ones and let the rest go. You put a killer like BoneMan in front of them and they went ballistic, but BoneMan was really only the tip of the iceberg, and agents like Ricki had to learn to bear that burden on their own.

They wound around a rare corner and she looked to her right to watch the two black Lincoln Continentals careening behind them. The train extended back to the seven highway patrol vehicles that flew around the corner, lights flashing in silence.

"Would you say it's morning?"

"First light," Mark said. "I think this counts. Hard to believe that we're actually going to find anything after all this time. You know you hound someone for years and they never give you a peek. Then you get one phone call and it's all over."

"Somehow I doubt that," she said. "You're forgetting that the phone call came from him. Why is BoneMan leading us to himself?"

"Because he's not the same BoneMan we went after two years ago."

ACCORDING TO THE stamp on the side of the sledge-hammer, it weighed seven pounds. How hard did you have to swing a seven-pound hammer to break the ulna and radius without forcing their jagged edges through the skin?

This was the question that clawed at Ryan's mind as he stood over Burton Welsh's heaving body.

The man had been wakened by Ryan's second blow, which had bounced off his forearm (the first had missed entirely). He'd given up on the screaming and now just glared up at Ryan, breathing hard.

"Sorry," Ryan said. "I don't want to do this."

The man yelled something that approximated a string of curse words, then settled back to his heavy breathing.

"I only have to break ten bones," he said. "I have to do it, I don't have a choice, he has my daughter."

Another string of curse words.

Ryan considered his predicament again, for the hundredth time, searching for any way around breaking these bones, but all of his reasoning ended in the same place. BoneMan was going to kill Bethany. The only way to possibly stop him was to hurt this man.

And morning was coming, maybe here.

He lifted the sledge to his shoulder and lined it up with Welsh's arm. If he stepped back and just took a full natural swing, he would hit the ceiling, and even if he didn't, he would likely smash the arm. Instead he had to line up the sledge and drop it with more force than the last time.

His arms shook. What was a broken bone? What was just one broken bone in the grand scheme of things? What was just one broken bone next to his daughter's life?

But Ryan couldn't stop his shaking, which now began to spread to his legs. He was suddenly terrified that if he didn't swing now, he might lose his resolve altogether. He might not be strong enough to save his daughter.

Pushed now by panic, he began to scream as he stood at the ready over the man's arm.

And when the scream began to run out of air, he closed his eyes and he swung the sledgehammer with all of his might.

"LEFT."

Mark turned left on Highway 83 and flew south, followed by the black Continentals and the cruisers with flashing lights. They drove in silence now, drawing closer, ever closer to the quarry the air patrol had identified as the likely target.

Cornstalks rose on both sides of the two-lane road, late-fall feed variety that looked gray in the growing light. It could be any lazy fall morning and no one would be the wiser that somewhere, someone was in trouble.

A young child prostitute in Bangkok.

A village of mothers in Afghanistan.

A district attorney in Texas.

Her radio crackled. "You're approaching the road."

The first two would have no cavalry to come to their rescue.

She was Burton Welsh's cavalry.

"Here, here!"

She pointed to the cockeyed sign that read LANDERS LANE, and Mark swung the Buick onto a dirt road, cutting between the fields.

They blasted over gravel, sending clouds of dust back into the cars that followed.

"Okay, slow down. You're about two hundred yards out. The quarry is to the right of the switching station."

Ricki keyed the radio. "Okay. Mark and I are first in. We're going for the door as soon as we've established close-in perimeter. I need a team on the car, clear it, then we go."

"Copy that," said Roger Clemens, with the tactical unit.

Mark brought the Buick to a slow crawl as they drove up to the fence surrounding the huge transformers and electric poles that made up the switching station.

"Follow the sign," Ricki said, voice low even though there really was no need for quiet.

He guided the car into a shallow quarry and the lights
played over the black Taurus parked at the center. The sky
was now gray and getting brighter by the minute, but the
sun hadn't yet broken the horizon.

"Hold up."

He shoved the stick into park and they both stepped
out into the cool morning air. Dust roiled past them as
the cars came to a stop behind them, forming a wide
arch across the quarry.

No sign of life from the car.

All eyes were now on the door that led into what the
electric company had identified as an unused storage
shed.

Ricki slipped a nine-millimeter Glock from her shoulder harness and covered the door as she waited for the rest
of the team to take their positions. The precaution would
cost them a few seconds, but it was well worth the delay
in any unknown situation, and this qualified.

Mark spoke in a whisper. "Ready."

She moved forward on the balls of her tennis shoes, not
bothering to crouch. More important to keep her barrel
trained on the door in the event that it flew open.

But it didn't fly open.

A soft wail, the sound of a man weeping, came to her
from beyond the door now. A chill washed down her
back. It sounded like a wounded animal. Maybe it wasn't
a man.

Mark reached the door just ahead of her, gripped the
handle, and, after a quick nod from her, threw it wide to
offer her a full view of the interior.

She stepped in, gun trained and ready, finger pressing
lightly on the trigger. Mark was already there beside her.

The first moment into a crime scene was always a moment stuffed with adrenaline and heightened sensitivity. You never knew if you would meet a slug, a victim, or a vacant room. None of them were particularly good outcomes, which made the moment of truth an unpleasant one, regardless.

No exception here; Ricki saw it all in less than a second and felt her stomach sink.

Orange light showed a nearly naked man whom she recognized as Burton Welsh strapped to a metal bed. His legs were stretched between two bedposts as was one of his arms.

The other was wrapped in a towel and cinched down to two blocks of wood. The forearm was folded between the blocks at an obscene angle. The DA's chest rose and fell, but he lay unconscious.

On the floor lay another man, facedown, hugging what appeared to be a large sledgehammer, weeping. "No, no, no, no . . ."

The man turned his tear-streaked face slowly toward her and stared up, disoriented. This was Ryan Evans.

"I can't." Tears streamed down his knotted face. "I can't do it. I can't."

He just kept saying that, and Ricki's heart broke.

Mark stepped past her, gun on the man's head. "Not a muscle, boy."

27

BETHANY LAY ON the bed, curled up on her side, shaking from the cold. It wasn't really that cold, she knew, but her skin had gone prickly a few hours ago and nothing she did seemed to stop the shivers.

Thing of it was, she'd been strong up to this point. She'd kept her head stretched just above the pool of fear and breathed as calmly as she could, careful to process as much information as she could.

Like father, like daughter. And she hated him for making her like him.

Then again, if she'd been more like Celine, she'd be a puddle of flesh now, overwhelmed by emotion.

Days had passed, she didn't know how many, but she did know that each passing hour lessened the chances of her being found alive in this tomb. How long could the human body go without eating? She'd seen a show on it once, a movie about the guy who'd starved to death in Alaska after trying to find himself by disappearing. Had it been days or weeks? She couldn't seem to remember. But he'd had water, right? She hadn't had food or water for a long time; hadn't felt the need to relieve herself for just about as long.

Even her tears had stopped flowing.

These were the least of her problems. The fact of the matter wasn't what she was or wasn't doing here in this concrete room. It was who had placed her here.

That was the issue. That was the problem.

That was what had been gnawing at her as the minutes crawled by and became hours without any change. And knowing a little about her captor, even without having seen him yet, she was sure that her being alone with the dread of knowing his identity was the whole point.

BoneMan was leaving her alone to break her down and it was working.

First her mind. But then her body. He was going to break her bones as he'd broken the bones of the other girls.

Why? Because he was who he was and she was who she was. And really, the more she thought about it, they weren't nearly as different as she might have once thought.

She hated him for who he was and she hated herself for being the kind of person he wanted.

Thoughts of suicide had come and gone over the days, but whenever she came close to convincing herself that running full speed into the wall with her head lowered would solve all of this, she learned that she didn't want to die yet. In fact, that was the whole point. If she didn't care, she wouldn't be so tormented, lying here thinking of the sick coward who'd taken her.

There was one thing that gave her hope. Only one that she could put her finger on, anyway. That was her anger.

She discovered while lying in complete silence that when herself-pity turned to anger her heart beat stronger, and when her heart beat stronger she wanted to live longer. It would make her stand and pace on occasion, clenching her hands into fists.

Her survival all came down to who BoneMan really was and who she really was, and how she could relate to the man.

When Bethany thought of him, of what she would like to do to him if he were sitting on the floor right now and she had a gun or a rock—they wouldn't be able to recognize him after she got through with him.

But his sitting down and handing her a gun so that she could shoot bullets into his face was about as likely as her growing teeth that could bite through the wall and tunnel to freedom.

More likely was that BoneMan would eventually walk into the room and begin preparations to break her bones. Until then, Bethany was powerless. When he came to her, she would change who she was so that he would find her unsuitable.

Or she would try to help him change who he was so that he no longer had the need to use her in the way he intended.

She'd spend endless hours thinking about what a sixteen-year-old girl could do to make the match between her and her abductor a bad match. His needs weren't sexual, she knew that from the news reports two years earlier. It was at least something to build on.

He wanted to be needed. Isn't that what they all wanted? The pain of not being wanted drove him to this. She could at least understand that part of him.

Or maybe revenge was driving him. Maybe his mother had beat him or kept him in a closet and only fed him on weekends. She'd decided long ago that this must be at least partially correct. Something had happened to the man as a child to make him the kind of person he was.

Maybe his father had abandoned him. It had happened to her. She hadn't stooped to this level, nor could she.

How far could someone go to be accepted and loved?

Or maybe he was trying to teach society a lesson. A crusader on the warpath, striking down girls to make a point that somehow made him feel like a hero. Justifying himself, and ultimately feeling needed as a result.

Or maybe he was just plain sick in the head and did this all for fun, like a child who lights the tails of cats on fire for fun.

It made her wonder what made people do evil things in the first place. Why did some bullies beat up on dogs? Why did fathers walk out on their daughters? Why did thieves shoot gas-station attendants in the head? Why did pimps prostitute girls younger than she was? Why did politicians hate those who got in their way?

In the end it was all about being needed. Being wanted.

Bethany moaned, rolled slowly over so that her left arm was under her body, and pushed herself up. Dizziness spun the room and she sat still for a moment until it passed, then lowered her feet to the floor.

Dirt from the mattress had smudged her blue plaid flannel pajama bottoms and turned her white T-shirt a light gray brown.

As odd as it might seem, perhaps her greatest desire now was for BoneMan to walk into the room and make his intentions clear. Until then, she was left with her own crumbling mind and she didn't know how much longer she could take it.

She'd been telling herself that since the first time she'd woken up here. But something had begun to change these last few hours. The anger that had given her a small amount of hope had started to fade, replaced by a sense of being totally alone. Forgotten even. Abandoned.

The feeling was what destitute must feel like. What if not even BoneMan came for her?

What if no one really cared if she lived or died; only that BoneMan be stopped?

What if all of her hopes and dreams and aspirations ended in a slow, mocking death in this oversized tomb?

Or what if . . .

A scrape outside stopped her thoughts. Her heart thumped harder in her chest. Could have been a rodent, or the wind, or her imagination.

But then the sound came again. Soft footfalls on a concrete hall.

She stood and stared at the door. Then quickly sat back down. Maybe she should lie down. What would please him, to find her standing and alert, sitting and patient, or curled up on the bed, exhausted?

She instinctively wiped her face, thinking it was probably dirty. She should have made an attempt to at least look presentable.

Presentable? What was she thinking?

Bethany sat down, folded her hands in her lap, and waited for BoneMan to open the door.

28

THEY STOOD AROUND the room, glaring and pacing, refusing to entertain that anything Ryan had to say could be something as simple as the truth. The interrogation room was outfitted with a single white table, six lightweight folding chairs set haphazardly about the table, and a large one-way window that allowed authorities to watch undetected from the adjacent room. A black television stared at him from a cart along the far wall.

The only other fixtures in the room were the people, who'd come and gone over the past hour. At the moment they consisted of one uniformed officer who stood in the corner; Ricki Valentine, the FBI agent whom Father Hortense had called; her boss, a man named Mort Kracker. And the district attorney, Burton Welsh, who'd just been released from the hospital and paced on the far end like a bull who saw only red. They'd told him he had no business being here less than twelve hours after suffering a broken arm, but angered bulls apparently didn't listen to doctors.

The DA had held a news conference in which he'd

come off like a war hero who'd broken out of a prison camp and single-handedly ended the war by delivering to justice the tyrant who'd terrorized them all.

Ryan knew that he was facing impossible odds, that besides the DA's arm nothing had broken his way, that even his frantic pleading and explaining now worked against him.

Within minutes of the FBI's entrance into the storeroom, he'd made his case abundantly clear through pleas for understanding. He couldn't do it. He couldn't kill an innocent man, no matter what was at stake. And that was a problem, see, because Bethany was at stake! They had to stop BoneMan.

But his urgency had fallen on deaf ears and he'd shut down, mind set on the hope, however thin, that he could still get to BoneMan by making his appointment.

His choices were limited. He could either go quietly behind bars and wait for an attorney to make his case while Bethany paid the price for his failure to meet BoneMan's demands.

Or he could make someone in this room believe and look for a way out.

"I don't think you understand how implausible this sounds," Kracker said, eyeing him with an arched brow. He tapped his cheek with a thoughtful finger. "If you've done all of this at the demand of this so-called other BoneMan, why would you jeopardize your daughter's life by calling Father Hortense? I would think you'd do exactly what he required you to do."

"Have you ever tried to break a man's bones, sir?"

"Okay, so you had trouble going through with it. But why call Father Hortense?"

"Isn't that the question I should be asking you?" Ryan demanded. "Why would I? Aren't you listening to a word I'm saying here? I have until morning to get to him. You have me trapped here while the real monster is out there with my daughter."

"The only reason we didn't put a bullet between your eyes when we had the chance was because you're the only one who knows where Bethany is," the DA spat through an ugly frown. "Don't press your luck."

Ryan slammed his handcuffed hands on the table. "I . . . am not . . . BoneMan!"

The DA was around the table and had his good hand on Ryan's collar before anyone could react. He jerked his face close so that Ryan could feel his breath. "I should break your neck right now, you slimy worm. I was there, remember?"

Ricki stepped up and pulled the man to one side. "Back off, Mr. Welsh."

He whirled on her like a wounded bear.

But she didn't back down. "We didn't put a bullet between his eyes because that would make us the killer, now wouldn't it?" she said. "He hasn't been convicted yet, no need to throw the switch."

"Convicted?" The DA released his collar. "This man took me from my home, knocked me out, broke my wrist, took a sledgehammer to my arm, and would have broken every bone in my body if he hadn't been stopped."

"But he was stopped, sir," she snapped. "And we're here to try to understand *why* he was stopped. Why he called the priest. Why he didn't just finish the job as BoneMan would have two years ago."

"Because he was *stopped*!" the man shouted. "Or is that too much for your small head to comprehend?"

"You're hurt," she said, challenging his fierce stare with her own. "But please don't use it as an excuse to sound small. I'm not excusing what the suspect did, I'm only pointing out that he may not be the same man who killed the seven victims we found two years ago. We don't have enough evidence to determine if he's an original or simply copying BoneMan due to his ordeal in the desert. Or, for that matter, a wounded father who's doing exactly what he claims he's doing."

Welsh took a step toward the FBI agent. "I was there. I looked into his eyes. There is no doubt in my mind who he is, and I assure you, when I'm done with a jury, there'll be no doubt in their minds. Do not try to stand in my way."

"Enough!" Kracker said. "We're on the same side here. Just step back, Burt."

The DA looked at the FBI boss, then reluctantly stepped away. "All I care about at this moment is saving that girl." He shoved a thick finger back at Ryan. "And he knows where she is."

Ryan sat back and spoke slowly, enunciating his words as if they contained the brittle truth. "You're about as dense as they come, Mr. Welsh. BoneMan called you the father of lies, and he wants you dead because he believes everything about you is a lie, beginning with your supposed love for Bethany."

Ricki blinked. "He told you that?"

He had to step lightly here. "Not all of it."

"He is *him*!" Welsh said. The DA swore. He placed a painkiller into his mouth and swallowed without water. He eased into one of the chairs at the end of the table.

"He wants you dead," Ryan said. "And he's out there.

You willing to gamble your life on the certainty that I'm BoneMan?"

No one took him up on the challenge and he pressed while he had them listening, focusing in on Ricki, who seemed to be the closest thing to an advocate in the room.

"You have to let me go."

Hearing it himself he knew this was wasted breath. He'd failed to comply with BoneMan's demands and now Bethany would pay the price. His chest began to tighten, restricting his breathing, but he was able to close his eyes and ease the beginnings of panic.

"He's expecting me." Ryan opened his eyes and looked at Ricki. "I can still save her."

"Where?"

"I . . ." He couldn't tell them, because any hint of police involvement would only end any hope he had of saving Bethany. They would go to the Crow's Nest, and BoneMan would know he'd talked, and then they would find his daughter's broken body.

"I can't tell you. He'll kill her, you know that. You can put a trace on me or find some other way to track me. But you have to let me go and meet him—he was very clear about that."

"If you think we're stupid enough to actually release you . . ." Welsh appeared too flabbergasted to finish his thought.

The door opened, but Ryan kept his eye locked on the DA. "You steal my wife. You steal my daughter. And now you're just going to stand by while that freak murders her?"

"I'm trying to save your daughter," Welsh said. "From you."

"Where have you put her?" It took Ryan a fraction of a second to make the switch from the DA to Celine's voice.

He turned his head. She stood in the doorway, dressed in a lime green skirt, a white silk blouse with a wide black belt, and black heels. Her stare was dark and flashed like a steel blade, giving her the appearance of hawk intent on its prey.

But she was his wife and Ryan hadn't fully accepted, much less understood, their divorce. Seeing her standing with her arms crossed, glaring at him, he felt momentarily overwhelmed by both his own sense of belonging and outright rejection.

This was the woman he'd wed over eighteen years ago. They'd moved into a half-dozen homes and raised a child together. He'd devoted himself to providing for his wife and child, and she'd devoted herself to mothering, and although they'd both failed a thousand times, they still belonged on the same journey they'd sworn to take together eighteen years ago.

But this was also Celine, the woman who had betrayed him not just once or twice or even a hundred times, but as a matter of practice. This was Celine, the woman who had allowed the predator to his right into their family, like a wolf.

This was Celine who hated him and very likely everyone who didn't love her the way she wanted to be loved, including Bethany, though she would never admit it.

She lowered her crossed arms and walked up to the table. "Where did you put my daughter, you pig?"

Her voice was cold and low and it cut through his chest so that he found he couldn't respond.

"Tell me!" she screamed. "Tell me where you have her!"

"I don't have her!" How could his wife accuse him of such a thing?

They said that absence makes the heart grow fonder. In Ryan's case, two years of absence culminating in a brutal encounter in the desert and the discovery too late that another man had stolen all that was precious to him had gilded his memories of Celine. She was at once a witch and a goddess.

But backed into his corner Ryan forgave her all her wickedness and embraced what hope the mother of his daughter could offer.

The realization that his own wife believed that he had the capacity to turn against their own daughter shut his mind completely off for a moment.

He couldn't think. So he just yelled what he'd already said.

"I didn't take our daughter!"

"Stop it!" she cried, on the verge of tears now. She waved the bandaged hand that BoneMan had broken. "Stop all of this lying! Don't you have any feelings at all? How can you be so cold?"

"I . . . I'm trying to save her."

"Trying to *save* her? You left her fifteen years ago! You think anyone actually believes this? That you would come in to save your daughter after being gone her entire life? That suddenly you would become the perfect father and move mountains to save her? You *abandoned* her!"

He couldn't stand to hear the accusations because he knew that some of them were true. He'd left Bethany . . .

If only he could relive the last fifteen years he would stay close and watch over her like an eagle. He'd sleep outside her door at night, he would set the table and feed her a feast before she left for school.

He would meet her for lunch whenever she wanted and talk to her teachers and invite her friends over every afternoon just so that he could be near her.

He would go without clothes to afford the best fashions that would tell everyone who passed her on the street, *There goes the daughter of Ryan Evans who loves her more than he loves his own life.*

He would attend all of the football games and cheer along with her at the top of his lungs, and he'd go get her a hot dog at halftime so she could stay at the side of the field with the other cheerleaders.

If only he could live his life again . . .

But he couldn't. He could only live his life now, and right now his daughter wasn't sleeping in bed or waking for breakfast in the morning or walking through the halls of her school while the boys watched.

Right now Bethany was in the hands of a monster and he would die before he allowed that monster to touch one hair on her head.

But even that was only an idea, because in reality, far more than one hair on her head *had* been touched.

Ryan's mind switched between the accusations being leveled at him by the eyes in this room and a nearly uncontrollable urge to break his chains, plow over whoever stood in his way, and run to where he knew he could find his daughter.

It occurred to him that they were all waiting for his response. Ricki Valentine paced silently, watching him with gentle eyes. Welsh fixed him with a defiant stare. The FBI boss, Kracker, stood brooding.

Celine's mouth was parted in utter contempt. She looked like she'd been forced to swallow a spoonful of mud.

Ryan took a deep breath and clasped his hands under the table. He had to straighten them out. He had to get them on his side. For Bethany's sake.

He looked at Celine and swallowed so that he could speak. "You're right. I haven't always understood what it means to be a father. But that changed in the desert." His voice felt as though it would fail him with each word.

"I saw that I'd abandoned you and Bethany and I vowed to change it all. When they tie you to a chair and force you to watch as they break the bones of innocent children because that's what we're doing to their children. They chose to use BoneMan because he was a high-profile case and they feel like his victims. And so do I. So do we all."

He felt dizzy but forced himself to continue speaking. "But I can't do what they did. That's not me any longer. I could hurt myself to save her, I could hurt BoneMan, but that's it. I'm finally the father I was meant to be, can't you see that?"

"By breaking my finger?" She stabbed that white-wrapped finger at Welsh. "By kidnapping the man I love at gunpoint, stripping him down, and taking a sledgehammer to his arm? Of course. It makes perfect sense now. How could I have been so blind? Just being a good father."

It was too much for Ryan. He bolted to his feet, knocking the table hard as he did so. "I owe her my life!" he cried.

"*Your* life, Ryan, not Burt's life," she snapped back. "You're not God."

He hesitated. "I know that now. So let me go, let me get her. I'm not BoneMan."

They stared at him.

He continued, speaking in a rush while he had their full attention. "Think about it. I learn that Bethany has been taken twenty-four hours after it's happened and you haven't bothered to tell me. Instead, the killer's left me a message demanding that I find him. I admit, I lost control. Then I find out I'm a suspect. But he's waiting for me." Ryan jabbed at the wall. "He's thrown down the gauntlet and I have no choice but to accept his challenge because I can't come to those sworn to protect and serve—no, because you all think I'm *him*, of all things! So I go after him myself."

He looked at Ricki. "How many times do I have to explain this before it starts to make sense to someone in this room?"

"I think the problem is that your explanation is only one of several that could make sense," she said. "And twelve hours ago we found you in a bunker with a hammer in your hands."

"But I'm here, look in my eyes, tell me I'm not telling you the truth. I took the DA only because I was under direct orders to take him, return him to the quarry, and break his bones by daybreak. And I have until morning to let him find me or this is all over. For Bethany's sake, you have to let me go. Then take me, prosecute me, do whatever you like. But give me this one chance." He was talking to Celine now even though she had no authority.

"I'm begging you."

Celine took another step forward, lifted her hand, and slapped his face hard with her good hand.

"You're a sick man twisted by jealousy," she said. "Who do you think you are to violate the man I love? I'm going to do everything in my power to make sure you fry in the electric chair. You hear me? You're dead to me."

She stomped for the door, leaving in her perfumed wake the stunning statement that in her mind, this was all more about her and her new lover than it was about her own daughter.

"Then so is your daughter," Ryan said. "I'm her only hope. You walk away from me and you're walking away from Bethany."

But he knew that her mind was so fogged that she couldn't possibly consider turning back. She exited without another word and was gone.

Ryan sank to his seat, crushed by the weight of the inevitable outcome facing them all. Bethany, his only daughter, whom he loved more than life itself, was going to die a terrible death.

"Get something out of this man or I will," Welsh said, following Celine. "He's scheduled for arraignment first thing in the morning. I trust you can keep him under lock and key until then."

He delivered the scathing indictment and closed the door.

Ryan put his arms up on the table and saw that they were shaking as they did when his emotions overtook his capacity for control. The handcuffs were vibrating. Something about the clasp around his wrist struck a chord deep in his mind.

Perhaps because it symbolized his limitations. A father could only do so much. Or maybe it reminded him of the shackles of humanity, bound by inevitable tragedy that ultimately ended in death.

He was not God. He could not rend the heavens and

sweep aside his enemies to save the lost child who cried out for help. He was a suspect in an interrogation room, shackled by . . .

His mind suddenly filled with one of BoneMan's drawings on the storage room walls. A broken hand.

"Tell me, Ryan," Ricki Valentine said, pulling out a chair opposite him. "Where do the crows fly?"

He looked up. "Sorry?"

"Where did you meet him?"

"You should know, you found me."

"You spent three days in the quarry?"

"Yes." It was a lie, but he couldn't reveal the location of the Crow's Nest yet. Not until or unless he was absolutely sure that there was no other alternative. "What else was I supposed to do? I had to wait for him."

"So your message on the radio told him where you'd be? But he drew you to the quarry? Forgive me being dense, but none of it adds up. Care to help me out?"

"We can get to all of that when we have time. It's already eight o'clock, right? I'm telling you, we're running out of time."

"Captain, if you really think we're going to even consider letting you go you're sadly mistaken," Kracker said, lowering his tall frame into one of the flimsy chairs at the head of the table. He crossed his legs and put both hands on his knee. "If you want to lead us to this so-called meeting point that's one thing. But the fact of matter is, you've committed a felony and the whole world knows it. There's no disputing what we found. You kidnapped a man and physically violated him. That's good for twenty years in prison. I don't think you're appreciating the limitations of your situation."

Ryan looked into Ricki's kind eyes. As much as he

wanted to believe that she would trust him, he knew her hands were tied. She wasn't in a position to help him.

"Ma'am, please, I'm begging you. He's going to kill my daughter unless I show up before sunrise."

"Well, that's a problem, Ryan. I hear you saying that, but I don't hear you telling us where she is. You can appreciate the inconsistency."

"I don't *know* where she is! And if I tell you where he wants me to meet him, he'll know. Can you guarantee me he won't?"

She frowned. "The way I see it, you don't have any good alternatives. Either you tell us and we check it out, and yes, maybe we do tip him off . . ."

"Assuming we find another BoneMan," Kracker added.

Ricki glanced at him. "On the other hand, if you don't tell us and neither you nor we show, he kills her anyway. What am I missing?"

Ryan didn't answer. She was right, but he didn't have to make the call until midnight, which would still give them time to get to Crow's Nest before dawn. Later, if they used a helicopter.

"Not telling us about this meeting point only endangers your daughter's life," Ricki said. "And knowing how you feel about her, I confess I'm confused by your silence. We should be talking about how to get to her, not shutting down."

Unless your knowing endangers her more than your ignorance, he thought.

"I'm sorry, I can't take that risk," he said.

"Because you haven't told us the full truth, have you, Mr. Evans?" Kracker said. "Because maybe, just maybe, you are guilty of taking your own daughter."

"No."

Ricki leaned over the table. "Okay, suppose we were to put an electronic tag on you and let you go. We could follow in a helicopter at a safe distance, say a few miles, and have support on the ground. You would agree to meet BoneMan?"

"Out of the question," Kracker said.

She held up her hand. "Hypothetically."

"If I was sure you wouldn't interfere. It's not just a meeting. I have no idea what he'll want to do. The tag couldn't be a recording device or anything large enough to find if he searched me."

"If he showed, we could sweep in and take him."

"He's too smart for that. How do I know you'd keep your word?"

"She won't keep her word because this is a nonstarter," Kracker said.

"Sir, if you'd just think about our current situation and—"

"I have thought about our current situation!" Kracker stood and walked to the door. "He's escaped us once; the public would go ballistic. The answer is no. End of discussion."

He could see by the bunching of her jaw muscles that Valentine didn't like being summarily shut down, but she let the matter drop.

She pushed her chair back and stood. "Then I suggest you come clean, Mr. Evans. If you're right, time is running out. You may be willing to move heaven and earth to save your daughter, but the fact is I'm the only one who can move anything at this point. And believe it or not, I'm as eager as you are to find Bethany before it's too late."

She turned to exit but turned back at the door. "Please, help me find her. Call me at any time; I'll be waiting." And then she too was gone and Ryan sat alone with the guard in the corner, who studied him silently.

He stared at the handcuffs and he wondered if BoneMan had broken any of Bethany's bones.

The thought made him want to throw up.

29

BETHANY SAT PERFECTLY still, eyes glued to the door latch as it rattled, then slowly lifted. Her heart pounded in her ears, and once again she considered lying down because her captor might be the type who was easily angered by anything less than absolute submission. If so, she would submit.

Or he could be the type who respected strength.

Strength, she decided, and sat still, facing the door as it slowly opened.

The man who walked in was tall with close-cropped hair and deep-set eyes hidden by the dim light that filtered through the cracks in the corners. He wore loose-fitting pants, the kind that had extra pockets on the thigh, and his shirt was tucked in, a normal cotton shirt like the ones worn by mechanics or janitors.

But the man who stared at her from the open doorway was no mechanic, unless you considered doctors to be mechanics, which in a way they were.

This was BoneMan. In his own way he was an orthopedist like Dr. Johnson, who'd set her collarbone two years earlier after she'd fallen during a routine dismount. And although Bethany's hands trembled in her lap, she had every intention of treating him with as much respect as she would show any other doctor.

"Nice of you to finally make it," she said.

Her voice came out tight, obviously emotional, but she could only control her body so much.

"Would you mind switching rooms?"

The question caught her off guard so she stood and answered the only thing that popped into her mind. "Okay."

The man stepped to one side and held out his arm. "Take my hand."

She walked up to him, hesitated for only a moment, then took his large hand. It was soft and cool, not rough like the hands of a man who lifted rocks and mowed lawns for a living.

She was speaking before she had time to really consider her words. "Your hands aren't what I expected," she said.

He just looked at her.

She'd been so eager for this meeting, knowing that her only hope for survival depended on her ability to change either him, herself, or both, that she was rushing into her ploy with far too much energy. He'd see past her actions and label them as manipulation immediately!

"They're soft. It's not the kind of place you expect to find a man who smells like lotion and has soft hands."

"Thank you," the man said.

He held her hand firmly but not forcefully as he led her from the room, down a hall, past a flight of concrete stairs to a door near the end.

"You can relieve yourself in this bathroom. The toilet doesn't flush; I'll have to do it later. I've taken out everything that you could use as a weapon, which is why the workings of the toilet are gone. But at least you'll have privacy." He pushed the door open and walked down the hall, where he turned and looked at her. "Please don't take too long."

She stepped into a small basement bathroom lit by the crack from the door. A single ceramic toilet that looked and smelled as though it might have been cleaned with bleach recently sat along the wall. The room had been stripped of everything else except for a small packet of Kleenex. Even the toilet seat was gone.

BoneMan was not only a clean man, he was a very careful man.

She tried to relieve herself, but the rim of the bowl was cold and her future was uncertain and she couldn't relax. Then again, taking the time to urinate would show him that she wasn't too uncomfortable to maintain her basic bodily functions. She'd already begun to bond with him by showing respect and strength. Relieving herself now would only help her.

So she took her time and finally managed to empty what was left in her bladder.

Satisfied that he knew she still possessed the frame of mind to carry on, she took the packet of Kleenex and stepped into the hall. He stood patiently at the end of the hallway.

"Do you mind if I take these?" she asked, holding up the Kleenex.

"Be my guest. Your room is the one at the end. The door's open."

The thought of going into another room, especially

one already called her room, was terrifying. But Bethany turned on her heels and pushed into the room without showing the slightest fear.

The man walked in behind her and motioned to a metal bed stretched out along the far wall. "Have a seat on the bed."

She obeyed him. He crossed to a lamp that hung from a twelve-by-twelve overhead beam, lit the flame, and blew out the match. Yellow light chased away the darkness from the corners of the room.

The man shut the door, latched it with a padlock, slipped the key into his pocket. This room was twice as large as the one she'd occupied for the last few days, but otherwise very similar, from the bed to the post that rose to the ceiling at the center. Same walls, same ceiling, latticed with brown roots that looked dead or dying.

The only difference was the strange crosslike contraption fixed to the wall to her left. Blocks of wood that looked like they'd been glued or nailed into the concrete behind them. There were gaps between the blocks and they formed an upside down Y with a cross member at the top. She wasn't sure what it was—likely the remains of something that had once been built against the wall.

"My name is Alvin," the man said.

She turned back to him and saw that he was standing with both hands buried in his pants pockets.

"Some people call me BoneMan. I also like to think of myself as Satan. You can call me Alvin, or Satan, but please don't call me BoneMan. It looks fine on paper, but I don't like the sound of it."

This was it, Bethany thought. The time had finally come. She didn't know his plans yet, but they hardly mattered now. What did matter was that she find a way to connect to this monster. To Satan. Alvin.

She was going to make a deal with the devil and he stood before her now with his hands in his pockets, smelling like lotion.

Bethany stood. "What kind of lotion do you use?"

"Noxzema," he said, removing his hands from his pockets.

"Never heard of it."

"My mother used to use it. She gave me my first jar when I was a boy and I've used it every day since. It has medicinal properties that keep the skin smooth. She used to mock me because my skin wasn't smooth like hers but that changed after I used the product. But we're not here to talk about lotion, are we, Bethany."

"No, I suppose not."

"Do you know why I brought you here?"

"To break my bones."

"Then you don't understand yet." He paused, wearing a shallow frown. "Or maybe you're stupid, like the others. If you're stupid then I will have to break your bones."

Bethany walked slowly toward the metal post that rose to the ceiling and placed her hand on it to steady herself.

"I think you know I'm not stupid, Alvin. I'm just at a disadvantage. It's not like you invited me here. I've been waiting for you to explain yourself to me for days now. How am I supposed to know why you brought me here if you refuse to tell me?"

He watched her with deep-set eyes, hands still in his pockets. She'd seen a thousand men like Alvin on the street, at the mall, in the stands at football games, and had never thought twice. But there was a quality deeply, darkly disturbing about the man's eyes.

If she'd seen him in the football stands and made direct eye contact, she would have undoubtedly shivered and certainly never forgotten the look.

It was a look of bottomless evil. His pupils fell into hell. Satan was a fitting name, she thought, and she was unable to suppress another shiver. But her hand was still on the steel post, steadying her, and she doubted he could see just how disturbed she was by his presence.

She had to break his relentless stare. "Well? Are you going to tell me why you brought me here?"

"If you're not stupid, you'll figure it out."

"I've been thinking for a long time and I can't understand why anyone would take someone they don't know from their bed in the middle of the night and lock them in a basement while they wait to break their bones."

It came out like an accusation, and hearing her mistake, she quickly changed tones.

"At least that's what I thought at first. Then I realized that you probably do know me. You probably have a very good reason for doing what you're doing. You're not a lunatic without purpose; you have a very deliberate plan and have killed seven other girls as part of that plan."

He didn't speak. She was talking too much. She needed him to speak. She needed him to feel connected to her so that ultimately he might, however unlikely, reconsider breaking her bones until she was dead.

"I want to understand, Alvin. I really do. None of the others did, but before I die, I want to understand."

The man's hands were by his sides, as if he was unsure what to do with them. When he spoke, he did so softly.

"The other ones I killed quickly. By now half of their bones would be broken and they would be all twisted up on the ground, trying to breathe. But you"—he breathed in through his nose and swallowed hard—"you're different. I hope you realize that."

He was shaking. He stood there five feet from her, looking with those brilliant blue eyes, and he was shivering like she was shivering.

A man and a girl, facing each other in this basement, silently shaking.

"Do you know what your name means?" he asked.

She knew from her theology class at Saint Michael's Academy. A derivative of Elizabeth. "My God is an oath," she said.

"And has your father been good to his promise?"

He was using father and God interchangeably.

"No."

"My mother failed me too. I hate mothers. I hate fathers. They're all liars."

"So we do share some things in common." Her tremors had passed and she was thinking again, and above all she was aware that she shouldn't threaten him by trying to gain control of anything, including the conversation.

He looked at her for a long time, as if trying to judge her sincerity.

"Do you like my eyes?" Alvin asked.

They were beautiful and deeply disturbing at once. "They're pretty."

"So are yours. I like blue eyes."

She shivered involuntarily.

"Would you like to see my skin?" he asked.

What struck Bethany most forcefully now was her lack

of fear in his presence. In a strange way she felt relieved to be with him. It was far better than the uncertainty that had stalked her for days. Standing here with Alvin was oddly comforting. She was going to embrace a part of him, she knew that, and it wasn't as horrifying as she'd imagined it might be.

The man before her was now her means of survival. He was her savior. Alvin was her only hope for life and she clung to it as he might.

"Yes. Yes, Alvin, I would like to see your skin."

He began to unbutton his shirt and when he'd unclasped the last button, he slipped it off, folded it in quarters, and gently laid it on the ground.

Alvin Finch's skin was white. A pasty translucent white that showed the blue veins just beneath the skin that stretched over his shoulders and arms. His chest was smooth and looked strong, though not cut like a body builder's.

There were many things about this moment that might have urged Bethany to begin crying. She was the captive of a man who shaved his whole body, applied lotion, and abducted girls so that he could break their bones. That man had just taken off his shirt and was staring at her with the scariest eyes she had ever looked into. And now he was approaching her. Slowly, like Stephan Hill on that first and last date, when he'd made a pass at her.

But crying was the furthest thing from her mind.

Alvin Finch stopped three feet from her, staring down, breathing steady. She refused to look into his eyes, fixing instead on his chest, which was eye level. The smell of his lotion was both sweet and medicinal and his skin seemed to glow in the flame's light.

She'd once read a series of books about a woman who'd fallen in love with a vampire, and the images of that seduction swept through her mind. But there was no temptation to taste the forbidden fruit here.

There was only revulsion.

A tear slipped down her cheek. She was crying? She couldn't cry! Not here right in front of him. The dark veins etched beneath his skin looked like they were filled with black brine, not red blood. His chest rose and fell, closely shaved, smooth, and the briefest compulsion to reach out and touch it crossed her mind, chased away by fear.

"Do you like it?" the man asked softly.

No, but I want to like it.

Confusion nipped at her mind. She swallowed and said what she knew he wanted her to say.

"Yes."

"I thought it might frighten you."

"It should, shouldn't it?"

"It's nearly perfect. The others were disturbed by me."

There was a sadness in his voice but there was also a soft crackle of anger, she thought. And in that moment she thought she understood Alvin Finch more.

She was in the presence of a powerful man who thought nothing of taking or giving life. A beast, a Lucifer, as he called himself.

Yet he was as needy as she was. Alvin Finch only wanted to be needed. Loved. And absent of either, he resorted to deflecting his pain by killing.

Just like a teenager might resort to deflecting the pain of rejection by cutting. People did a lot of crazy things to be wanted.

"How could anyone be disturbed by your skin?" she asked.

He only breathed. She couldn't make the mistake of sounding patronizing, as mother would say.

"When you force girls from their homes and tie them up, they don't react in reasonable ways," she said. "They would be disturbed by anything."

"Or they were jealous," he said.

She lifted her hand, saw that it was shaking, and lowered it. "Could I touch it?"

It took him a moment to decide. "Yes. Yes, I want you to touch it."

"My hands are shaking. I'm not used to this. I'm nervous."

"It's better that way."

She reached out her trembling hand and touched the flesh above his right nipple. It was cold, and when she traced the tips of her fingers over the skin, she was surprised by how smooth it felt.

For a dizzying moment Bethany felt more wonder than fear. She told herself that it was because she wasn't thinking clearly after being trapped down here for so long. That the sudden comfort she felt by touching his skin was because her mind had been broken by him.

That he broke bones, but more than bones. He broke minds and he'd already started on hers.

But she didn't resist his pull.

"What kind of lotion did you say you use?"

"Noxzema," he said.

There was a connection between them, she thought. He'd chosen her and now in her own way she was choosing him. The seven girls before her had not responded this way.

She ran her fingers over his skin, distracted by the thought that she wasn't repulsed by the feeling. This man had the power to give her life or take it and for the moment she set her mind and emotions on his power to save her.

She lifted her other hand, responding to a strong desire to slide her arms around his large chest and pull him to herself. To beg for his mercy. To vow her companionship.

The emotions were all mixed up and she hated herself for feeling even the slightest attraction but she also knew that her life was at stake.

So she placed both hands on his chest and drew them slowly down his sides.

"Your mother must have known what she was talking about."

He didn't immediately respond, perhaps surprised by her boldness.

"She had very beautiful skin," he said. "I killed her."

Bethany felt a jolt of alarm course through her veins. Of course, that was it. Alvin Finch was jealous of his mother and her skin. She made him feel bad about his failing. Unable to make himself look like her, he even killed her and was killing his mother with each girl he killed.

That's why he called himself Satan. Alvin was Satan, who'd fallen from the grace of the one who'd given him life.

And in her, he'd found someone who understood that betrayal, surely not to the degree that had pushed him to such rage.

"Does your father deserve to die?" he asked.

Bethany looked up into his eyes and let the darkness behind them pull at her.

"He's already dead to me."

"And does he deserve to be dead to you?"

"He was never there. When I was young I used to call out and he was never there to hear me. He's been dead to me for a long time."

"Then would you break his bones?"

She didn't like the direction he was taking her, but she felt powerless to resist. And here with BoneMan, having touched his flesh and understood his rage, she felt she could be brutally honest.

"I try not to think of him."

"Why? Because he angers you?"

"Yes, that's part of it. I don't like the thoughts I have when I think about him."

"What thoughts?"

She shrugged. "Sadness."

"Anger?"

"Yes, some anger."

"Because he abandoned you."

"Yes."

"Then would you break his bones?"

She wanted him to stop these questions so she said what he wanted her to say.

"Yes."

"Then you know how I feel."

She was surprised to see a tear snake down his right cheek. There was a bond between them. Surely he hadn't done this with the other girls.

Encouraged and even a little hopeful, Bethany slowly slid her hands over his sides toward his back, aware of the gooseflesh that now covered his skin.

"What do you want from me, Alvin?" she asked softly.

He was breathing heavily and his flesh was quivering under her fingertips.

"What will make you happy?" she asked.

He lifted his hands, gripped her wrists in a steel-like vise grip, and pulled them off his body. He stared at her wrist, the back of her right wrist where she'd cut herself.

"What is this? You . . . you cut yourself?"

His sudden anger terrified her.

"You filthy whore, you cut yourself?"

"No . . ."

"How could you do such a thing?"

"I. . . ." What could she say? She felt a fresh tear slip down her cheek.

Alvin stared at her and slowly his face softened. "I would never let this happen to you. I would never leave you alone to feel that kind of pain."

He breathed steadily, easing his grip on her wrists.

"If you ever do that again, I will break every bone in your body."

"I won't."

He was trembling.

"I would like you to be my daughter."

Then Alvin Finch turned, left the room, and locked the door behind him, leaving his neatly folded shirt on the floor.

Bethany walked to the bed, sank slowly to the thin mattress, and began to cry.

30

THERE WERE TWO reasons why Ryan didn't finally break down and tell Ricki Valentine that BoneMan was waiting for him to show at the Crow's Nest Ranch in western Texas. The first was that he knew that for all their good intentions, the FBI could not save Bethany.

The second was that he knew there was a chance he could. However small the possibility, as long as he could wrap his mind around it he would keep his mind, his body, everything that was within him singularly focused on giving that possibility room to grow.

He'd learned that he couldn't break an innocent man's bones to save his daughter, but he would break every bone in his own body to save her.

Under any other circumstance he would never look at iron shackles and think of them as a possibility, but he'd put his mind to just this possibility from the moment they moved him into the holding cell in the downtown precinct and locked the restraints around his wrists.

The cell was one of five used to hold prisoners in

transit, not the kind he'd seen on television with a bunk bed, a toilet, and a sink. Steel bars ran along the hall wall and white concrete completed the ten-by-ten room. A single bed sat in the far corner and a chain shackled to the prisoner's wrist kept them from being able to reach the bars.

"Why the chain?" he'd asked the two guards who'd accompanied him to the cell.

"To keep you from running home to mommy," one said with a grin.

The other was more directed by protocol. "Prisoners stay chained at all times in the cage. You need to use the bathroom, you let us know. You stand facing the wall, we come in, secure you with handcuffs, take off the chains, lead you to the toilets, and return you." He dropped a bucket on the floor. "Need to piss, use that—we're not orderlies."

The guards had shoved him roughly into the room and attached the chain to his left wrist using an inch-wide strap of steel that locked into place with a keyed latch.

A new facility that gave each prisoner his own toilet was near completion. In the meantime they had the system down to a science that Ryan tested within ten minutes of his arrival.

"What is it?"

"I have to use the bathroom."

"You just got here. Why didn't you go while we had you out? Now you want me to drag you to the latrine and wait for you to mess yourself?"

"Unless you want me to do it here."

The guard, a short balding man who liked to walk with his hand draped over the forty-five on his waist, swore.

"Palms on the wall."

Ryan faced the wall and placed both hands on it while the man opened the cell door.

"Hands behind your back, one at a time."

He complied. Handcuffs were quickly latched to his wrists and the shackle unlocked. It fell to the floor with a loud clang.

"Turn around."

He was marched to the latrine, where he faced another set of procedures, but his mind was back on the cell. Back on the shackles.

Five minutes later he was secured by them once again.

As long as he was fixed to the chain, there was no way out of the cell. Once out of the shackle the guard took other precautions that would make a struggle a losing proposition.

He sat on the bunk, stared at the thick band of steel that ran around his wrist, and let BoneMan's drawing fill his mind. On the drawing had been one bone that supported the thumb, the ball at the base of his thumb, the trapezium. He rubbed it, feeling the faint outline beneath his flesh.

If he could break the trapezium, his whole hand would collapse a full inch. The drawing on the wall had made as much clear. He might also need to collapse one of his metacarpals to squeeze his hand through the shackle.

But if he could stomach the pain, he stood a better than even chance of surprising the guard and taking his weapon.

A strange notion occurred to him as he sat on the bed, lost in the prospect of breaking his own bones. His daughter had suffered nothing less at the hand of BoneMan. In a way his own pain in breaking the bones in his left hand so that he might have at least some hope of going to her felt justified.

It was the least he could do. And he knew how to do it. Right here using the leverage provided by the bed, the shackle itself, and his full body weight, he might be able to break his bones.

The idea swallowed him.

"I DON'T LIKE it." Ricki lifted the bottle of Corona as if to take a drink. Instead she waved it to punctuate her point. "This feels like the Phil Switzer takedown to me. Right circumstances, right motive, right everything, but wrong man."

Mark Resner shook his head. "He may not be BoneMan, but he's guilty, isn't he? And I agree with Kracker, this town needs a guilty man behind bars right now, even if he isn't the one who we were after two years ago."

They sat in the Tattle Tale, a Fourth Street pub in downtown Austin that would be standing room only on weekends thanks to live music and college students from the nearby University of Texas. Tonight, a lone piano serenaded a sparse, more mature crowd.

To their right the hour hand on a three-foot antique clock had nearly completed its climb to the midnight mark. Even on weeknights, Austin, Texas, live music capital of the world, did not sleep. She and Mark, on the other hand, did, and they'd agreed to call it quits at twelve.

"You know the DA's gonna do everything in his power to pin it all on him. And while we're at it, you know he was the one who did this the last time."

"Did what? Plant the blood evidence?"

She took a drink and set the bottle down without bothering to respond. "Problem is, nothing eliminates Evans. I've been through the evidence we have on BoneMan a hundred times—the times, the places, the forensics— none of it clears Evans. Not even the phone we found in the quarry. The calls came from another cell phone in the same area. He could have called himself."

"But?"

"But you look in his eyes and you tell me."

A wry smile slowly spread over Mark's face. "You *like* this guy?"

"Please. Like you said, he's guilty." She lifted her bottle again, turning it in her hands, peeling back the corner of the label. She felt . . . respect. Nothing romantic in the least.

Mark leaned back. "You gotta admit though, there's something pretty compelling about a father who's so desperate to save his daughter."

"Assuming that's what he's doing," she said.

"Isn't that what you're saying?"

She sighed and leaned back to match his posture. "There was a look in his eyes when I interviewed him two months ago in his hotel room, before all this went down. He'd just laid out the DA, which I can't say disturbed me too much, and his marriage was on the ropes. He had a hundred reasons to be furious. But he just sobbed. It broke my heart."

"Like I said, you do think he's telling the truth."

She looked at him for a moment. Not so long ago she might have retreated into his arms for comfort on a night like this. Now she was alone, not so unlike Ryan.

Ricki shifted her eyes away from Mark and watched

the piano player. "If I had to pick a side? Yes. I think he's telling the truth. I think he took Welsh because he was told that if he didn't, his daughter would die."

"And we're making a mistake by not taking him up on his offer."

Eyes back on him. "If I'm right, yes."

"Well, we'll know soon enough, won't we?"

"How so?"

"When we find the girl's body, the coroner will tell us if her bones were broken before or after we took Evans into custody. With any luck, you'll be able to safely conclude that she was killed after Evans was taken into custody and clear him of at least that much. You still have the DA to contend with."

It was an ugly prospect but true. The fact that they were sitting here with their feet up while Bethany was still out there was enough to make Ricki swear off this cursed line of work for the last time.

"If he's not BoneMan, a jury will excuse him for what he did to the DA. After what he's been through— probation, maybe a short sentence, but no one's going to lock up a tormented father for too long, not after so many fathers have lost their daughters to BoneMan. He'll be public hero number one when this is all over."

"That's a big if."

"What is?"

"If he's not the BoneMan."

She set the half-empty bottle down and checked her phone in case she'd somehow missed a call in the ruckus.

"No call?"

"No. But he claims the killer gave him until daybreak. We can be anywhere in the state in matter of a couple hours. He's got till three or four in the morning before he runs out of time."

"What could possibly change between now and three in the morning? Why not just tell us now, assuming he's going to tell us anything at all?"

"*We* could change," she said. "We could change our minds. The DA could have second thoughts. After leaving Evans, I laid out all of the reasons for letting Evans take this last shot, wearing a location transmitter, and Kracker promised to pitch my reasoning to Welsh one more time."

"Not a chance, not after his dog and pony show with the press this afternoon. Welsh already has his mind on the next election."

However depressing, neither of them could argue.

Ricki dug out a five-dollar tip and set it on the table. "Then let's hope we get a call from Evans before four this morning. I have to get some sleep."

"You talk to anyone down at the station lately? He awake?"

"Half an hour ago, just before I got here, and yes, he's awake. Just sitting there. You coming?"

"Go ahead, I'm going to finish my drink. Call me if you hear anything."

Ricki walked down Fourth Street toward the Trulucks, where she'd valet parked her car. She handed the attendant her ticket and called the station while she waited. Johnson, one of the guards on night shift, answered and agreed to take a quick look.

He returned thirty seconds later and confirmed that Evans was still awake, lying down now, but he wasn't going to sleep any time soon.

"How's that?"

"He just don't have that look," Johnson said. "He staring up at the ceiling like he's expecting it to cave in at any minute. Sweating up a storm."

"Sweating?"

"His whole shirt is wet."

She frowned. Good. He was sweating it out, literally. Maybe he would change his mind.

Ricki reached her apartment at twelve-forty in the morning, called Kracker one last time on the chance he would pick up, and sat down in front of the television to let off some steam when he didn't.

She checked her TiVo and watched a bit of Letterman, then kicked off her shoes, lay down in the corner of the couch, and let exhaustion push her slowly toward sleep. They would call; she'd given them all her numbers.

If there was any change at all, they would call.

LETTERMAN STILL GRINNED on the monitor when Ricki jerked upright out of a dead sleep half an hour later. *Two AM.* She grabbed her cell phone on the coffee table.

"Yes?"

"Agent Valentine?"

"He's talking?"

"I'm sorry?"

"Evans! Evans is talking."

"Um, no . . . no ma'am, no. I'm calling for Assistant Director Kracker. Can you hold the line?"

"Kracker? Sure."

Kracker? At two in the morning. The DA had agreed then. If so, they had to hurry. She kept the phone to her ear and pulled on her boots.

Dropped the phone. Picked it up off the carpet and lifted it to her ear. "Hello?" Nothing.

Then Kracker's familiar low voice filled her ear. "Ricki?"

And she know immediately that something was wrong. She stood.

"What is it?"

"Ricki, I'm at Burt Welsh's house. God help me, I don't know how we let this happen."

"What?"

"He's dead. It looks like the work of BoneMan."

Her heart hit hard and seemed to stop, then kicked in steady. "Dead?"

"He was found a few minutes ago after an anonymous call reported a murder at his house."

"Found how? How do you know this was BoneMan?"

"He was found on his bed, tied off to the posts, naked. All of the bones in his extremities are broken. God, he looks like. . . ." Kracker's thick voice failed him.

"No blood?"

"No. No bleeding except from his head where he was hit, hard enough to put him out. I hope he was out."

The revelation made her legs feel like rubber. "Ryan told us this would happen."

Silence.

"He warned us that BoneMan wanted Welsh dead. The father of lies. Right? When Ryan failed to meet his demands he went after Welsh himself and then he made the call because he wanted us to find him. He doesn't want us pinning his work on Ryan."

"He's dead, Ricki. For God's sake, the district attorney of Austin, Texas, was just brutally murdered in the same manner as the victims he'd sworn to avenge. And it happened right under our noses! Do you have any idea how this looks?"

But Ricki couldn't care less how it made anyone look. Her mind was suddenly full of one thought, and one thought only.

"What about Ryan?"

"He's locked up in—"

"Have you called down there?"

"He's in a cell, Ricki."

"But have you checked?" she demanded with enough force to rattle her phone.

Pause. "No. My first call was—"

"I'll call you back." She pressed the end button. Quickly scrolled down the recent calls log, selected her last outgoing call, and hit send.

The phone rang seven times without an answer. She hung up, checked that she'd dialed the right number, and called again. This time a receptionist picked up after ten rings.

"Please hold." That was it. The woman abruptly cut the line and placed her on hold. Ricki holstered her Glock and headed to her car. Fired it up and pulled out onto the street. Still nothing but a silent line.

She cursed, hung up, and called Kracker back.

"Kracker."

"I need your help. Do you have an alternate line to the Eighth Street station? The main line isn't responding."

"What do you mean, not responding?"

"I mean something's going down there and I need you to connect me!" she yelled.

"Hold on."

He punched her off. She pulled onto MoPac and headed south. The highway was nearly empty at two in the morning, and she took the car up to a hundred. According to state law, any speeding infraction over a hundred miles an hour earned the driver an immediate escort to jail. That's where she was headed anyway.

She'd covered a mile before Kracker came back on with the sound of a ringing phone behind his voice.

"Ricki?"

"Here."

"I'm conferencing. This is the only number I have on me so I'm not—"

"Fourteenth Street Prison Division, please hold—"

"Mort Kracker, FBI here. What's your name, son?"

"Sergeant Joseph Spinelli."

"Fine, Joseph. I need to speak to someone in charge."

"I'm . . . This is about the incident?"

"What incident?"

"I'm sorry, it's a bit of a zoo down here. We had a prisoner break out of a cell. He knocked out a guard and managed to get out of the station before an alarm was sounded. The night chief—"

"What prisoner?" Ricki demanded.

"Evans," the man said. "The prisoner who took the district attorney."

But of course. They should have expected nothing less. She took the car up to a hundred and ten.

"When?"

"About half an hour ago," Spinelli said.

"As of now, consider the scene part of a federal investigation," Kracker snapped. "Lock it down. Do you understand me, Sergeant Spinelli? We'll have an evidence response team there within half an hour. Don't let anyone touch anything. This is a federal matter now."

"The chief would like to talk to you, sir."

"Put him on."

"Hold on." He set the phone down with a clunk.

"Ricki?"

"I'm already on my way, sir. Tell them I'll be there in ten minutes."

RICKI HELD THE shackles in her gloved hands, slowly turning them over, mind spinning with the story they told. Mark Resner had just arrived after she'd woken him with the news.

A crime scene investigator was already dusting and probing, but there were very few unanswered questions to investigate. They all knew what had happened.

They knew who the prisoner was; they'd put him in the cell themselves.

They knew that he'd managed to get out of his restraints. They knew that he'd called for the guard so that he could use the bathroom. They knew that Johnson had responded to the request and had, by all appearances, followed proper protocol by unlocking and entering the cell only when the restrained prisoner was safely against the wall with his shackled hands in plain sight.

They knew that Evans had overpowered Johnson and rendered him unconscious before the guard could raise an alarm. The prisoner had then taken the man's gun and his uniform and made it all the way out of the building before another guard had gone looking for Johnson and found him in the cell in his boxers.

They also knew that Ryan had taken Johnson's keys and that his white Honda Accord was missing from the parking lot out back.

What they didn't know was where Ryan had gone.

Or how he'd managed to get out of his restraints.

Mark stared at the flat steel ring in Ricki's hands. "You'd think they could come up with a more efficient way of restraining prisoners."

"It's a temporary arrangement. They don't hold prisoners here very often, only special parties on the request of the DA."

"Special parties? Is that what our man is?"

"Their term, not mine." She turned the black shackle over and tried to slip her hand into the small opening, but it wouldn't go. Maybe with a little Vaseline.

"Evans isn't a small man. His hands have to be quite a bit larger than mine."

"Only one way out."

"He broke his thumb."

"At the very least."

She handed the restraint to Mark. "That's what I call commitment."

"He seems to be developing a taste for this."

Ricki looked at him. "I don't think anything could be farther from the truth. I think there's nothing in the world that terrifies him more than the thought of his daughter's bones being broken. To the point where he's willing to break his own with his own hand, for the slimmest chance to save hers."

"Well, that's one way to look at it."

"He was here, locked in chains when BoneMan killed Welsh. Ryan Evans is a father who will do anything to save his daughter. That is now the only way to look at it."

Mark nodded, point conceded, and dropped the shackle on the bed, where it clanked in its chains. "Back to square one," he said.

"A Honda Accord speeding on a back highway somewhere. At least it's not black."

"Somehow I don't think it'll matter. By morning the Accord will be long gone and Evans will be with BoneMan."

The idea sent a shudder through her bones.

"God help him."

31

THE NIGHT WAS dark, the night was cold, the night was hell there just ahead, beyond the car's long-reaching high beams, around the next corner, at the Crow's Nest. Ryan held the accelerator pedal to the floor, gripped the wheel tightly with his right hand, and prayed he was not too late.

Pain throbbed up his arm from the bone he'd broken next to his thumb. He'd wedged the shackle between the bed frame and one of the posts and positioned his hand so that all of his weight would fall on his thumb when he threw himself backwards, but even then the bone had survived two failed attempts.

When it had finally popped, he passed out from the pain.

And he'd passed out a second time trying to slide his collapsed hand through the shackle. But he had succeeded, and after a five-minute reprieve to collect his senses, he'd wound the chain around his wrist so that it appeared he was still bound by it, and he'd called the guard.

If there was one bit of grace in breaking a hand bone,

it was that the swelling was limited because there was far less flesh to tear around a thumb than around many other bones, like the femur or the radius.

His left hand was still puffy, as if it belonged to someone a hundred pounds heavier than him, and it throbbed like a steam train struggling up a long hill, but the pain was bearable next to the true pain that he faced.

No amount of nerve damage could compare to the terror that had drummed itself into his mind as the Honda roared due west over vacant predawn roads.

A dozen potential scenarios whispered like serpents, most with sinister flickers of the tongue, suggesting that she was already dead. That Bethany, the child whom he'd ignored in his passion to serve his own career, was dead and broken in a hole somewhere.

And if she was alive—which he finally convinced himself she must be, if for no other reason than that BoneMan was too fixated on tormenting them both to end it so quickly— she could be badly hurt. Disfigured for life. Broken and twisted even now as he pushed the car to the breaking point.

He'd already decided that if the police found him before he reached the Crow's Nest, he would not stop until he reached Fort Davis, where he would surrender and demand to speak to the FBI agent Ricki Valentine about leading them the last few miles to the meeting spot.

To Crow's Nest Ranch.

Trapped for four hours in a car with only his thoughts proved to drive him only further from the calm, reasoned state that would serve him in this crisis. He found himself unable to hold back tears on numerous occasions, and because he was alone with nothing to do but drive, he allowed them to run down his cheeks. But then they began to interfere with his ability to drive at high speed, so he wiped his eyes, set his jaw, and swallowed his fear.

The faintest hint of gray edged the eastern sky as he left Fort Davis in his wake and brought the car back up to speed.

By the time he hit the dirt road that led into the ranch, the horizon was brighter, unquestionably so, but he still needed his lights to see the road ahead. BoneMan had said first light, or was it dawn? Either way, this was neither dawn nor first light. This was predawn.

Ryan slowed when he crossed under the arching Crow's Nest Ranch sign—he'd made it this far undetected. Just a few hundred more yards. And now he began to worry in earnest that he really was too late.

He drove the car into the same camp he'd used two days earlier, turned off the engine and the lights, and stared into the darkness.

He opened the door and stepped out into the dirt, between the door and the car. Faint night sounds, crickets, breeze, a lizard or two. The car's engine cooling.

But the night sounded vacant to him, and the memory of his previous long wait pushed him into a sudden panic. He rounded the car and stared at the camp's perimeter.

"Hello?"

Nothing but silence answered him.

"I'm here."

But BoneMan was as unlikely to step out and take his hand as he was to release Bethany for good behavior. What was he thinking?

"Hello? I'm here, for the love of God!" His voiced carried into the night and a lizard took flight to his right, but nothing else seemed to take note that he was even there.

Ryan loosened his fists and walked to the same tree he'd sat under the last time he'd waited. He stood there and looked around, mind ragged after being battered for over twenty-four hours without sleep.

There was nothing else he could do now. Nothing.

So he slowly sank to his seat, rested his arms on his knees, and sagged, exhausted. He took several deep breaths in an attempt to calm his frayed nerves, but nothing seemed to still the palpable throb in his hands and arms.

Nothing would except sleep, and he didn't dare fall asleep now. The man had said first light, and first light was approaching. Then it would grow warm and he would be alone again, at the whim of a man who might very well be watching at the moment, or might decide not to come for another day or two or never.

And what would Ryan do then? Whom would he confide in? What brilliant decision would he make except to wait, and then wait some more until finally, a day later, a week later, he finally accepted the terrible truth that Bethany was gone? Or had been found.

No father could do this. No mind could withstand this much . . .

The blow came then, like a locomotive from the night. It struck his head from behind with enough force to jerk the light from his mind and drop him to the ground like a side of butchered beef.

32

Eden, Texas

ALVIN FINCH PULLED the Ford F-150 pickup truck into the barn and hauled both doors closed, shutting out most of the light. He stood there for a moment, collecting his thoughts, grateful for his fortune.

But it wasn't just fortune that had brought him to this place of such unprecedented opportunity. Luck had little to do with the fact that the FBI hadn't come sniffing anywhere near him yet. It wasn't chance that he'd just driven a third of the way across Texas in broad daylight without being stopped.

He was here in the musty old barn with the father of lies because of meticulous planning and he was here because he was Alvin Finch who had become Satan for this day.

Even he hadn't understood it all until that moment, standing before the girl, Bethany, while she placed her hands on his chest. When the final knowledge had come he'd begun to shake, an uncommon reaction for him.

The girl who would be his daughter was the most beautiful creature he had ever shared space with, a perfect specimen of unblemished flesh, a pristine vessel that contained everything that was desirable in life.

Bethany was a perfect creation and Alvin hated her more than he'd hated anything in his life, including his mother, whom he'd hated very, very much. However beautiful Alvin was, he'd seen that she was far more than he could ever hope to be. The realization had forced him to bring the last reserves of his control to bear for fear that he would reach out and snap her forearms as she tried to seduce him.

Only the fact that she was going to be his daughter stopped him. And now he wanted more than ever to win her undying love, her complete devotion.

He must be her father! She had to be his daughter. It was the only thing that could possibly satisfy him now.

There were two things that Alvin loved; three that he would kill for. The adoration of a girl who would be his daughter. The unflinching devotion of that daughter. The opportunity to share a jar of Noxzema with a daughter who would rather die than upset him.

He knew that these truths were all wrapped up a metaphorical mess that mind-prodders would call mad, but wouldn't they also call Satan mad?

The thought brought a flutter of contentment to his belly. Although his was often a tortured existence, there were some fringe benefits that came along with being Satan.

He lowered the tailgate and eyed the prone form he'd wrapped in the blue tarp. The father was conscious inside, but immobilized by the drug. It was important that he be fully aware of just how terribly he had failed.

Alvin pulled off the tarp and pulled the man out by his heel. But the boot tore free, leaving only a brown sock to cover the man's foot. He grabbed the heel and tugged him.

He paused when the body was halfway out, struck by the feel of the heel in his hand. The calcaneus. He'd never broken a heel bone before, preferring instead metatarsals in the toes. The heel would require a hammer blow. Holding Ryan's heel, Alvin decided that this would be where he started.

The man's eyes were open, staring at the ceiling, and his eyelids fluttered once. The drug was wearing off.

Alvin lowered the foot with both hands and dragged him out of the bed. The body landed on the old barn's straw floor with a thump. No grunt, no snap because the man wasn't able to use his vocal cords and the fall was too small to break bones.

He leaned over the man's face, knowing that the wide eyes could see. "They call me BoneMan," he said. "But I'm really Satan and I have your daughter."

He offered the man a smile, but the man did not return it.

Alvin picked up the body and slung it over his shoulder and grabbed the fallen boot. He walked out of the barn without checking to see that they were alone. The old farm that his mother had left him was ten miles off the nearest paved road and visited only by the occasional hunter who ignored the NO TRESPASSING signs that Alvin had erected around the eighty-acre lot.

Cypress trees formed a natural boundary around the barn and house and an acre of brown, long overgrown lawn. After burying his mother in the back over twenty years ago now, he'd locked the property down and left for the cities. He hadn't bothered to keep the house up and it had become virtually unlivable for a man of his tastes. He now used the house only for its basement, where he'd perfected his craft.

He stopped halfway to the house and turned around, studying the perimeter. They could be out here for a year and no one would know. All around Texas they were looking for BoneMan, and here he was, twenty miles south of Eden, in the basement with the father and his daughter.

Alvin entered the house and walked down the hall to the door that blocked off the basement. He'd carefully scrubbed the kitchen and the bathroom and the smell of bleach filled the house still. As soon as he placed the man in his own room, he would take a shower and clean himself. It was best to be clean before he talked to his daughter again.

He left the door open and descended the concrete stairs. The electric power to the farm had been cut off a dozen years ago, but oil lamps suited the place. They hid all the dirt.

Alvin stopped at the bottom and looked down the hall to his daughter's door, which remained locked. He wondered what she was doing now. Had the lamp burned out? Was she wondering how she might please him? Or was she examining the cross he'd fixed to the wall?

His breathing thickened and he turned away. The door to the second room, the one in which he'd kept the girl for the first few days, lay open to the darkness beyond.

Alvin shifted the body on his shoulder and walked down the hall into the room. He dumped the man on the bed and left him as he landed, with one arm across his neck and the other under his back, staring up at the ceiling.

He considered talking to the man but decided it would

be a waste of time. The basement room was dimly lit by daylight that entered through several cracks in the foundation at the corners. The sedative would wear off soon and the man would discover his room. He'd proven to be quite resourceful.

But they had plenty of time. It might be days before he talked to the man on the bed. His fate now hung in the balance of the daughter's mind.

Alvin Finch, aka BoneMan, who was really Satan, stood over the bed, lost in thoughts of the daughter again. Again his breathing thickened.

He wanted to drag her into this room now and break her bones as the man who would be her father watched. Snap her arms and legs using his knees as a fulcrum as he had on occasion. The sudden break would likely tear through her flesh and ruin her skin, so he wouldn't, but he wanted to.

Filled with sudden rage, he bent down and slugged the man in his face. He may have broken his nose, he didn't know, he didn't care. Before this was over, a broken nose would be completely forgotten.

Then he walked out of the room, locked the door, and retreated to the upstairs bathroom to take a shower and apply lotion.

33

THE SCENT OF camphor lingered with the oily smell of lamp oil from a flame that had burned out many hours ago. Bethany lay in a curled ball on the sagging mattress, staring at the thin cracks of light that cast a gray hue through the cell.

She could just see the strange wood blocks that formed a large Y with a cross member on the wall and she absently wondered about the crosslike structure. But her mind wasn't putting the pieces together with ease any longer.

How long had she been in the basement? Five or six days? Maybe longer. At least a day since Alvin Finch, the BoneMan, had introduced himself to her. She'd been alone with her fear for what felt like an eternity since he'd left, battling the certainty that it was only a matter of time before he began breaking her bones, one by one.

Funny thing how one incident can turn your entire understanding of life on its head. How one week you're planning on going to New York to smile for the camera and the next you're thinking that anyone who would waste even a moment of their lives trying to impress anyone for any reason is a fool.

But aren't you interested in impressing Alvin?

Well, if you called trying to survive in Alvin's world trying to impress him, then yeah, maybe she would try to impress him.

The thought crawled through her mind and then left and she tried to get it back, but it was gone. Something about trying to impress Alvin.

Yes, that was right, she was interested in impressing Alvin. Or Satan or BoneMan or whatever he wanted to be called.

The one thing Bethany had learned as she waited in the dark without food or a pot to piss in was that she was powerless down here. Completely, utterly worthless and unable to change a thing about it.

No contract from New York could save her.

No FBI would rescue her.

No father to come to her salvation.

No mother to do anything but scream at the world about how they weren't doing enough to find her little model who was going to be famous, for heaven's sake! Still, Mother was the one person she owed her life to and she missed her. What she would give to hear a cynical, cutting remark from her now.

The idea of worrying whether or not she would miss cheerleading practice felt like an obscenity in her mind, a little cockroach that scampered around the edges of her reality, offering her nothing but pointless distraction.

She watched a roach climb up the wall.

Another thing Bethany had learned was just how much her father's failure bothered her. She might even say she hated Ryan more than anyone she knew for not adequately occupying the role of her father. She could only have one father. Where was he when she needed him? For all of his talk about how he wanted to be her father, where was he?

Her father was about as helpful as God. *I'll be there, I'll be there, I'll be there, I'll be there*, but never, never, never there. Not even the theology professor at school really expected to serve a God who would actually rescue her from a bad day, much less Satan's pit.

What she would give to be able to rely on a huge, wonderful God who would reach down and swat Alvin aside and scoop her up into his chest. What if there was such a thing? Where a paternal father failed, there would be God to rescue her.

The thought choked her up with desire and she even whispered a prayer to the ceiling.

But the roots that had snaked their way into the darkness were the only thing she saw. No thunder. No one who loved her. No father.

No, the truth of the matter was that Alvin Finch was the only one who had any power to save her skinny, worthless neck. Alvin Finch and Bethany Evans, they were the only two who mattered now.

This was the reason she found him strangely attractive. In Alvin's world, Alvin held all the cards. And the only way to win in Alvin's world was to play Alvin's game and win some of those cards for yourself.

Like Celine said, "You want to get ahead in the world, you have to play by the world's rules." And Celine did.

In this world Alvin was as much an angel as he was the Satan he professed to be. And although Bethany was fearful of him, she was also very aware of his power to save her, and as the hours slogged by she found herself wishing he would return. She thought she understood him nearly as much as she understood herself now, which wasn't very much, granted.

The odd thing about her feelings was that she understood that they'd been manipulated, but this knowledge didn't help her stop them. Being the daughter of a Naval intelligence officer had filled her head with the stories that Ryan talked about when he was home. She knew about Stockholm syndrome, an acute sociopathic response to intense trauma, usually expressed by victims identifying with, even siding with, their oppressors.

Ryan had once told her about a project or operation called Red Cell that he'd been involved in. Naval Intelligence had pretended to be terrorists, taken over a class of midshipmen, and psychologically tortured them for twelve hours. The class members began to suffer psychological breaks as soon as six hours into the ordeal.

Stockholm syndrome, individuals' desperate attempts to become like their captors. On a lesser scale it was why good German citizens followed Hitler, Ryan said. Or why any person might compromise his or her convictions without realizing he or she was doing so to be accepted. To be wanted.

The world was suffering from Stockholm syndrome.

She knew that something along these lines was happening to her, but knowing you're worthless doesn't give you value any more than knowing you are a captive sets you free.

Given the choice she would either cut Alvin's throat or thank him, depending on whether she was being sane or not. Cutting his throat was sane, very sane.

Thanking him with a soft kiss was anything but sane. So was she insane? Was she really that far gone?

Yes. Yes she was. Because there were times that she really would do anything to please Alvin. Like now, right now Alvin didn't strike her as being so bad at all, really. Not really, now when you considered the alternative, which was broken bones and all. He'd shown her mercy, hadn't he? Or was she just—

The lock rattled softly and Bethany jerked upright on the bed. The door swung open.

She watched, shocked by the suddenness of Alvin Finch's entrance as he walked to the lamp and lit it without bothering to shut the door behind him. Not that he couldn't easily cut off any escape attempt in two strides.

He faced her, shirtless, breathing in long, loud pulls. His skin was the color of watered-down milk, silky smooth, with faint hints of veins on his upper chest. His cotton slacks were held up by a black belt that was cinched tight just below his belly button, higher than she was accustomed to seeing except on older men, and he wasn't old.

He wore black shoes that had been recently shined.

Alvin was showing off, she realized. Her captor thought enough of her to go to some trouble to be sure she was impressed. She'd struck a chord with him the last time, maybe surprised him with her boldness. Nothing else made sense.

Encouraged, Bethany felt an uncommon urge to rush over and throw her arms around him. Monster or not, he alone had the power to save her. This was his pit. She still couldn't see his deep-set eyes well, but she imagined that he was eying her with kind desire. Though it would also be stern. He knew what he wanted.

Alvin walked back to the door, locked it, then approached her. "Will you stand up for me?"

Stand up?

She slid her legs off the bed and stood, strengthened by the adrenaline now coursing through her veins.

"Will you step out into the middle of the room?"

She did so. He walked behind her slowly. Then around her left side. His hands carefully lifted her T-shirt and he stared at her bared side for a few seconds before lowering the top. She could smell his lotion and found herself drawn to the refreshing scent.

There was no way to know how long he would stay this time. He might simply inspect her and then leave her alone with her emptiness again. She couldn't let him do that, not this time.

Alvin stopped in front of her, naked down to his belt. "You are a very special girl," he said.

"Yes, I know," she said, searching for the right words. She couldn't seem to think clearly so she said what she'd been thinking in her nightmares.

"And I know that you're hurt. You killed your mother because she made you feel bad for not being as beautiful as she was. That's why you killed the other girls."

He stood still. But she could see into his eyes now, and she saw no denial. Only those bottomless pits of black.

"But I'm different, Alvin. I'm more like you. I'm the one beautiful thing that you can have. I can thrive in your world and we can be together."

When he still didn't respond, Bethany stepped forward and reached for his right hand. She touched his fingers. Held his hand and drew it toward her. Against her belly.

"Is that what you want? Hmmm?" She said it lightly

with complete sincerity because she knew that she would gladly fall into his embrace to escape the helplessness of her captivity.

"You don't want to hurt me, Alvin. You want to love me."

She pulled up her shirt and placed his cold, trembling hand on her belly. "I can be yours, all yours. That is what I want, Alvin."

He left his hand on her skin for only a moment, then pulled it away. "Is that the way a father would treat his daughter?"

Of course! She was still looking at the world through her eyes. In his eyes she was a daughter and he wanted to be her father, he'd said as much. How stupid of her to assume that because he was a man he would be interested in seduction.

Yet it *was* a seduction, just not a sexual seduction. Alvin wanted to lure her in as his own. And he wanted to be loved the way a daughter loved a father. But Bethany didn't know how to love a father. The thought began to panic her.

BoneMan stood over her, breathing steadily, showing no signs that he was disgusted with her.

"You see, that's the problem," he said. "All the fathers are liars, and none of the daughters know what it's like to loved by a father. Or how to love one."

"Then why do you come in here without a shirt on?" she asked.

"I wanted to impress you. Your skin is so much like mine. We are already the same. I could be your father, Bethany."

"But you confuse me," she said. "How can you expect

a girl to do what you need her to do if you send so many mixed signals?"

"What do you mean?"

"Walking in here without anything covering your chest, knowing full well that your skin is so beautiful, for example. Or leaving here, talking about how much you would like to break my bones. It's hard to tell if you love me or hate me."

"That's because I love you and I hate you," he said without a hint of anything but pure sincerity in his voice.

"I . . . I thought you liked me."

"I do. But I find myself wanting to break your bones at the same time. It's hard, you know, standing in the same room with you and not letting my desires take over."

"So you really want to kill me?" she cried.

Their eyes seemed to be locked in a trance, finally broken by BoneMan, who looked at the door.

"Can you be honest with me?" he asked.

"Yes."

"Would you be afraid to walk down the street with me?"

She wanted to be truthful and had to think.

Alvin faced her again. "Would you be grateful to have me by your side to guide and love you while others looked on?"

"Why would you think I wouldn't?" she returned. "Isn't that what everyone does? Pretend to be someone they aren't? Driving their fancy cars and wearing the latest fashions? They all sleep with the devil every day."

"Is that what I am?"

"You told me that you were Satan. Isn't that how you think of yourself?"

He was back on his heels and Bethany assumed it was

her boldness and unapologetic acceptance of him that he found so jarring. This was her advantage.

She took a step closer and placed one hand on his shoulder.

"You're already like a father to me, Alvin. In some ways more than my own father was ever a father to me."

"Do you mean that?"

"You have the power to save me," she said. "To protect me. Isn't that the least a father can do?"

He frowned for a moment, then stepped over to the blocks of wood on the wall and spoke quietly.

"I've brought him here."

"Brought who here?"

BoneMan ran his hands along the cross. "The man who has pretended to be your father. I brought him here yesterday."

"Burt Welsh?"

"No. I killed that one because he was a liar. I brought the other father of liars."

Ryan? She felt her heart skip a beat.

"He abandoned you, didn't he, Bethany?" BoneMan turned around. "Now you're all alone. So I brought him to you."

"You . . . you brought Ryan here?"

"He's in your old bedroom."

She felt as if he'd struck her with his fist. Ryan, here?

On the one hand she wished this kind of entrapment on no one. On the other hand she found herself thinking he deserved it more than she did.

And the idea that she could even think such a thing disturbed her more than either thought.

Still, in her state of insanity, trapped in Alvin's world, there was some truth to her feelings.

"I can see that it bothers you," he said.

"Are you going to kill him?"

"Should I?"

"No. No one deserves to die like this."

"You can't have two fathers."

In the end it all came back to that. To having a daughter.

"Is it really so important to have a daughter? You're overreacting."

Alvin Finch stood very still and at first she thought that he wasn't responding because she'd asked a good question. But then she saw that his jaw was locked and his hands shivered by his sides. Maybe he wasn't speaking because he was fighting off waves of rage. She didn't know what to say or do, so she just stood there while he shook.

Then Alvin walked up to her, lifted her left hand, gripped her pinkie finger between his own, and snapped it.

Pop.

Pain screamed through her hand and up her arm, but she clenched her jaw and stared at him, refusing to make a sound.

He dropped her hand and backed away. "I'm sorry, but that was a stupid question."

Tears stung her eyes, then rolled down her cheeks. But she held her eyes on his face, determined not to show her fear. She wanted to ask him how he could even think about being her father if every time he got angry he broke her bones. Instead, she apologized.

"I'm sorry."

"It's too much to ask a young girl to understand why her love is so important. I should just kill you now."

"Then you'd never know what it was like to have a daughter," she said, taking her broken finger in her good hand.

The man's chest was now covered in a layer of sweat that had mixed with lotion, leaving thin white trails as it ran down his body.

"Would you rather I kill your mother?"

"No. It would hurt me more than you breaking my bones. If you want a daughter who knows how to love, then you can't expect me not to love the mother I already have."

"I've watched your mother. She is a witch and my mother was a witch."

"That doesn't mean you can kill her!" Nausea from the pain in her hand crawled up her throat. She stepped back to the bed and sat to still her dizziness. "You can't just kill people because you're jealous of what they have."

"I can do far more than you think I can. That's who I am. The man who calls himself your father has never been by your side when you needed him. I would never let you out of my sight."

His reasoning had its own kind of compelling sense. "But that doesn't mean Ryan deserves to die."

"Only I have the power to give you and your father life. You're in my world now." He took a deep, catching breath. "If you don't want me to kill your father, then he has to stop being your father, because you can only have one father."

She was confused by the train of emotions that now ran through her exhausted mind. Her hand ached and her mind struggled to stay on a particular line of thought.

"I want to break your bones, and I want to break his bones," BoneMan said. "I hate you and I hate your father even more for being your father. But more than either of those things, I want to be your father."

She swallowed, no longer able to follow his thoughts. "So what do you want from me?"

"I want you to hurt him. The way I would hurt him. And then I want you to send him away so that he will never want to come back for you."

"How . . . how do you expect me to do that?"

"The way I would do it."

"I can't do what you do."

"You already do. I am Satan and you're my daughter. Now we're just going to be honest with each other."

"And if I can't?"

"Then I will do what I always do. It might be best anyway."

She didn't know how to respond to what he was suggesting. She could express her outrage, but after six days in this hole, even her outrage was confused with eagerness to please him. She could argue with him, but she didn't want to anger the one person who could save her.

She could agree to his terms, but she didn't think she could bring herself to actually hurt anyone for any reason. Certainly not Ryan. He was a lousy father, but no one deserved this except maybe her.

Or did he? No, of course not.

"Could I have some water and some food?" she asked. "I haven't eaten in a long time."

The question seemed to sidetrack him.

"If you were my daughter I would never let this happen to you," he said.

*   *   *

DARKNESS HAD FALLEN. Ryan Evans knew this because the room had grown pitch-dark again, the third night since he'd awoken in the room. So, if he was right, he had been in BoneMan's basement for two and a half days now.

For the second time in three months he'd been taken captive and held against his will in a room below the earth. What the man who'd taken him couldn't know what that his method of capture, injecting Ryan with drugs that rendered him immobile but fully conscious, had actually played to Ryan's advantage.

He'd broken out of jail, stolen one of the guard's cars, and cut across the state of Texas like a bat out of hell, riddled with more emotion than he'd suffered since this madness had begun. The fear that he wouldn't be taken captive had been taken away the moment he'd been hit. And the long, forced wait in the back of BoneMan's truck had given him time to accept his new challenge with the same calculation that had saved him in the desert.

Exhausted from lack of sleep, he'd fallen asleep after being dumped on the bed and when he'd awoken many hours later, the effects of the drugs had worn off.

He'd examined his room carefully, found no potential avenue for escape, then retreated to his bed where, except to drink water from a large bottle by the door and urinate in the pot, he'd lain in near perfect stillness for nearly two days.

He would have to say *near* perfect stillness, because he found himself unable to contain his grief for more than a couple hours before he broke down and let himself weep.

His chest shook and his eyes flooded and his mind

could not shut out the image of his daughter, Bethany, whom he loved more than he had ever thought possible.

He passed the hours thinking through what he knew of her life, which was so little it must be criminal. His first memory of her was as a baby wrapped in a pink blanket that Celine had purchased at Target a week before they'd finalized the adoption.

He thought about the small face in that pink blanket, those tiny hands batting aimlessly at the air, and he rolled over on the bed and wept. He'd wept because a week later he'd left for a two-month assignment.

He could remember the time that Bethany had run into the house with skinned hands and knees, crying after a spill on her skates. They were only superficial wounds and with a stoic nod he'd slapped her on the back and told her it would make her tough.

But his encouragement did not take away her red face or her squinted eyes spilling their tears. That face haunted him now and he wept.

If he could go back to that day, he would fly to the door and sweep his angel off her feet and rush her to the kitchen sink, holding her tight and whispering that everything would be all right. He would carefully bandage her small, superficial cuts and then take her to Dairy Queen to celebrate her being such a brave little girl.

Dear God, what have I done? Why was I so blind?

He remembered the time his dear little child, only ten at the time, had come into his office and asked if he would play a game of chess with her. He'd been gone for two weeks, at an intelligence conference in Norfolk, and had just returned, tired. He'd said what he always said. Maybe later.

But he never had played chess with her. Never, not once!

If only he could do so now. Just one game. He would sell all he owned to buy back that one day.

Ryan searched his mind for memories and as they came, he stored up the pain that came with them. Then, when he could no longer hold so much pain, he lay on his side and he wept.

This was his penitence. His heart was being slowly and painfully sliced and these memories were the salt poured into each cut.

Then he'd run out of memories and he found this even more disturbing than the memories themselves. But finally, after two days, Ryan had finally come to the bitter end of himself, corralled his emotions, and now lay perfectly still on the bed.

But he wasn't doing nothing. He was still thinking. Calculating, controlling, saving his will and his resolve for that moment he knew was coming. He would need to leave his emotions behind then and do what was necessary to save Bethany, no matter what the cost.

He was calculating, and for the first time he was praying. Begging God to understand his pain and save his daughter. No matter what the cost.

Because for the first time in his life he thought he understood what God must feel like. He would feel like Ryan who was out to rescue his daughter from the Satan who wanted her for his own. Who wanted to break her bones and crush her spirit and possess what was not his.

34

RICKI VALENTINE SAT on a metal folding chair, feet planted flat on the concrete floor, hands folded on her lap, staring at the chalk drawings of the human skeleton illuminated by two three-hundred-watt halogen lamps that ran off the portable generator out in the quarry. Father Hortense stood beside her, arms crossed. The artist, almost certainly BoneMan, had used white chalk with a fine point, not the thick one-inch variety that kids used to draw on sidewalks. And he'd applied remarkable skill.

She was back for her third visit, including the first when they'd taken Ryan Evans into custody, four days earlier. At first viewing the drawings on the wall had shed no new light on the case. She already knew that the killer was obsessed with bones and knew his anatomy well. That he'd proven his knowledge by filling the walls as if they were an anatomy textbook only reinforced what they all knew.

Following Ryan's escape a day later, she'd driven back out to take a second look. Admittedly, she was motivated by more than pure investigative curiosity. She was never more than a step away from scrutiny in a case that had literally blown up overnight. She needed the break.

Three days ago the city had woken to news that District Attorney Burt Welsh had been brutally murdered by the BoneMan or a killer mimicking BoneMan, on the very eve of his announcement that he had BoneMan behind bars.

To exacerbate the matter came the stunning admission that Ryan Evans, the supposed BoneMan, had escaped from his holding cell an hour after Welsh's murder. Theories abounded on how, if, and why Ryan Evans, who some still speculated was BoneMan, did what he did. And until more data came in, Ricki wasn't in the position to be absolutely conclusive one way or the other.

She knew that Ryan wasn't BoneMan.

She knew that the handwriting analysis that had just come in this morning had eliminated him as the author of the notes on these concrete walls.

She knew that Ryan was a distraught father who was doing exactly what she herself might do were she in his position.

She knew far more than the public could know about the case because BoneMan was still out there somewhere, plotting his next move. Austin was coming apart in a panic, but her first priority was stopping the man, not holding the public's hand, and for the time being that meant keeping a lid on certain details.

Mort Kracker was left with dealing with a city gripped by fear. She'd seen a number of cases terrorize regions of the country before. The DC sniper had virtually shut down Washington, DC. The I-9 killer, the Candy Man in Houston, a long list had left their mark on communities.

And now BoneMan had left his mark on Austin. Coverage of the astounding series of events that had led to the dead end they now faced blanketed all of the major networks. Blogs and news stories on the Internet had logged tens of millions of hits. In today's tech-savvy world, information could hardly be contained.

All of this had only fueled the fear of those in what the media was now calling the *kill zone*. Not surprisingly, because many of BoneMan's victims had been students, all public and most private schools in Austin had canceled classes until the FBI could assure them it was safe to return, something Ricki would have done two days earlier. But Kracker was treading water after so many apparent failures in the case.

A camper had found the white Honda Accord Ryan had stolen in a small campground called Crow's Nest Ranch in western Texas yesterday. Ryan's radio message now made perfect sense. He'd likely found the location and sent out a message on the radio waves, challenging BoneMan to meet him at the Crow's Nest Ranch, precisely as he'd claimed.

The evidence response team from the Dallas field office had done well to locate and take plaster casts of tire tread that proved to be an exact match to the Ford F-150 pickup truck that BoneMan had used two years earlier.

He wanted them to know that he had taken Ryan Evans.

But that knowledge, like the Crow's Nest crime scene, had led them nowhere. So Ricki had convinced herself to escape the tensions mounting in Austin once again this morning by asking Father Hortense to join her here, in the quarry, to give her his take on the drawings that filled the walls. He was both a religious man and psychiatrist, and as such was uniquely qualified.

"What stands out to you, Father?"

"The crosses, naturally. He's clearly obsessed with them."

"As much as the bones?"

"Well, yes, the skeletons go without saying."

"No proof at this point but I think we'll find that this writing belongs to BoneMan."

The priest walked up to the image they were both studying: a full body-length drawing of a complete skeleton floated before a hastily drawn cross with its arms spread wide and its feet pointed down. No nails or rope fixed the skeleton to the cross. Its skull stared at them with two round, empty eye sockets and smiled with a perfect set of large teeth.

"Is his moniker his own or did someone else name him?" The priest leaned forward and looked more closely at the wrists.

"The newspaper in El Paso was the first to call him BoneMan. It caught on."

He traced a line written in Latin next to the image. "Not one of his bones shall be broken."

"Meaning?"

"The Romans always broke the bones of those they crucified with a heavy hammer." He indicated the fibula with a curved finger. "Breaking the legs made it impossible for the victims to support their weight, forcing them into suffocation quickly. But not so with the crucifixion of Christ, one of the most remarkable aspects of his death.

It seems that our man is determined to do it right this time. I would say he's breaking bones in a fitful rage, like a spoiled child."

Ricki nodded. "That might explain his method. But why?"

"I would say he wants to punish the fathers and take their place. He wants to be the father."

"All this from a drawing on the wall?"

He shrugged. "Why else hasn't he killed Ryan? He's had ample opportunity. I think he's playing both Ryan and Bethany. Punishing the father and drawing the daughter."

"And he kills the girls why?"

"Because they don't measure up to his ideal of a daughter," the priest said. Then he shrugged again. "But that's just me."

"One very sick puppy," Ricki said.

They stared at each other, lost in the notion. It gained them no ground on BoneMan for the moment, but understanding the man would pay dividends soon enough. Assuming Hortense was in the ballpark.

Her phone rang. Kracker. She slipped it open.

"Valentine."

"Ricki, we have another victim."

The basement seemed to tip under her feet. She could feel her face cool. The first name that screamed through her mind was Bethany. Then Ryan. Surely BoneMan hadn't taken the time to search out an unrelated victim.

She couldn't find the voice to respond.

"The neighbors found Celine Evans facedown in the swimming pool after she failed to answer her phone this morning. No blood. All of her primary bones, including her spine, were broken. It's his work. I need you back here immediately."

"God help us. Does the press know yet?"

"They will within the hour. Just get back here,

Valentine." He sounded as if he wanted to say more. But he disconnected.

The priest was staring at her. "What is it?"

Ricki closed her phone. "BoneMan killed Celine Evans last night."

35

RYAN HEARD THE footsteps in the hall first, but his mind was deep in a well of sorrow and he was applying all of his energy to staying afloat in the black, inky emotions trying to suck him under. The soft padding of feet sounded more like his heart slogging through the stuff.

And he was succeeding. The pain was there, all around, pressing in on his flesh, but he could tread these brackish waters with relative ease so long as he kept his mind focused and strong.

Even the pain of his broken hand, now badly swollen, had abated.

He'd stopped his weeping and gnashing of teeth many hours ago and applied himself exclusively to the task of preparing himself for the moment he knew would eventually come, like the coming of the first winter storm.

He was the father and BoneMan had taken him for the exclusive purpose of tormenting either him or Bethany or, more likely, both to drive them apart.

Evil was predictable, always painfully expected. Even

so, whenever the enemy came, whether it be in the form of a suicide bomber bent on blowing up a bus full of women and children or in BoneMan's form, the shock and pain could be immobilizing.

Ryan knew that Bethany's life (assuming that she was still breathing, a prospect that he clung to without regard for the alternative) would likely depend on his ability to disregard those debilitating emotions so that he could do what was needed to save her.

He would throw himself at this singular objective. And if for any reason he failed, he would live or die with the pain of that failure, but also he would live or die as a father. The father he'd never been. The father he was today, in the deep black pit, where he could only hope for one chance to hold his daughter's hand and lead her out of darkness.

Ryan kept his eyes closed and listened to the padding of his heart. To the feet. His eyes sprang wide.

What was that? Was that—

All of his reasoning, the hours of careful deliberation, the days of pining for an opportunity to come face-to-face with the one who'd violated his offspring fell away for an instant and his heart bolted against his chest.

BoneMan. Those were the feet of him, walking toward his door.

He very nearly threw himself from the bed, intent on rushing the door. Instead he quickly gathered himself, re-capturing the practiced resolve and calculation that their lives now depended on.

Ryan lay perfectly still and swallowed his impulse to panic.

The rusted latch clicked as the lock disengaged. He heard the door hinges squeal softly. There was a moment of silence as his visitor paused at the door, then walked in. He didn't close the door.

And all the while Ryan refused to look. Refused to quickly acknowledge his captor. He lay still, staring at the sea of hairy roots on the ceiling, knowing that BoneMan was watching him with curiosity, courting a sliver of uncertainty.

Ryan spoke first, for his sake, not for his captor's. "Hello, BoneMan."

The man waited a few seconds before responding. "My name is Alvin Finch."

Alvin. For some reason Ryan found the name sickening.

"Hello, Alvin. Nice of you to finally come."

"You may also call me Satan."

The suggestion hardly surprised Ryan. That it was spoken with such sincerity, as if by a boy who was showing a neighbor his marble collection, was disturbing; but not even this should have surprised him.

"You may stand up now," Alvin said.

Ryan sat up, let his head clear, then lowered his feet to the concrete floor. He was still dressed in the same tan slacks he'd been wearing for over a week now and they were badly smudged. His brown boots were dusty and his socks had dried to his feet.

In contrast, the man who stood by the door looked as though he'd just stepped out of the shower before slipping into a freshly pressed shirt. Even from this distance Ryan could smell the soap he'd used or the cologne he'd applied.

Alvin was a tall white male with close-cropped hair who had a face you might see looking into any shopwindow at the nearest mall. His eyes were set deep and hidden by shadows.

Ryan stood slowly, undisturbed by the sight of the man who'd brought hell to them, though everything within him knew he should be disturbed. Deeply distressed. Raging with fury.

What was more disturbing to him was the open door that let in a small amount of light. BoneMan blocked his path, but the hallway beyond was screaming to Ryan, begging him to rush through the basement in search of his daughter.

"Before we finish this, I want you to acknowledge a few things to me," Alvin said. "I've been wanting to break your bones from the first time I read about you in the papers two months ago. It's been very difficult for me to show my restraint, but I've done it and I think it's been worth it."

The man was intelligent, not some clumsy butcher who just happened to evade the FBI for years.

"But first I will make my confession. Okay?"

That the man was asking his permission meant something, but Ryan was having a difficult time keeping his mind off the empty hallway beyond him.

"Okay."

"I appreciate the fact that you broke his bones. It was a noble beginning. I went to his house and I broke the rest of his bones the next night."

He'd killed Welsh?

"That father of lies is dead now," Alvin said.

Ryan didn't know what to say, so he said nothing.

"Last night I went back to your house and I broke the witch's bones. They will find her floating in the pool, full of chlorine."

Celine?

A fist of nausea rose into his throat. He wanted to

scream out his protest, but he knew that he could do no such thing. He refused to weaken his control now, while the hall behind the monster was empty and begging.

Celine? Dear God, Celine was dead. . . .

"The whole state is having a fit," Alvin said. "They seem to be more disturbed than you are. You didn't love that witch."

He wouldn't speak. He couldn't speak.

"You were never a good husband and you were an even worse father. It's important to me that I hear you confess your sin."

No! No, I will not confess my sins to you! How dare you judge me?

A voice whispered through his mind, warning him that he wasn't behaving as he knew he must. He had to be calm and reasoned and ready to move when the moment of opportunity presented itself.

For a long time BoneMan stared at him. Finally his shoulders sagged just barely and a faint frown bent his lips. "Then she was right, you are the father of lies. Do you deny your failure?"

"No."

"But you refuse to acknowledge that you don't deserve to be her father."

"Because I do. I'm trying to be her father."

"It's too late," BoneMan said.

"I wasn't her father before. Not the way I want to be her father now. She isn't my seed, I adopted her, but I never became her father. But that changed in the desert."

"So you admit you're not even really her father."

"Yes."

His answer seemed to confuse the man. This was the

kind of reason and control that would give them hope, he realized. And although BoneMan knew how to hate with more passion than most men, real love would confuse him.

"I admit, I'm not her father, not really," Ryan said. "But that's changing now."

"Now that you're in my house."

"Now that I'm pursuing her love."

The words seemed to take Alvin Finch off guard. He was a man of exceptional control but now he blinked; he began to sweat.

"She hates you," BoneMan said.

No. No, she couldn't possibly hate him. Maybe on a hot afternoon when harsh words about who she was dating were exchanged, but not now when they were both fighting for her life.

Alvin Finch was so devoid of love that he didn't know how to recognize it. He was indeed the Satan in the mix, bent upon winning the heart of his victim, though no one could possibly love him. His victims might show him a mirror of love to win his kindness, but they would never be able to return real love any more than he could receive it.

"You are the father of lies," Ryan said. "You can't be a true father."

The man's breathing thickened. "She wants me to be her father."

"But deep inside she wants me to be her father."

"You're lying. You're the father of lies! We both have the same soft skin. She's the most beautiful person I've seen. I want to be like her. She wants to be like me."

"Given the chance, she would kill you."

"You're lying. You're a filthy liar."

"Given the chance, she would come to me."

Ryan knew that he was departing from his resolution to remain perfectly stoic for her sake, but realizing that BoneMan saw himself as a kind of Satan, he thought it only prudent to point out that in the real world, everyone fled the terrors of evil and ran for the loving father.

The thought stopped him cold.

BoneMan withdrew a pair of handcuffs and tossed them onto the concrete in front of him. "Place them on your broken wrist and turn around."

He did as the man ordered, hands together behind his back. When Alvin had clasped the second cuff on his right hand, he grabbed a fistful of Ryan's hair behind his head and turned him around. Holding him with an outstretched arm, BoneMan pushed him forward, maintaining a tight grip on his hair.

How many other victims had he experimented on to perfect this effective hold? He steered Ryan from the room and down a hall toward a door at the end. Reached around him, removed an unlocked padlock looped through the latch, and shoved the door wide.

Lamplight filled the room beyond with orange light.

He steered Ryan inside and slammed the door behind them.

Already Ryan was looking, searching the room with wide eyes, but his head was tilted back and he couldn't turn it to see the entire space.

He was only interested in seeing one thing and his heart felt like it had lodged stubbornly in his throat, refusing to resume its beat until he saw her.

But she wasn't here.

Bethany wasn't in the room!

BoneMan unlatched his handcuffs and released his hair. Ryan spun around looking, searching.

He saw the lamp.

He saw the bed.

He saw something fixed to the wall.

He saw a pot on the floor.

He saw Alvin behind him.

But he did not see . . .

A thin girl dressed in dirty flannel pajama bottoms and a filthy T-shirt stepped out of the shadows from behind a wood post that had blocked his view of her.

This was his daughter. Her face was soiled and streaked with dried tears. Her long hair was tangled and matted and her eyes looked like they'd been pushed deeper into blackened eye sockets.

This was Bethany.

And then Ryan saw that her left hand was swollen. Three of her fingers were crooked. Alvin had broken three of her fingers.

Ryan had spent two days calming himself; sinking slowly into the place of reason and reckoning where mindless knee-jerk reaction was laid to rest so that even the cleverest of opponents could be outwitted and dismissed. He knew that he was working not only *against* BoneMan but *for* Bethany, hoping to outmaneuver the one while drawing out the other. He was unequivocally committed to bringing to bear on this matter the last reserves of his considerable skill, developed over countless hours in many continents, having saved too many lives to count.

But in that moment, seeing Bethany for the first time in two months, the cords that moored his arms and legs to the harbor of reason snapped and he felt powerless to hold his emotion at bay.

He was sobbing immediately, blubbering like a child as he stumbled forward, arms wide.

He couldn't even say her name. He shouldn't be overwhelming her like this, he was likely to terrify her, but he just couldn't stop himself.

Ryan fell upon her and wrapped his arms around her and pulled her into his chest. His mouth opened in an involuntary wail, but he had no breath to weep with, no voice to cry out; his chest and throat were locked in a vise.

She didn't move.

Behind him, BoneMan didn't stop him.

Then he caught his breath and he began to cry aloud, shaking like a fool while his body enfolded hers. He kissed the crown of her head and he held her close and he wept. He could smell the musky scent of sweat mixed with soap or lotion in her hair.

Tears streamed from his eyes and wet her hair as he sobbed, but he was too far gone to stop now. Nothing mattered more to him now than this moment, clinging to his daughter.

She was alive. She'd been lost but he'd found her and now she was in his arms. No matter what happened, he would have this moment.

"I love you," he managed to say. "I'm so sorry. I love you so much."

A hand pressed against his chest, her first gentle embrace. What had the monster done to her? She could barely move! He'd beaten her into the ground and now she stood like a drugged doll, barely able to move!

The thought brought a chill to his bones and he kissed her head again, then again.

Dear Bethany! Dear Bethany, I love you so much, oh God, how I love you!

Her hand was pressing against him with surprising strength. She still had her strength, that was good, that was good to know. And now her other hand, the one that was broken, pushed against his stomach.

"Don't," she said.

Her voice was strong as well. And it was bitter.

"Don't!"

She pushed him harder and only then did it occur to Ryan that his daughter, who'd been in captivity for more than a week now, was pushing him away. He was smothering her and she needed space to breathe.

But she was in his arms now; how could he dare let go of her now?

"Stop it!" She shoved hard. "Get off me!"

She was rejecting him? How was that possible? What had BoneMan done to her? He wouldn't let her go, not after everything. Not after seeing so many children die in the desert. Not after breaking Burton Welsh's wrist. Not after breaking his own hand and rushing here to save her.

Something slapped his face and he let go instinctively. Bethany glared past him, scorn etched deeply in her dirty face. He turned and followed her stare, expecting to see that she was looking at BoneMan, but it was only an empty wall.

Ryan spun back. "Bethany?" His mouth and throat felt like sandpaper. "What . . . what did he do?"

Her eyes slowly turned to him and in them he saw not even a flicker of grace or kindness.

"He's only going to kill us both now," she said.

"No, he would have already—"

"You've never been a father to me," she bit off in a low voice. "You were never there when I needed you. I've hated you most of my life. What makes you think you can come in here and expect me to care what he does with you now?"

"Bethany, I . . . please—"

"He says you can live if I show you how I feel and send you away, and that's what I'm going to do. It's the only way now." She glared at him. "You do want me to live, don't you?"

"Yes! Yes!"

"Then let's get this over with."

It was all happening too quickly, like some sick initiation in the middle of night. He hadn't expected her to be so harsh or calculating. What she was saying might make sense; it might if he knew everything. But the bitterness in her voice, the darkness in her eyes . . .

She might be doing what BoneMan had insisted she do, but she was doing it as if she were BoneMan herself! How could she be so cold?

To save him? Yes. She was granting him his life perhaps. But more than this she was doing it because her psyche belonged to Alvin. The man had won her over. She couldn't know what she was doing!

"Bethany—"

Something hit the side of his head and he fell to the ground, unconscious.

36

THERE WERE TWO things that Alvin Finch, aka BoneMan, wanted; nay, three that he would cut off his own hands to possess. His daughter, because Bethany was the seed of his life and all that was beautiful in him.

To crush the father's heart who, having been rejected, would be forced to live out a terrible life with the knowledge of his utter failure.

To break both of their bones if he couldn't have Bethany's love.

Naturally, he would allow her to express that love in new ways—for example, maybe she could take to breaking bones with him on a regular basis as they sought other daughters.

Alvin remained calm as he always did when he broke bones, but this time, controlling his pleasure was more difficult than he remembered it being. The idea that had grown in him was now before him, illuminated by the lamp's flame.

He'd hoisted the man up on the cross upside down,

then strapped his ankles spread-eagle to the frame by running rope through a hole he'd drilled in each block of wood for this purpose. He'd also tied the man's hands to the bottom portion of the cross frame and strapped his mouth with tape.

Then he'd asked Bethany, his promise of God, to wake him, and after looking at him with long eyes, she'd done so by slapping his face.

The father now hung awake, face red and eyes bulging, silent because of the tape, but inside surely screaming. Screaming with enough force to expel his lungs and his intestines.

This was what Alvin Finch had learned: you can break their bones, but it is far better to break their heart.

Suffice it to say that he had broken the father's heart.

Satisfied, he picked up the sledgehammer leaning against the wall and walked over to the daughter, who stared at the cross without expression. He held out the hammer to her.

She took it with her right hand and supported its weight with her left, though it was badly swollen. The sledgehammer was longer than her arm and the black iron head was the thickness of her calf. Seeing her frail frame gripping such a large hammer was an interesting sight.

He nodded his encouragement and indicated the short stool he'd placed by the man's head. "I'll hold his foot steady."

She just looked at him, lost. Was she thinking about backing out?

A shot of adrenaline washed through his blood and he felt his neck grow suddenly hot. If she backed out now, he would not be responsible for the pain he would inflict on her skeleton. No judge could blame him for what he would do to the father. Every bone, not just those that could be broken in the extremities, but all of them would have to be cracked or crushed. If she betrayed him now . . .

The daughter walked away from him and mounted the stool, hammer in hands.

His anger fell away like dead leaves in the fall. In fact, he regretted his doubt. How could he doubt such a lovely daughter who had agreed with him at each turn, though he'd had to break three of her fingers to convince her that he was right?

He hurried up to the cross, grabbed the bared right foot, and pulled it away from the cross so that she would have ample room to land the blow.

"Right on the heel. You'll have to swing the hammer hard and land it square or it'll slip off. Don't hit me."

She held the hammer over her shoulder and stared at the heel. "The heel," she said.

"Just the heel."

"And you let him live?"

"We agreed on that."

"I can't kill anyone. I'm not like that."

"Not yet, no. Just the heel, I promise, my child."

The last two words came out awkwardly, but with time they would flow from his tongue like honey. And with time she would beg to break all of the bones of anyone they took.

He'd thought about the possibility that she could direct the hammer's blow to his head, of course, and standing here beside her the concern reasserted itself. She was a clever little pig. She might just try it. It's what he would do and she was very much like him.

"Hold on."

He bent and picked up a five-foot length of rope left over from strapping Evan up. He quickly looped it around the man's toes and stepped back, pulling the foot flat so that the father couldn't ruin Bethany's blow by twisting.

He was now slightly behind her, making a blow to his head impossible.

She looked at him dully.

"There," he said. "Remember, swing as hard as you can."

She faced the father again. He was trying to talk through the tape, but she ignored him and brought the sledgehammer back.

There were tears in her eyes, but her jaw was fixed. Her arms were trembling, but the hammer was heavy and her left hand wasn't entirely functional. And besides that, striking that first blow was always the hardest. It had taken him three months from the time he'd decided to kill his mother to work up the courage to break her bones.

He'd wept with each blow.

"It's okay, my child. You'll get used to it. I'm right here behind you."

She held the hammer cocked above his foot for a long time, trembling so badly that Alvin doubted she could swing straight. She would miss and lose her resolve.

But she had to swing! She had to break his heel! Alvin wasn't sure he'd ever wanted anything so badly as he wanted her to smash Ryan's heel now, while he watched.

He glanced down. The father had quieted and closed his eyes. He would accept this fate because he knew that he'd lost her already. Now he was at their mercy.

Later, a day from now, a month from now, he didn't

know when, Alvin would walk into the father's house and kill him. But today he wanted only to break his heart.

And he wanted Bethany's full adoration.

"Swing it," he said.

A soft, terrible wail came from the girl's mouth and Alvin began to panic.

"Swing! Swing, you dirty little pig. Swing!"

Bethany swung the sledgehammer.

BETHANY FELT AS little as she thought she could possibly feel without it being nothing and as much as she'd remembered feeling, all at once. It sounded impossible, but it was as though her mind had been split in two when she swung.

Part of her cried out in horror at the action she was taking.

Part of her screamed with rage.

But part of her wanted to do only what made Alvin happy. What would endear her to him, even though she was loosely aware that she shouldn't feel that way. She was siding with him even though she knew deep down where thoughts are hidden that he was a monster.

She would rather be a monster and with him than be dead and nowhere.

So when Alvin screamed *swing*, she felt both horrified and compelled to swing the hammer with all of her might.

It landed hard on the flesh of his heel and bounced off.

Crunch.

Something had broken.

She was panting from the exertion. Ryan was still, except for scattered staccato jerking movements, like a freshly slaughtered pig.

Something had broken, all right.

Bethany's strength left her legs and she stepped back to steady herself, only too late remembering that she was on a stool. BoneMan caught her and set her straight before she fell.

He leaped up to the form on the cross and quickly examined the heel. "You did it." His voice was thick with pleasure. "I think you did it."

Bethany stared at her father, sickened. He'd stopped shaking and she thought that he might have passed out. His face looked at peace now. He was stretched on the wood frame and his shirt had slipped down to reveal his belly with his ribs sticking out. He was breathing quietly.

He'd come to save her. He'd come to hold her. She was sending him away and she didn't understand why or what she should do.

She was looking at his face when his eyes suddenly opened and he looked directly at her. She blinked, and when she looked at him again, his eyes were closed again.

But in that one moment she'd seen her father. Not the man who'd abandoned her for the navy. Not the man who did not love Celine. But a man who would die to be her father. To hold her and make her life right again.

But she'd chosen. The only way to survive in BoneMan's world was to become like BoneMan, the man who would kill to be her father.

She walked over to her piss pot and threw up in it. Her gut was empty so only bitter yellow bile came out.

Then she walked to the bed, lay on her side facing the wall, and closed her eyes. She was in hell, she thought.

And Alvin Finch really was Satan.

37

"WAKE UP." A hand slapped Ryan's face. "Wake up."

He blinked and opened his eyes. A man dressed in a clean cotton shirt with a close-shaved jaw leaned over him. His mind was trying to tell him who this was, what was happening, where he was, why he was on his back, how long he'd . . .

BoneMan.

Ryan blinked again and the details of the last week flooded his mind. He'd come to save Bethany and landed in hell.

She'd pushed him away. She'd swung the hammer. She couldn't possibly be in her right mind, but she had rejected him and this should have been no surprise to him because they'd never been close.

"Stand up," BoneMan, who was named Alvin Finch, said.

The smell of gasoline stung Ryan's nostrils.

"Stand up."

Ryan struggled to his knees, wincing. His right heel

throbbed and he saw that the man had wrapped bandages around his ankle for support.

"Stand up."

He pushed himself up on his left leg and stood, carefully applying weight to his right leg. The smell of gasoline was thick in the air. A heavy layer of clouds shut out the sun. Not a sound from the compound that he could hear. He'd been able to see the place when BoneMan had brought him, and he knew they were far from the nearest town because he'd paid attention to the sounds as they drove. But standing at the edge of the deathly still compound now, he felt utterly abandoned.

BoneMan had a machete in his right hand. He glanced down the gravel road, then returned his bright blue eyes to Ryan.

"In a mile the road runs into a paved road. I'm going to give you twenty minutes to reach it. Then my daughter and I will burn this place to the ground and drive out. If you're not gone, we'll kill you. Don't bother calling the police, we'll be long gone before they can get here."

Ryan couldn't think straight. They were setting him free and would then vanish.

"Why didn't you pay more attention to her when she was yours?" Alvin asked, but there wasn't a hint of curiosity in his voice. He was only inflicting more pain by pouring salt into Ryan's wound.

"You're dead to her. She killed you. This is your hell now. Wander around and regret every breath, but if you come back for her, I will break every bone in her body and I will begin by snapping off her teeth, one by one. Then I will burn both of you and go find myself another daughter. Do you doubt me?"

Ryan made no attempt to push back the fear that spread through his bones. He'd lost. He could either lie down here at BoneMan's feet and die or he could run.

Run as fast as his bruised heel would carry him into the hell that would be his life.

"Are you deaf now?"

"No," Ryan croaked.

"Do you doubt me?"

"No."

"Then leave. And if you try to find us later, I will find you and break your bones in your bed while you sleep. Do you doubt me?"

"No."

"Then leave," he said again. "Go."

Ryan limped the first step and then another, unsure.

Alvin Finch landed a loud blow on his back with the machete's broad side.

"Run!"

BoneMan's voice echoed across the compound.

Ryan ran. More precisely he stumbled forward, jaw set, holding back tears. And with each step he found the pain in his leg less bothersome and the barrenness in his heart less confusing and then he did begin to run, albeit a jerky, limping run.

He was like a dog, chased out of the house with a whip. He was not wanted here. He'd come for his daughter and was leaving without his daughter or his heart.

This wasn't the way it was supposed to end. How could she turn away from her own father who'd come to save her?

You're not her father, Ryan. They're right, you never really were her father.

No. No, but I want to be. I came here to be her father and to take her away from this monster and to hold her tight and to chase away all of her fear. To cherish her and lavish her with gifts.

He cast a quick look over his shoulder. Alvin Finch stood on the edge of the compound, staring at him like a watchdog. To think that he could still go back and do anything but demolish any last hope was utterly foolish. The worst kind of denial.

Ryan put his head down and plunged down the road, ignoring the pain in his foot now, pushed forward by a flash of anger. Gravel crunched with each footfall.

One mile. In one mile he would come to the road and flag down a car and call Ricki Valentine. But Bethany would be gone long before any help could arrive. He pushed on, breathing hard through his nostrils now.

Bethany's captivity was a terrible tragedy that had filled him with fear, the kind of horror most refused to even consider for all of its pain. But her rejection of him was even worse.

His mind was numb with rage.

He pushed himself faster, clenching his teeth to push back the pain in his heel. The gray ground passed by underfoot, but it was only an abstraction behind the raw emotions now throbbing through his mind. The paved road stretched across the horizon and he would reach that line in the sand. He would go on with his life, he had to, he had no other choice but to die and he was tempted, so tempted to run off the road and throw himself into the ditch.

But that was impossible. Killing himself wasn't in his psyche. No, instead he would cut her off from his emotions.

Ryan was panting now, gasping for reason as much

as air. Thumping down the road in an uneven gait, like a wounded horse headed for slaughter. He'd made it half-way to the road ahead, and he could see a truck shimmering along the blacktop.

The only way to survive was to accept the fact that Bethany was dead to him. It was the only way. It was the only way to live with this pain.

She'd rejected him. Crushed his heart. Destroyed him. He would return her favor by searing his emotions and putting what was left of his love in a box, never to be opened.

Ryan came to an abrupt stop, panting, terrified by the thought. An image of the broken children in the desert ran through his mind. Of Bethany standing over him with the sledgehammer while Alvin Finch held the rope and screamed for her to swing it.

How could he dare to think of shutting her out of his mind? How could he feel even a moment of bitterness toward her? How could he leave his one and only daughter in the hands of that monster? How could he take even one more step toward the safety of the road? How could he live with the pain now spreading from his bones into his chest and heart and mind? He would rather be dead.

He stood immobilized in the middle of the dirt road as the world tipped crazily around him.

But he didn't dare go back so that BoneMan could break her teeth off. So that he could take that sledgehammer to her frail bones. So that he could brutally murder her and leave them both for dead!

So then what?

He could do nothing. Nothing! *Nothing!*

Panic overtook him. His limbs felt like they were on fire. Nothing . . .

The trembles hit him suddenly, his whole body at once, and he knew that he was going to have a nervous breakdown right here in the middle of the road. A groan broke from his parted lips because he didn't know what else he could do but stand and shake and groan.

His daughter was alive but now she was dead. His daughter was alive and now she was going to die. She was dead already, not at BoneMan's hand, but in her own mind. She was becoming him, sick with deception, wallowing in her own desperation to live, even if it meant the death of herself. She needed to be saved from herself now as much as from him!

Before he fully realized any implications of what he was doing, Ryan was screaming, full-throated, at the sky.

The moment he realized he could be heard back at the house even from this distance he shut his mouth. But in that moment, screaming at the sky, Ryan knew something.

He knew that he could not survive alone in BoneMan's hell. He could not live in this walking death.

Ryan turned around and faced the distant compound now hidden by trees. BoneMan had left the road. He'd gone back in for his daughter.

A slow calm settled over Ryan's body. No, he could not live in BoneMan's hell. And so he would not.

Ryan began to run. Back to the house.

Back into hell.

FIVE DAYS HAD passed since Ryan Evans had vanished. Two days since Celine Evans had been found floating in her pool. And Ricki had turned up nothing that seemed to lead the investigation closer to stopping whatever was happening in BoneMan's world.

She sat at her desk, twirling a pencil, watching Greta Van Susteren on *Fox News* break down the case with a retired profiler from the FBI, Marybeth Arnolds. The media had been dancing around all kinds of speculation, but they were slowly putting together the pieces with the public.

Evans most likely wasn't the BoneMan.

BoneMan had Bethany and she was probably alive.

BoneMan might have Evans in captivity as well.

If Evans wasn't the BoneMan, he had gone to great lengths to save his daughter and had been used as a pawn when he took Welsh captive and broke his arm. If so, and they kept repeating the word *if*, Ryan Evans might be one of the bravest fathers who'd made the news in a very long time. They should give him a medal.

The toolshed drawings of crucified skeletons had been withheld from the public, and they had shed some light on the killer's motive—this reasoning that BoneMan justified everything he did as a natural part of a worldview that rotated around God, Satan, and their battle over the children. Typical pattern-killer psychosis.

Psychotics often believed the rest of the world was twisted, when in reality it was they who were tied up in knots. But there was always enough truth in their worldview to support reason.

Case in point: Kahlid, the terrorist who'd emulated BoneMan and thrown Ryan into his psychological tailspin to begin with. That Kahlid would equate the death of so many of his country's wives and children to a few children he was willing to sacrifice to make his case could be at least understood on some broad scale.

BoneMan was doing the same thing in his world. He

was inflicting perfectly reasonable punishment on a segment of society to make a point.

"Anything?"

Ricki lifted her head and looked at Mark, who had just poked his head in. "Nothing."

"Nothing. The world is screaming for answers and all we can tell them is *nothing*."

"Tell them they created BoneMan. Then tell them that it's out of our hands now."

"I wasn't aware that we were giving up. Who's going to save the world from BoneMan?"

She tapped the pencil eraser on her desk and nodded. "The father," she said. "Ryan Evans."

38

THERE WERE THREE thoughts pounding through Ryan's mind as he sprinted back to the compound. The first was that he had saved Bethany. The other seven daughters had died by BoneMan's hands quickly, but by giving Alvin Finch another target on which to inflict his sadistic rage, Ryan had kept his daughter alive.

The second was that his daughter had surely embraced Alvin Finch's game because she was blinded by his world and didn't see the alternative. Classic Stockholm syndrome.

The third thought was that the only way to save his daughter was to end Alvin Finch's bid for her, and the only way to do that now was to kill the man.

In the end only this thought mattered: Kill him. Kill the monster. Kill the BoneMan. Crush him so that he can never, never stalk another daughter in the darkness again.

How to kill BoneMan wasn't the issue. How a man with a broken heel and no weapon, worn to a thread from days without food, could possibly hope to kill a large man like Alvin Finch hardly entered his mind.

Live as Bethany's father or not at all. Kill or be killed.

Then he sprinted into full view of the house with not a soul in sight and he realized that he wouldn't be killing anyone because in reality this was BoneMan's world, and in BoneMan's world, BoneMan did the killing.

But Ryan didn't stop or slow because Bethany was inside that house and he was her father.

He, not BoneMan. *He was Bethany's father!*

He nearly cried it out as he sprinted across the yard, but a wedge of reason stopped him and brought with it the realization that he couldn't just crash into the house and expect Alvin Finch to step aside while he liberated his daughter from his basement.

He came to a jerking halt thirty feet from the front door, wheezing. His right foot throbbed with pain but he refused to give it any space in his mind. He limped up the broken path, keenly aware that he had no plan other than to kill BoneMan.

Kill or be killed.

Paint that had once been white peeled away from the house in flaking strips, revealing rotting gray wood beneath. The front door hung at a slight angle on only one hinge, following the whole house's tilt to the right.

Gasoline fumes wafted from his right. The barn. The house hadn't yet been soaked. Alvin Finch was busy wandering around inside, paying his last respects to the house of hell. Or in the basement with Bethany, putting her in chains.

For a few brief moments, stumbling up to the house, Ryan's mind cleared. He saw the glassless windows, the empty hall beyond the front door, the darkening sky. He felt the breeze on his face and smelled the scent of gasoline. And for a single second he considered stopping and developing a more stealthy approach.

But then his emotions pushed the thought aside and he grabbed a rusted handle, pulled the door open, and stepped into BoneMan's house.

The hinge squealed as the door shut behind him and slapped against the frame. He turned to his right and walked quickly, not because he knew where the hall led, but because he wasn't here to know anything any longer, he was only here to act. His breathing came in steady pulls through his nostrils and he held his hands in fists without regard for his broken thumb.

There had to be a stairway. Somewhere a stairway that led down.

The interior of the house was in no better repair than outside but there was a floor under his feet and under that floor there was a basement and that was all he cared about now.

He rounded the corner at the end of the hall, saw the kitchen, saw the opened door next to an old rusted refrigerator. Saw the opening in the wall on his right and the wood railing sloping down.

There were other details now, the smell of bleach, a crooked picture of a rooster on the wall, an old cookbook with a red-and-white checkerboard cover.

But there was the door, open to the basement, and Ryan was already halfway across the kitchen.

The floor moved under him and he knew that if Alvin was directly below him, he'd already heard the weak foundation moving. Like the creaking hinge and the banging door, the protest from the floor only seemed to push him.

He was known now. There was no chance of outwitting

BoneMan any longer. There was only Ryan's rage against the man who had broken his daughter's fingers and corrupted her mind.

Ryan was about to enter the stairwell when an image seen through the opened door next to the refrigerator stopped him. Through the doorway he could see a bedroom with a bed. But it was the pictures on the wall beyond the bed that sent a chill down his neck. There was no mistaking the black-and-white photograph of Bethany, standing in her window at the house in Austin. The freak had stalked her and taken this picture with a zoom lens?

A newspaper clipping hung next to his trophy. *BoneMan Takes Another Victim.*

A second picture had been pinned to the wall on the other side of the larger image. An old, yellowing photograph with a crease running diagonally across the upper left corner. And even from this distance Ryan knew the small child grinning with chubby cheeks.

This too was Bethany. When she was only a baby.

Ryan blinked. Walked into the room and stared at the wall, mesmerized. He knew that he should be rushing down the stairs. He knew that at any moment BoneMan could rush up behind him and put his hammer through his head. He knew he had come to kill or be killed.

But he also knew something else that now rendered him immobile. The picture of the baby was his baby, his Bethany, his angel, but it was a photograph taken before he'd adopted her.

He'd never seen this picture before. This wasn't something that BoneMan had taken from their house. So then where had he found it? And why was it on his wall? The larger one showing Bethany within the last year he understood. But the small, worn photograph reached into Ryan's chest and tightened a fist around his heart.

Ryan moved around the bed, like a man walking dead and unseen, fixated on the picture. He stood before the image and lifted his hand to the wall. Ran his fingers over the image of Bethany as an innocent angel, smiling dumbly. It was paper clipped to an envelope addressed to a post office box.

The postmark was just over one month earlier. BoneMan had received this picture just thirty days ago?

A knot was already locked in his throat, but now something else joined it. Nausea.

The rest of the room was very plain, but the bed was made with white sheets, and four half-burnt candles the thickness of his arm sat on an old dresser. BoneMan slept here. He lay here and he dreamed of being Bethany's father.

Ryan plucked the picture off the wall. The envelope floated to the ground.

Surely there was no real significance behind finding a baby picture of Bethany in this monster's room. No, that . . . that wasn't right. No, no, no, that just couldn't . . .

He flipped the small picture over and stared at a note scrawled in fresh blue ink.

> *Here's you daughter, you ingrate.*
> *I put her up a month after this picture*
> *was taken caus she wouldn't shut up.*
> *Rot in hell. Betsy.*

A red line was drawn through the name.
Ryan couldn't stop the tremble in his hand, but he

had to read the note again because he was sure he'd misread the words. There was a mistake. He had to read this again!

He grabbed the picture with both hands and scanned the lines again. This could not be, not his angel, not born to that . . .

Revulsion smothered him all at once. He realized that he'd stopped breathing, and now he sucked at the air in loud, halting gasps. The nausea he'd felt a minute earlier rose through his throat and he couldn't stop himself from heaving. His stomach was empty so they were dry heaves, but they watered his eyes and contorted his body.

Bethany was Alvin Finch's daughter by birth. He'd discovered it only recently and gone after her. And he would as soon break her bones as love her because in BoneMan's twisted mind there was no difference.

Ryan lost his reason then. He almost screamed his rage. Under any other circumstances the mere thought that Bethany was born to the man in the basement would have inspired him to smash the windows and bloody his hands, breaking the walls as an expression of his fury over the injustice of it all.

But at this very moment BoneMan's daughter, who was now Ryan's daughter, cowered in the basement, giving her soul to him!

Still gripping the picture between white fingers, he leapt over the bed and tore from the room, only barely caring that he might be giving himself away now.

He grabbed the wall at the stairwell, spun through the doorway, and plunged down a flight of concrete stairs built as part of the foundation. Down into darkness. With each step he felt the end rushing up at him. This was BoneMan's world, where BoneMan killed. But the realization didn't slow him.

This was where Bethany was, captive to the father of lies.

The room he'd been held captive in sat at the end of the hall, door opened to empty darkness. Bethany's room was the other way, at the other end.

He reached the bottom of the steps, spun around the bottom rail, and stopped. An empty hall ran up to the same door BoneMan has shoved him through. The doorway to Bethany's room was open and glowed with orange light.

They were waiting for him. Ryan's heart crashed in his chest. BoneMan was waiting to fulfill his promise.

Or they were already gone, on another road out the back way.

He released the railing, shoved the picture in his belt, and limped down the hall, mind clouded with rage and fear and Bethany.

He was halfway down the hall when he heard the voice. BoneMan's voice. A low and kind voice that sounded like the weeping of children in Ryan's mind.

"It looks very pretty on you."

Ryan covered the last ten yards without being able to think. And then he was in the open doorway staring at the room with the cross on the wall.

He saw the entire scene as if it were a single snapshot that his mind had studied for long seconds, not the mere moment it took for him to comprehend what he was looking at.

Alvin Finch stood shirtless with his pale, veiny back to Ryan, blocking his view of Bethany. The man was so completely absorbed by the object of his jealousy that he didn't turn.

The rest of the room was as Ryan remembered—the lamp hung from a nail on the overhead timber. The bed ran along the wall across the room, empty now, and beside it the piss pot. The sledgehammer leaned against the cross, thick steel head resting on the concrete.

"My mother was short," Alvin Finch said. "You'll grow into it in a year or two."

He took a step forward, and when he moved, Bethany came into view. She stood in a white wedding dress, hemmed in lace and yellowed by time.

"Do you want to touch my chest?" Alvin asked.

The fury coursing through Ryan's body now felt like the intense, dry heat of a sauna blown in his face. The sight of the white monster who called himself Satan standing over his daughter made him instantly ill and he felt as though he was going to throw up. He could not breathe, he could not think, he could not move.

He could only shake.

"I've just applied lotion," Alvin said.

Bethany saw Ryan then, and her eyes shifted ever so slightly.

And Ryan started to turn.

Ryan wasn't sure why or how or even that he was moving, but he was. Grunting and panting he leaped across the room to the cross.

With both hands, Ryan grabbed the sledgehammer by the long handle and began his swing from the floor as he turned.

He bolted for them, roaring like a bull, and swung the hammer, adjusting the trajectory of the head as best he could, given the energy he'd already thrown into the swing.

BoneMan still had his back to him and was turning with a stunned stare. The head of the sledgehammer landed on the side of the man's head with a sickening *crack*.

A sharp jar ran up Ryan's arms. He felt the hammer slip from his grasp and drop on the concrete next to Bethany. His nemesis stared from bulging eyes that peered from a skull bleeding on one side.

And then Alvin Finch, aka BoneMan, aka Satan, toppled to his left. He bounced off the post in the middle of the room, struck the concrete next to the hammer's head with a loud slap, and lay still.

For three long seconds Ryan stared at the form, still uncertain that he'd caught him flat-footed. The man's own sickness had killed him. If he hadn't been so consumed with possessing what he could not have, he might have heard Ryan coming.

Instead, he lay on the floor, either dead or close to it, and Ryan felt nothing even remotely similar to remorse.

Bethany was looking at him. He glanced at the hammer by her feet, then back at her lost eyes. Finish it . . .

A wave of rage washed over him. The hammer was there, by Bethany's feet, and the beast who'd abused her was there, on the floor. Ryan wanted to scream out for his daughter to pick up the hammer and slug this bull in the head again and again, until there could be no doubt that he'd been appropriately punished for his indiscretion.

"Kill him," he muttered.

But Bethany just looked at him. She stood still like a limp doll swimming in the mother's wedding dress.

It occurred to him then that even now, BoneMan's hooks

were still in her mind. She really had given her captor a part of herself and would have to wrestle it back. The rage would come later.

"You came back for me," she said. Without shifting her eyes from him, she reached up and pulled the dress off her shoulders. It fell to the floor around her feet, but she just stood there in her pajamas staring at him and he wasn't sure if she was angry or glad. Her face slowly twisted into a knot, and tears sprang to her eyes. Her shoulders began to shake.

A knot crowded his throat so he couldn't tell her how much he loved her, although that was all he wanted to do.

Bethany looked at the fallen form to her right, then up at Ryan again and now began to wail. Panic washed into his mind. She was crying over his death? Over *BoneMan's* death?

No! No, Bethany dear, it's not like that! I saved you. Don't cry, please don't . . .

Bethany lifted both arms and stumbled forward and only when she reached him did he realize she was coming with an embrace.

Blurting a sob, he stepped forward and threw his arms around her. She wrapped her thin arms around his body and rested against his chest.

"Thank you," she managed to whisper. Then again, a strained whisper, "Thank you." She held him with more strength than he imagined possible after her extended captivity. And then she wept unreservedly.

"I'm sorry," he said.

"No!" she cried. "No!"

"I want to be your father. I—"

Bethany put her arms around his neck and kissed his cheek. "You came back for me. You are my father and I'll never leave you."

It was almost more than he could bear. He couldn't speak so he held her close and wept into her hair.

But another sound joined their cries of remorse. Behind them BoneMan groaned.

Bethany jumped at the sound.

He wasn't dead?

Ryan turned slowly and stared at BoneMan's face. The man's eyes shifted about, darting from Ryan to Bethany and back. Despite his broken skull he was clearly conscious. And in his blue eyes Ryan could see that he clung stubbornly to a desire.

For a long moment he stood still, allowing the blood in his veins to grow hot, gripping his hands slowly into fists so tight he might have cut his palm with his fingernails.

BoneMan was alive still. And with every lustful breath the monster took, Ryan felt robbed of life. The man's display of raw evil was even worse now for expressing itself in those hideous eyes despite his utter failure to win the daughter.

Ryan roared and threw himself blindly at BoneMan.

Gripping the man by his trousers and shirt, he hefted him up like a weight lifter snatching up dumbbells. He twisted, roaring still, and slammed the body against the wall.

Onto the blocks of wood.

Bethany was shrieking now, diving in, grabbing at the ropes still fastened through the blocks that had held Ryan's arms and legs.

"Tie him!" Ryan cried. "Tie him!"

She sobbed and she bound him in quick short move-ments, spinning from limb to limb. It only took a few seconds and in those seconds Ryan and Bethany were one, undivided in their purpose.

It was enough to make him want to cry.

Bethany leapt back, eyes wide on Alvin Finch, who was strapped to the wooden blocks. Ryan let him go and stepped back. The man's body sagged, then hung still, unmoving except for the slow rise and fall of his chest.

Bethany grabbed the lantern from the beam and held out her hand. "Come on."

Together they staggered from the room, leaving BoneMan incapacitated on the wall, watching them with desire. When Ryan looked back at the door he had to fight back a strong urge to pick up the sledge and close those eyes once and for all.

"Come on," Bethany said, tugging him.

They limped down the hall and up the stairs without a word.

She let the door slam shut behind them and squinted in the light. Ryan took her hand again and hurried her away from the house, toward the driveway, toward the large oak that spread its long limbs over the road. He stopped and turned back, still unsure if they really had escaped the monster.

Crickets screeched. A gentle breeze rustled the leaves overhead. The old, dilapidated house stood in the setting sun, quiet and serene, belying the horror that it had harbored for so many years. Cracked windows, crooked door, flaking paint—just another house set far back from the well-traveled roads that wound unsuspecting through Texas.

Beside him, Bethany sniffed, then shook with a sob. Ryan's mind snapped back to the child, back to his daugh-

ter, and for the moment the house ceased to exist. All that
mattered now was Bethany.

He grabbed the lantern from her free hand and set it
down on the ground. Then swung around to face her. He
was only halfway around when her arms wrapped around
his neck and pulled him tight. She buried her face in his
neck like a leech, drawing life in a desperate silence.

Ryan stood immobilized. Slowly he put his arms
around her waist and held her close. Father and daughter.

They clung to life as one, and Ryan couldn't remember
ever feeling so grateful, so full of love, so blessed as he
did now holding his daughter, Bethany.

The afternoon heat smothered them, a welcome furnace of love kindled by deep, deep longing and relief. If
Ryan died then of a heart attack, he would have lived a
full life, if only in these last few moments. No heaven that
awaited could possibly be any more satisfying than the
gratitude that now swept through his mind and body.

"I love you, Daddy," Bethany whispered into his neck
through trembling lips. "I love you so much."

He wanted to push her away so that he could look
into her eyes and tell her that she didn't need to feel any
guilt. This was all his fault now. He would never let her
go again.

But he realized that she wasn't clinging to him in order
to deflect guilt. She was holding tight to him, her savior,
her father, the one who'd moved heaven and earth to rescue her.

And then it struck him: they *were* in heaven. Not literally, but just as real. He was the father who'd come to
rescue his lost child from this Lucifer's hell. He was the
father embracing his prodigal child.

"I will never leave you, Bethany. Never!"

Ryan wasn't sure how much time passed as they embraced under the oak's majestic branches; it had either sped by or slowed to a crawl, he didn't know which. But gradually the sound of crickets and rustling leaves became realities again.

Bethany pulled back, kissed his cheek tenderly. "Thank you," she whispered.

His throat was still in a knot; he didn't know what to say anyway.

She turned and faced the house, holding tightly to his arm. An image of BoneMan strapped to the beams below filled Ryan's mind. The thought that they'd left the man— the beast, this Lucifer who came from the pit of hell— alive. How could they do that?

What if he was still alive? What if he'd managed to escape? What if the wall had some kind of safe passage built in? What if this father of lies lived to hunt down his daughter once again?

He swallowed hard, aware of a growing ringing in his ears.

"Will they come for us?"

"There's a road nearby. We can walk out."

But she made no move to flee. Her breathing had thickened and her hands were steady.

"I hate this place," Bethany said.

"I hate it too."

They stared at the house.

"This house is hell to me. It will haunt me."

Yes, he thought. And, *No, he would not let anything like this haunt his daughter.*

"Then burn it," he said.

*   *   *

"HE'S IN THE basement."

Ryan bent over, lifted the flaming lantern, and walked toward the house, outraged by the realization that they hadn't yet finished. "I'll burn it." He stumbled forward, mind fixed.

"No!" Bethany cried. She raced up to him and grabbed the handle. She was going to stop him? Finally confronted by BoneMan's demise, she was unwilling to see him die? His hooks were so deep in her mind that she—

"I'll burn it," she said.

Ryan could hardly contain his relief.

They exchanged one long look of understanding, then turned as one and slung the lamp through the nearest window with a pronounced grunt.

It smashed against the interior wood wall and doused it with oil, which burst into flame. They watched the flames crackle down the hall, licking at the ceiling. The house was like a tinderbox. Pillars of smoke rose into the sky for all the world to see. It was only a matter of time before the authorities arrived now.

"Take me away from this hell, Daddy," Bethany said, turning away.

Ryan took his daughter's hand and together they walked away from the burning house.

The End

ABOUT THE AUTHOR

TED DEKKER is a *New York Times* bestselling author of more than twenty novels. He is known for stories that combine adrenaline-laced plots with incredible confrontations between good and evil. He lives in Austin with his wife and children.

ARE YOU THE BONEMAN'S DAUGHTER?

AS WITH ALL of my novels, *BoneMan's Daughters* has a unique story behind it, this time, as you might guess by the title of the book, a story involving my own teenage daughter.

Now, I would like to think that I am a good father. That I have raised each of my children in the way they should go, and given them freedom to make their own choices once they have enough of a sense of the world not to be crushed. But when my daughter began to fall for this one particular creep at the tender age of sixteen, I began to sweat.

No one else saw him as a creep, mind you. He was the kid at her birthday party who could break-dance and smile ever so charmingly. He seemed kind and thoughtful and all of the girls thought he was, for lack of a better word, hot.

I don't know, maybe it was the way he kept looking at me with piercing eyes, or the way he yelled at me when I asked him not to date my daughter (go figure) but this kid scared me.

Fast forward two years. It was three days before Christmas. I'd learned that my daughter, now eighteen and in college, was madly in love with this boy. By this point I was certain that the kid was not only a punk, but truly dangerous. He'd yelled at me on numerous occasions. He'd told me I had no right to my daughter. He'd threatened my family.

But most of all, this kid, now twenty, had won the heart of my daughter and for that I began to hate him. My anger was directed at him, not my daughter, you see, because he was the monster and she was my precious baby and the fact that he'd found a way to seduce her was infuriating.

And that night three days before Christmas, everything came apart, because that night my daughter informed the family that she was leaving our home to live with this monster. There are six of us in the family; five of us stood there at the door, crying, while the monster led the sixth out the front door. I can still see his face—he was carrying her suitcase and he was smiling.

But what could I do? My wife and I, and the other children had all begged her not to go with him. But, like a victim of Stockholm Syndrome, she had given her heart and mind to the monster, unable to see the wolf under that sheep's clothing.

LeeAnn and I tried to comfort our other children. Our youngest, only a small child at the time, was devastated and we couldn't stop her weeping. For hours she cried and hiccupped and all we could do was hold back our own tears for her sake while we held her.

Then, like the twin dead, we walked to our own room, closed the door, fell on our bed, and sobbed. And we sobbed.

For the next two months our bedroom was the weeping place. The monster had our child and there was nothing I could do about it. I talked to the police, I called all of our friends, I dialed the FBI, I would have called the President if I thought it might help. I begged our daughter to reconsider every time I talked to her, but it was her life and I could only pray that she came to herself before he destroyed her.

It stuck me then that I would do anything to save my daughter. *Anything.* And every time I thought about the monster my outrage at his trickery grew. In my mind he was BoneMan. My daughter was now BoneMan's Daughter.

In the end all I could do was stare at my blank computer screen for hours, lost in desperation. I knew then that I had to discover the meaning behind this terrible love I had for my daughter through a fully fleshed story. I had to write a story that made absolute certain in the mind of every daughter how precious they are to the father.

My pain was intensely personal and I needed to understand that pain in the context of every father who loses a daughter, be it in Iraq or in Hollywood or in Colorado. Is this how God loves each of his children?

I still remember the day the call came. It was my daughter. She was crying so hard she could hardly get the words out. She wanted to come, oh how badly she wanted to come home, she'd wanted to come home for weeks, could we please, please take her back? Heaven filled our home that day.

And then we learned the terrible truth. The monster *had* abused her. That devil had crushed her! She was too ashamed to call, too proud to come home, but she'd laid awake in bed many nights crying for home.

Years have passed and now. Rachelle will tell you that she was snatched out of hell itself that day. I cringe to think what might have happened. And I cringe to think what goes through the mind of a father who has lost his daughter forever.

I've dedicated BoneMan's Daughters to Rachelle, but this love story is for you. For every daughter, every son, every father, every mother. For my part I will continue to rip the sheep's clothing off of those wolves in my novels, exposing them for who they are despite occasional objections from those who would rather turn their eyes from the ugly truth.

For your part, go to your daughter, your father, your son, your mother. Hold them close, and cherish them forever.

"THANK YOU, DETECTIVE. We'll take it from here."

FBI Special Agent Brad Raines stood in the small barn's wide doorway and scanned the dimly lit interior. Dusk fell on an ancient wood floor covered in dust disturbed by numerous footprints.

Shafts of light streamed from cracks in a sagging roof.

Long abandoned. A natural choice.

"With all due respect, Agent Raines, my team is here," the detective replied. "They can work the scene."

"But they won't, Detective Lambert."

Raines turned his head slowly, taking it all in.

One rectangular room roughly fifteen by forty, covered by a tin roof. Interior walls formed by six-inch graying wooden planks. Ten, twenty, thirty, thirty-two on the narrow side. Fifteen feet, as estimated. Two shovels and a pitchfork on the floor to his right. A single window with dirty, tinted panes, crowded by empty cobwebs.

A dust-covered wooden bucket rested in the corner, its rusted handle covered with filth. Several old rusted tin cans— GIANT brand peas with the label mostly missing, HEINZ canned hot dogs— scattered on the floor, left by campers long gone. An old plow blade lay against the near wall. An even older worktable sat to the left, near the far wall.

All unsurprising. All but what had brought Brad.

The woman's body was glued to the wall to his left, arms wide, wrists limp. Like the other three.

". . . Chief Lorenzo for clearance." The detective's voice edged in on his thoughts. Lambert was still here.

Brad looked over his left shoulder where Nikki Holden, a leading forensic psychologist, stood staring at the woman's body with those wide blue eyes of hers. She caught his get-rid-of-the-cop glance and turned to face Detective Lambert. Brad returned his gaze to the shed's interior as she spoke.

"I'm sorry, Detective," she said in her most reasonable tone of voice, "but I'm sure you can appreciate our position here. Give my team a few hours. If this isn't our guy, you'll be the first to know. The police department's been more than helpful."

Brad looked up to mask his knowing grin. One of the rafters was cracked, and its gray husk revealed a lighter, tan core. Freshly broken.

"I don't like it," Lambert said. "For the record."

Brad pulled his eyes from the crime scene and smiled at the detective. "Thank you, Detective. Noted. There's quite a bit about this job not to like. If your men could secure the perimeter, that would be helpful. Our forensics team will be here any minute."

Lambert held his gaze for moment, then turned away and addressed a man behind him. "Okay, Larry, cancel the forensics, this is now an FBI investigation. Tell Bill to secure and hold the perimeter."

Larry muttered a curse and flicked away a bit of straw he'd taken from a pile of old bales. A white unmarked van rolled over the yellow perimeter tape and slowly crunched over the gravel driveway. It had taken the forensics team an hour to reach the scene, just south of West Dillon Road, from the Stout Street field office in downtown Denver. A farm had evidently once occupied this empty field in Louisville, twenty-plus miles northwest from Denver up the Denver-Boulder Turnpike.

Brad glanced at Nikki. "Tell them to start on the outside," he said flatly. "Give us a minute. Bring Kim in when she arrives."

Kim Peterson, the forensic pathologist, would determine what the body could tell them postmortem. Nikki headed for the van without comment.

Brad turned his attention back to the small barn. The shack. The farm shed. The killer's nest. The rest of the story was here, in the dark corners. The walls had watched the killer as he'd methodically ended a woman's life. The worktable had heard his words as he confessed his passions and fears in a world turned inside out by his compulsions. It had witnessed her pleas for mercy. Her dying moans.

Careful not to step on the exposed markings in the dust, Brad entered the room and approached the wall on which the woman was affixed. He stood still, filtering out the sounds of voices from a dozen law enforcement personnel outside. The hum of rubber on asphalt from the main road two hundred yards down the driveway settled in with the sound of his breathing. Both faded entirely as he brought his senses in line with the scene before him.

Her nude torso rose pale in the glow of a single light shaft. As though by magic, her body seemed perched on the wooden wall behind her, both arms stretched out on either side. Two round dowels that supported much of her weight protruded from the wall under her armpits. Her heels were together, each foot angled away from the other to form a V.

A white veil of translucent lace had been carefully arranged to cover her face, like a bride.

The outthrust posture sent a collage of art-history remnants cascading through his mind— the *Venus de Milo*, a thousand renditions of the Crucifixion, the Louvre's *Winged Victory* statue, her marble bosom jutting forward as if it belonged on the prow of an ancient ship plowing through a Mediterranean surf.

But this was no museum. It was a crime scene, and the mixture of cruelty and ostentation pouring from the garish exhibit filled him with a sudden wave of nausea.

Slowly, his analytical faculties began to reassert themselves.

She was naked except for thin cotton panties and the veil. Blond. White. Everything about the placement was symmetrical. Each hand was set in identical form, with thumb and forefinger touching, each shoulder, each hip had been carefully manipulated into perfect balance. All but her head.

Her head slumped gently to the left so that her long blond hair cascaded over her left shoulder before curling under her armpits. Through the veil he could see that her eyes were closed. No blemish, no sign of pain or suffering, no blood.

Only blessed peace and beauty. She could as easily be an angel painted by da Vinci or Michelangelo. The perfect bride.

Brian Jacobs, seventeen, had brought his girlfriend here after school for reasons unrevealed and found the Bride Collector's fourth victim. Brad preferred to think of them as angels.

He peered closer and felt strange words of empathy well up inside of him.

I cry with you, Angel. I weep for you. For every strand of hair that will never again blow in the wind, for every smile that will never brighten someone else's day, for every look of desire that will never quicken another man's pulse. I am so sorry.

"She's beautiful," Nikki said behind him.

He felt a momentary stab of regret for having been pulled away from his connection with the woman on the wall. Nikki walked past him, eyes fixed on the woman, touching his arm gently with her fingers as she passed. Her breathing was steady, slightly thicker than usual. He knew the cause: the dark waters of the killer's mind, which she now probed by staring at his handiwork.

Like an avalanche, the poignancy of his relationship with Nikki crashed through his mind . . . and then was gone, replaced by the image of her standing next to the woman. A blond angel hovering over a brunette. One with arms stretched wide in complete resignation, the other with arms folded. One nearly naked, the other dressed in a blue silk blouse with a black jacket and skirt.

She's beautiful, he thought.

"What a shame." Kim Peterson's voice cut softly through the room, gasping what the other two were too proud to verbalize. The forensic pathologist stepped up next to Brad, withdrew a pair of white gloves from her bag then set it down. "What do we know?"

Brad would have preferred to spend more time alone with the victim, but the opportunity had passed. "No ID. Discovered an hour ago by two teenagers."

They stared in a moment of silence.

"She's beautiful," Kim said.

"Yes."

"This makes four."

"Looks like it, doesn't it?"

The pathologist approached opposite Nikki, who remained quiet, lost in thought as she studied the body with searching eyes.

Kim sank to one heel and gently lifted the woman's toes for a better view under the foot. "Care to tell us how you think it happened before I begin my preliminary examination?"

He wasn't ready, of course, not yet, not without a complete analysis of evidence still to be gathered. But he'd been credited with an uncanny ability to accurately judge events from the thinnest of evidentiary threads. He'd cracked three major cases in the Four Corners region since leaving Miami and joining the Denver field office a year ago. At thirty-two years of age, he was on the fast track for high ground—much higher ground, according to his superiors.

But unlike them, his motivation had nothing to do with climbing an organizational ladder.

"Male, size eleven by the shoe prints. They were here for a while, maybe a day . . ."

"How so?" Nikki asked.

A distant murmur carried to him: an officer speaking to the curious driver of an approaching car outside, instructing him to head back to the main road. The roof over their heads ticked as it began to cool in the late afternoon.

"That smell. It's baked beans. He was hungry, so he ate. You won't find the can. He wouldn't leave any DNA evidence in here."

"She was alive when he brought her here?"

"Yes. And he killed her like the others, by draining her blood from her heels. No struggle. A tarp under the table caught most of the trace evidence—bodily fluids, skin cells, hair. He was careful not to use too much force, keeping her on the edge of control and submission. She was lying prone, sedated, conscious and fully aware when he numbed her heels and drilled up into them. He was forced to clean up the blood on the table and floor where it ran off the tarp. Then he sealed the wounds, lifted her into position, held her long enough for the glue on her shoulder blades to cure on the wall, reopened the wounds on each heel, and watched her blood drain into a three-gallon bucket."

All of this, Brad had guessed from the markings on the table and floor, the ring from the bucket beneath the woman's heels, and the lack of bruising. The physical evidence had painted a picture in his mind as clearly as if he were staring at a Rembrandt.

"He did it out of respect, not rage," Brad said.

"Love," Nikki said.

He nodded, even willing to go that far. "Love."

"Both heel wounds are plugged with the same fleshy putty we found on the other three," Kim said, standing. "And what kind of love is this?"

"The groom's love," Brad said, savoring his response.

Special Agent Frank Closkey spoke from the door. "Sir?"

Brad held up his hand without looking back. "Give us a few more minutes, Frank."

The agent retreated.

Kim continued her initial examination, gently

prodding the woman's flesh, checking her eyes, lifting her hair, inspecting the backs of her shoulders. But Brad already knew what she would find.

The question was, *Why?* What motivated the Bride Collector? How did he make his selections? What good or evil did he think he was doing? What had been done to him to motivate his taking of life in such a manner? Who had he decided to kill next? When would he take her?

Where was he now?

The questions spun through Brad's mind as one, yet distinguishable. Some were clearer than others, but all whispered from beyond, tempting him to listen because each question already contained an answer. He simply had to find it and unpack it.

Nikki paced with one arm pressed against her belly, the other propping up her chin. It struck him that like her, two of the victims had been brunettes. Like her, all four had beautiful complexions.

What would enter the killer's mind if he were staring at Nikki through a hole in the wall at this moment? Brad pushed back a fleeting impulse to check the wall behind them to see if there might indeed be a hole, filled with a single eye peering in at them.

Instead, he let his eyes wander over Nikki— her calves well defined beneath the hem of the black skirt. Her wavy long hair cascading on her shoulders, her eyes bright with question. Her forefinger absently brushing full lips. A perfectly symmetrical face.

Would the killer feel any desire?

No. No it wasn't desire, was it? She was beautiful, but beautiful women filled the world. Something else drew the Bride Collector, in the same way that something else was drawing Brad now, though he had a difficult time putting a finger on it.

Of the numerous women he'd dated over the past ten years, only four relationships had lasted two months or more, each ending sooner than the previous one. Nikki had once accused him of playing the role of bad boy. He thought picky was a better label. He had taste, after all.

After what he'd been through, he needed to be picky.

Nikki was thirty-one, married once at age nineteen, divorced six months later. She held her doctorate in psychology from CSU. Highly intelligent, witty, reduced to deep introspection by scenes that left most people heaving.

This would excite the killer, wouldn't it? And if Nikki came on to the killer, would that excite him?

No, Brad thought.

"He would like you," Brad said.

Nikki glanced back at him, arm still around her waist. "Excuse me?"

He caught himself. This was one of those frequent times when honesty might not be so wise.

"I was just thinking that he liked her. You. That is, speaking to the victim. He. *He* would like *you*, meaning he would like *her*. "

Kim saved him. "Speaking to cadavers now, Brad? Don't worry, I do it all the time."

"You were looking at me when you said it," Nikki said.

"So I was. I tend to do that."

"What, stare at women? Or specifically at me?"

"Both, on occasion."

A faint smile turned the corners of her mouth up. She winked. Not a full wink, but the movement in her right eyelid was unmistakable. Or was it?

Nikki turned to face the wall, leaving Brad to feel somewhat dirty. In an attempt to help the woman on the wall, he'd somehow violated her privacy. Yet her story was still unknown and demanded respect.

Silence. Remorse. Shame.

"Sir?" Frank's voice intruded again.

Brad turned from the wall and walked to the door. "Bring the team in. Photograph every inch, dust every exposed surface. Blood, sweat, spittle, hair; bag and tag the air if you have to. I want preliminaries from the lab this evening."

"Um . . . It's getting late. I don't—"

"He's staring through a peephole at another woman already Frank. We have less than a week to stop him from showing that woman his love. Preliminaries tonight."

Brad left the shack thinking he might have chosen better words to express the urgency burning across his nervous system.